If Wishes Were Horses

If Wishes Were Horses

Patricia Glen

PIATKUS

If wishes were horses,
beggars might ride.

ANON

First published in Great Britain in 1989 by
Judy Piatkus (Publishers) Ltd of
5 Windmill Street, London W1

British Library Cataloguing in Publication Data
Glen, Patricia
If wishes were horses.
I. Title
823'.914 [F]

ISBN 0-86188-875-8

Phototypeset in 11/12 pt Times Linotron by
Wyvern Typesetting Ltd, Bristol
Printed and bound in Great Britain by
Mackays of Chatham Plc, Chatham, Kent

PART ONE
(1954–1955)

Chapter One

It was very late when I took out the sports car, and the drizzle which had been falling all day had turned into a steady downpour. It was not a night for driving, but I had to get away and be by myself for a while. I took the quickest route out of London, and found an unlit country road which suited my mood.

I started to relax. I turned on the radio, and was fumbling in the glove tray for my cigarettes when the music changed to the all too familiar 'Sad Man'. I cursed, and reached forward to switch it off. My eyes must have left the road for no more than a few seconds, but when I looked up again the car was already into a hairpin bend.

I slammed on the brakes, which was the worst thing I could have done, for the tyres skidded on the wet tarmac, and the back end spun outwards, out of control. I struggled with the wheel, but it was too late, and with a scream of ripping metal the car crashed through a hedge into a field. It was a light vehicle which had been made for speed, not durability, and it started to roll. I braced myself, feeling no fear, only mild surprise that death should come so ingloriously. Then I must have hit my head, for I lost consciousness.

Chapter Two

Chris Steinberg was pacing the hallway when the tall, fair-headed woman stepped from the lift. He recognised her immediately, even though they had never met, for it was like looking at a mirror image of her son. They both had the same oval-shaped face, with a finely sculptured nose, generous mouth, and eyes of vivid blue. Her hair was not so bright a gold, but as she walked towards him Chris realised this was due to a sprinkling of natural silver.

'Are you Mr. Steinberg?' she asked hesitantly. She had assumed that he would be young, not a middle-aged man with thinning hair and a paunch.

'Yes,' said Chris, smiling at her. 'I'm pleased to meet you, Mrs. Hanley.'

She stripped off a glove, and as he took her hand, he saw that too was the same, thin, with long sensitive fingers.

'How is Mark?' she asked.

'He's conscious,' he said. 'He was badly knocked about, and has a broken arm. It's a miracle he came off so lightly. The car was a total write-off,' He paused. 'They won't let me see him yet, but you'll be allowed in. If you wait here, I'll find a nurse to take you to him. This is a surgical ward and they don't like people wandering round.'

'Surgical?' she asked, her voice trembling.

'They put him here because it was the safest place after some kids went on the rampage downstairs,' Chris explained. 'And it also gives me more control over who is allowed to come up. The boy is a celebrity, Mrs. Hanley. He's the biggest pop phenomenon ever to hit this country, and he's about ready to make the same impact in America. There's nobody there who can touch him.' He would have said a lot more, but she was looking impatient. 'I'm sorry. You must be anxious to see him. Why don't you sit down for a moment? There's nothing to worry about. The worst is over now, and I'm sure your coming will make the world of difference.'

'I hope so, Mr. Steinberg,'' she said, smiling weakly. He squeezed her hand, and then turned away.

As Mary Hanley watched him go, she thought about the son whom she had not seen in four years. The teenagers outside the gates had come as a shock, for they had thrust home to her the person Mark had become and the life he had chosen. They had mostly been girls, waiting in silence for news of their idol. Some were crying, and most of them held pictures of him. And there were flowers everywhere; thrust through railings and scattered over the pavement.

She found it impossible, even now, to think of the so-called Mark Anthony as her son. He had always been strong-willed and constantly bickering with his father, but only when he started working at the family textile mill had the head-on clash occurred. The two of them had quarrelled once too often, and Mark had not only walked out of the mill, but out of all their lives as well. He had left behind him a fire which—even though Paul Hanley eventually made it clear to everyone that his son was not to blame—had destroyed Mark's reputation, as well as part of the mill. He had disappeared, and nobody had known anything about him until a year later, when a singer named Mark Anthony exploded onto the music scene.

She had followed his remarkably successful rise to fame, but during the past few months had begun to suspect that something was wrong. She had watched helplessly, unable to discuss her fears with anyone, for Paul would barely acknowledge the existence of his son, while their daughter, Francesca, was too involved with her fiancé to worry about a brother of whom she had always been jealous.

But when Mary Hanley heard of last night's accident on the early morning news, she had known that this was her opportunity to re-enter Mark's life. 'I want him to come home,' she had said over breakfast that morning. 'I ask very little of you, Paul, but I am going to bring him back, and I want you to forget your grudges and accept him for what he is. It's no good thrusting the mill down his throat. He never was interested in it, and never will be now.'

'Mill has been handed on to Hanleys from generation to generation,' he said. 'What would you have me do? Give it to that upstart journalist Fran wants to marry?'

'Will there by anything left to give anyone?' she shrewdly retorted. It was a nasty remark, for Hanley Mill, one of the most reputable textile mills in southern Yorkshire, was in financial trouble. In order to rebuild and replace badly outdated machinery, Paul Hanley had borrowed heavily from a number of banks, and now there was talk that the loans were about to be called in. If that happened, he would have no option but to sell out. 'Well?' she persisted.

'This is still his home,' he said. 'But you're chasing shadows, Mary, for he'll not come, not now. I doubt you'll even get to see him.'

But see him she certainly would...

'Mrs. Hanley,' said Chris Steinberg, startling her. There was a young nurse with him. 'You can go in now. If you need anything I'll be out here.'

The nurse turned away. 'Please follow me,' she said.

Mary Hanley stood up, her eyes resting on Chris Steinberg's tired face. 'I think you ought to know that I am going to try and persuade him to come home,' she said. 'This life isn't really for him, and I think that, deep down, you already know it.'

Chris gazed at her, his face expressionless. 'He'd be a fool to give up now,' he said.

'Aren't we all fools at times?' Mary Hanley asked as she walked past him. 'Even Mark?'

She was taken to a small room which smelt of medicine and carbolic soap. His eyes were closed, and his face looked pale and drawn beneath the heavy bruising. His left arm, encased in ugly plaster, was lying flat beside him, with only the still fingers visible.

'It's the concussion which is making him sleep so much,' the nurse explained. 'You'll find that he wakes for short periods, but is quite lucid during those times. If you need anything, use the bell.' She said it without much conviction, for celebrity or not, there were other patients more in need of her attention.

Mary Hanley walked across the room and, pulling a hard-backed chair close to the bed, sat down. She watched his unmoving face, and shuddered more than oncc at the thought of how easily he could have been killed.

She sat there for an hour, listening to his steady breathing. At some stage the nurse reappeared with a welcome cup of tea. She had drunk half of it when he suddenly stirred and, taken by surprise, she almost dropped the cup on the linoleum floor. Her hands shook as she put it on the small bedside cabinet.

'Mark?' she murmured.

His head moved almost imperceptibly. She repeated his name, and his eyes opened abruptly, staring at her in confusion.

'Mark, darling, it's me,' she said, leaning forward to kiss him.

'Mother,' he said, his voice a whisper. 'What on earth are you doing here?'

'You are still my son. You should have known I would come.'

He smiled, and she took hold of his right hand, tightly gripping the long fingers between hers.

'I hoped you would,' he said. 'But it seemed unlikely after what happened.'

'Why did you run away?' she asked. 'It wasn't like you, and only made everything look so much worse. You must have known the fire couldn't have been your fault. The wiring was pre-war, and it could have happened any time.'

'It wasn't the fire which made me leave,' he said quietly. 'I didn't even know about it at the time. I simply had to get away from father's domination. When I found out, I didn't really care whether it was my fault or not. And I certainly never gave a damn about what other people thought.' He closed his eyes, as though the memory was still painful to him. 'What would have been the point of staying? Father and I would have only had another show-down. Was it a bad fire?'

'He had to cut down on production for a while, and then, because he was hopelessly under-insured, had to take out large loans to buy more modern machinery. That meant mortgaging everything we own, something he never wanted to do.'

'I warned him of the consequences if he didn't start a gradual modernisation programme,' Mark said. 'But he wouldn't listen to me. He never did. He wouldn't even give me any responsibility.'

'That's because you never seemed to take anything seriously,' his mother said. 'I think he lived in terror of you going off the rails.'

'Didn't I?' he asked, bitterness edging his voice.

'No,' she said. 'If you had, all those people would not be patiently waiting outside for news of you. Part of your trouble is that you have never been satisfied with what you have. You're like your grandfather. He always wanted to do more ... to be better. He burnt himself out in the end, and didn't achieve very much for all his efforts. I know your father's faults better than anyone, but it was his dogged determination which kept the mill going during the war, and through the depression before that. You're not unintelligent, as you have proved again and again, yet you always seemed to take a perverse pleasure in defying him in everything you did.'

He smiled. 'Only because he was so damn serious. It started out as a game, but eventually became a way of life.'

'And more often than not, it was hell for the rest of us,' she said acidly.

He seemed to hesitate. 'Why do you think I backed down so often?' he asked. 'In the end I had no option but to stand up to him.'

'I know that too,' said his mother gently. 'I could see your frustration.'

She reached forward and swept a few strands of fair hair from his forehead, and then they talked a little longer, until a nurse brought in some medicine and he drifted back to sleep. When he awoke again it was dark outside, and the room was lit by a shaded bulb.

'How do you feel?' his mother asked.

'Sore.' He shifted a little, and managed to raise himself on the pillows. 'Will you be staying?'

'Only if you want me to. I've booked into a nearby hotel.'

He frowned, the strain visible as he tried to pull together his jumbled thoughts. 'You aren't exactly a poor relative, Mother. I have a comfortable flat in central London which you are welcome to use, and there's a chauffeur-driven car which can bring you back and forth. Chris will be happy to make the arrangements. I'm sure he's still out there.'

'No,' she snapped, blue eyes clashing with blue. 'I came here to see my son, not some trumped-up image who goes under the name of Mark Anthony. I want nothing whatsoever to do with that side of your life, and would prefer to remain at the hotel.'

He shifted away from her in the bed. 'I should have known you would disapprove,' he said after a moment. 'It wasn't planned, it just seemed to come about by accident. I suppose I could have stopped it, but I'm not sure whether I wanted to at first.'

'Well, I consider it to be an absolute waste of an expensive education, and of a more than adequate brain,' said his mother. 'And just look at you. You're far too thin. What have you been living on? A large dose of nervous energy?'

He turned his head again to face her. His eyes were half closed with weariness, but he returned her stare. 'Chris wants me to make an American tour early next year. What with one thing and another, the pressure has been building up. But I promise to take some time off.'

'I want more than that,' she said sharply, 'I want you to come home.'

He stared at her for a moment.

'What does Father say to that?' he asked. 'I haven't noticed him rushing down to find out whether I'm still alive. And electrical fault or not, I expect he still blames some of the fire on me.'

'I have spoken with Paul,' she said gently. 'He won't turn you away. And as for the fire, it's forgotten. Come home, Mark. I think you need its sanity far more than you realise.' She paused. 'You look exhausted. Get some sleep and we'll talk again later.'

'You will not talk,' he said. 'You will bully me until I give way.'

From the moment he opened his eyes and saw his mother sitting beside him, he knew that Mark Anthony had ceased to exist. He was prepared for strong resistance from Chris, but was surprised to receive nothing worse than a mild protest; nor did Chris try to stop his use of an almost non-existent health clause as a way out of an otherwise watertight contract. But then Chris had always been more of a friend than a manager, and Mark suspected that he had sensed this crisis was coming long before the accident brought it to a head.

There were also other contracts to be broken, and a lot of people were justifiably furious; but it was the fans who suffered most, for after the much publicised car crash, Mark Anthony simply disappeared. A rumour began to circulate that he had been badly disfigured; it was a rumour which those who knew better made no attempt to quell.

Mary Hanley had been home a fortnight when her son turned his back on London. He left quietly, and arrived at Manchester in equal anonymity. Nobody met him, for he had told nobody when he was coming.

Manchester was cold and cloudy with the promise of rain later in the evening, or even snow if the wind dropped. The Hanley home was an hour's drive from the city, and Mark struggled to find a taxi driver willing to undertake the long journey. He did find one eventually, but only because the man recognised the expensive cut of his heavy overcoat and, against all regulations, asked for and received half the fare in advance.

It was strange to be back after all this time. They left Manchester behind, and after passing through some scattered villages, reached the small town of Steelton. Mark was surprised to see how it had grown, with rows of houses where he could remember green fields, more shops in the main street, and a cinema with flashing neon lights. Steelton owed its existence to the Hanley Mill, but as he peered out of the taxi window, Mark thought he could detect the beginning of a slow eradication of the strong Hanley influence.

Then Steelton was gone, and after travelling a few more miles they came to Oldenshaw, a tiny one-street village with two neat rows of slate-roofed cottages. The taxi bumped over a small patch of cobblestones which still remained in front of the smithy, then passed the Jolly Farmer, the pub most favoured by what was predominantly a farming community.

From Oldenshaw, it was only a mile and a half to Olden Manor, an elegant house set amidst a rambling twenty acres, heavily wooded around the borders, and impossible to see from the road. As the driver slowed down to negotiate the open gateway his passenger leant forward and, touching him on the shoulder, asked him to stop.

The driver looked at him as though he were mad. 'Are you sure?'

'Yes. How much do I owe you?'

Mark handed over the remaining fare, together with a generous tip. The man counted the notes, pushed them into his pocket, and then, smiling broadly, wished the young man good luck.

Mark felt he needed that luck as he watched the taxi speed back towards the village. A bitter wind cut through him and, realising how cold it was, he turned up the driveway, the gravel crunching noisily beneath his feet. It was a longer walk than he remembered, and above him the wind sighed through the rows of tall pine trees. An owl hooted, and he froze for a moment before recognising thc sound; and then he laughed at his foolishness.

The house came into view. It had no clearly defined shape in the darkness, but looked like an enormous shadow set amongst deeper shadows, with only a few of its many windows reflecting light. A lamp glowed above the old oak door, hewn, it was reputed, from a tree in the then much larger estate. He cut across the lawn, the short grass crisp with the promise of a cold winter, and then hesitated on reaching the four wide steps which led to the front door. He wondered, for the first time, whether he had been so wise to come without warning. But he was here now, and there was no going back.

He climbed the steps, put down his suitcase, and reached for the old-fashioned bell-cord. As he pulled it, the first snowflake of winter blew against his cheek. Shivering from a combination of cold and exhaustion, he leant against the wall behind him, listening to the reverberating clang of the bell and, further away, a barking dog. He wondered whether it was Whisky. The border collie had been eleven when he left.

The snow was coming down in angry clouds when the door was opened by a young girl of about seventeen who had a moon-shaped face and rosy cheeks. She looked annoyed, and kept the door between them.

'Good evening,' she said, none too politely. 'If you've come to see the master, he's at dinner, and won't like being disturbed.'

He had not expected the fatted calf, but even so he stared at her in astonishment, unable, for a moment, to grasp the fact that she did not recognise him. And then he remembered the bruises which still discoloured his face, and the hat which he had worn to hide the conspicuous golden hair.

'This one time you will have to disturb him,' he said. 'And if you don't mind, I should like to come in.'

She pulled the door a little wider, peering suspiciously beyond him as though expecting a horde of bandits to appear. 'He won't like it,' she sullenly repeated, stepping aside to let him pass.

He halted just inside the door, gazing around the hall which was virtually unchanged, except that it was warm enough to suggest his father had finally installed central heating. It was a magnificent hall, crowned by a grand sweep of stairs with an intricately hand-carved balustrade; but it had always been draughty and nobody ever lingered here long.

The ugly Victorian coatstand which has father would allow nobody to throw out was still behind the door. There were some coats on it now, and an old gardening mac which probably belonged to his mother. He took off his hat and hung it on a spare hook, and was starting to peel off his coat when he heard the maid gasp. He swung round, and saw that she was staring at him with distended eyes. She knew now who he was, and although she had never met Mark Hanley, she recognised Mark Anthony.

'What's your name?' he asked, struggling to free himself of the cumbersome coat.

'Elaine, sir,' she stammered. 'But everyone calls me Elly.'

'Well then, Elly, could you tell my parents that I am home?'

'Wouldn't you prefer to go straight in?' she asked, her cheeks scarlet.

'No,' he said. 'I think it would be best if I stayed here.'

'I'll not be a minute, sir,' she murmured, and bobbed a curtsey before dashing away.

It was not long before voices drifted down the passage; his mother, sharp and enquiring; his father, more ponderous. There were footsteps, neither slow nor hurried, which did not belong to the maid. He knew then that his father was coming alone.

Paul Hanley halted beside the staircase, one hand resting against the bannister. In four years he had grown old, and was no longer the tall imposing man Mark remembered. His body seemed to have shrunk, and there were deep lines in his face which had not been there before. But his eyes were bright, and the aura of authority undiminished.

'Hello, Father,' Mark said.

'Mark,' he replied, and although he did not return the greeting, his voice was not angry like the last time they had confronted each other. 'You look different. More mature. Your mother said you would come back, but I thought that was your way of getting her out of your life.'

'I couldn't leave immediately,' Mark said. 'Do you object to my being here? If so, I'd rather go now.'

He was surprised when his father smiled. 'And have your mother never speak with me again? Even Fran is excited, and you and her never did nowt but fight. Nay lad, this is your home, and despite our differences I'd not put you out. How did you come?'

'By train.'

His brows rose, for the boy could not be lacking money. But he refrained from making a caustic remark. 'You should have let us know,' he said instead. 'Come along now, your mother's waiting.'

In the impressive dining room, Mary Hanley had risen from the table and stood beside a coal fire. Mark hesitated inside the door, aware of his father breathing down the back of his neck; and then his mother stepped forward. They clung together for a few moments, letting their emotions speak for them.

Mark was smiling when he turned towards his sister. Francesca Hanley had inherited none of her mother's grace and beauty, and at twenty years old, she was still an awkward, overweight girl. She had always resented her brother because not only had he been endowed with good looks, but had a personality to match. But time had helped bridge the gap, and she was genuinely pleased to see him now. She got up from the table and kissed him affectionately before proudly introducing her fiancé.

Eric Stewart was a small man with greased-back hair and sharp eyes which missed nothing. Mark was unimpressed, for plain though she was, he thought Fran could have done better for herself. Eric Stewart, on the other hand, could not believe his luck. He had known there was a brother, but not until Mary Hanley returned from her mysterious trip to London did he learn who that brother was. It was an added bonus for someone who had clawed his way up from the slums of Glasgow, for here was someone who might, perhaps, take him all the way to the top...

Paul Hanley, in the meantime, had told the maid to set another place at the table, and when she came into the room a few minutes later, the dog came with her, pushing through the door, and running to Mark. It was Whisky, fifteen years old and squirming like a puppy.

'Get that dog out of here!' Paul Hanley bellowed. 'I'll not have animals at dining-table.'

'Let him be, Paul,' said his wife, laying a restraining hand on his arm. 'After all, he is Mark's dog.'

'Excuse me, ma'am,' Elly said nervously. 'Maude and Albert are in the hall.'

Maude was the housekeeper and Albert the head gardener. They had come to Olden Manor when Mary Hanley was a young bride, had married and stayed, and were now part of the family.

'Tell them to come in,' Mary Hanley said as her son broke free from the ecstatic dog. Mark looked at her, smiling still, and then gazed around the familiar room, thinking how good it was to be home.

Chapter Three

Lisa Crowder was nearly home when she was forced to abandon the old Morris and struggle the rest of the way on foot. The snow had come early this year, and her father would be furious, for it meant keeping the valuable dairy herd inside the barns, eating their way through expensive winter fodder, and growing restless with inactivity.

It took her half an hour to reach the yard, where the going was easier because pathways had been cleared between the buildings.

'Who's there?' a gruff voice shouted as she passed the smaller of the three barns.

'Me,' she said, peering round the door at a wizened old man with bow legs who was pitching hay. The other farmhands came in daily from Oldenshaw, but Harold lived in a small cottage behind the pigsties, and had done so for as long as she could remember.

'Why, Miss Lisa!' he exclaimed in horror. 'Your dad never expected you home so soon, and in this weather.'

'I know,' she said. 'But exams are finished, and I wanted to surprise him. Where is he?'

'In the house, where you ought to be. I never heard the car come in.'

'Because I couldn't get it in,' she said. 'It's lovely to be home again, Harold. And I think we're going to have a white Christmas.'

He snorted. 'Cows will be eating their heads off. And you'll be spending Christmas in bed if you don't get out of those wet clothes. Anyhow, it's still three weeks away.'

She grinned. Harold was always happiest when he had something to complain about. 'And how are the horses?' she asked as she was about to leave.

'Like cows,' he moaned. 'Eating their bloody heads off.'

Her irrepressible laughter echoed through the yard as she ran to the granite-built farmhouse.

'I'm home!' she yelled, flinging open the kitchen door and dropping her small holdall as she fended off the delighted dogs.

'As if we couldn't tell,' said a dour voice. 'And if you don't hurry up and shut that door there's going to be more snow in here than out there.'

Lisa kicked it with her foot, and then ran to the housekeeper and kissed her on the cheek. Orchid Livingstone had been employed by Richard Crowder on the untimely death of his wife when Lisa was only four years old. She was an austere woman with a quick tongue, but she loved the girl like her own daughter.

Richard Crowder had been dozing in his favourite chair before the open range, and awoke with a start when the door slammed. He saw his daughter, and was surprised, as always, by how like her mother she looked. She was twenty-one now, a slim girl with long coltish legs, and a pale skin which was smooth as porcelain. Her thick hair was naturally red, not an ugly carroty colour, but more like burnished copper, and she had her mother's laughing eyes which saw nothing but good in everything.

Those eyes were watching him now. 'Aren't you pleased to see me, Daddy?' she asked.

He stood up and held out his arms. She ran to him, and he hugged her affectionately.

'How's university?' he asked, holding her at arm's length.

'The bugs and bacteria are about to drive me to drink,' she said. 'I sometimes wonder why I decided to become a vet. It's beastly hard work.'

Before she could evade him, her father lifted her chin, and gazed into the emerald eyes. 'Roads will be impassable soon,' he said. 'Why didn't you phone you were coming?'

'Because I wanted to surprise you,' she said, pulling away from his gentle grasp. 'But I'm afraid someone will have to dig the car out in the morning. It got bogged down in Tanner's Lane, and I had to walk. I haven't missed supper, have I, Orchid?'

'If you had you'd get me to cook another,' came the scolding reply. 'It'll be a half-hour yet, but I'll brew a pot of tea while you're waiting. Go and sit by fire with your father. And take dogs with you. I don't know why they have to come in house. There's not another farm in the district where the dogs aren't kept outside where they belong.'

'That's cruel,' said Lisa. 'Especially in weather like this.'

'Aye,' her father agreed. 'It would be now, after you've gone and spoilt them silly all these years. Come and tell me about the bugs and bacteria, and what else you've been up to since you were last home.'

She curled up on the rug at his feet, the palms of her hands stretched towards the fire. 'I'd much rather hear about the farm,' she told him. 'And the horses.'

'Aye, it's always the horses,' Orchid said as she spooned tea into a china pot.

Neither of them would admit it, but for Richard and Lisa Crowder their lives revolved around each other and their beloved horses.

It was much later in the evening. Orchid had gone to bed, and Richard Crowder only stayed because he was as eager to listen as his daughter was to talk. They were sipping a last cup of tea when he suddenly said, 'Malcolm Dunnett was on telephone yesterday. I told him you'd be home soon.'

Lisa frowned into her cup. Malcolm was sweet enough, but could be a bit of a dim-witted clot at times. She had only agreed to go out with him because her father approved, and now he was becoming a pest every time she came home.

'Then thank goodness for the snow drifts,' she said. 'With luck, he'll be stuck on the other side of Steelton for a while.'

'I thought you liked him, lass.'

'In small doses,' she said. 'And you needn't look so worried. I want to be a career woman, and the last thing I'm going to do is settle down and have a family.'

'Good God!' he exclaimed, 'I don't want you married. I just like to see you going out and having some fun, and not sitting with us old folk all the time.'

'I like sitting with you old folk,' she said. 'In fact, I must go and see Aunt Mary tomorrow morning. I want to tell her about ...' She stopped abruptly when she saw her father frown. 'What's the matter?' she asked anxiously. 'Is she ill?'

'Nay,' he quickly replied. 'But if you're going to the Manor, you ought to know that he's back. He came about three weeks ago.'

'Mark?' she asked, her voice a hoarse whisper.

'Aye, Mark,' he said. Lisa had been remarkably devoted, collecting a thousand and one pictures of her childhood friend, and subjecting her father and Orchid to a repertoire of records which consisted solely of hits by the so-called Mark Anthony. Richard Crowder realised that fantasy and hero-worship were a part of growing up, but now the illusion was about to become reality and he felt frightened for her.

Lisa, in turn, was aware of her stomach churning. 'You've seen him?' she asked.

'Aye, when I was taking Ben and Betsy to plough Lark Meadow.

He was walking in the lanes with that old black dog he got from us. We chatted for a while, and he asked after you.'

She felt her cheeks burning and quickly looked down so that he would not see. 'It he ... is he very different?' she asked.

Richard Crowder took her hand and squeezed it gently. 'No,' he said. 'Not really. He's thinner, I think, and older.'

She looked up at him and smiled. 'I'm glad he's come back, if only for Aunt Mary's sake. But what am I going to do now? I can't go there tomorrow as though I don't know. And what on earth am I going to say when I meet him?'

Her father stared at her with astonishment. 'That's plain silly,' he said.

'I expect so,' she agreed, and took a deep breath. 'I don't suppose you noticed whether he tints his hair like all the magazines say?'

Richard Crowder threw back his head and roared with laughter, wakening the sleeping dogs, and alarming a ginger cat which was curled in the hearth.

The next morning Lisa took out her horse Kingston, while Richard Crowder and Harold went to fetch the car.

'Stick to high ground,' her father warned. 'Don't let him get cold, and don't stay out long'.

It was bitterly cold and, keeping the horse at a brisk pace, she went to one of her favourite places, a small scattering of trees which was filled with childhood memories. She and Mark had often come here during the summer months, she mounted on the ill-tempered Snowy, and he on his flashy and headstrong pony, Tuppence. It was from here that they had been able to watch the formations of planes from an airfield further north going out on bombing missions over Germany. At other times, when the skies were clear, they had sat talking, or else pretended to be famous show jumpers, putting their ponies at fallen logs and branches. That had been a long time ago, and he would probably laugh about it now. But it was a world from which she had never grown away.

As she approached the trees, startled birds broke noisily from a bush, and a deer, caught in the act of stripping bark from a young sapling, fled in panic. Kingston watched it with bulging eyes, and holding him still, Lisa watched too. It was a long time since she had last seen a deer in these parts.

She walked the horse between the trees, and on seeing the uprooted oak, turned him towards it. The tree had come down in a storm over a decade ago, but although most of the roots were dried out and exposed to the elements, there was still enough life left for it to sprout a few leaves each spring. It was not high, and even Snowy had managed the jump in her younger days. Kingston knew it too, and sprang eagerly forward. But as he was about to lift off, something frightened him and he shied to the left. Lisa automatically corrected him, but he was off balance and decided to stop. He was practically sitting on his haunches as his forelegs shot out before him, and Lisa, who was leaning forward, fell off. She landed on her back and, the breath knocked out of her, lay gasping.

'I have him,' said a familiar voice. 'Are you hurt?'

'No,' she wheezed. 'Except for my pride.' She sat up. 'I was wondering how to make an impact.'

'Well, you've succeeded,' Mark said, and offered her a hand. 'I only wish you would remember not to let go of the reins. You always did. Every time you fell off, Tuppence and I had to chase Snowy most of the way home.'

He pulled her to her feet, and as she stood brushing snow from her jodphurs she decided that he had not really changed all that much. He was taller than she remembered him, and although he had always been good looking, he had matured into the most handsome man she had ever seen. It was little wonder that he created hysteria wherever he went. His windblown hair bore no trace of unnatural colour, and his eyes were so vivid a blue that she found them hypnotic.

And then she saw his lips twitch with irrepressible humour, and smiling at him said, 'What are you doing here? It's miles from anywhere.'

'Walking. I enjoy the exercise, and so does Whisky.'

She took the reins from him. 'How long will you be staying?'

'Long enough to shake off the shadow of Mark Anthony,' he said abruptly. 'Other than that I don't know.' He was looking at the horse. 'He's shivering. Why did you have him clipped?'

'Daddy had him done for hunting,' she said, frowning. 'And I'm cold as well, so you must be frozen. Are you coming back to the farm?'

He shook his head. 'I'm expected home, and you ought to keep him moving.'

'You can telephone,' she said. 'Please come, Mark. We've so much to catch up on, and Kingston will be all right if we walk quickly.'

He looked at her for a moment, remembering the tomboy with plaits who had been his closest friend. The plaits had gone, but he suspected the tomboy had not. He smiled at the thought. 'All right,' he said. 'But I can't stay long.'

They fell into step, with the horse and dog plodding behind.

'I thought you would be different,' she said after a while.

'I've changed, Lisa,' he admitted. 'but coming here is like taking a step back in time.'

'But won't you miss being a celebrity?' she asked.

'No,' he said again, his voice flat, as though he found the subject distasteful.

'But surely it was exciting and glamorous?' she persisted.

He laughed. 'Perhaps it was once, but in the end it was just a job. Now can't we talk about something other than what I have been doing?'

She stared at him with rounded eyes. 'What do you expect?' she asked. 'After all, your choice of career was rather extraordinary.'

His eyes met hers. 'I suppose I deserved that.'

'No,' she said. 'Not really. But I'm glad you're back.'

'Storm's about to break,' Harold said as he walked into the barn. 'They'll not be clearing the roads today.'

Richard Crowder glanced up. 'Is she home yet?' he asked.

'Nay. But the horse won't want to stay out long in this.'

The farmer nodded, his mind with the work which still had to be done. 'Can you see to pigs?' he asked. 'I'll not be finished here for another half-hour.'

'Aye,' replied Harold, and pushing his hands into his pockets, went back outside.

The wind was blowing furiously, carrying on it fresh snow, when Richard Crowder heard a trumpeting whinny. He pushed open the barn door and peered out. Lisa was struggling to close the gate, while somebody else held the excited horse.

'Oh, let him go,' she shouted.

It was Mark Hanley. There was no mistaking that hair as the tall young man threw the reins across the saddle and then slapped the horse on the rump. Kingston leapt forward, gave another deafening whinny, and trotted across to the stable block where he rubbed noses with Snowy.

Richard Crowder felt a twinge of anxiety as he wondered what fate had brought them together so soon. Mark had been a trustworthy, if headstrong boy, but now he was a self-confident young man who, according to the press, only needed to snap his fingers to have any woman he wanted. Mark Anthony had lived a life which Richard could not begin to comprehend, and so it was only natural that he should fear for his daughter.

Orchid Livingstone was watching from the kitchen window, and when they turned towards the house she put on the kettle.

'I've brought Mark back,' Lisa said, bursting into the kitchen. 'I fell off Kingston and he came to the rescue.'

'The original knight in white armour,' Mark said from behind her. 'Hello, Orchid. You've not changed a bit.'

'And I see you're still one with the words,' she said, pleased nonetheless. 'As for you, young lady, bring those dogs in, or else shut them out.'

'They're excited because of Whisky,' Lisa protested.

'They're nowt but spoilt silly. Now get upstairs and change into some dry clothes. And I'll take that wet coat, Mark Hanley. Your mother won't be thanking me if you catch a chill.'

'Really, Orchid,' said Lisa. 'We're not children any more.'

'I'd never have known it,' Orchid said.

Lisa scowled, and then fled. Mark kissed Orchid on the cheek. 'I'm sorry for barging in like this,' he said. 'But Lisa swept me up like a lost puppy.'

'And when did you not cause disruption in this house?' she demanded. 'Running off to London with never a word to anyone, and Lisa crying and moping for weeks afterwards, and waiting for letters which never came.'

'I never knew,' he said, genuinely surprised.

'Aye, and there's a lot more you'll not be knowing,' she snapped. 'Now go and sit by the fire while I make some tea.'

A heavy fall of snow kept Mark at the farm for the rest of the day, and it was past three before he was able to leave. They were drinking tea in the kitchen, and Richard Crowder took another slice of cake before turning to Mark. 'Parts of the southern fields are high,' he said. 'You'd best cut across them. Lisa can take you to the lane.'

'I can find my own way,' Mark said.

'Aye. But it'll be dark soon and everything looks different in the snow.'

'I was going to come anyway,' said Lisa.

They left soon after, accompanied by the dogs, who scampered through the snow and chased startled birds with shrill yaps. The wind was bitter, and heavy clouds hung low with the promise of yet more snow. They were two fields away from the lane which led to Olden Manor, and walking alongside a low stone wall, when Lisa suddenly stopped. 'It would be much quicker to go over the top,' she said. 'Can you manage with one arm?'

'I'm not totally crippled, you know.'

'All right,' she said, wrinkling her nose at him. 'But be careful, as it's sure to be slippery.'

She scrambled up the wall and perched on top, gazing across the empty fields.

'Do you know where we are?' she asked.

'Yes,' he replied, and climbing over the wall, turned to offer her his hand. She took it and jumped down beside him.

'Then surely you've not forgotten,' she said. 'Look over there.'

He followed the swing of her arm, and saw the willow tree, its trailing branches weighed down by a mantle of snow. 'Your magic pond,' he declared, eyes sparkling. 'I'd never forget that.'

'You're teasing me,' she said.

'No I'm not.'

Her lips pursed. 'Then let's go and make a wish.'

'My dear girl, do you realise that it's half a mile in the wrong direction?'

'But we have to make a wish,' she insisted. 'You know it brings bad luck not to.'

'I have no intention of walking all that way just so that I can look at a patch of ice.'

'Really, Mark!' she exclaimed. 'You've become citified and dull.'

He looked at her, seeing the excitement and anticipation in her eyes. The pond had always been a magical place for her, and she rarely passed it without making a wish.

'All right,' he said. 'But we'll have to be quick.'

He was right about the pond. It was frozen solid, and although Lisa tried, she was unable to break the ice. 'Use this,' said Mark, handing her a wet piece of wood which he had found. With it she managed to make a small hole.

'Do you have a penny?' she asked.

'I doubt it.' He searched his pockets. 'Will a green threepenny bit do?'

'That's even better. You throw it in and we'll both wish.'

He dropped the coin through the hole, then turned to her, smiling.

'You're laughing,' she objected. 'You shouldn't laugh. It'll bring bad luck.'

'Lisa,' he said, 'it would be a tragedy if you lost that sweet innocence.' He pulled her towards him, but did nothing more alarming than hold her close for a moment. 'I hope your wish comes true. Do you still ask for a pitch black Arab stallion which runs fast as the wind?'

'You're not meant to know that,' she said indignantly. She looked up at the darkening sky, suddenly aware of how late it was. 'Come on.

We'd better run. I'll race you to the gate.'

She broke away from his grasp, and together they ran, the excited dogs yapping at their heels, and their laughter echoing across the countryside.

Chapter Four

I had not cared for Christmas since leaving home, but I was now caught up in the spirit of the season as I watched age-old preparations which had laid half forgotten at the back of my mind. Everything was as I remembered it: Maude barricaded herself in the kitchen, Albert strung rows of coloured bulbs through the pine trees alongside the drive, and Elly ran back and forth like a demented creature. The tree was installed in the drawing room, and Mother worked herself into the usual panic over the Christmas Eve party. It was an annual affair, and the only time Father opened his doors to the elite of the industrial north. There had been a pointed informality about these parties when I was a child, but they were now regarded as a social event and invitations had become precious as gold.

Christmas Eve came, and Father went to the mill to preside over a staff party, while Fran slipped away with Eric, no doubt to the two-roomed flat he was renting in Steelton. My little sister, I suspected, was no longer an innocent virgin; I had several times seen her sneaking in very late with a brilliant glitter in her eyes. For her sake, and Eric's, I hoped Father would not find out.

As I would not be seeing Lisa until the evening, and because Mother was frantic about the caterers being late, I took refuge for the morning in the library. It had always been my favourite room and, fascinated by the rows of books, most of which had been lovingly collected by my great-grandfather, I had come here often as a child. I could lose myself for hours in a well-thumbed volume of 'Stories for Boys' or one of John Buchan's gripping novels.

About half past eleven, Mother burst into the room. 'This has come Special Delivery for you, dear,' she said. 'I thought it was the caterers. Really, this is the end. We'll never be ready on time.'

I took the package from her. 'It's early yet,' I said. 'This happens every year, but everything always works out. Your guests go home highly impressed and wondering if they'll get an invitation next year, but you worry the whole time and never really enjoy yourself.'

'I can't help myself,' she said. 'Aren't you going to open it?'

'It's a present for Lisa.'

She sat on a chair-arm, her hands smoothing down the folds of her skirt. 'My curiosity has got the better of me,' she admitted. 'It was delivered by a messenger from one of Manchester's higher class jewellers.'

'They were only couriers,' I told her as I stripped off the outer paper. 'It was made by a small jeweller I know in London. Do you think she'll like it?'

The emerald bracelet was quite superb. Mother took it from me and ran her fingers over the perfectly matched stones. 'The poor child will be terrified to wear it,' she said. 'When do you intend giving it to her?'

'Tonight.'

She shuddered. 'Then you'd better watch her like a hawk. And the house will be full of strangers all afternoon—don't you think you should lock it away in your father's safe? Look, I'll show you the combination.'

The safe was an old-fashioned affair located between two ranks of book-shelves and concealed by a gloomy, gilt-framed portrait of my great-grandfather. When we had stowed the bracelet safely away, Mother resumed her perch on the chair-arm and looked at me with serious eyes. 'You've always been fond of Lisa, haven't you?'

'She grows on you.'

'That's not an answer,' she said, frowning. 'But when I think about it, I can't really remember a time when you were not together. She's a charming girl who tends to be a little naive, but Richard adores her, and I don't think there's a soul in the district who dislikes her... What I'm trying to say, Mark, without sounding too much of a prude, is, don't take advantage of her.'

'We're friends, Mother, and we enjoy each other's company. We always did. I can see nothing wrong in that.'

'Of course not. I'm pleased you have got together again. We always had high hopes for you and her.'

'Oh, my God,' I mocked. 'I'm giving her a bracelet for Christmas, not a wedding band for life!'

'I am perfectly aware of that,' she snapped. 'But you seem to forget you are no longer children. If you must take up most of her time, which you have certainly done these past three weeks, then you must equally expect rumours to be rife.'

I stared at her. 'Don't tell me ... the village is agog with speculation!'

'The entire village and surrounding countryside are taking bets that you will be walking up the aisle by Easter. You are no longer in London where such things are of no importance.'

'Then heaven save us from the bigoted minds of insular people,' I said.

Mother frowned. 'I am not in the slightest bit concerned about your already dubious reputation. You can come and go as you wish, and your image will remain untarnished. But Lisa intends staying here, and she can't do without local good feeling and respect. Remember that.' She gave my arm a squeeze. 'Why so serious, Mark? I'm not necessarily suggesting you see less of her. Just don't engulf her too much ... for both your sakes. And now I really must find out where those wretched caterers are.'

Father came home for lunch, a flung together hotchpotch which we ate in one of the smaller rooms. Mother was too busy to join us, and afterwards I was surprised when Father asked if I would go with him to the study.

'Why?' I asked.

His face clouded. 'Can't I ask the simplest thing of you without my motives being questioned?' he demanded.

'It just seems a strange request when we can talk just as freely in here,' I said.

'With Elly clattering the dishes?' he said more calmly. 'And your mother likely to commandeer the room at any moment for a cloakroom or a buffet or some such? What I have to say won't take long, and I'd prefer to get it over with now, and in private.'

I went with him, wondering what all the secrecy could be about. He offered me a brandy, which I refused. I sat on one of the leather chairs, pulled out my cigarettes, and then put them away again as I recalled the last time we had been together at the mill.

'I don't object to your smoking,' Father said. He was standing beside the desk and had picked up a large envelope which he was turning over in his hands.

'I can do without,' I said. 'I need to cut down. I was going through two packs a day before I came back.'

'That's not surprising, considering the unnatural life you were leading,' he said. It was the first direct reference he had ever made to my past. 'Have you thought about what you're going to do now?'

'No,' I said, although it was something which had been constantly on my mind. 'There's no point in doing anything until this bloody arm comes out of plaster.'

'Would you consider coming back to the mill?' he asked.

'No, Father,' I said. I stood up, prepared to leave the room rather than be drawn into an argument. 'I have no interest whatsoever in the mill, and even if I did, it would never work for the two of us to be there together.'

'It would be different from the last time.'

'Perhaps it would at first, but we would never be able to agree.'

'Is that your last word on the matter?' he asked heavily.

'Yes,' I said.

'I won't say I'm not disappointed, because I am. Somebody has to take it over. I'm getting old.'

'Give it to Fran as a wedding present,' I said.

He frowned, his mouth forming a grim line. 'You always were flippant,' he said. 'I had hoped you'd grown out of it. Here, take this now before I change my mind.' He held forward the envelope.

'What is it?' I asked.

'My Christmas present to you, and proof that I bear you no hard feelings,' he said. 'Are you going to insult me by refusing it?'

'No,' I said. I took the envelope from him, tore it open and tipped the shares onto the desk. 'How many are here?' I asked.

'Twenty per cent of the total holdings. They were meant to come to you on your twenty-first birthday. But before you accept them, I'm imposing one condition. If you ever want to sell, I'm to have first option. If you won't agree to that, then you can return them now.'

I wanted neither his money nor his shares, but to refuse would only provoke a full scale row. I offered him my hand, which pleased him, and said, 'I wouldn't mind that drink now.'

He was smiling as he poured two generous brandies. 'Here's to better understanding between us,' he said.

I raised my glass, but said nothing.

I was ready too early and as I wandered downstairs saw Elly lurking behind an elaborate flower arrangement. She looked self-conscious in her new uniform, and on hearing my steps she darted back like a frightened rabbit. I walked over to where she was hiding.

'The first guests won't start arriving for at least another half hour,' I said. 'Is this your first party?'

She stepped forward, her cheeks scarlet and eyes downcast. 'Yes, sir,' she said. 'I'm sorry, I shouldn't be up here yet, but Maude has her hands full with the caterers and I was only in the way. Everything looks so grand and I didn't think anyone would be down for a while.'

'They won't,' I said. 'There is usually a last minute panic with everybody dashing down as the first car draws up. Are you as nervous as you look?'

'No,' she said unconvincingly.

She seemed very young and vulnerable standing there, reminding me of Lisa four years ago. It had been her first party and my last.

'You need a drink to steady your nerves,' I said.

'Oh no, sir, I couldn't possibly.'

'Of course you can,' I said, glancing at my watch. 'You can't stand around here doing nothing, and a little Dutch courage never hurt anyone. Come along.' She did not move, and so I took her by the arm and led her into the library.

I handed her a glass of sherry and as she refused to sit down, I also remained standing. She was reluctant to talk, partly I think because she was still in awe of me. But the sherry helped loosen her tongue, and after a great deal of persuasion she told me she was the daughter of a farm worker, one of seven children, and fortunate to be working in a large house such as this. She spoke respectfully of my mother's kindness, and was genuinely grateful for the way in which she was treated. Mother had always been like that. One of the earliest lessons she had taught Fran and I was not to treat servants as inferiors.

'Another?' I asked as she drained the glass.

'Good heavens, sir, you'll make me tipsy!' she exclaimed.

I laughed. 'You'd need a bottle of that stuff. And Elly, I really would prefer it if you didn't keep calling me sir. It makes me feel a hundred years old.'

She blushed. 'Yes, sir ... er, Mr. ... er ...'

'Mark,' I told her. 'Otherwise you'll be confusing me with my father.'

'Yes, sir ... Mr. Mark,' she stammered. 'I think I ought to go back to the kitchen. Maude must be wondering where I am, and the guests will be arriving soon.' She backed towards the door. 'Thank you,' she said.

'Enjoy yourself, Elly,' I told her. 'After all, this is Christmas.'

She slipped out, and I poured myself another brandy before sitting down. I seemed to recall saying much the same to Lisa all those years ago. Richard had said she was too young for a ball gown, and she looked terrified yet perfectly enchanting in a sleeveless party dress, her hair tied back with a red velvet ribbon.

It was not long after that night when I walked out. How different my life might have been had I stayed. My father had always made it clear that I would eventually take over Hanley Mill, and even when I was very young I resented him for giving me no choice. I rebelled by deliberately doing whatever he explicitly told me not to. Like the time when I was seven and forbidden to climb trees as it was dangerous. I shinned up the tallest oak I could find, slipped on the way down, and fell fifteen feet to the ground. I was unconscious for five hours and lucky not to have split open my skull.

It seemed that I was never able to please him, whatever I did. Even when I got Whisky everything went disastrously wrong. He was a heavy puppy, the largest of a litter produced by one of Richard Crowder's collies. I carried him into the study to show Father, but my arms were aching and so I put him down on the carpet, where he promptly squatted with a large puddle spreading from beneath him. Father was furious. He yelled and the puppy took fright, bolting into a low table and knocking a decanter of whisky over himself. I'm not quite sure what would have happened if Mother had not walked in. She quickly calmed down Father and then picked up the puppy, laughingly saying that from now on he should be called 'Whisky'. The name stuck, as did the pungent aroma.

I was smiling at the memory of Maude washing him in an old tin bath on the kitchen table when the doorbell rang, startling me. I glanced up, wondering if Lisa had arrived. Elly knew to send her in here. But the voices which mingled with those of my parents were unfamiliar, and finishing the brandy I stood up to pour myself another. I lit a cigarette and sank back into the chair, trying to recall when it was that Lisa and I first became friends.

I had known her all my life, as she often came to play with Fran. But they were an ill-suited couple, for Lisa was not interested in dolls and tea parties, and when she became bored with Fran's make-believe she would often come to see what I was doing. But it was not really until the outbreak of war that we drew close. Fate was obviously working against Father, for his plans concerning my immediate future were thwarted. I should have gone to Rugby where he had been educated and his father before him, but because of the possibility of bombing, plans were hastily altered and it was decided that I should attend Steelton's small co-ed school. Before that I had gone to a private school on the outskirts of Manchester where I was treated no differently to the other boys. But in Steelton I was Paul Hanley's son and heir to the Hanley Mill. As the majority of pupils were the children of mill-worker families I was either treated with awe or ignored altogether. I very soon learnt about loneliness and rejection, and began to detest the name Hanley because it was instrumental in setting me apart from the others.

I suppose that in this isolation it was natural I should draw closer to Lisa, but it was not until the Christmas of 1939, when her father bought Snowy at an auction, that our friendship was sealed. Fran was not the least bit interested in the pony, whereas I was as enthusiastic as Lisa. Together we learnt to ride and then, quite miraculously, Father agreed to let me have a pony of my own. By then Maude and Albert had virtually taken over our upbringing. I saw less and less of Father as he worked long hours at the mill, battling to complete urgent government contracts with a badly depleted, under-skilled staff. Mother was equally involved with charity work, so I think it was meant to be a way of making up for their loss.

I certainly did not miss my father, and for Lisa and me those were good years. We had our ponies and our freedom, and were never really touched by the horrors of war. During summer we would disappear for daylong trips with packed lunches, while in winter there was hunting, a sport which continued throughout the war years. But the lull could not last forever, and in November of 1942 I fell foul of Father again. But I was growing up and this time I answered him back, with consequences I had not anticipated.

We had house guests for the weekend; two pompous men with their wives who were here arranging future contracts for the mill. Many mills were being forced to close down and I knew Father was fighting for survival. When they heard I was hunting on Sunday, they expressed a desire to follow on foot. Father managed to arrange for Richard Crowder to accompany them, as well as himself, while much to Mother's relief, the women decided they would prefer to remain in the house. Father had never intruded in my domain before, and I was nervous about him being here now. It was Lisa who pointed out that we were sure to lose them if we raised a fox.

But everything went wrong. The fox doubled back and hounds killed it in practically the same spot we had started from. To make matters worse, I found myself well to the front, which was something I had always avoided. As the hounds fought over the bloody carcass I turned Tuppence away, which was when Richard Crowder appeared.

'It's about time you were blooded,' he said to Lisa. 'And you too, Mark.'

'No thank you,' I said curtly. 'I think it's a barbaric custom.'

'It's tradition,' he said. 'And foxes are vermin. You know that.'

'Which doesn't mean I have to be splattered with their blood,' I said, kicking Tuppence on.

I did not see my father standing in our path, and had to pull up so sharply that Tuppence tossed his head angrily. He was frowning, and not far behind him stood his two guests, their trousers mud-stained.

'You'll not shame me in front of all these people,' said Father very quietly. 'You're a Hanley, and it's about time you damn well started behaving like one.'

He reached for the reins, but he knew nothing about horses, and I was easily able to pull Tuppence round. The excited pony sprang into a canter, and then a gallop. I leant forward and let him go, only stopping when white beads of sweat started to form on his neck. I dismounted, and led him for a while. I couldn't go home yet. I knew Father would be furious.

Lisa found me an hour later. I was sitting on the wet ground beside the pond, hugging my knees.

'Uncle Paul is awfully angry,' she said, sitting down beside me. 'You shouldn't have gone off like that. It wasn't that bad. Don and Nancy had it done as well. Don got the brush.'

I looked at the dried blood which was smeared across her forehead. 'Wash it off,' I said, giving her a handkerchief.

'It's meant to stay on all day,' she protested.

'Wash it off, Lisa, or else go away and leave me alone.'

She took the handkerchief and dipped it in the pond. 'Here, you do it,' she said. 'I can't see.'

I wiped away the blood and then stared at the handkerchief in disgust. There was nowhere to throw it, so I shoved it back into my pocket.

'Did they send you to look for me?' I asked.

'Of course not. What are you going to do now?'

'What can I do except go home?'

'You could run away,' she suggested.

I almost laughed, but I didn't. After all, she was only nine years old and deadly serious.

'Where to?' I asked. I glanced up at the sky. 'It's going to rain. You'd better go home.'

'What about you?'

'I'll go too,' I said, standing up.

'Make a wish first,' she said. 'It'll help.'

'Nothing will help,' I said dismally. 'And I don't have any money on me.'

'I've got a penny,' she said.

A penny could buy a lot in those days, but she threw it into the pond, closed her eyes tight and made her wish. 'Everything will be all right now,' she assured me before we said goodbye and went our separate ways. I watched her coax Snowy into a trot, but despite the pouring rain which caught me less than halfway home, I kept Tuppence at a steady walk.

Albert was waiting for me in the stable. He tutted his disapproval and took the reins as I slid to the ground. 'Even if you don't mind getting soaked, it won't do him no good,' he said, nodding at the pony. 'Your father's waiting for you in the house. What have you done now? He came back in a flaming temper.'

'What I always do,' I said, unbuckling the girth. 'I answered him back.'

'Well, it's about time you learnt how to handle him proper,' he told me.

When I walked into the study, Father was sitting behind his desk, and Mother in a chair beside the fire. She was very pale, and I thought her welcoming smile was tense. I wondered whether they had been fighting.

'Good God, Mark, you're soaking,' she suddenly said, rising to her feet.

'Sit down, Mary,' Father said. 'This won't take long.' Water dripped onto the carpet as he purposely kept me waiting. 'You knew those people were important, but you still went ahead and made me look a fool, not only in front of them, but half the district. You wanted a pony, and you got one. You wanted to hunt, and we let you. Well, you can't expect to do things by halves. You either do them properly, or not at all. If you don't like the customs, stay away from the sport.'

'Everyone knew I didn't want to be blooded,' I told him. 'None of them ever tried to force me before.'

It was not the right thing to say.

'It's high time you learnt what discipline is,' he angrily declared. 'Your mother and I have been far too easy on you, but that's finished now. Given the choice I'd sell the damn pony tomorrow, but your mother has persuaded me that it would do more harm than good. So I've decided to send you away to school. You'll be leaving in the morning. I'll take you to the station, and you'll be met at the other end.'

'But it's only three weeks to the end of term,' I protested.

'I don't give a damn!' he shouted. 'You're going!'

And so I ended up at Rugby after all ... and after Rugby I spent a year at Oxford before deciding I didn't really want to be a full-time scholar, and going into the Air Force to do my two years national service. I was a good student, and I enjoyed flying, but none of these places or experiences seemed to leave much impression on me, and I made no lasting friends. What stayed foremost in my mind was the time spent at home, with the familiar pattern of ponies, dogs; and Lisa.

But then Tuppence died, heralding yet another change in my life. Three months before my discharge from the RAF he contracted pneumonia, and Lisa wrote to say that medication didn't seem to be helping. I came home on a weekend pass, to find him being nursed by Lisa and Harold. The stable was warm and echoing with the sick pony's rasping breath.

'We hoped you would come,' Lisa said quietly. 'I'm sorry, Mark, but he'll have to be put down. He can't go on like this for much longer.'

That afternoon the vet shot him. I did not stay to watch the hound van take him away, but walked aimlessly through the nearby countryside with Whisky padding behind me. When I finally stopped, it was to sit at the base of the uprooted oak tree in the copse. Whisky laid his chin on my knees, and I fondled his ears. I was too old to cry, but with Tuppence had gone a large part of my childhood.

Lisa came as the sun was beginning to set. 'Come home, Mark,' she said. 'You can't stay here. Orchid has a steak and kidney pie keeping warm in the oven. I don't suppose you've eaten since you got back.'

'I'm not hungry,' I said ungraciously.

'Then come anyway,' she said, taking hold of my hand.

I looked up at her. I think it was the first time I realised that she was no longer such a little girl. I stood up, and still holding hands, we walked back to the farm.

It was soon after that I went into the mill. It was a disaster from the very beginning. The machinery was antiquated and badly in need of replacement, which was not entirely Father's fault, as the war had made any kind of renovation impossible; but now was the time for improvement and change. I was fired with an initial enthusiasm, but every suggestion I made, whether practical or not, was thrown aside. I think I could have done a lot for the mill, but Father never gave me a chance, and it was only a matter of time before the inevitable explosion occurred. When it came, it was over a trivial incident. Smoking was forbidden in most parts of the mill, but Father enjoyed the occasional cigar in the privacy of his office, and one morning when I was feeling particularly irritated, I lit a cigarette.

'Please put that out,' he said crisply.

'Why?' I asked, immediately on the defensive.

'Because I told you to. And because this is my office.'

'For Christ's sake!' I swore. 'I am not a child.'

'Then stop behaving like one.' He deliberately pushed forward a cheap glass ashtray.

I knew that if I spoke I would say something I would later regret. Instead, I walked out of the office, slamming the door behind me. I stood in the narrow passageway. To the right of me were the storerooms where the bales of cotton were kept, to the left the working area with its constant throb of machinery. I heard the door open behind me.

'Put out that bloody cigarette! You know smoking isn't allowed out here.'

I swung round. I was taller than him now, so that he had to look up at me.

'You can keep your mill, Father,' I said slowly. 'I want nothing further to do with it.' I dropped the cigarette and ground it beneath my heel. The fateful cigarette which was to bring about my condemnation.

Father's face was red with anger. 'Get back into my office this instant.'

'No,' I told him, and turned away.

'Mark, come back here!' he shouted after me. The men working the looms nearest to us looked up. 'If you leave now you can also get out of my house, for I'll not have you there.'

'That suits me fine,' I called over my shoulder.

'Mark ...'

But I kept walking. I left behind everything I knew, determined that whatever I did, I would be a success.

I put down my empty glass. Yes, I had certainly been a success.

I must have been halfway through a pack of cigarettes and well into the brandy bottle when Lisa arrived. I glanced up as she slipped into the room, and my breath catching in my throat, rose silently to my feet. To put it mildly, she looked absolutely stunning. She wore a full-length green gown of some irridescent silk material which was cut low from the shoulders, revealing curves which I had not realised existed. Her hair had been piled on her head in a becoming style which complimented her neck and highlighted her cheekbones and luminous green eyes. The awkward young girl in a party dress was now a woman, and a very beautiful one.

I walked towards her, and taking hold of her hand raised it to my lips. 'Congratulations,' I said. 'You have rendered me speechless. I can see that I shall have to fight off hordes of lovelorn young men.'

She laughed merrily, and was at once the Lisa I knew so well. 'I'm sure you'll manage,' she said. 'You look morbid.'

'I shouldn't drink alone. Would you like something? I'm afraid there's only sherry or brandy in here.'

'Sherry will be lovely,' she said, sitting down and watching me. 'How many brandies have you had?'

'Three,' I told her. 'Four if you insist on counting. But you needn't worry, I never get drunk.'

'I don't care if you do,' she said. 'You'll be the one who makes a fool of yourself by falling flat on your face. It's Christmas Eve, Mark, and you should be spilling over with goodwill. What's happened?'

I handed her the sherry, and then leant against one of the tall bookshelves. 'As a show of faith, or goodwill as you would probably say, Father has given me twenty per cent of the Hanley Mill shares.'

She sipped the drink, her eyes on mine. 'It may not be your idea of the perfect Christmas present, but it's better than a pair of socks,' she said. 'And I'm sure it was done with the best intentions.'

'But I don't want to become involved with the mill,' I told her. 'I left in the first place because of it.'

'Was there a precondition that you must become involved?'

'No. He stressed the shares were mine with no strings attached. It's up to me whether I go back or stay away.'

'Then why are you so miserable?' she asked. 'Uncle Paul never says anything he doesn't mean. And it won't say much for my company if you're going to look like that all night.' She sprang to her feet, and taking the goblet from my hand, slipped her fingers into mine. 'Cheer up,' she said. 'I want to have a marvellous time, and see everyone turn green with envy when I walk in on the arm of Mark Anthony.'

'Lisa!' I protested.

'Well, it's a bit hard to ignore the fact that your other self has taken over the top three spots in the record charts,' she said.

'That is Chris trying to lure me back,' I told her. 'He and my recording company are releasing songs which I was compiling for a new long-player. Unless I'm mistaken, there's only one left. I finished it on the day of my accident.'

She let go of my hand, and stared at me with incredulous eyes. 'You're a hypocrite,' she said. 'I only heard that on the radio this afternoon, so unless you have a hot line to London, you must listen just as much as I do.' She paused, her head a little to one side. 'At least I've made you smile.'

'You always make me smile,' I said. 'And now, before we join the party, I have a little goodwill for you.'

I handed her the package.

'What is it?' she asked.

'Open it and see.'

She tore impatiently at the wrapping and then looked at me. 'You must have spent a fortune,' she said.

'On a pretty box?'

She opened her mouth, but closed it again, and opened the box.

'Oh, Mark.'

I scooped up the bracelet.

'See,' I said, 'they sparkle as bright as your eyes. Here, give me your wrist.'

'You'll never manage,' she murmured. 'Not with one hand. I'll do it.'

Her fingers were trembling, and it seemed to take her a long time. 'There,' she said, holding up her wrist. 'Thank you, Mark. It's the most beautiful present I have ever been given. Now bend down so that I can thank you properly.'

I think she only meant to kiss me on the cheek, but somehow our lips met, and when I drew her close she did not pull away. We came together naturally, as though we had always belonged; which I suppose we had.

I don't know if everybody was trying just that little bit harder or whether it had always been like this, but Christmas was an enchanting mixture of everything good that I remembered; and it was nicely rounded off by the traditional Boxing Day Meet in Oldenshaw. Lisa was riding Kingston, but I had to make do with Richard's draughty Land-Rover.

Ours had always been a small Hunt, whose main support came from the farming community. There was also a sprinkling of nobility, the most prominent amongst them being Lord Charles Latchcham who owned a run-down estate to the north of the Crowder farm.

The Hunt had changed in four years, and although the same old cronies blocked the entrance to the Jolly Farmer, the majority of people crammed into the single street were strangers. Horseboxes and cars were parked on every verge, and groups of children on shaggy ponies got in everyone's way.

'I remember when we thought a field of thirty was big,' I said as Richard Crowder parked the Land-Rover between two horseboxes.

'Aye,' he agreed. 'I don't know where they all come from, but the Committee aren't complaining as there's plenty of money coming in.'

We were almost at the pub when Lisa arrived. She was barely recognisable in breeches and knee boots, with her hair hidden by a rarely worn riding cap. She saw us and, waving, turned the plunging horse in our direction. A hound which had strayed from the main pack passed a little too close to Kingston's hind legs, and he lashed out at it. The animal was not hurt, but yelped with fright, attracting the attention of Toby Goodson, the Huntsman.

'Get that bloody horse away from here,' he yelled at her. 'It should be wearing a red ribbon.'

'He's excited,' Lisa yelled back, not in the least subdued. 'And I want a drink.'

'Take him to the side,' Richard Crowder shouted. 'Mark will bring you one.'

I somehow managed to greet the men I had known all my life, and then, with two glasses balanced precariously in one hand, I made my way to where Lisa had dismounted and was trying to stop Kingston from spinning round in circles.

'Thank you,' she said, taking a glass from me. 'Don't you wish you were riding?'

'Only on something a lot less hysterical than Kingston. Will you be able to hold him?'

'Of course,' she said. 'But I suppose it would be wiser to join some friends. I passed some of the old crowd by End Cottage. Would you like to come and say hello?'

'No,' I said. 'I have escaped detection so far because the older generation don't give a damn about Mark Anthony. But I am certainly not going to be thrust into the midst of a gang of gawping teenagers.'

'Nancy and Don are engaged, and Tina got married last year, so I would hardly classify them as gawping teenagers,' said Lisa with asperity. 'And anyway, I warned them that you're sensitive about the past, so the conversation will be restricted to the weather and horses.'

I laughed, and went with her. As Lisa had promised, they accepted me for myself, and after exchanging greetings, their chatter turned to the world of horses to which I no longer belonged. I half listened as I took in the colour and excitement of the Meet, revelling in a surge of half-forgotten memories.

I'm not sure when I became aware of the man watching me, but I instinctively swung round and stared back at him. He was small and wiry, with pasty skin and thinning brown hair which jutted out from beneath a cloth cap. There was a pretty girl of approximately half his age with him, who would have looked better had she been less heavy-handed with both make-up and peroxide. I thought, for one horrible moment, that Mark Anthony was about to raise his ugly head.

He walked towards me. 'Good morning, Mr. Hanley,' he said, squashing my fears. 'I'm sorry for intruding, but was told you might be here, and wondered if I could have a word, private like?'

I glanced at Lisa who was on her fourth glass of sherry and arguing over the treatment of spavin. 'Over here,' I said, and led them to a line of deserted cars. I leant against a bonnet which was still warm. 'What can I do for you, Mr. ... er ...?'

'Bennett,' he said. 'Arthur Bennett. And this is my fiancée, Sally.' As I greeted the girl he glanced over his shoulder. 'Do they always carry on like this before going out and killing some poor sod of a fox?'

he asked.

'Usually,' I said. 'But they don't always catch a fox, and the majority of people come for the love of the chase. Should I know you, Mr. Bennett?'

'I work at mill,' he said. 'I'm only a foreman, mind, but my family have always worked for mill. I was there the day you walked out. Took guts, that did. As you've not been near the place since coming back, I suppose you don't know what's going on, or that your father is in financial trouble.'

'No,' I said, staring at him. 'No I don't.' I was shocked, and stalled for time by offering them both a cigarette. The girl shook her head but Arthur Bennett took one. Toby Goodson gave an experimental toot of the horn, and bits jangled as restive horses shook their heads. 'What sort of financial trouble?' I asked, composed again.

'Your father is up to his ears in debt, with at least three banks carrying large loans. Much of the machinery was hopelessly outdated and he had to replace it or go under. But that's not where the root of the trouble lies. A year ago Lester Mill at Talon-Under-Water was bought out by a large company called RIEL. You'll probably remember that Lester was always badly managed and running at a loss, but under new management it's trying to compete with Hanley Mill, and the present owners don't much care how they do it. Last week I learnt that RIEL is trying to pressurise the banks to foreclose on the Hanley Mill loans. If that happens, the mill will go for sure. There's no way your father can fight back.'

'You seem to be remarkably well informed for a foreman, Mr. Bennett,' I remarked.

'I have connections,' he quickly countered. 'I dabble in real estate, and a bank clerk I know told me in confidence. I'd rather give no names, but you can check it out for yourself.'

'Why did you come to me?' I asked.

'Because the mill is your inheritance, and I guess you've managed to put aside some pennies these past few years. Enough, I'm sure, to cover those loans. Hanley Mill has a reputation for turning out some of the best cloth in Yorkshire. Will you be the one to let it go?'

It was an unfair accusation, for it was my father's problem, not mine. But it was also frightening when heard from the lips of a man who would probably never get off the floors.

'Thank you for coming here to tell me, Mr. Bennett,' I said.

'You'll do something?' he asked. 'I know old Mr. Hanley is a proud and stubborn man, but it would break his heart if the mill were lost. And there are a lot of us who are dependent on it.'

The horn sounded again and there was a scurry as riders prepared to leave. Arthur Bennett looked round. 'They're going?' he asked.

'In a few minutes. You should stay and watch for a while, it's a beautiful sight when hounds run.' I ground my half-smoked cigarette beneath my heel. 'Have you any idea how widely known this is?'

'There's nowt but rumours on the floor,' he said.

I saw Lisa tighten Kingston's girth, swing into the saddle, and then look round for me. Sally also saw, and gave Arthur Bennett's arm a jerk. 'We'd best be going, Arthur,' she said.

The man nodded, and bade me farewell. I lost sight of them as Kingston halted in front of me. 'Who was that?' Lisa asked.

'Nobody important. I think I ought to find Richard. Have a good day, and remember not to overdo it.'

'Really Mark, I know what I'm doing.'

I smiled at her, and without much effort pushed Arthur Bennett to the back of my mind.

Chapter Five

The cast came off my arm in the second week of January and three days later Lisa persuaded me to ride Kingston.

'It's like swimming,' she said. 'You can never forget. And you needn't look so worried. Daddy rides him when I'm not here, and you're a much better horseman than him.'

'I haven't ridden for years,' I told her. 'And Kingston isn't exactly a placid riding school hack.' But once mounted I found that Lisa was right, and when the horse began to dance sideways, I controlled him without much effort.

As Lisa was riding Snowy, we did not go very far, and came back through the southern fields. We stopped at the pond, and dismounting, let the horse and pony graze.

'We can sit here,' I said, spreading my jacket under the willow tree.

She sat beside me, her hands clasped about her updrawn knees, and for no other reason than a desire to do so, I put an arm about her shoulders.

'Penny for your thoughts,' I said. 'You've been unusually quiet this morning.'

'Have I?' she asked. 'The trouble is that I've been so happy these last few weeks. But like everything, it has to come to an end. I have to go back to Liverpool, and you ... What about you, Mark? There's been something on your mind since Christmas. Are you going back?'

'Back where?' I asked, startled.

'To being Mark Anthony?'

I looked at her. 'No,' I said. 'I grew to hate Mark Anthony. He became a sort of alter ego which didn't really belong to me. He was expected to have no thoughts of his own, no identity. He was like a celluloid image.'

'Then what are you going to do?' she asked.

'Go back to London,' I said, running my fingers along her cheek. 'I love it here, but there is nothing for me other than being Paul Hanley's son. I want more than that, Lisa. I always did. I need the stimulation which can only be found in the city. Can you understand that?'

She nodded, staring at me with solemn eyes.

'I know the music business inside out, so I've decided to try and establish my own recording company. I'll be taking an enormous gamble, and if it doesn't work out, I could lose everything. Would you marry me if I were penniless?'

'Marry you?' she gasped.

'Yes, darling,' I said gently. 'Did you think I was about to go away and forget you ever existed?'

'I was too terrified to contemplate what the future would be like without you,' she said. 'And you know I don't give a damn whether you're rich or poor. It's you I love, not your money.'

I took her in my arms and kissed her. Her partly open lips seemed to mould into mine, and through our thick layers of clothing I could feel her soft, rounded breasts pressing against my chest. God, I wanted her! More than I had ever wanted any woman.

I pulled back abruptly, holding her at arm's length.

'What's wrong?' she asked, looking surprised.

'Nothing,' I replied, hoping she couldn't hear my wildly palpitating heart. 'I wanted to see your face so that I could remember this moment.'

'Let me come to London with you, Mark. Please.'

'No,' I said. 'You have to finish University, if only for Richard's sake. He is so proud of you. And I can't tie myself down to a wife. Not yet.'

'Why not? I'd never interfere or get in the way.'

'It's not you, Lisa. It's me,' I said. 'I'd have no time for you. I'll have to work impossible hours, perhaps travel around the country. You would have to take second place. No marriage could stand up against that strain for very long.'

'But we love each other,' she protested. 'That must mean something.'

'Love can very quickly turn into hatred. And I'm not about to let that happen to us.' I took both of her hands in mine. 'At the right time I shall buy you a ring and say all the correct things, but for now I only want you to know how I feel, and that I'm not deserting you.' I paused. She was gazing down at our clasped hands so that I was unable to see her face. 'I don't think we should say anything to Richard just yet. He may not understand.'

'Probably not,' she agreed. 'He still thinks of me as a little girl. But if you're going to live in London, when will we be able to see each other?'

'I'll come up often,' I promised, and releasing my right hand I gently lifted her chin. It was then I saw the tears coursing down her cheeks. I took a handkerchief from my pocket and carefully wiped them away before I kissed her again.

'When will you be leaving?' she asked me later on, as we slowly rode home.

'After Fran's wedding. But I want to go down to London next week to sort out some problems relating to Mark Anthony.' Kingston was plodding and I reached down for her hand. 'I love you, Lisa. Just remember that we won't be apart forever.'

'I know,' she said sadly. 'It just seems as though we will.'

With only eight days before Fran's wedding, I had no time to waste in London. The first night I spent with Chris, who was as enthusiastic as I had hoped about my plans; and the next morning I went over my finances with my bank manager, Stephen Tate-Jones, who assured me that on the strength of my assets the bank would be willing to extend whatever loans I might need. I told him, last of all, about the mill. I had already decided to help my father, but had no idea how to do it; for I knew he would never accept my money.

'You should talk it over with a company lawyer,' said Stephen. 'I can recommend an excellent one. And in the meantime, I'll put out some feelers and find out the amount of Hanley Mill's indebtedness to the banks.'

Stephen made the appointment and two days later Alan Weston came to my hotel. He was a thin man of medium height with an intelligent face rather than a good-looking one, and he had hazel eyes which were surprisingly intense. I judged him to be about a decade my senior, and liked his straightforward manner from the outset. He had obviously done his homework, for he came armed with facts and figures, and the alarming information that my father had put up forty per cent of the mill shares as collateral, shares which had never before been out of Hanley hands. If the banks foreclosed now, and sold them to an outsider, his only way of retaining control would be through me. I suddenly began to wonder whether he had given me the shares in order to keep them out of the hands of his debtors.

'Your father has fallen back on his repayments,' Alan Weston said in a matter-of-fact voice. 'Interest is mounting and the banks, three of which are already strongly influenced by RIEL, are beginning to get nervous. RIEL, by the way, consists of a group of companies which have enough financial clout to get anything they want when they want.

This is their first venture into the textile industry, and they seem to think they will have more success if they can get rid of their nearest competitor—a formidable competitor, I might add.'

'Hanley Mill has worked hard to earn its reputation,' I said. 'What do you suggest I do?'

'If you refuse to become directly involved, then I would advise you to form a company which can intervene by making a takeover bid for those shares. It will, of course, need your present shareholding to give it credibility and bargaining power. Your father will never be able to raise enough capital to repay the loans, even if he mortgages everything he possesses. I think there will be little practical resistance, certainly not from the banks, if you make it clear that present management will not be interfered with. It goes without saying that the company will need to look impressive, on paper at least.'

'I expect Stephen can help put together a board of bogus directors,' I told him. 'Form the company immediately, and call it whatever you want, so long as there is no connection with me. Its only function will be to finance the mill, indefinitely if need be.'

Alan Weston frowned. 'It will be impossible to hide your involvement altogether. Superficially, yes. But if he delves deep enough into the company, your father could find out. I still can't understand why you don't simply tell him what you are doing. It would save a considerable amount of time and money.'

'He would never accept my help unless I was working with him, and even then he might refuse. He's a proud and stubborn man; he's gone to great pains to ensure that I remain ignorant of what is happening.'

'Do you have anyone in mind who you can trust to handle this?' Alan Weston asked.

I'd always been considered rash, even as a child, just because I wasn't frightened to make hasty decisions. I was rarely wrong, and doubted I would be now.

'Yes,' I said. 'You.'

He continued to stare at me. 'I am a lawyer, Mr. Hanley. It's out of the question.'

'You are a junior partner in an extremely large firm. If and when you get to be a senior partner, you're going to be an old man on the verge of retirement,' I told him. 'I'm going to need a permanent legal man whom I can trust. I'll give you a salary equal to what you are earning now, together with a five per cent shareholding in the new recording company.'

The man gave no indication of what he was thinking. 'You are offering me a five per cent share of nothing,' he said.

'It may be nothing now, but I intend to compete with the biggest and the best.'

This time a flash of shrewdness passed through his unemotional eyes. 'I believe you will, Mr. Hanley. Do I have time to think this over?'

'I'm returning to Yorkshire next Thursday. I'd like to know before then.'

Alan Weston accepted my offer two days later. He had to work out a month's notice, but while doing so he would attend to the business of the mill. I suddenly found that I had time on my hands, and purchased an extravagant present for Fran and a house for myself.

Thursday quickly came. It was a cold day with a mist hovering over the city. I had arranged a private flight, and Chris was taking me to the airport. When he picked me up at lunchtime the mist had thickened into a sluggish fog, and by the time we got there all flights had been cancelled. I told him to try the trains. If they had also been cancelled, then I would have to hire a car and drag myself northwards as best I could. I could not afford to wait, not with Fran being married on Saturday.

They were still running, although badly behind schedule. There was an express leaving for Manchester in three hours, or a slow train to Liverpool in ten minutes. I chose the slower train, and quickly telephoned home to let them know I was on my way. The train left twenty minutes later, not ten, and was one of the last to leave London during the next forty-eight hours. It crawled through goods yards and intersections, and then on into the miserable yellow fog through which nothing was visible.

It was after nine when it finally reached Liverpool, and there, beyond belief, was Lisa. She saw me immediately I stepped onto the platform, and yelling, ran to me. I caught her, and swung her in a half circle before our lips met.

The platform was empty when we broke apart. Lisa was breathing heavily, and had a wild look in her eyes which was totally out of character. I stroked her cheek and would have kissed her again had she not shivered when a gust of freezing wind swept down the platform, blowing some old newspapers before it.

'Good God, girl, you're frozen,' I said. 'How long have you been standing here? And what one earth are you doing here anyway?'

She screwed up her nose. 'I only came out of the waiting room when they announced the train was coming,' she said. 'You know I had to come into Liverpool and sort out my curriculum. I don't need to move back here yet, but there are some lectures which I must attend. Actually, I was going home this afternoon, but Aunt Mary telephoned and suggested we drive back together.'

I put my arm around her shoulders. 'You can drop me off at a hotel,' I said. 'But first you need some brandy to warm you up.'

'I detest brandy, but I'll settle for a coffee in the buffet.'

'It'll taste ghastly,' I told her. 'Railway coffee always does. They brew it all day in enormous vats.'

She laughed as we hurried down the platform. The buffet was empty except for an old man sipping tea in a corner. We sat beside a window and drank the tepid liquid which passed as coffee, and nibbled cheese and tomato sandwiches with hard crusts which were beginning to curl up at the edges. We talked about the horses, the farm and Fran's wedding, but not London nor what I had been doing there, for that was a chapter of my life which would separate us soon enough. It was after eleven when we left, arm in arm, our footsteps echoing hollowly behind us.

I offered to drive, but she said I must be tired. I wasn't, but found it pleasant to lie back with my eyes closed. We were now so completely in tune that words were no longer necessary.

I did not open my eyes again until she switched off the engine. We were not where we should be, but in a dimly lit back avenue, where the pavements were lined with chestnut trees which shaded the old Victorian houses. I turned to Lisa and saw that the devil-may-care wildness was back in her eyes.

'Lisa,' I said, reaching forward to touch her cheek.

She moved quickly, her hands imprisoning mine. She held my fingers to her lips. 'Don't be sensible,' she said. 'Not tonight. We're going to be parted soon enough, and I want a memory; something which only we can share.' She paused. 'You want it too. I may be inexperienced, but I'm not stupid.'

I looked at our clasped hands, and then kissed her cheek. 'Are you sure?' I asked.

'Yes.'

Her room was on the fifth floor. It was large and pleasant, with old-fashioned furniture, and a kitchenette hidden behind floral curtains. There were some personal touches: a couple of hunting prints which I recollected having seen in Richard Crowder's office; some dried flowers in a vase; four small china horses; and photographs of Kingston and Snowy, and of her father standing with Ben and Betsy. The narrow bed was covered by a patchwork quilt which looked like the handiwork of Orchid Livingstone, and above it on the wall was a rectangular shape as though something had recently been removed.

The room was cold, and while I took off my overcoat Lisa poured coins into a gas fire.

'What was there?' I asked.

She looked at the wall, then back at me. 'A poster,' she said a little too quickly. 'Do you want something to drink?'

'No thank you. A poster of what?'

'Mark Anthony. I took it down after your mother rang.'

'Oh Lisa,' I said, and walking forward, gathered her in my arms.

We made love by the red glow of the hissing gas fire. Her body was pale and lithe and lovely, and her small breasts with their hard nipples were tantalising mounds which thrust hotly against me. She lost her virginity with barely a murmer and afterwards we slept, her head buried in the crook of my arm, and her hair spread over my chest.

I awoke to the sound of rain beating against the window panes, heralding a grey and unappetising dawn. The gas fire had long burnt out its sixpences and the room was freezing. Lisa was still asleep, and I kissed her forehead before moving her gently to one side and covering her naked body with the quilt.

She kept a supply of coins in a jar and I poured as many as I could into the slot. The flames burst to life, and I stayed crouched before them, warming myself.

'Mark.'

I glanced round. She lay on her side, one hand cupped against her cheek.

'God, you're beautiful,' I said, rising to my feet.

'So are you,' she replied, her eyes travelling over my body. 'I thought it would be different. A bit like a bull having a go at the cows. But it's nothing like that at all. Come back to bed, Mark.'

We made love again, gently this time, with none of last night's passionate fervour. We drew out every possible moment and it was mid-afternoon when we finally left, walking hand in hand down the stairs, and running through the pouring rain to the car.

Chapter Six

It rained all day, and Fran gloomily predicted that her wedding would be a disaster. 'It'll stop,' said her brother. But it was still pouring when she went to bed.

She awoke next morning to see an insipid sun peeping through fluffy white clouds. 'I told you everything would be all right,' Mark said as they were about to leave for the church. 'And remember those old flagstones can be treacherous. Don't trip up the aisle and fall flat on your face.'

'Nobody but you would think of such a thing,' she said, kissing his cheek in a rare show of affection.

The ceremony went off like clockwork, and afterwards everyone returned to Olden Manor for the reception. This was Fran's day, and nobody noticed that her brother stayed deliberately apart. Mark and Lisa only had eyes for each other, and longed to escape. Their moment came when Fran and Eric left on their honeymoon. Lisa was one of the small circle of friends who went upstairs to help the bride change, but she did not come down with the others. She put on corduroy trousers and a jumper which had been left in Mark's bedroom earlier, and when everyone was outside seeing the couple off, she ran down to find him waiting.

'We'll use the old tradesman's entrance,' he said. 'I left an anorak and wellingtons there, and Mother's car is hidden behind the garage.'

'Can we walk?' she asked. 'I could do with some fresh air after all that champagne. How do you manage to stay so sober? It's indecent to stay sober at a wedding!'

'I told you once before that I never get drunk,' he said. 'We'll go through the trees to avoid being seen, and then cut across the fields.'

The ground was muddy and hard going in places, but the sharp air soon cleared Lisa's head. They walked hand in hand, talking rarely, and stopping once to watch a fox pick its stealthy way across a ploughed field. Then, beneath a sycamore tree, Mark spied an early snowdrop and wanted to pluck it for her.

'No, don't,' she said. 'It'll only die.'

They walked on through a herd of cows which insisted on following them; and then, with only one field between them and the Crowder farmhouse, the skies opened and the rain came down.

'We'd better run,' she said as he wrapped his anorak around her shoulders.

She had forgotten that her father had put the horses in that field for a change of pasture. They were at the far end, sheltering beside a hedge. Kingston recognised Lisa's voice and, wanting his stable, trotted away from the others. Snowy followed him, and then Ben realised that he had been left behind and lumbered into a clumsy gallop, with Betsy just behind him. Kingston tossed his head, and suddenly it was a race to see who would reach the gate first.

Mark heard them and swung round. He tripped on a clump of grass and fell flat on his face.

'Mark!' Lisa yelled, slithering to a halt. She screamed at the horses as well, but beyond caring, they sped past, splattering mud as they went. 'Are you all right?' she asked, crouching beside him.

'I'm filthy,' he said, rising to his knees. 'And my suit is ruined!'

'They didn't mean it,' she said, laughing. 'They only want to go in.'

'I sometimes wonder whether I'm secondary to those damn horses,' he muttered, and staggered to his feet.

'Of course you're not,' she said. 'And ... oh dear, you're sopping wet as well. Come on, you'll catch a chill if you don't get out of those clothes.'

She took his hand and they ran the rest of the way. The horses rushed through the gate immediately it was open, and Lisa hesitated as she watched them file into their stables. But Mark was beginning to shiver, and before she could follow them he pulled her towards the house.

'The yard is shut off,' he said. 'They can't come to any harm.'

Lisa put on the kettle while he took off his soaking jacket.

'I think you ought to have a bath,' she said over her shoulder. 'I'll find you something of Daddy's to wear. We can put your clothes in front of the fire to dry.'

He didn't argue, and while he was in the bath she changed into dry trousers.

'The tea's brewing,' she said when he came down in her father's dressing-gown. 'Have you got anything on under that?'

'Brazen hussy,' he retorted. 'It's none of your business.'

He sat in her father's old chair by the range, the dressing-gown wrapped primly about him. She poured the tea and bringing them both a cup, sat on the floor, resting against his legs. He reached down, his strong fingers gently massaging the back of her neck.

'What were your other women like?' she asked.

'My other women?' he said, his voice trembling with laughter. 'You make me sound like a first-class rake. What other women?'

Her eyes were serious as she gazed up at him. 'Those glamorous females who clung to Mark Anthony like so many leeches!'

'Don't tell me you're jealous?' he asked, the humour gone.

'Why not? The newspapers delighted in publishing photographs of you with them, and speculating on which one you would marry.'

He put down his cup and bent forward to kiss her. 'They were a part of the life I was leading,' he said. 'A necessary part. But none of them meant anything to me. While you ... well, you're special. I've never felt like this about anyone before.'

She took his hand between both of hers, and pressed the palm against her lips. 'Come upstairs and prove it,' she said.

His brows lifted. 'We've taken enough chances already. It wouldn't be very clever if you became pregnant.'

'Don't be such a prude,' she said, jumping to her feet. 'Only characters in books get pregnant that quickly. This will probably be our last chance anyway. I know Daddy won't be back for ages, he was thoroughly enjoying himself; and Orchid is away until Monday.'

He did not protest as her hand slid beneath the dressing-gown caressing his thigh.

'What if Richard comes home early?' he asked.

'We'll hear him.'

'If we don't, darling, it'll be a shotgun wedding, and tomorrow morning to boot!'

He stood up, and swept her effortlessly into his arms.

Mark had been in the summer room all morning, making preliminary plans for the launch of the new recording company. He sat at his mother's writing desk, unsuccessfully trying to stop his mind from wandering. He had decided to return to London in a fortnight, at the end of February, and dreaded breaking the news to Lisa. At least she would have moved back to her bedsitter by then and be fully involved in her studies.

Today, she and Orchid were shopping in Manchester. He was taking her to dinner tonight, and would tell her then. He was gazing through the window when his father's unmistakable step caught his attention. He glanced round as the door was flung open.

'You bloody bastard!' Paul Hanley swore. 'You sold them! The whole damn lot!'

The attack was so unexpected that it momentarily knocked Mark off balance. He stood up, aware that he must remain calm. 'Are you referring to the shares?' he asked in a matter-of-fact voice, which infuriated his father even more.

'Christ! What else would I be talking about?' Paul Hanley yelled. 'I gave them to you in good faith and, as always, you've let me down. Some bloody firm I've never heard of is about to make a takeover bid, and I'm powerless to stop them! You deserve to roast in hell for what you've done.'

Mark's thoughts raced ahead. Damn Alan for rushing this through so soon, placing him in an impossible situation. He was left with no alternative but to admit the truth. 'I own the company,' he said without any trace of guilt or alarm.

'What the hell are you talking about?' Paul Hanley asked, his voice furious but more controlled. 'I'll not let you squirm out of this by telling me a pack of lies!'

'I'm not lying,' his son told him.

'Damn it, I've seen the list of directors.'

'From which I was deliberately excluded,' Mark said sharply. 'Why didn't you tell me the mill was going under?'

Paul Hanley exploded. 'Why the hell should I tell you anything? You refused to come back there, and by doing so, forfeited all right to interfere in my affairs.'

'Someone had to interfere,' Mark said, his expression hardening. 'Otherwise you would have lost it.'

The boy was so bloody sure of himself, so confident. What he'd done was unforgiveable and he couldn't even see it.

'I want you out of here. Now. You've always caused trouble, and I was a fool to let you come back.'

Neither of them noticed Mary Hanley until she walked into the room. She had only heard her husband's last words, and was horrified by them.

'Paul, what's happening?' she asked.

He swung round. 'I don't want him here,' he said harshly. 'He's an arrogant, self-seeking bastard, and he'll never change.'

Mary turned to her son. He was pale, but other than that his face showed no emotion whatsoever. 'What have you done?' she said.

'Father will tell you,' he said coldly. The die was cast and he would not grovel, even to her.

'He sold the shares,' Paul Hanley said. 'And now he's concocted some cock and bull story about still retaining control of them. He'd stoop to anything in order to save his own damn neck.'

'Oh, Mark,' Mary said. 'How could you?'

He did not attempt a reply.

'Come along, Mary. There's nothing more to say. He's leaving.' Paul Hanley took hold of his wife's arm and led her from the room.

Mark did not move immediately. His emotions were running riot, for he had never wanted this to happen.

His movements were deliberately slow as he sat down at the desk and reached for a sheet of his mother's embossed notepaper. The letter he wrote Lisa gave no satisfactory explanation for his sudden departure, nor did the words convey any of the warmth she would expect from him. But as he struggled to still the involuntary shake of his hand, he knew it was the best he could do. She was sure to understand, and he would make it up to her later.

Richard Crowder was making himself a cup of tea when Lisa came in and flung a couple of carrier bags onto the kitchen table.

'We had a lovely day,' she said. 'And bought all sorts of things which I don't really need. Would you like an impromptu fashion show while Orchid makes supper?'

'I'd love it,' he said, and caught hold of her arm before she could dash away. 'Wait up, lass, there's something you ought to know first. Mark's gone. He left a letter for you. It's on the hall table.'

'Gone?' she said, her eyes widening with disbelief. 'Gone where?'

'Back to London.'

She felt as though the bottom had dropped out of her world. How could he possibly leave without saying goodbye? After all they had shared together. 'Why?' she asked, the gaiety gone from her voice.

'I don't know,' Richard said gently. 'But if his expression was anything to go by, I'd say there's trouble brewing.'

'But surely he's coming back?' she asked. 'Exactly what did he say, Daddy?'

'Only that he had to go,' he said. 'Don't get your hopes up, sweetheart. The last time he left here nobody heard from him until he found it convenient to come back.'

'But this isn't anything like the last time!' she gasped, pulling away from him.

He watched helplessly as she rushed into the hallway.

'Why didn't you tell her the truth?' Orchid asked. 'Bad news travels fast, and she's sure to know by tomorrow.'

He turned round. 'That was the truth. He said nowt to me. And I don't think his letter will tell her any more. I only wish she wasn't so fond of him.'

'It's developed into something more than fondness,' Orchid said softly. 'For her at any rate.'

A door slammed and they both glanced up.

'Should I go to her?' Richard asked.

'No. Leave her be. She'll probably want to cry.'

But Lisa was crying already. She lay across her bed, still clutching the letter, with tears streaming down her cheeks.

The day his son left, Paul Hanley suffered a mild heart attack, which only fuelled the rumours that Mark was a good-for-nothing who had brought the mill and his family to the brink of disaster. Two weeks passed.

Orchid was worried about Lisa, who waited for a letter which never came, and slipped deeper and deeper into an uncharacteristic depression.

'We'll have to do something,' she said to Richard Crowder.

'She's going back to Liverpool next week. She'll soon work him out of her system.'

'I don't think it will be that easy,' she said. 'Although being in the company of young people may help. I saw that Malcolm Dunnett at market last week. He's a nice lad, and he's sweet on Lisa. He'd show her a good time, without expecting anything in return. I could have a word with him. And I think you should talk to her.'

'I'd do anything to see her smile again,' he said. 'Where is she?'

'In her room. She's spending far too much time up there.'

'I'll speak with her now,' he said.

She was sitting by the window, reading some handwritten notes.

'Studying?' he asked.

She glanced up. 'Yes. I can't afford to fall too far behind.'

He was aware of the strain in her voice, and the way her eyes deliberately avoided his. He sat down on the bed, within arm's reach of her.

'He's gone, love, and he won't be back now. He'd not want to show his face here again, not after what he did to his father.'

'He couldn't have known what he was doing,' she said dully. 'He couldn't have meant it.'

'He knew,' said her father. 'He's too clever not to have figured it all out. He was making himself a quick profit. He was thinking of himself, and be damned with everyone else.'

'I don't believe that!' Lisa said. 'You don't know him like I do.'

'I know he was your first love,' he said. 'But that's all part of growing up, and there'll be others. Keep a special place for him in your heart if you like, but don't let him ruin your life. He could have telephoned, but he hasn't even bothered to do that. And don't you make excuses for him. Nobody can be busy for twenty-four hours a day.'

'There has to be a reason,' she insisted.

'Aye. He's back in London and has probably forgotten we exist. We were a convenience for him, Lisa. Somewhere to hide away after that accident.' He took hold of her cold hands. 'You've got to forget him and start enjoying life again. Did you know that young Malcolm has been asking after you?'

'Don't push me, Daddy. Please,' she said.

'I'm not pushing you. I only want you to be happy. Go out with him. You might even enjoy yourself.'

'With *Malcolm*?' she asked.

'Aye, with Malcolm,' he said patiently. He lifted her chin and kissed her forehead. 'Give it a try. For me.'

'I'll think about it,' she said evasively.

'Good girl. Now leave that for a bit and come on downstairs.'

She went with Malcolm to the Jolly Farmer because it was what her father wanted. He was dull and irritatingly slow; but he was kind, and she needed kindness. And he made no demands; he didn't even seem to mind that she spent half the evening in silence.

She returned to her bedsitter in Liverpool, but almost at once came down with a bad bout of flu which kept her in bed for the next three days.

She had only been up for an hour, and was still wobbly on her feet when there was a knock at the door. She opened it to find Malcolm standing there, holding a large bunch of chrysanthemums in his left hand, and smiling his hopeful smile. She had no choice but to ask him in.

'I'm sorry about the mess,' she apologised. 'I've had the most awful flu.'

He looked at the unmade bed and her books scattered over the table. 'I don't mind,' he said. 'You look poorly. Have you taken anything?'

'Aspirin. The worst is over now, but I feel utterly drained. You should have telephoned before coming all this way.'

'I nearly did, but decided to surprise you,' he said. 'Now have you been eating properly?'

'Mainly toast,' she said. 'I couldn't face anything else.'

'Do you have any eggs?' he asked. 'I make an excellent omelette.'

'I couldn't possibly let you,' she protested.

‘I’d enjoy it,’ he said, thrusting the flowers at her. ‘Why don’t you lie down and rest until it’s ready?’

She did as he suggested. She still wasn’t feeling too good, and sometimes it was nice to be cosseted.

Chapter Seven

I had no time to think of Oldenshaw and what had happened, for there was too much to be done. I was inundated with documents which had to be carefully studied, and there were endless meetings to attend. And then the press discovered I was back and began to haunt me.

But my biggest headache was finding suitable premises for the company. I wanted somewhere within reach of central London and Heathrow, with ample room for expansion; but after three weeks of searching I was beginning to think that such a place did not exist. It was Chris who heard that Manna Records was up for sale. I'd never heard of them, but he assured me it was a legitimate company which specialised in third rate remakes of current hits. The owner had health problems and wanted to sell out. There was one recording studio, record pressing equipment, and a small suite of offices. It was situated in Hammersmith, on three acres of land running alongside the Thames. I looked at the ridiculously low price being asked.

'What's wrong with it?' was my first reaction.

'It's run down and a bit shabby,' said Chris with a diffident shrug. 'But there's no harm in making an appointment to look it over.'

Manna Records was situated in part of what looked like a derelict warehouse at the end of a short cul-de-sac, with rubble-filled properties to either side of it. The whole lot looked as if it should have been condemned years ago, and the small section of warehouse which Manna Records occupied was no more appealing than the rest of the place. The offices were cold and dingy, with cobwebs festooning the ceilings and paint peeling off the walls in long strips. The machinery for cutting the discs seemed adequate, but it was situated in a dark room which had no windows. I soon told Chris I had seen enough, and would have skipped the recording studio altogether had he not persuaded me otherwise. I dreaded what we would find, but it was certainly better maintained than the rest of Manna Records, and although much of the equipment was old, it was in good condition.

'It has possibilities,' said Chris as we drove away.

'It's appalling,' I told him.

'You'll never find anything better at the price.'

'The entire place needs demolishing and rebuilding from scratch,' I said. 'The overall cost would be exorbitant.'

'Initially, you could manage with what's already there.'

'What about the rats?'

'Haven't you ever heard of exterminators?' he asked.

I talked it over with Alan, and we decided to have the place surveyed and a proper assessment made. Alan Weston and I worked well together, whereas Chris, invaluable though he was, tended to forget that I was no longer the boy he had once managed.

Ten days later, when it looked as though the deal would go ahead, Chris and I were sitting in the Kensington flat I had rented, studying Manna's balance sheets. Chris had procured them by means known only to himself, and although I was grateful, I wished he would leave me alone for a while. I had been on edge all morning and when he suddenly picked up a newspaper and thrust it in front of me I barely managed to control my temper.

'You're not even mentioned in here,' he said.

I glanced up. 'Should I be?' I asked.

'Didn't you attend that ball at Grosvenor House last night?'

'I didn't feel like going,' I said. 'I'm sure I wasn't missed.'

'Good God, there are people who would give their right arm to get invited to a function like that!' he spluttered. 'If you want to get your business off the ground, Mark, you're going to need all the publicity you can get. You have to go to that sort of function, you know. It's not much different from the Mark Anthony days. You have to cultivate friends in the right places.'

'I do not intend to live my life in a glass bowl,' I told him coldly. 'When I need publicity I'll ensure that I get it. And whether I am successful or not is going to depend on me alone, not the people I cultivate.'

But Chris was nothing if not persistent. He picked up a pile of invitations which were lying unopened on the desk. 'You need a secretary to deal with these,' he said. 'Then perhaps you'll be better organised. And another thing, it's not right for you to be seen without a partner. You should take your mind off work once in a while and get yourself a girlfriend.'

'No,' I snapped.

His eyes narrowed.

'Why not?' he asked. 'Or do you already have someone tucked away?'

'That's enough, Chris,' I warned. 'Drop it.'

But like a dog gnawing at a bone, he did not know when to stop.

'You do have someone!' he said. 'She can't be here, otherwise we would have seen her. You're not making a fool of yourself over some farmer's daughter, are you?'

I sprang to my feet.

'What I do in my private life is none of your damn business. You are employed to help me run a company, and nothing else. If you don't like it, I suggest you find another job.'

He paled. 'I am fully aware of my position,' he said in a flat and unemotional voice. 'Do you need me for anything else today? If not, I'll go home.'

I wasn't proud of what I had said, but it had been necessary. 'No,' I told him. 'And I won't need you tomorrow either. I shall be unavailable all day.'

It had been long enough. Too long. I was going to see Lisa tonight.

I could not be bothered with the hassle of getting onto a commercial flight and so I hired a private plane to take me to Liverpool. I slept the entire way and as the plane touched down awoke refreshed and wondering whether my impulsive urge to come here had been such a good idea. But I was committed now, and to go back without seeing Lisa would be ridiculous.

The taxi driver obligingly found a flower stall where I was able to buy her two dozen red roses. And then I was in the quiet back street with the chestnut trees and the tall Victorian houses. A feeling of calm swept over me as I vividly remembered the last time I had been here. When we made love by the red glow of the gas fire.

It was still early enough for the front door to be unlocked, and as I walked in, I visualised her expression when she saw me. The way her eyes would widen and that delighted, infectious laughter.

I climbed the stairs slowly, and was breathing hard when I reached the top. No sound came from her room, but light seeped from beneath the door. I smiled. She was probably studying. I shifted the roses into the crook of my arm and knocked.

She did not come immediately and I thought I heard a murmur of voices, but so brief an exchange that I decided it must be my imagination. I resisted an impulse to knock again, and leant back against the wall, foolishly wondering how I could sweep her into my arms without dropping the roses. The door opened, but only by a few inches.

Lisa stared at me and I at her, neither of us attempting to speak. I saw the way her knuckles whitened as she gripped the door, and how the colour drained from her cheeks. Her eyes did widen, but not with the pleasure I had anticipated. They were red-rimmed and puffy, while her hair was tousled and her clothes crumpled. She looked, quite literally, as though she had just got out of bed.

I don't know if the shock was reflected in my own expression. I straightened up, gazing at her still, and unable to find the appropriate words. It was as though I had stumbled into a nightmare. Perhaps I was still on the plane, and none of this was happening.

'Hello Lisa,' I said with an effort.

'Mark,' she murmured hoarsely. 'I thought you weren't coming back.'

'You should have known better than that,' I said flatly.

'But you never even bothered to phone,' she said, her voice bearing no trace of accusation. 'You simply walked out. Do you know that your father had a heart attack after you left?'

'Yes,' I said. 'But it didn't keep him out of the mill for long. Aren't you going to ask me in, Lisa?'

Her cheeks reddened, and she glanced guiltily over her shoulder. I felt uneasy. This had started all wrong, and it wasn't getting any better.

'I have someone here,' she said. 'You might remember him from years ago.' As her words penetrated I felt myself stiffen. 'It's Malcolm Dunnett. He's an old friend who also popped in unexpectedly.'

Something Richard Crowder had said, some careless or perhaps deliberate remark, rang a warning bell, but I couldn't grasp it immediately. And then, as she stepped back and opened the door wide, I saw him. He was a stocky young man. His sleeves were rolled up and he was standing by the cooker prodding at something in a frying pan. The room was untidy, with books stacked on the table. They had been pushed back to make room for two place settings. My eyes travelled to the china horses and photographs on the sideboard, and then to the wall with the fading marks from the poster. A print of two horses standing beneath a tree hung there now.

He had been courting her. That was what Richard Crowder had told me when we had been alone together for a few minutes. He even hinted that they would have become engaged had she not dropped him when I came back. His voice had echoed his displeasure; the fact that he did not really approve of me and his daughter being together, but was helpless to do anything about it.

I looked at the bed.

'What's the matter?' Lisa asked.

The quilt lay in a heap on the floor. The blankets had been thrust back, and the sheets were crumpled. Malcolm Dunnett was smiling at me. I could smell cheese and eggs and deceit, and I instinctively recoiled from them all.

'Mark?'

I gazed into her bloodshot eyes.

'I trusted you,' I said slowly. 'You are the one person I have always believed in.'

'What are you talking about?' she asked, confused and a little frightened.

'Him,' I said coldly. Malcolm Dunnett turned beetroot-red, opened his mouth as if to say something, but didn't. 'And that.'

She followed my gaze.

'I was lying down,' she said. 'I've ...'

'I don't want to hear excuses,' I said, viciously cutting across her words. 'Not when I can see perfectly well what has been happening.'

'Dear God, what are you saying?'

She grabbed hold of my arm. It was an instinctive reaction, and the first physical contact between us. The pressure of her fingers sent a bolt of lightning through me. But I had been in too many beds not to recognise the signs. I pulled away from her in disgust and anger.

'When it comes down to it, you're as cheap as every other woman I've known.' I threw down the roses. 'A parting gift,' I said.

She looked at the crushed flowers and then at me. There were tears in her eyes.

'Mark ...'

I didn't want to hear. Her betrayal cut deep, much deeper than anyone would ever know. Her voice followed me down the stairs, but I didn't stop until we were separated by two blocks of buildings.

I was in a busy main street, and ignoring the curious stares of passers-by, stood with my back against a lamp post. I closed my eyes, mustering every bit of self-control to stop myself from breaking down altogether. An integral part of my life had been shattered and I knew that after today, never again would I be so vulnerable. That part of me was lost forever.

PART TWO
(1960–1961)

Chapter One

I arrived in London at the unearthly hour of three in the morning, only to find that there were no northbound connections for another six hours. Tim was waiting instead, insistent we drive direct to Oldenshaw.

I had been in a meeting in San Francisco when the telegram found me. Alan and I had been there since early June, negotiating to take over a failing California record company, and so establish our first American base. The telegram said nothing more than that my father was dead. I glanced over it briefly before continuing with the delicate discussions. I didn't want to return to the home I hadn't seen for five years, and it certainly wasn't a good moment for me to leave the American negotiations, but when I thought about it, I knew I had to go—and so I went, leaving Alan behind me to cope as best he could.

Thank God for Tim, I thought now as I sat back in the Rolls. I had taken him on as my chauffeur four years before. He was still in his twenties, and had come down from Liverpool with a wife and baby in search of the legendary pot of gold. I presumed he had come close enough, for he had stayed; and although at times he tended to be blunt and opinionated, and had a natural fondness for gossip, his loyalty was unwavering. Even the most persistent reporters were unable to get anything out of him.

It was five years since I had travelled north. As the car surged smoothly onwards, I thought about what I had achieved. I hadn't long turned thirty, and the business I had built from nothing was now rated among the top four recording companies in the country, with branches operating throughout Europe. I had high hopes for the American venture, too. No British singer had so far successfully crossed the Atlantic, but I knew it was only a matter of time before there was a breakthrough. Perhaps Mark Anthony could have done it, for Elvis had not come on the scene then, swinging the pendulum round to the pulsating sounds of rock and roll. Everywhere, the record business was booming. Both here, and in the States—where John F. Kennedy looked likely to be the youngest man ever to be offered Presidential office—the rigid barriers of the Fifties were breaking down, and the young were determined to speak out and be heard.

We passed through Oldenshaw shortly after nine on one of those rare sparkling mornings which give the promise of a hot day.

Olden Manor looked the same as it always had; this was summer, and the gardens were a profusion of colour. Some cars were parked in front of the garages. They probably belonged to the relatives whom Father had always hated. I straightened my tie and combed my hair as Tim stepped out to open the door. He stood with no expression on his well-schooled face, for Tim took pride in his work, and our easy informality died a sudden death in public.

'Go round the back and get some breakfast,' I told him.

'Yes, sir.'

The front door opened and Fran came out. 'Thank goodness you got here,' she said. 'Alan telephoned to say you were on your way, but we didn't know whether you would make it on time.'

I started up the steps towards her. 'How is Mother?'

'I don't think it's hit her properly yet. She's still in a daze.'

I kissed her cheek. 'Was it his heart?'

She nodded and said, 'He had a massive coronary. On the stairs. Mummy heard him fall, and when she found him he was already dead. The doctor said the attack would have killed him even before he hit the bottom. It was she who insisted that you should be called back for the funeral. She knew Eric could get in touch with you.'

Eric worked for me now. I knew it was unwise to employ a relative, but the man was practically a stranger and so I had decided to make an exception in his case. Three years ago his newspaper had gone insolvent, leaving him and many others jobless. He couldn't find employment in the area, and so Fran had swallowed her pride and contacted me. Her plea had come at a time when I was looking for somebody to run my publicity department. Eric was sharp and ambitious, and I decided to try him out. I had never regretted my decision, for he was excellent at what he did. But as he grew in stature and affluence, so Fran changed from a sour north country girl into a disagreeable London matron. When he had his first affair with a young model, I turned a blind eye. After all, what Fran did not know could not hurt her.

The two of them seemed to manage to walk their fine domestic tightrope fairly convincingly, and regularly took the two children up to visit their grandparents. But neither Mother nor Father had ever come to London. I was there, and the separation between us had seemed final.

'Come in,' said Fran now. 'You look tired.'

'Lack of sleep,' I told her. 'I lost a whole day between California and here. You're looking a little rough yourself.'

Her hands flew self-consciously to her swollen stomach. 'Same complaint,' she said. 'It kicks all night. Your room is ready. But I think you should see Mummy first. Eric is in Steelton. He had to make all the arrangements in your absence.'

'What time is the funeral?' I asked.

'Eleven o'clock.' We walked into the hallway, and as Fran closed the door, shutting out the sunlight, I felt a chill pass through me. There was no barking, as there had been the last time I came home. I knew from Fran that Whisky had died six months after I left, and Albert had buried him in the orchard.

There was a hum of voices coming from the drawing room. Fran touched my arm. 'She's in the summer room,' she said quietly. 'You go ahead. I'll have your luggage taken up, and make arrangements for Tim.'

'Thank you,' I said. And with the ghosts of the past peering over my shoulder, I walked through the house.

I could not find it in me to shed a tear for my Father, nor do I think he would have expected it. But Mother sobbed terribly as she leant against my arm.

Father had always been respected, as was proved by the people who crowded into the sweltering graveyard. Many of his employees came, and the textile industry was strongly represented.

'. . . ashes to ashes, dust to dust . . .'

The vicar's voice droned on like a sleepy bee. Then it was over, the silence punctuated by intermittent sobs, and far away the bored bark of a lonely dog. I threw a handful of soil onto the casket, and Mother did the same before I led her away. Eric followed with Fran.

I sent them home with Tim, and told him to come back for me. I watched the car accelerate along the street, and then turned to the people who were clustered at my back.

Some preferred to slink away without fuss, while others insisted on enlarging upon Father's better points; but mostly, with eyes downcast, their condolences were brief. I was replying automatically after half an hour, my eyes no longer focusing on the sea of faces. I knew Tim was back, patiently waiting for me to finish.

'I'm sorry, lad. Deeply sorry. Paul Hanley will be sorely missed around here.' Richard Crowder was looking hot and uncomfortable in a dark suit which obviously did not see much wear. But it was not on him that my gaze fell, but on his daughter. Lisa flushed, and turned her head away.

'Thank you,' I said, still staring at her. She had matured, and there was an assurance about her which I found startling. I looked quickly at her left hand. No ring. 'Will you be coming to the house?' I asked.

'Nay lad,' he said. 'There's work to be done.' He said something else, but I only half listened, and was thankful when he turned away.

Lisa looked up, and although I searched her eyes, I could read nothing in them. 'Hello, Mark,' she said evenly. 'I'm surprised you came.'

'He was my father,' I said. 'We didn't hate each other. We just couldn't see eye to eye. Are you working round here, or did you come for the funeral?'

'I'm not working anywhere,' she said, her cheeks burning. 'I'd like to talk to you. But not now. This is neither the time nor the place. Can you come to the farm tomorrow morning at about ten?'

'Yes,' I said.

'Thank you. Goodbye, Mark.'

I should have forgotten after all this time, but as I watched her walk away I fought back a mixture of emotions. It was only when she and her father had gone that I realised they were the last to leave. Two labourers had started to fill in the grave, and Tim was standing beside the car, watching me. I took a deep breath and walked towards him.

The will was to be read at five, and there was little likelihood of our relatives departing until then. I was still thinking of Lisa when I got back and, not looking where I was going, collided with Elly in the hallway. A silver tray clattered to the floor.

'Damn!' she swore. She looked at me, her cheeks scarlet. 'I'm sorry, Mr. Mark. I should have been paying more attention. Thank goodness there was nowt on it.'

I picked up the heavy tray and handed it to her. The nervous girl of five years ago was now totally self-assured, and had more or less taken over the running of the house from Maude.

'Where's the family?' I asked.

'Miss Fran is lying down in her room, and Mr. Stewart went up to her just before you came in. Mrs. Hanley is waiting for you in study.'

'Thank you, Elly.' I glanced towards the drawing room. 'I suppose I'll have to join them later, but until then, keep the food and drink flowing.'

'Aye, sir.'

The study was still Father, even down to the stale tobacco smell which was ingrained in the walls and furniture. Mother was sitting by the fireplace, gazing at the desk and its empty chair. She looked up when I walked in.

'You shouldn't be alone,' I said. 'Especially not in here.'

'When I am in this room I find it hard to believe he's gone. He was a hard man, Mark, but a wonderful man nonetheless. I shall miss him.' She paused for a moment. 'Don't worry, I'm not going to cry. He's dead, and I have no more tears left. Come and sit down, dear. I have something for you. But first you can pour me a sherry.'

I poured sherry for her and a large brandy for myself, then sat in a chair which faced the windows. 'Do you mind if I smoke?' I asked. She shook her head and I lit a cigarette while waiting for her to begin.

'He wanted you to have this,' she said shortly, and as her hand moved I saw the envelope lying on the small table beside her.

'What is it?'

'An apology, I think. You know, he was quite ill for some months before the coronary; he had a feeling that time was running out for him, and that's when he wrote this. I wanted to call you home and let there be some sort of reconciliation, but he wouldn't let me. I think he was afraid you wouldn't come.'

'Five years, Mother,' I said. 'And another four before that. We tried once, but couldn't make it work. Of course I'd have come had you asked. But he was right. What good would it have done?'

'You ought to know that he left the mill and all the other property to you, but none of the money. You already have enough of that. Fran and I have been well taken care of, and also the servants. I know the house should rightfully be mine, but I don't want it, and told him so. It's too large and too full of ghosts. I'm moving into Heatherdown Cottage. It's been empty for some time and always was one of the prettiest of Oldenshaw's cottages.' She must have seen my puzzlement. 'Of course, I forgot that you didn't know about Oldenshaw. I think Paul was embarrassed about it. But ownership of the majority of cottages came as part of the parcel when the first Hanley purchased the Manor. They are not worth very much, and the rents are ridiculously low. Your father never made any profit from them. Richard Crowder also leases some of the land. It would all have been lost if you had not stepped in when you did. Everything was already mortgaged to the hilt, as he had been borrowing on the property for years in order to modernise the mill and keep it going. He knew that you were the only one capable of carrying on. I am too old, and Fran . . . well, would you trust Fran and Eric?'

The mill . . . this house . . . even the village . . .

'I don't want them,' I said.

'I know, dear, but there is precious little you can do now. Here, read the letter.'

The envelope had my name written across it in his bold hand. I slit it open and removed the single sheet of paper. It was undated, and began with my name followed by a hasty dash. I glanced at the bottom. There was nothing written there which gave even a hint of any kind of sentiment, and he had signed it with his initial. As I read it, I heard Mother murmur, almost as if to herself, 'You were so alike, you and he. The tragedy was that you never realised it.'

Chapter Two

When he had not come by ten-thirty, Lisa told Orchid Livingstone she was going for a walk. But she had not gone far before she began to feel vulnerable, especially when she recalled his voice yesterday, pleasant, but distant. She stopped, afraid of what she was getting herself into. It was almost eleven, and he was obviously not coming. Why should he?

There was a stile close by and she scrambled up, pausing to stare down the deserted lane before swinging round and dropping into an empty meadow which was blanketed in daisies. 'Lisa Crowder, you are an idiot,' she said out loud. And then she laughed, and falling to her knees, started to pick daisies.

He would have missed her altogether, except that he was looking through the window. He caught a glimpse of her green shirt, and her copper-coloured hair, which was as conspicuous as his own fair head. He tapped Tim on the shoulder, and the car halted a short distance from the stile.

'Wait here,' he said.

He walked back, and leant against the stile, smiling a little as he watched her.

'Hello, Lisa,' he said. 'You wanted to see me?'

She leapt to her feet, startled. 'I thought you weren't coming,' she said accusingly.

'And decided to make daisy chains from frustration. I'm sorry, I should have telephoned.'

She studied him as she looped the chain over her left arm. He was smiling, but apart from that his expression was guarded. And he never changed, damn him. His hair shone like spun gold, and in his youthful, suntanned face the eyes were more intense than the deepest blue of the cornflowers which grew alongside the hedges. But there was a difference in him; he looked harder, with a firm set to his mouth which was now a part of him. Mark Anthony had long gone, and in his place was a man who had built the beginnings of an empire from nothing but dreams and hard work, and no doubt a good injection of the money he had earned as Mark Anthony. But it took more than money to guarantee success, and Mark Hanley was undoubtedly successful.

It seemed strange he had never married. There must have been ample opportunity, for since she had last seen him his name had been linked with a number of women, many of them successful in their own right. Once bitten, twice shy, she wryly thought. She was suddenly aware that he was staring at her, sizing her up like she was him. The business columns of the newspapers said he possessed one of the keenest brains in the country, and now that brain was turned on her Lisa felt dim and inadequate.

'You look like a deer at bay,' he said. 'Am I that formidable?'

'Of course not,' she retorted, disconcerted that he could still read her innermost thoughts. 'Did you walk here?'

'Good God, no! I have a car waiting down the road. Why did you want to see me?'

She took a deep breath and walked towards him. He placed a hand beneath her elbow as she climbed over the stile, hastily withdrawing it when she landed on the grass beside him. 'Thank you,' she breathed, her eyes on the Rolls Royce. 'Why did you come in that?'

He glanced towards the vehicle. 'Because it is the only car I have here, and I'm on my way to the airport. Would you rather walk?'

She gazed into those cool eyes, fancying for a moment that she caught a brief glimpse of the Mark she knew. But it was gone too quickly for her to be sure it had ever been there. 'Yes, if you don't mind,' she said. Today, she needed to face him on her own terms.

He nodded. 'Excuse me a moment, I'll tell Tim to wait at the farm.'

She waited while he spoke to the driver. As the car pulled away he turned back to her.

'Well, Lisa, it's just you, me and some cows on the other side of that hedge. Now will you tell me why you wanted me to come? You seem to be avoiding the subject like fire-water.'

'I want to move down to London,' she said. 'But Daddy won't let me because he says I don't know anyone there. And before you say anything, I'm asking nothing more from you than friendship.'

'I came today, didn't I?' His voice softened, giving her the courage she needed.

They started to walk.

'Has Fran told you anything about me?' she asked.

'No. Why?' He suddenly stopped, and took hold of her arm,

swinging her round to face him. 'What's happened, Lisa? Why aren't you working?'

'I never got to be a vet,' she said. 'I had a baby instead.' She saw the shock in his eyes as he stared at her. 'It was no great feat on my part,' she quickly continued. 'After all, women have been giving birth since the year dot. She's illegitimate because I didn't want to marry her father, and truth to tell, he didn't want to marry me either. He ran a mile when I told him I was pregnant.' Still Mark did not speak. 'Her name is Marian. She is four years old and the scandal of the entire district. Fran never told you because I made her swear not to. Perhaps now you can understand . . .' She broke off on a gasp. She was going to make a fool of herself and cry. She turned away from him, and running to a nearby gate, stood sobbing into her open hands.

Mark waited, using his intuition, his discomfort in the face of feminine tears, and a lot of common sense. Had she turned then, she would have caught him unawares, with every feeling he still had for her written across his face. But she did not turn, nor did he go to her.

It was the cow which jolted her back to her senses. It had detached itself from the grazing herd, edging closer and closer until it had worked up enough courage to jab her elbow with a cold nose. Lisa leapt back, and the cow retreated a few steps before uttering a low of indignation.

'Stupid beast!' the girl yelled. But the tears stopped, and after searching in vain for a hanky she steeled herself to meet the coldness of Mark's stare.

There was no need. 'Here,' he said, handing her his handkerchief. 'I think we ought to discuss this sensibly. Let's sit under that tree.'

She blew her nose. 'The cows will pester us.'

'Not if I arm myself with a handful of pebbles and launch an attack if they come within range.'

'They're dairy cows. If you start a stampede Daddy will be furious.' He did not reply, but taking hold of her arm, swung open the gate and led her into the field. 'I'm sorry,' she said. 'I'll be all right now. Do you want your handkerchief back? I'm afraid it's covered in mascara.'

'Keep it,' he said. 'I hate to think what that stuff does to your eyes. It stains like boot black.'

He sat with his back against the rough bark of the tree, while she lay full length on the grass, chin cupped in her hands.

'The daisies were for her?' he asked.

'Yes. But it doesn't matter now.'

'Lisa . . .' he began after a moment.

'No Mark,' she said. 'Please don't ask me about her father. It's a period of my life which I prefer to forget. I'm only sorry that I hurt you so much.'

He turned his head away. 'I came back three weeks later . . . after I'd thought it all out. I wanted to believe I'd made a mistake. But when your landlady said you'd moved, the whole thing seemed so bloody hopeless that I went back to London.' He paused. 'Why did you have the child? There must have been someone who could have helped with an abortion.'

'I was frightened! I didn't want to have my insides mucked up, or else bleed to death like a girl who tried it the year before. I don't think I actually wanted an abortion at all.' She could not see his face, but his hands were clenched together, the knuckles white. 'I'm sorry,' she said, at a sudden loss for words.

He turned to her then. 'I am the one who should be sorry,' he said gently. 'None of this might have happened if I had only waited for you to come home that day.'

'It's too late for recriminations,' she said, her green eyes level with his. 'The best we can do is forget that the past ever existed.'

Marian was a pretty child, with red-gold hair and her mother's green eyes. Lisa left her in the parlour with Mark, and when she came back, she heard their voices mingling in song, Marian shrill and tuneless in comparison with the sweetly moderated tones which had beguiled a nation. She paused outside the door, instinctively knowing that this was something which Mark would not want her to hear. She stood listening until the tray grew heavy in her arms, and then deliberately rattled it before walking into the room.

Marian was sitting on his lap. ' "Oranges and lemons . . ." ' she chanted. But this time Mark did not join in.

'Marian, there's milk and cake for you in the kitchen,' Lisa said, putting the tray on the nearest table. A vase of roses tottered dangerously near the edge, and swooping them up, she placed them on top of a bookcase.

' ". . . say the bells of St. Clement's" . . . I want to stay here,' said Marian defiantly.

'Well, you can't. Uncle Mark and I have to talk.'

The child's face puckered dangerously. 'I want to stay!'

Mark swung her to her feet. 'Why don't you go and sing that song to Aunty Orchid?' he suggested. 'I'll still be here when you come back.'

A delighted smile lit Marian's face. 'All right,' she agreed. He walked with her to the door, watching as she ran to the kitchen.

'I wish I had your knack,' said Lisa. 'She can be so obstinate at times. We already have the most frightful rows.'

'You must be very proud of her,' he said, closing the door.

'I am. I made coffee. There's also cake and biscuits.'

'Only coffee, thank you. Do you mind if I smoke?'

'No, of course not.'

He wandered to the window, looking out at the grazing horses and cattle, at someone pushing a barrow of manure across the yard. 'Does Richard still work the horses?' he asked.

She looked up. 'He's got a new pair of matching greys which he's training. Ben and Betsy are semi-retired now. They were supreme champions for two years in a row, you know. It was quite an achievement.'

She handed him the coffee, and then sat on the sofa, a little afraid of this self-confident man who was the Mark she knew, and somebody else as well.

'Why do you want to go to London?' he suddenly asked. 'Why not Manchester or Liverpool? They're both nearer home.'

'I thought about them, but I want to go far away where nobody knows me. Daddy's done his best for us, but I'm turning into a recluse . . . the people here don't approve of me, and they never will now. And Marian will have to start school soon. I don't want her going to a local one where the other children will tease her because she doesn't have a father. London would be a new start.'

'You would be desperately lonely.'

'No more than I am here,' she said. 'The only person I ever visit is your mother. It's about time I started to be self-supporting. Daddy would help me in the beginning, but I don't want to rely on him forever.'

'You know Richard will do everything to stop you if he thinks I am the only person you can turn to.'

'I can handle Daddy,' she said. 'I just want you to be my friend.'

'I shall always be that,' he said, a smile softening his features. 'There are ways of allaying Richard's fears, and I think for the time being you should say nothing to him. Now I really must be going, otherwise I shall miss my plane and foul up every connection between here and the States.'

'What do you mean?' she asked.

'Trust me, Lisa.' And that was all he would say.

Richard Crowder saw the letter fall through the letter box as he came downstairs, and picked it up from the mat. It was addressed to Lisa and he saw by the postmark that it was from London. He frowned, and glanced upstairs, from where he could hear the sound of laughter, of splashing, and of Lisa lightly scolding. Mark Hanley came immediately into his mind, but the writing certainly wasn't Mark's. He weighed the letter in his palm for a few moments longer, and then tossed it onto the table and walked into the kitchen.

Lisa brought Marian down for breakfast soon afterwards. She was holding the letter. 'I wonder who it's from,' she said to nobody in particular.

Her father looked at her. 'You don't know?' he asked.

'I haven't the faintest idea,' she said. 'And don't worry, it's not from him. The writing's all wrong.'

The envelope held a single sheet of paper which she read slowly.

'Fran wants me to stay with her and Aunt Mary for a while,' she said. 'Eric will be in America for a month.'

'She never asked you before,' her father said suspiciously.

'That's because I didn't want Mark to know about . . . about what happened.'

'Uncle Mark,' said Marian, hearing the name. 'Is he coming here again?'

'No, darling. Now eat your breakfast like a good girl.' Lisa looked at her father. 'It's what I need, Daddy. You can read it if you want. She has a nanny for the children, which means I would be free to look round at flats and job prospects. And you wouldn't have to worry, for Fran is as staid as Yorkshire pudding, and Aunt Mary will be there as chaperone. Please don't try and stop me from going.'

He stroked his rough hand across her cheek. 'Nay lass, I'd not do that. Just remember your home is always here should things not turn out the way you hope.'

'I know,' she said, and hugged him.

Chapter Three

It was a long journey, and by the end of it Marian was behaving so badly that Lisa gave her a hard slap, horrifying the elderly woman with whom they were sharing a compartment. While Marian sat sniffling beside the window Lisa packed away the toys and magazines, and when the train slid into the station she called Marian over and wiped her face.

Their travelling companion stood up. She swept a beauty case from the rack, straightened her hat, and then glared at Lisa. 'I certainly hope you learn a little more tolerance, young lady. Children need love and understanding.'

'Good heavens,' said Lisa. 'I would have moved to another carriage a long time ago had I been less tolerant.'

There was a hiss of indrawn breath and the woman left, clattering the door as she went.

'I didn't like her,' Marian said. 'She was like a witch. I bet she rides a broomstick at night.'

Amusement twitched her mother's lips. 'Yes, she was rather nasty,' she agreed. 'Come on, let's see if we can find Aunty Mary.'

They searched the crowds. Among all the shifting faces, not one seemed familiar, and Lisa had to quell a moment of panic before drawing Marian to a nearby bench and sensibly sitting down to wait.

'Kevin crawled into the bathroom and drank half a bottle of bleach before he was found,' Mark said from behind her. 'Fran was looking after him while the nanny dressed Kim, but she went off to answer the telephone and forgot to shut the door. It's a wonder he didn't fall down the stairs and break his neck. She was hysterical, so Mother went with them to the hospital. Did you think you had been forgotten?'

Lisa leapt to her feet, but it was Marian, breaking away from her loose grasp, who ran to him. 'Uncle Mark!' she cried, delighted when he swung her into the air and then settled her in the crook of his arm.

'Hello, Marian,' he said, and kissed her flushed cheeks. He turned to Lisa. 'You look stunned. I thought you'd be pleased to see me.'

'I am,' she said with feeling. 'Will Kevin be all right?'

'Oh yes,' he replied. 'He's as tough as old boots. Now, would you mind waiting a bit longer while I find a porter? I had to leave Tim guarding the car because he insisted on parking next to a line of no stopping signs.'

It was a relief to let him take over. A porter quickly appeared, and then Mark was steering her towards the car, one hand on her arm. When she saw the Rolls Royce, with the liveried chauffeur arguing with an angry policeman, she shuddered and stopped. Mark was preoccupied with what was going on and did not notice.

'Would you mind taking your offspring, Lisa? The last time Tim got into an argument with the law, the result was a twenty pound fine or a week as guest of the Crown.' Lisa took Marian, and lowered her to the ground. 'The punishment would have done him the world of good, but I had to pay the fine because I need him. Excuse me.'

'Where's Uncle Mark going?' Marian asked, pulling against her mother's hand.

'To talk with the policeman,' Lisa said. 'And then we're going for a ride in his car. Won't that be fun?'

But Lisa Crowder was out of her element, and knew it. In Oldenshaw she had thought it possible for her and Mark to be friends, but now she no longer felt so sure. He was obviously at home here, enjoying an affluence which she found intimidating.

Whatever argument Mark used to settle the dispute, it was certainly an effective one, for by the time she and Marian and the baggage reached them, the policeman was smiling. Tim gave Lisa a stilted greeting, but not until they were in the car and ready to leave did Mark join them.

'Next time that happens I'll leave you to your fate, even if it's a year behind bars,' Mark told the chauffeur.

'I'm sorry, sir,' he said. 'It'll not happen again.' But Lisa heard no regret in his voice, and saw that Mark was smiling.

'What's this?' Marian asked. She had found a small cupboard but was unable to open it.

'Marian, come and sit beside me this instant!' Lisa said.

'I don't mind,' said Mark, pulling open the door. 'It's only a bar, and as you can see, it's empty. The car was in for a service yesterday and Tim doesn't trust a soul. He removes everything which isn't bolted down, and then forgets to replace it for at least a week.' He leant forward and said something to the chauffeur. The man nodded, and Mark closed the glass partition between them.

Marian was busy exploring something else and Lisa frowned at her. 'If you don't sit down I'm going to get very angry.'

'You seem,' said Mark, 'to be lacking in . . .'

'. . . tolerance. I know. But if you had been cooped up with her in a confined space for hours, you would be driven to distraction too. Marian . . .!'

The child scrambled onto the seat next to Mark, well beyond her mother's reach. 'Why don't you look out of the window,' Mark suggested. And much to Lisa's amazement, she did just that.

Mark turned his attention back to Lisa. He noticed the fine lines of exhaustion about her eyes, emphasised perhaps by the way she had pulled back her hair. Her cotton frock was badly creased and she was nervously kneading the thin leather straps of her handbag.

'Do you still want to move down here?' he asked.

He spoke as gently as the old Mark would have done, but she was too preoccupied by her own anxious feelings to notice. She nodded, and self-consciously smoothed down the folds of her frock. She knew Mark was only doing all this for her because of what they had once shared, and it made her feel deeply awkward. 'Yes, I think so,' she said. 'Thank you for speaking to Fran.'

'Actually, I talked it over with Mother, who agrees that the further away you are from Oldenshaw, the better.' He stopped, sensing her constraint. 'Have we really grown so far apart?' he finally asked.

She turned then, only too aware of his overpowering presence. On the far side of him the child still had her nose pressed against the glass, fascinated by the ordinary London world going about its ordinary business outside the confines of the car.

'You have moved on, Mark, while I have stayed still. I can't help this feeling I have that we — we belong to separate worlds.'

He was staring at her. 'Five years ago you were willing to share my life.'

'I know, but a lot has happened since then,' she said, more harshly than she meant. 'I was very young, and the future seemed unimportant. But I have responsibilities now, and even if . . . even if things were different, I don't think I could become a part of all this. It's far too late to go back, Mark, and we would be fools to try. Wouldn't we?'

She felt a sudden coolness, as though an opened door had suddenly been shut in her face. 'We're nearly there,' Mark said quietly. 'After today, I'll not interfere with your life, Lisa. But despite what you may think, I do keep my promises, and if you are ever in need of a friend I shall always be here.'

Fran lived in a narrow, four-storeyed house with a back garden which bordered on Holland Park. She had a cleaning woman who came in daily and the nanny, a pleasant girl in her mid-twenties who was happy to take Marian under her wing.. Lisa was now free to decide what her next steps would be; not that the decisions were hard, for she had all of Mary Hanley's common sense to guide her.

Mary had changed since her husband's death, and for the first time Lisa saw how alike she and her son really were. When Paul Hanley was alive, she had been content to take a back seat and involve herself in home, family and local charities. But with him gone she had blossomed into a frank, at times startling person, who was totally self-sufficient. Fran had insisted her mother stay with her for a few weeks, until she got over the shock of Paul Hanley's death. She had not wanted her to fade away from grief, but very soon Fran began to wish she had left her in Oldenshaw to settle into Heatherdown Cottage. Lisa, on the other hand, liked this new Mary Hanley, and they soon became close friends, despite the difference in their ages. It was three weeks after her arrival that Mary asked whether she had decided to stay or not.

'I'll be going home after Fran's baby is born,' she said. 'Eric will be back from America by then, and two of them together will drive me mad. I know Fran's my daughter, but you must admit that she's a dreary girl. And Eric spends his life trying to be something he's not. I swear the man is turning into a snob. He must be good at his job, otherwise I'm sure Mark would never put up with him—I hear he does a little freelance journalism on the side, just to keep his hand in.'

Lisa gazed at the elegant woman who did not look right with knitting needles in her hands.

'Does Mark know about the freelancing?' she asked.

'What do you think? Mark has offices throughout Europe, and now one in America, yet he still seems to know what's going on in them all. I'm sure he is aware of what Eric does under his nose. And now, my dear, can you tell me whether you will be returning to Oldenshaw or staying here?'

'I want to stay.'

Mary looked at her. 'You're sure that is what you want? That you will be happy?

'I miss the farm, I miss the horses, and more than anything I miss Daddy,' Lisa said. 'But I think it's time I learnt to stand on my own feet. I can always go home if things don't work out.'

'Yes, I know, with your tail between your legs!' Mary said kindly. 'I hope everything does work out. You might even find yourself a husband. Now there's no need to blush. It's a sensible answer to your problems. But enough of that. Mark . . .'

'Mark?' Her startled eyes flew to the older woman's face.

'Yes, Mark,' said Mary firmly. 'He telephoned me a couple of days ago asking for a report. I told him you were not one of his balance sheets, but that I would find out whether you wished to stay. He can help you, Lisa.'

'I know,' she said. 'But I don't want his help. It won't work any more, Mary. Our worlds are too far apart. I could never live up to his, any more than I could expect him to come down to mine.'

Mary laughed. 'Foolish child, it does him good to come down to earth once in a while! God knows, it's something he does little enough of these days. He has the connections to enable him to find you a job and somewhere decent to live. Don't turn him down because of foolish pride.'

'If you and brother Mark aren't exactly on talking terms, then he'll probably send one of his many yes-men to do your bidding,' said Fran from the doorway. 'He lives in the same city as us, my husband works for him, and he's uncle to Kevin and Kim and this nameless object here, but he never damn wells bothers with us. He took Mother to dinner and the theatre during her first week here, but since then she hasn't seen him either.' She walked over to the sofa and dropped heavily onto it. 'I honestly don't think he gives a damn about any of us.'

Mary glared angrily at her daughter. 'He has a business to run,' she snapped. 'I don't expect him to rearrange his life to suit me. And I haven't noticed you suffering from his apparent lack of interest.'

But Fran didn't feel like fighting, and turned to Lisa instead. 'Well,' she said, 'Mark has gathered a select little entourage about him, including Eric, who all sit up very prettily when told to do so. If you accept his offer of help, and find you've got one of those at your beck and call, then you're not on his blacklist.'

Mary threw aside her knitting. 'Fran, you're turning into a first class bitch,' she said. 'Come along, Lisa. I was thinking of purchasing a new hat. A stroll along Kensington High Street would be very pleasant.'

Mary told her son of Lisa's decision over the telephone. 'Will you come yourself?' she had asked.

'I am neither an estate agent nor an employment bureau,' he had said. 'I shall have somebody look into it.'

Fran was jubilant. 'I told you this is what he'd do,' she said with childish triumph while they waited for whoever Mark had delegated to this task.

Lisa looked attractive in a green blouse and beige trousers, with her hair falling loose below her shoulders. She stood next to the window, feeling like a sheep about to be paraded at an auction, and wishing she had never agreed to this ridiculous idea. Mary Hanley, however, had no such misgivings. She knew Lisa needed help, and had enough confidence in her son to know that he would not humiliate the girl.

The car arrived on the dot of ten. Fran heaved herself upright and waddled over to the window, where she pulled aside the lace curtain. Lisa remained well back, her face pale and hands trembling. Mary placidly continued to knit.

Fran found herself paid back for her earlier venom. 'My God,' she hissed, 'He's sent Alan.'

Lisa looked alarmed, and Mary smiled at her. 'What else did you expect?' she asked. 'Shall I let him in?'

Alan Weston was doing this as a special favour for Mark. All he knew was that the woman in question was an old family friend, alone with a young daughter, who wished, for reasons of her own, to settle in London. For Mark to go to so much trouble meant something, but the woman couldn't be all that special, or Mark would be doing the dirty work himself. She was probably a buxom country girl with a thick Yorkshire accent.

He rang the bell of the Stewart house, and after a brief pause the door was opened by a tall woman of indeterminate middle age. He knew immediately who she was.

'Mr. Weston?' she said pleasantly. 'Please come in. I'm Mary Hanley.'

She studied him, and approved of what she saw. He looked a stable sort of man, who would undoubtedly be as good for Mark's extrovert ways as Mark must be for his sobriety. Alan and Fran knew each other, and their greeting was brief, but he was unprepared for the girl. The picture he had formed was shattered when Lisa stepped forward to greet him, her voice accented by a faint but pleasant burr.

'Would you like some coffee?' Fran asked. Alan was Mark's right-hand man and the only one he trusted to run the business in his absence. He was no yes-man, and he never ran errands. Fran was already having second thoughts about the nature of her brother's attachment to his childhood friend.

'No, thank you,' he said. 'I think we ought to get going. There's a lot of ground to cover, and I have to be back in the office this afternoon.'

Lisa snatched up her handbag, her anxious eyes resting on Mary's face.

'Everything will be all right,' Mary assured her. 'Listen to what Mr. Weston says, for I'm sure he knows what he's talking about.'

Alan smiled, and was about to follow Lisa from the room when Fran's voice halted him.

'I don't suppose you know when Eric will be back?' she asked. 'The baby's due in a fortnight and he seems to have been away for an awful long time.'

'I expect Mark will bring him back next week,' he said.

'Mark is away?' Mary asked.

The brown eyes turned to her. 'He left a couple of days ago. Didn't you know?'

'Do we ever?' said Fran.

Lisa Crowder did not speak again until she was in the car, and then she said, 'I think you ought to know that although I'm grateful for your assistance, I don't intend taking anything unless I consider it suitable in every way, particularly financially. And even if nobody thinks I'm capable of finding a flat, I can get myself a job, so please don't try and force any of Mark's ideas on me in that respect.'

He admired her courage, and sensed she would say as much to Mark were he here. 'I understand, Mrs. Crowder,' he said.

Her cheeks flushed. 'My name is Lisa.'

'And I'm Alan.'

She laughed. 'I think we ought to call a truce,' she said. 'I'm sorry if I was rude. It's not your fault that we're stuck in this predicament.'

The last flat on his list was situated in Bayswater, only half a block from Hyde Park, but had she liked any of the others he would have skipped it altogether. The flat itself sounded ideal, but it was situated above some stables, and he couldn't imagine anyone in their right mind wanting to live there.

'What's this place like?' Lisa asked. She had reached the conclusion that Fran was lucky to own a house with its own garden, for living in a flat was obviously going to be a dreary existence.

'It's a mews house,' he said.

'Mews house?' she repeated. 'Aren't they built over garages, or something like that?'

'Yes,' he agreed. 'Something like that.'

A middle-aged man was bawling at his four pupils to sit properly when they arrived. He then mounted his own horse and reached down to tighten the girth, ignoring the car which was waiting to pass. Alan cursed his luck and resisted the temptation to hoot the horn. He knew nothing about horses except that they kicked; and he had no intention of having his expensive car dented. The man gave some instructions to his pupils, and then they moved off towards the other exit. Alan turned to apologise for the delay, but the words stuck in his throat when he saw Lisa's face.

'Is it down here?' she asked.

'The one with the yellow door, next to the stables.'

'Well, I hope you're right about the rent being cheap, because I love it already.'

She was able to move into the flat the following week. Her father sent some money, and Mary helped buy mostly second-hand furniture to fill it. She introduced herself to the owner of the riding school, and two days later he was letting her ride in exchange for some help in the stables. By the weekend she had the pick of the horses and was taking out some of his classes, leaving Marian in the care of his wife. She had no time to pine for the farm, and in the evenings she had Alan. He was attracted by her quiet charm, and asked her out; and because she liked him and knew hardly a soul, she accepted his invitations. The only black cloud in her life was the lack of a job.

She refused to accept help from anyone, for this was something she had to do for herself. But a half-trained vet of twenty-seven had no chance of worming her way into even the most humble clerical position.

Fran gave birth to a daughter, and breathing a sigh of relief, Mary Hanley returned to Oldenshaw and the task of redecorating Heatherdown Cottage. Richard Crowder sent more money down to Lisa, but she hated to rely on him and dipped into her own meagre savings. She put Marian into a nursery school, a necessary move, but one which cut deep into her pocket at a time when she didn't have a job. Alan wanted to line up some interviews with firms known to Hanley Recordings, but she refused his offer. Something was sure to come up.

June Halliday was sub-editor and fashion editor of a prominent monthly magazine aimed at the in-betweens, the adolescents who were groping their way towards adulthood. She was excellent at her job, but it was becoming too much for her to cope with single-handed and she needed an assistant. None of the present staff were interested in the position, for June Halliday was known as a bitch, and had quarrelled with them all. So she contacted an employment agency who sent over a selection of girls. She worked her way through twelve of them in less than two hours, ending up with a foul headache and a stinking temper. She would have exploded had she known that a thriving betting shop had been set up in the post-room.

'There's one more,' said Moira, the receptionist.

Unlucky thirteen, June acidly thought, and said, 'Wheel her in.'

'Miss Crowder,' Moira announced.

June looked up, and the pencil she was rolling between her fingers came to an abrupt halt. The girl was slim and attractive, and well dressed, if perhaps a little behind the more fashion-conscious. She was obviously nervous, but retained a distinctive poise, and unlike the twelve before her, she looked moderately intelligent.

'Good afternoon,' June said. 'Please sit down.'

The agency had sent Lisa because the job was for a Girl Friday with no specific needs such as typing, but on seeing the woman who was to interview her, what little confidence Lisa had sank rapidly to her feet. Lisa had always imagined that people involved in fashion would be fashionable themselves, but June Halliday was short and fat, with badly cut hair and clothes which looked as though they had been purchased from one of the cheaper chain stores.

'You look very young,' said June. 'What experience have you had?'

'None in this sort of thing,' Lisa said, trying to dodge the question.

'In what sort of thing, then?' the woman snapped.

'Well . . . nothing, actually.'

'For God's sake!' said June Halliday. 'My dear girl, I have no intention of training somebody who is straight out of school. Goodbye, Miss Crowder.'

Lisa bit her lower lip. She had come all this way only to be thrown out without being heard. She felt something rebel inside her. Why should she be browbeaten? She could stand up to Mark—and Alan had told her that nobody crossed Mark, and that he himself would go to any length to avoid a head-on confrontation with him. Lisa told herself now that if she wasn't afraid of Mark, then there was no reason for her to be frightened of this woman either.

'I think that having come here, I deserve a proper interview,' she said, settling deeper into the chair. 'I'm sorry if you think I am wasting your time, Miss Halliday, but if I am also to waste mine I don't want to be cheated from the outset.'

June Halliday was amazed. 'You are an insolent young lady,' she said, putting down the pencil. 'If you're as aggressive as this at every interview you attend, I don't wonder you've not found yourself a job yet.'

'I've never before been cut off with barely a word said.'

'All right,' said June, 'Tell me about yourself.'

The entire office staff lost their wagers that day. Lisa did not take long to learn about her new boss. June was a fair-minded woman who lived for her work and hated stupidity. One day she was sweet as honey, the next viperish, and learning to assess her moods, Lisa knew when to ask advice and when to plod along as best she could. Perhaps June's best attribute was that she was never jealous of other women, and when Lisa began experimenting with clothes, she was generous with her advice. However, when one or two young men started hanging hopefully around the office, she chased them away with a few choice words; she had no intention of losing an assistant who was actually becoming a great help.

Initially, Lisa had been delegated to running messages and proof reading, but she caught on quickly and in no time at all was helping with the basic compilation of articles. She also had a keen eye for fashion, seeming to know instinctively what would appeal to the average teenager. She did not have June's aggression, but given time, would probably be good enough to command a position on any fashion magazine in the country.

It was autumn when the young designer came begging for an interview. The magazine had been running a series of articles on up-and-coming designers, and armed with a portfolio of his best work, he was making a direct approach.

June had been in a bad mood all day, and Lisa was concentrating on a backlog of work. Late in the afternoon she was called to June's office, and as she walked in, a sheaf of loose papers was flung at her. She caught them as best she could, but some of them floated to the floor, so that she had to drop on her knees to gather them up.

'Rubbish . . . utter rubbish!' June was shouting. 'I don't know how anybody could have the cheek to hand me things like this . . . Lisa, please tell the young man we are not interested, and that he should change his ideas or else get out of this business altogether.'

Lisa snatched up the last sheet, crushing it as she did so. She looked at the sketch. It had a flair which appealed to her, but the dress itself was shapeless and indecently short. It was quite different from anything she had ever seen.

'Have you finished that layout yet?' June asked.

'No.'

'Then stop dawdling and get on with it.'

Lisa rushed into the passage, wishing June would do her own dirty work. She expected to meet a brash young man, and was taken aback when she saw a fidgeting youth who looked no more than eighteen. He had sandy hair which flopped over his brow, and there was something haunting about his finely sculptured face and large eyes.

'Miss Halliday?' he asked.

'No, I'm afraid not,' she said. 'I'm her assistant, Lisa Crowder. She's very busy at the moment and can't see you.'

'She doesn't like them?' he asked.

She wanted to soften the blow, but the look in his eyes stopped her. 'No, I'm sorry, she doesn't. But I do,' she said, and handed him the drawings.

'You didn't have to say that.'

'I know, but I meant it. I'm sorry about this one. It got crushed.'

'That's all right,' he said. 'You can keep it if you want.'

She took the drawing from him. 'Look,' she said, 'why don't you write your name and address on the back. I might be able to catch June in a better mood. No promises, but you never know.' She watched as he bent over a low table. 'And don't give up. Perhaps you should try and conform a little more. Make them a bit longer for a start. If I wore a dress like this, just imagine the eyeful it would give every boggling male!'

He laughed. 'I think you'd look marvellous in one of these, Miss Crowder. You have lovely long legs. But I'm sorry, I've wasted enough of your time already. Goodbye.' He fled.

Moira glanced up from manicuring her nails. 'My mum always said there were more nuts out than in,' she said. 'And they all come in here looking for instant fame.'

His name was Martin Henderson, and it was a long time before Lisa was able to forget his earnest face.

Chapter Four

I did not turn when Alan sat down beside me, and he, knowing better, did not interrupt while Marty Pole was straining for the high notes. Marty missed, and I raised my hand, stopping the ill-fated session for the umpteenth time.

'What the hell is wrong now?' Marty shouted angrily, glaring at me through the glass which divided us.

'It still doesn't sound right,' I told him. I switched off the connecting speaker and turned to Tony Crane, a top technician who could work wonders on the mixing desk. 'Can you fake it?' I asked. 'If not, we'll have to dub over the bad parts.'

'I'll try,' he said. 'But can I have a clear run first? And then you'll have to get him out of here. I won't be able to do a thing with him peering over my shoulder.'

Marty Pole had been a bricklayer before Chris discovered him in a pub in the East End. Two years ago he had been a fresh-faced kid with a good physique, but now the muscle was turning to flab, and the freshness had been replaced by an unsavoury mixture of self-indulgence and conceit. Of course, the kids who worshipped him only knew what we told them, and during the past year all his records had reached number one in the charts. Now he was watching me sullenly, and I knew that if I hadn't been there, he would be giving everyone hell.

'Go through it one more time,' I told him. 'And then we'll pack it in for the day.'

Tony was giving instructions to his assistant, and as Marty turned his attention to them I suddenly remembered Alan.

'What do you want?' I asked. He never came to recording sessions unless it was absolutely necessary; he hated pop music and the people who performed it.

'Something important has come up which we need to discuss. But I think you'd prefer privacy rather than this goldfish bowl.'

'Let's get this finished first,' I said. 'And then we can go up to my office.'

Tony signalled he was ready and the band hit the first chords. I shuddered as Marty came in late.

'Did you hear they want him for the next Royal Command?' I asked. 'God only knows how he's going to get through it. His voice is starting to go.'

'He doesn't sound bad to me,' said Alan.

Tony grimaced, and I smiled. Alan had never been able to differentiate between one song and another, let alone between singers.

It must have been almost an hour before Marty left. 'Give me a few hours, and then I might have something for you,' Tony said.

Alan and I walked over to the office block. The original warehouse had been demolished four years ago, and now there were two interconnected buildings which sprawled over most of the three acres of ground.

'How's Lisa?' I asked. I had taken a calculated risk when I sent him to help her three months ago, but it had worked, and she had him to lean on now.

'She's fine,' he said. 'She loves the job, and she spends all her spare time in the stables, refusing to accept a penny in payment.'

'Horses run in the Crowder blood,' I told him. 'As children we practically lived on horseback.'

'You rode?' he asked.

'Yes. Didn't she tell you?'

'No.'

I glanced at him, then dropped the subject when I saw a shadow of doubt cross his face.

Norma looked up as we walked through her office. 'I have a number of telephone messages,' she said. 'And Chris wants you down in rehearsal room three.'

'Later,' I told her.

Norma was a godsend. I'd worked through a succession of six secretaries in as many months when Stephen Tate-Jones recommended her. She had worked in a bank for a number of years, and then taken a year out to look after her terminally-ill mother. She was forty-five years old then, and a spinster in every sense of the word, from the tight bun at the back of her head to the sensible brogues on her feet. She obviously disapproved of me, and had already decided to refuse the position—but then I noticed that the suit she wore was one of the high quality Hanley weaves, and that broke the ice. I would be lost without her now.

'What's on your mind?' I asked Alan when we were in my office. I was standing beside a large picture window which looked down upon the Thames.

'The mill.'

I swung round. My father had been a crafty bastard, for although the mill was left to me, he had ensured that Mother retained trusteeship of the shares for five years. The deeds were so intricate and well drawn that not even Alan was able to untangle the mess. I had saved it for Father's sake, but wanted nothing to do with it now. So I had chosen to ignore it altogether, leaving it to run under its own steam. But judging by Alan's expression, something had gone wrong, and I was now going to have the whole damn mess dumped in my lap.

'There have been five strikes in less than ten weeks,' he said. 'If something isn't done quickly, you're going to lose money. A lot of it.'

'What do you expect me to do?'

'How about running the place?' he asked abruptly. 'You've not done a bloody thing since you inherited it. God only knows why, considering the trouble you went to five years ago. You poured in money which you could ill afford at the time, and now you're letting it rot.'

'I hate everything about that mill,' I told him. 'It brings back too many bad memories. You seem to know what's going on there. You go up and sort it out.'

'I'm not a Hanley,' he said stiffly. 'It's a family business. They'll respect you, but won't pay any attention to me. And I don't know anything about textiles.'

I did know about textiles. Some things never leave you, no matter how hard you try and rub them off.

'Let me have a detailed report,' I told him. 'If you won't go up there, will you go to America in my stead? I want to know how the new studios are coming along.'

He looked uneasy. 'You can go afterwards,' he said. 'It's not an important trip.'

I stared at him for a moment. It was the first time Alan had tried to avoid anything, and it took me a while to work out why. 'Lisa?' I asked.

He did not reply, and I felt unaccountably depressed.

'You ought to consider buying your own plane,' he said suddenly, breaking the awkward silence. 'You're going to be travelling a lot once the American studios become operational, and in the long run it'll save you money and time.'

The worst shock was seeing how badly neglected the Manor grounds were. Falling leaves were piled beneath the trees, hedges were shapeless, and the lawn was ragged. The house was not much better. My home had become an empty shell of its former self, the whole place reeking of desertion. In all the rooms, white dust-cloths were draped over the furniture, carpets had been rolled up, and clocks were silent. From the kitchen I could see the stable block, and beyond it the overgrown orchard where Tuppence had once grazed. Maude and Albert's cottage was hidden behind the trees, but there was no smoke coming from the chimney, and when I picked up the kitchen extension, the telephone rang without anybody replying.

I wandered back to the main part of the house, colliding with Mother in a dim passageway.

'Do look where you're going, dear,' she said, taking hold of my arm and kissing me on the cheek. 'Doreen Barlow saw you pass through Oldenshaw and couldn't resist phoning to find out if I knew you were back. I thought it best to come straight over. Maude is in Steelton shopping, and I borrowed Albert to do some gardening. I brought him back with me and told him to get the heating on. I don't know how we ever survived without it.' We walked arm in arm to the main hall. 'Sad, isn't it?' she asked.

'I never realised,' I said. 'I thought it would be the same.'

'And so it is beneath the covers. I took very little, mostly sentimental pieces. Everything in this house belongs here, and I don't want to be surrounded by too many memories. If you had let us know you were coming, you would never have seen it like this.'

'I was feeling peevish,' I said. 'I've just heard that there's trouble at the mill.'

'Ah yes, I thought that would bring you back. I'd ask you to stay with me, but the painters are in and only one bedroom is usable. But come for dinner. Elly is with me now.'

We went into the drawing room. I drew back the heavy curtains, while Mother pulled some dust-sheets from a couple of chairs and a table.

'We have to cover it, otherwise everything would get ruined,' she said. 'You should live here, Mark. I love this house, and hate to see it go to waste.'

'You should have stayed.' I looked across the lawn. 'How many gardeners did Father employ? Albert can't cope alone at his age.'

'One in winter and two or three in summer, depending on how ambitious he felt towards the flowerbeds. Come and sit down, dear. I can't stay long, and I want to talk to you about the mill.'

I did not sit, but leant against the mantlepiece. 'What about the mill?' I asked.

'As it only happened late this afternoon I'm not sure whether you know yet.'

'Know what?'

'That there were some nasty scuffles and the police were called in. Some of the men have been arrested and the rest are in an ugly mood. I don't think it's safe for you to go there, Mark, and it would be wiser to arrange for management, union officials and whoever else you want to speak to, to come here.'

'Is that what Father would have done?' I asked. She did not reply, but in her eyes I saw the answer I sought. 'I'll be careful,' I promised. 'But if I don't face them now I shall never win their respect. Is there anything else you can tell me? What about Frank Logan? Father made him manager, but he seems unable to deal with these troubles.'

'I know very little,' she said. 'Your father rarely discussed business.'

But she told me enough to substantiate the gross mismanagement Alan had hinted at in his report. After she left I made some telephone calls, and dusk was falling when I went out. Mother did not expect me for a couple of hours, which gave me plenty of time to drive into Steelton.

The house was a two-storey semi-detached situated in one of the new estates. I parked outside the gate, and after checking that there was nobody about who might recognise me, walked quickly to the front door and rang the bell.

Sally Bennett opened it. She was prettier than I remembered, despite the peroxide hair which was bunched about her face in a fall of loose curls. Her mouth fell open when she saw me.

'Good evening, Sally,' I said. 'Is Arthur home?'

'There could be bad trouble if you were seen here, Mr. Hanley,' she said, peering nervously to left and right.

'I know, and letting me stand on the doorstep isn't the best way of avoiding it.'

She stood aside. 'Arthur's in the parlour,' she said. 'It's over here.'

'You have no children yet?' I asked, seeing none of the clutter associated with a family.

'Nay. Neither of us are keen on kids,' she said, and swung open a door. The only light in the room came from a television set. A figure was slumped in a chair before it. 'Arthur!' she called, switching on the overhead light. 'Arthur!'

'What?' As he swung round I think he was more shocked than she was to see me there. He switched off the television and stood up.

'Bloody hell!' he swore. 'What are you doing here?'

'You did me a favour once, Arthur, and I'm now in a position to repay it.'

He was a shrewd man. 'Did anyone see you come in?' he asked.

'No. And I'm driving a hired car, so I don't think your neighbours will be suspicious.'

'You'd better sit down,' he said. 'I suppose you came about the mill?'

'I want to know what's been happening since my father died.'

He shrugged. 'A lot of things, and none of them helped by your apparent lack of interest. Old Mr. Hanley was always there, but since he's been gone the union have got too strong a hold. They're practically running the business, and will fight you every inch of the way.'

'What about Frank Logan?' I asked.

'It's rumoured he's skimming cream from top of milk. He's also the wrong man for the job. He was all right when your pa was overseeing him, but he's no feeling for the people on the floors, and tries to lord it over them, and him no better than the rest of us. A few days ago a couple of lads were larking about a bit, and instead of giving them a good telling off like they deserved, he sacked them. That's why we're out now.'

Sally brought in a pot of tea and some biscuits, and later on Arthur produced a half bottle of whisky. We drank it all, and smoked cigarette after cigarette as I questioned and he answered. The staff was in chaos, and production lower than it had ever been. I would have to intervene in the strongest possible way; and I would also need Alan, whether he liked it or not.

'I can see I made a mistake in not becoming involved before this.' I said when we had thrashed out most of the problems. 'I understand you have taken a partner in your real estate business, Arthur.'

His eyes narrowed. 'Not a partner in the legal sense,' he said. 'It's still not much more than a hobby which brings in a bit of extra cash. Sam Tucker had money to invest and asked my advice. We've stuck together since then.'

'Sam Tucker is the chief union man,' I said. 'From what I've heard, he's a bully who could be manipulated by the right person. I think you are that person. I have other interests which need my attention, and can only be here for short periods of time, so I need a manager who will be trusted by everyone. The job is yours if you want it.'

He did not speak immediately, but then said, 'I know nowt about top brass management.'

'How much do you know about cloth?'

'As much as any man you can name.'

'Then your qualifications are better than most,' I said. 'I shall be available to sort out the thornier issues, and if I'm away there are other men I can trust. My immediate problem is getting the mill back into full production. I want to be fair, but as this strike is illegal, I cannot agree to negotiate until they return to work.'

'I'll get them back if you give me a free hand,' he said.

'You have it,' I said. 'I'll speak with Frank Logan in the morning. You won't be having any more trouble from him.' I glanced at my watch. Mother had been expecting me two hours ago. 'Do whatever you must, Arthur. Just get them back.'

Technically, I didn't sack Frank Logan. He was in his early fifties and had served my father well, so I forced him into early retirement. That left the way open for Arthur Bennett, who had the mill back into production within two days. Alan and I had already decided what must be done, but first I needed to go there alone and let them see that I was ready to step into my father's shoes.

Hanley Mill had sprung out of the cottage industries in and around the village of Steelton. The individual weavers had been brought together by my far-seeing great-grandfather in a large shed-like building with looms which were driven by a water-wheel. Over the years the water-wheel had been replaced by a steam engine, and then my father had converted to electricity. But the building, although much extended, never rose above its present single storey, spreading out into an untidy series of interconnected sheds.

The offices were situated on the west side of the main building where the weaving was done. There were two ways to reach them, and I deliberately chose the longest, most conspicuous route, which led through the entire length of the working floor, between the looms and the men and women who operated them. I had walked this way with my father when I came to work here. But now I was alone, and as I passed through the doorway I realised that this was the first time I had set foot in the mill in over nine years.

The silence stretched out before me, the only sounds coming from the machinery, which was left untended as the operators watched me walk by. Some of the elder men bowed their heads, half respectful and half ashamed, and I greeted those I knew, seeing their pleasure at my recognition. The younger men tended to be more sullen, while the women crowded together, smiling and giggling.

It was a long walk, and I was relieved to reach the end of it. My father's office was at the beginning of the passage. I pushed open the door. Nothing had changed, and I almost expected him to be sitting at the desk. I went over to the window. When I was last here the view had been of green fields and grazing cattle. Now there was a rapidly expanding industrial estate. I turned away and ran my fingers over the desk top. My great-grandfather stared down at me from a portrait across the room.

'I never thought you'd have the guts to come in that way,' Arthur Bennett said from the doorway. 'You took a chance. They're back, but it won't take much to get them out again.'

'You told me once that it was my inheritance,' I said. 'You're right. It is. I've shirked my responsibilities for too long, and if I want their respect I have to win it. That was only the first step. What about the unions?'

'They're ready to meet you this afternoon. Sam Tucker is the only one you have to worry about, and he's willing to be reasonable if you meet him half way.'

I nodded. 'Three o'clock,' I said. 'This office should be large enough. My lawyer will be coming over later, and you are also to attend.' I suddenly realised he was clad in overalls. 'Good God, man, you're no longer a labourer.'

He smiled. 'Production has gone to pot over this past month. They need all the help they can get. I expect you'll want to look over the books?'

'Yes,' I said. 'I would also like a list of all our customers and the amounts of cloth they regularly purchase. And then I think it would boost your new status if we went on an inspection tour together. But change into some suitable clothes first.'

'I'll see to books beforehand,' he said. He paused. 'If you don't mind me saying so, it's good to have a Hanley back in this office.'

I sat on my father's chair. But it was no longer his. It was mine. 'Thank you, Arthur,' I said.

Chapter Five

Eric Stewart took Angie to Covent Garden because she wanted to flaunt the new fur coat and diamond bracelet which had set him back far more than he could really afford. She wasn't interested in the opera, only the people there, and afterwards he took her to one of London's best restaurants where she picked sulkily at the exorbitantly priced food.

Angie Clements was eighteen, although she claimed to be twenty and looked at least twenty-six. Eric wasn't the first man she'd had, nor would he be the last, but he was better situated than the two before him, and had promised her the opportunity of a recording session. That was months ago, and she was getting annoyed because nothing had materialised.

'I have a headache,' she said when he took her home, and then walked straight into the bedroom.

'So do I,' he said, 'from your perpetual nagging. I took you to that bloody awful opera, and the food gave me indigestion. Now come to bed and shut up.'

She looked petulant as he peeled off his shirt. 'If Mark Hanley really is your brother-in-law, why can't you get me in for a try-out?'

'Because it's not that easy. I'm not involved with that side of the business.'

'You must know the people who are,' she shouted. 'Or is it all a lie about your wife being his sister?'

'No,' he said angrily. 'But even if I got you in, Mark has the final say.'

She thrust out her hips. 'That would suit me fine. I'd like nothing better than to meet the famous Mark Hanley.'

If she had expected a reaction she was disappointed. She was a pretty girl and sexy, but Eric knew Mark would not give her so much as a glance.

'Stop being so bloody-minded,' he said. 'You know I have to leave in a couple of hours.'

'No,' the girl said. 'Not until you promise to try and do something.'

He sat down on the bed. 'You seem to forget that I've bought everything you are wearing, and I also pay the rent for this flat.'

'It's no palace,' she said defiantly. 'And these diamonds aren't up to much either.'

He gritted his teeth. He had made that promise in a fit of passion, and had regretted the careless words ever since. 'I can't do it, Angie. Nobody will go to the expense of a recording session on my account.'

'You won't know unless you damn well try!' she cried. 'And if you're going to do nothing, I'm walking out of here right now.' She picked up her coat. This time she wasn't bluffing.

He stood up. 'I'll try,' he said.

'You'd better,' she told him, her hard eyes glittering. 'Otherwise I really will leave.'

'Do you know when Mark will be back?' Eric asked. 'He said he was going for a fortnight, and it's been practically six weeks.'

They were in the passage, and Chris Steinberg continued to leaf through the papers he was holding.

'I thought you were happiest when he was away,' he said. 'At least we get to shuffle along at our own pace for a while. I swear I've aged twenty years since working for him.'

'And you love every nerve-wracking moment of it,' Alan Weston said, joining them. 'We all do, or we wouldn't be here.' He turned to Eric. 'The last I heard, Mark was shacked up with some Hollywood starlet. But he's sure to be back before Christmas, and if you've not done your stuff on Patsy Hart, he's going to hit the roof.'

'I'll do it when I'm good and ready!' Eric snapped. 'I have to make most of it up anyway. Patsy Hart might be this year's top female singer, but she's about as interesting as a lump of clay.'

Chris glanced at Alan. It was always the same when Mark was away. Give him a little rope, and Eric would start throwing his weight about. Give him enough, Alan thought, and one day he'll hang himself.

'I'm sorry, I've had a rough day,' Eric apologised. He knew what they were thinking. They all underestimated him, even Mark. But now that he had Alan and Chris together, this might be a good time to broach the subject which had been occupying his mind for the past few days. 'Chris, I'd like a demo made some time this week. Have you got a free studio? It'll also need a back-up group.'

'Who do you have in mind?' Chris asked unenthusiastically.

Alan leant against the wall. Eric had tried this before, but Mark refused to bring in a succession of his brother-in-law's star-struck mistresses.

'Someone who could turn out to be pretty good,' Eric said evasively.

'Who?' Chris insisted.

'A girl called Angie Clements.'

'Bring in Angie Clements and Mark will have you flayed, and us as well,' Alan said. 'And I doubt if Fran will be very pleased if she hears about it.'

'Exactly what are you insinuating?' Eric demanded.

'No Angie Clements,' said Chris. 'I'm sorry, Eric, but it's not worth the risk.'

'You should have been a little less obvious when escorting the lady about town,' said Alan diplomatically. 'We'd be the laughing stock if she came within a mile of this place, and Mark would sack the lot of us on the spot.'

Eric got around Angie by telling her that he was going to make a direct approach to Mark on his return. But the longer she waited, the more sceptical she became, not believing that he had no idea where his brother-in-law was. Mark had apparently tired of his current love nest, moved over to Europe on a whirlwind tour designed to put the fear of God into his employees, and then had simply disappeared. Alan knew where he was, but was disinclined to make it public knowledge, while Eric callously presumed him to be with another in the long line of women who would sacrifice their souls for the privilege of sharing his bed. If only Fran had thought to telephone her mother she would have discovered that, on the contrary, Mark was staying at Olden Manor, from where he was launching his excessive energies into the mill.

Christmas was only eight days away when, staggering into the office at eleven-thirty, after a night with Angie, Eric found Mark impatiently waiting for him. Alan and Chris were already there.

'Suffering from lack of sleep, Eric?' Mark sarcastically asked. 'I certainly hope no more little Stewarts are on the way. Do give Fran my love when you see her.' It was obvious he knew exactly where Eric had been. Eric coloured, and the other two men looked everywhere but at him. 'Oh, for God's sake, sit down,' Mark said abruptly. 'We have a mountain of work to get through. What you do in your own time is your own business, Eric, but I strongly object when a senior member of my staff decides to stroll in halfway through the morning looking as though he has just rolled out of bed. As to whose bed it is, I don't give a damn.'

Three hours passed before the three of them were dismissed, and Eric would have been first out except that Mark called him back. He caught a fleeting glimpse of sympathy on Alan's departing face before the door closed.

'I won't keep you long,' Mark said. 'I hear you have been trying to promote yet another of your mistresses. Don't look so surprised, Eric. Neither Alan nor Chris told me, but if you insist on conducting conversations in passageways, you must expect every word of them to be faithfully transmitted throughout the building, and eventually to reach me. I want your promise that this is the last of it. I don't care if you keep a harem, but I will not have my business reputation jeopardised because of your regrettable sexual appetite.'

He had been staring through the window, and when he swung round, his eyes were deadly bright. 'Well?' he said.

'All right,' Eric begrudgingly agreed, seeing that it would be unwise to cross him now.

Mark smiled. 'Is she any good?' he asked.

'I don't know,' Eric admitted. 'I've never heard her sing.'

'By the time that girl is thirty, she's going to be washed out and hard as nails,' Mark said without malice. 'But I'm willing to strike a bargain with you. If I can arrange for her to have a session with another company, will you renew your contract when it expires next year?'

Eric stared at him for a moment. 'That's blackmail,' he said.

'It really depends on how infatuated you are. I get the impression that Miss Clements is on the verge of packing her bags and leaving.' That information really startled Eric. How the hell did he know all this? Mark saw the effect he was having and carried on smoothly. 'You realise, of course, that if you accept the correspondent's post which I happen to know you've been offered, your salary will be somewhat depleted. You will certainly not be able to support a family and a mistress. Something will have to go, presumably the nymphet.'

Eric let that pass. 'How did you find out about the job?' he asked.

'The same way I find out about everything. Someone told me. I also know about the little bits of journalism you do on the side. If you stay here, that too will have to go. I will not put up with a conflict of interest, nor your work suffering because of it.'

'And if I go?' Eric asked. 'What are you threatening me with?'

'Why should I threaten you with anything? I certainly can't stop you from leaving. But I think you'll be making a mistake, especially as I shall soon be branching out into new fields where your literary talents can be put to good use.'

'What fields?' Eric asked.

'I am not prepared to divulge that information yet.'

Alan would know, but he was as tightlipped as Mark . . . 'Can I think about this?'

'As much as you want,' said Mark pleasantly. 'But please find somewhere else to do it.'

The trouble was that there was very little for Eric to think about. If he stayed he could have everything. And everything was what he wanted.

Chapter Six

Steelton was known for its lack of traffic, but today the streets were packed with hooting vehicles as everyone tried to get home early. Arthur Bennett was sitting in a traffic jam, listening to Christmas carols over the car radio. He was happy because he had finally got hold of the meadow next to the new housing estate. Ned Crawford had not wanted to sell it, but now he needed the money to rebuild the wooden barn which had burnt down, killing seven prize dairy cows. There was also the store of winter hay to be replenished, most of which had been destroyed by the fire, which had mysteriously flared up on a night when the family was out. Arthur had waited a couple of days before making an offer for the field, and as it was a fair offer and the only one the farmer received, he accepted it.

Steelton had not expanded enough for there to be a rush on available land, but Arthur Bennett was buying as much property as he could, knowing that the day was coming when he would make a fortune. He had ambitions in other directions as well, and next year was determined to get on the Town Council. He was already serving on a couple of local committees, one of which might bring him the publicity he needed. The Anti-Blood Sports Society had done little more than hold monthly meetings until Arthur joined them, but he had breathed in new life, and membership had trebled over the past couple of months. Their main target was the local Hunt, which retaliated by meeting at secret rendezvous, sometimes successfully, sometimes not. So far nobody had been able to discover where the Boxing Day Meet was to be held, but Arthur was not going to give up without a fight, for he had already planned that it was going to be a day which nobody would forget.

Lisa took Alan to the farm for Christmas. Because he was a city man he found it fascinating, and he also saw Lisa in a new light. The house was bursting with people, for Richard Crowder's two brothers and their families were staying until after New Year, and Mary Hanley would come on Christmas Day. She was alone at the cottage because Fran did not want to come to Oldenshaw, and Mary had turned down a half-hearted invitation to spend Christmas with her daughter in London. Mark had flown to America at the last moment. Larry Pine, who was presently topping the American charts, had appeared drunk on a television programme, and although the programme had come to an immediate halt, the harm was already done and Larry Pine had been banned not only by the station in question, but by the entire American television network. It was a legal hassle which Alan would normally deal with, but with Christmas almost upon them and plans already made, Mark had gone himself.

It rained on Christmas Day. After church Lisa went out on Kingston for an hour, leaving Alan to his own devices. The various Crowders split up, the men going out to the barns, the women to the kitchen, and the children crowding noisily into the parlour. Although the men had invited him to look over the cattle, Alan preferred to stay inside, and wandered aimlessly about until he found what appeared to be an office. It was small and cluttered, but there was a well-stocked bookcase which caught his eye. He looked through its bulging shelves, and spotted a photograph album which he picked up. He flicked through a few pages, wondered if he had the right to snoop like this, and then, overcome by curiosity, settled in an old armchair in front of a two-bar electric heater. He turned the pages slowly, learning more about the Crowder family than Lisa or her father could ever have told him.

The album went back to pre-war days, with pictures of a younger Richard Crowder and a pretty girl, her hair piled on her head, and in her eyes and delicate features something of Lisa. There were not many pictures of Elizabeth Marian Crowder, and the pages which held them were dog-eared. In some of the later photographs she was holding a baby and then, page by page, Alan saw the baby growing. A striking blonde boy appeared, and as Alan turned the pages he saw them grow up together.

'What's that?'

He leapt up, and the album dropped to the floor. Lisa stood in the doorway, her cheeks glowing from the cold and her faded jeans wet beneath the knees. Then she recognised the album and pounced on it as though it were a long lost friend. 'Where did you find it?' she asked.

'Over there,' he said, 'I'm sorry. I didn't mean to pry.'

She laughed. 'Good heavens, there's nothing private in here. I haven't seen it in years, that's all. I really ought to stick in some photos of Marian. How far did you get?'

She thrust the album back into his hands, and he sat down, Lisa dropping to her knees beside him, smelling faintly of horse and rain and a sweet dampness.

'You ought to get changed,' he said.

'Later. I'm warm as toast.'

He stopped at a page filled with photographs of her, Mark and two ponies, and she commented on every one with a memory for detail which he found amazing.

'I never realised you and Mark were so close,' he said half an hour later. 'There's hardly a picture where you're not together.'

She had enjoyed going through the album, but it had made her feel sad as well. She blinked back a tear and stretched her hands towards the fire. 'We were practically inseparable,' she said. 'You never knew him then, but he was nothing like he is now. It was the conflict with his father which changed him.' She paused. And me, she thought. I cannot be blameless. She stood up. 'I'd better get changed. Mary will be here soon, and Daddy has finished with the livestock, at least until this evening. Come on, everyone must be wondering what on earth we're doing.'

Alan had never before encountered the close-knit farming community, and Richard Crowder did his best to include the lawyer in their conversations, thus avoiding the usual topics of cattle and pigs. The conversation drifted even further afield with the arrival of Mary Hanley, but throughout the afternoon Alan noticed how no mention was made of Mark's name. He thought it a damn shame that Mary was alone for the first Christmas since the death of her husband. He had no illusions about Mark, but it was Fran's refusal to come here that he could not understand.

Lunch was served at four and eighteen people, including Orchid and Harold, were spread around three tables of varying heights. The children were at one end of the long board, and the adults at the other. Alan was placed between Mary Hanley and Tina Crowder, with Lisa opposite, beside her father. The meal progressed with a lot of merriment and so much noise that nobody heard the sharp rap at the front door. When Orchid Livingstone took some dirty dishes into the kitchen a short while later, she almost dropped the laden tray.

Lisa, who was facing the door, halted in mid-sentence, her face pale. Alan was discussing the legal aspects of poaching with Richard's younger brother, and when he saw her expression he hesitated, then lost his own train of thought. One by one they fell silent, even the children.

'I'm sorry,' said Mark. 'But the entire village was falling over itself to tell me that Mother was here.' He was standing in the doorway, his head almost touching the lintel. A damp overcoat was flung over his shoulders and drops of rain clung to his sun bleached hair.

Lisa's breath caught in her throat. He looked magnificent. He had a rich golden tan, and his eyes were unbelievably blue. She glanced towards Alan, who had swivelled round in his chair. He was so steady and reliable, yet, given the choice between them, would it be him that she really wanted? It was a terrifying thought. And then Marian, bless her heart, called out Mark's name and ran to him, shrieking with delight when he swept her into the air, kissing her cheeks before lowering her to the floor.

By then, Lisa was also on her feet. 'Mark,' she said. 'You came home.'

His eyes rested on her face, and as she walked towards him, it was only Mary Hanley who sensed a moment of helplessness before he put an arm about Lisa's shoulders and hugged her gently to him.

'Where else would I go?' he asked.

Lisa said nothing, and watching them, Mary realised just how much a part of each other they still were. Mark knew it too, but dissembled well. Mary turned to Alan Weston and, seeing his pained expression, pushed back her chair and stood up.

'You always did have a habit of walking in halfway through meals, Mark,' she said. 'Have you popped in to pay your respects, or are you staying?'

Miraculously, the tension broke, and as Lisa moved away from the shelter of Mark's arm, Richard Crowder stood up. 'You're welcome to join us,' he said.

'Thank you,' said Mark, and gave a rare, brilliant smile.

This was the first time since he had known Lisa that Alan had seen her and Mark together, and he tried to show neither hurt nor surprise as he watched them. Mary felt sorry for the lawyer; Mark invariably stole the limelight, whether knowingly or not.

'Remember they are old friends who have not seen each other for a long time,' she said to him softly. 'Don't begrudge them a little pleasure, Alan. They both have difficulties enough to contend with, and a little laughter can do no harm. I haven't seen Mark so relaxed in ages, and Lisa is the sparkling child I remember. She made one tragic error in her life, and to have to pay for that mistake to the end of her days would be unfair.'

'You know how I feel about Lisa,' Alan said. He did not add that in Lisa there was something he knew he had never captured, nor ever would.

'You can rest assured that Mark will wake up tomorrow morning as his normal, sarcastic self,' said Mary. 'I suggest you make an effort to attract Lisa's attention; brooding will only force everything out of proportion. Half the neighbourhood will call in later, and they're sure to make a party around the piano. I know it sounds provincial, but they do the same thing every year. And . . . oh dear, they're back on the subject of horses!'

But it was a subject which brought Lisa and Mark back into the general conversation. 'What a shame you can't hunt tomorrow,' she said. 'It would be like old times.'

'I'd probably fall off.'

Richard Crowder looked up. 'Have you ridden lately?' he asked.

'A few months ago in America,' said Mark warily.

'Then could you manage a day's hunting?'

'Perhaps. If I had a horse, and the clothing.'

'You could ride Kingston. I've already had him out a few times this season.'

Mary Hanley heard the challenge in the farmer's voice. He wasn't blind either, and this was his way of bringing Mark down a peg or two.

'What about Lisa?' said Mark. 'Or would you expect her to join the foot followers?'

'Lesley Barlow has gone to her gran's in Durham for Christmas,' Richard Crowder said. 'I'm sure if I telephone she'll not mind Lisa taking out Gremlin.'

'I know where your riding clothes are,' his mother said, knowing it had gone too far now for him to back out.

Mark's expression was unreadable. 'If you can get hold of another horse for Lisa the matter seems to have been settled,' he said. 'Is it being held in Oldenshaw?'

'Yes,' said Lisa. 'But it's all very secret. Daddy says they've been having a lot of trouble from this new Anti-Blood Sports Society.'

'Damn nuisances,' Richard Crowder swore. 'We've had to spread the rumour that the Meet will be held at Lord Latchcham's estate at ten. While they're watching there, we'll be at Oldenshaw by nine and well into the field by ten.'

Events began to move almost too quickly after that. As the first of Mary Hanley's promised visitors arrived, Richard Crowder was bellowing down the telephone to a bad line in Durham.

'It's all right,' he said, putting the receiver down. 'You can taken Gremlin. And I've phoned the farm. They'll feed him in the morning, but you'll have to get him ready. Mark can see to Kingston.'

Lisa caught Alan's eye and beckoned him over. 'You can run me to the Barlow farm,' she said. 'It's on the other side of Oldenshaw.'

'I hope you realise that she's trying to involve you in her hopelessly horsey world,' said Mark. 'You'll be hauled out of bed at some unearthly hour in the morning, and worked to death without even a warm drink to sustain you.'

'I'll survive,' said Alan staunchly.

'I'm glad one of us will.'

The doorbell was ringing again, and Tina Crowder purposefully broke into the circle.

'Stop hogging the best men, Lisa,' she said. 'Mark's already in demand, and I think Alan deserves better than horses.'

Lisa smiled at her aunt. 'You can have Alan,' she said. 'I want to check Kingston's rugs, and Mark might as well come with me.'

Mark let the horse nibble his fingers while Lisa checked the surcingle which held the blankets in place.

'Do you want to tell me something?' he said.

Lisa's face was colourless. 'Alan has asked me to marry him. He also wants to adopt Marian. I've accepted his offer, and wanted to tell you before anyone else did.'

'I think you have made a wise decision,' he said. 'Congratulations, Lisa.'

He kissed her cheek, and was about to turn away when her voice stopped him.

'Will you still be my friend, Mark?'

'For always,' he said, and held out his hand.

'Thank you,' she said, slipping her hand into his.

He took it, and saying nothing more, they went back to the house.

Mary Hanley insisted Mark stay with her at the cottage. They stopped at the Manor to collect his riding clothes, which smelt of mothballs, but were unable to find a hard hat. Mark could barely keep his eyes open, and finally persuaded his mother to leave by promising that he would borrow Richard Crowder's bowler, whether or not it fitted.

She left him in the drawing room with a mug of coffee while she made up a bed, and when she came downstairs ten minutes later he was asleep. She felt ashamed to wake him, and she was still hovering uncertainly when his eyes flew open, momentarily bewildered.

'I'm sorry,' he said. 'What time is it?'

'Almost three. How much sleep have you had during the past twenty-four hours?'

'None. Nor for the twenty-four preceding them. Does it show that much?'

'It will by tomorrow. I don't know why you gave in to Richard. You know perfectly well he only did it because you were monopolising Lisa. And talking of Lisa, what happened in the stables? She was very quiet after you came back.'

His eyes became strangely blank. 'She told me she was going to marry Alan.'

'There's something else,' she said. 'I know you too well. Lisa still means a lot to you, doesn't she?'

She had the dubious satisfaction of seeing his cheeks flush, and knew that had he not been so tired, she would have been unable to batter into him like this. His defences were beginning to totter, and she had no intention of giving him the opportunity of rebuilding them.

When he did speak his voice was flat. 'I came back because I didn't want you to be alone. Unfortunately, my own plane will not be delivered until next month, and flights at this time of year are impossible. I managed to get on a plane, but it developed engine trouble over the Atlantic and had to go back to New York, where we eventually transferred to another. I should have arrived sometime during this morning, and thereby avoided walking in halfway through lunch. Does that satisfy your curiosity?'

She could see he was annoyed, but she gritted her teeth and pressed on. 'You've told me why you're here, but not about you and Lisa. If you're going to be evasive I shall ask you a direct question. I think you still love the girl. If I'm right, why are you letting Alan marry her?'

He sat very still, but she did not press him further, and after a short while he said, 'Alan is a bloody good lawyer and the only person I trust to run the business in my absence. He is certainly too valuable to be sent traipsing about London hunting for flats. So why do you think I put him in charge of Lisa in the first place? She needs someone to look after her, and Alan is the best man I know. She will have a good life with him. It won't work for her and me any more, Mother. We've grown too far apart, and in the long run we'd only succeed in making each other miserable.'

'You must have had something very special to keep the flame alive for so long.'

She saw a glimmer of light pass through his eyes. 'We did,' he said. 'Maybe you had it with Father, I don't know. Fran and Eric never did. They never will.' He stood up. 'Goodnight, Mother. Happy Christmas.'

She watched with troubled eyes as he walked up the stairs, and when he had gone she sat in the chair he had vacated. It was four fifteen before she stirred and went up to her own bed.

* * *

Alan had seen nothing like it.

'Wait until you see them in full cry,' said a voice behind him. Mark was standing beside Kingston, holding Richard Crowder's bowler and a hunting whip which he had not wanted but the farmer insisted he take. The breeches and knee boots suited him, and he looked unusually relaxed, with a hint of happiness in his eyes. 'Where's Lisa?' he asked as they were joined by his mother and the Crowder family.

'Over there,' said Alan, pointing.

Toby Goodson started to call the hounds to him, and Lisa glanced round. By the time she reached them Mark had mounted, the bowler making him unrecognisable.

'At least we've shaken off that awful Society,' she said.

'You shouldn't say things like that,' said her father. 'It'll bring bad luck.'

'Charles Latchcham was telling me he had to sneak his horses out at four this morning,' Mark said. 'Do I really have to carry this thing?'

Richard Crowder looked at the hunting whip. 'It looks smart,' he said.

'I know, but one tap on the rump and he'd be in the next county.'

It was then that the cry went up.

'They've bloody well found us!' someone shouted.

Everyone fell silent as six cars containing at least twenty-five men and women drew up.

'Damn!' Richard cursed.

'Let's move hounds out before they can get started!' said Charles Latchcham. People were already spilling from the cars, many of them carrying banners.

Mark looked about him, feeling the uncertainty and something very akin to fear. That so many should be intimidated by so few puzzled him. He knew, of course, that these Societies often went to extremes and it had not been unknown for hounds or horses, or occasionally riders, to get hurt. The village constable was still inside the pub, but with a crowd this size, all he could do was issue a warning. Even Lisa was pale, gripping the reins too tightly, so that Gremlin was snatching at the bit, his front hooves alternately pawing the ground.

'Can't something be done?' somebody was asking.

'After all,' said another voice, 'we don't go and muck up their bloody football and darts.'

Mark suddenly saw who was leading the protesters and knew then that something could be done. He was certainly not afraid of them. He couldn't remember ever being afraid of anything in his entire life, even those vast auditoriums filled with screaming, hysterical girls.

Alan heard a movement beside him, and when he looked round he saw Kingston was walking forward. Mark did not go far before stopping the horse. He was staring straight ahead, and following his gaze Alan saw Arthur Bennett, with a pretty blonde woman in over-tight trousers beside him. Without hesitation, Mark went forward to meet them.

Lisa sensed something was wrong and slid to the ground. She reached for Alan's arm, and he laid a hand over hers.

'Mark . . . ' he said, but the rider did not seem to hear.

Arthur Bennett's plan had worked. They had missed Lord Latch-cham's box departing at the unearthly hour of four-fifteen, but another box had been sighted heading for Oldenshaw. And they had only just arrived in time, for the riders were obviously about to move off. Arthur smiled as he fingered the small object he was holding. Today there would be no hunt. This would guarantee it.

Sally was sulking. She clutched a rolled banner in her cold hands and wished she had the courage to bash Arthur over the head with it and go back home. If these people enjoyed chasing after a pack of dogs, it was all right by her. And now, instead of making a dis-organised retreat like they normally did, some fool on a brown horse was coming towards them. Sally Bennett was terrified of horses.

'Perfect,' Arthur said. 'Let's show them we mean business, shall we, darling?'

Sally laid a restraining hand on his arm. 'You shouldn't, Arthur,' she said, a little afraid. 'It's dangerous.'

He shook her off. 'Don't be bloody ridiculous. It'll do the bastard good to fall off on his well padded arse.'

Mark Hanley could not see what his mill manager was holding; not until it was too late, and all he could do was try and stay on. The world exploded about him as Arthur threw the firecracker at Kingston. The terrifying noise was more than the horse could stand and, panic-stricken, he leapt high into the air. He crashed into a parked car, leaving a large dent and smashed wing mirror; he twisted and turned and skidded on the tarmac, but was unable to escape the strong hands which held him.

Sally clung to Arthur's arm, knowing that this time he had gone too far. A lot of riders were struggling to control their nervous horses, and a child fell off her pony onto a grassy verge and burst into tears. Even Gremlin was tossing his head, and Richard Crowder wisely took the reins from Lisa's shaking hand. Mary Hanley was trembling as she prayed that Mark would fall off before the horse fell on him, or took it into his head to bolt.

The firecracker burnt itself out as the rider's hat came off and, ashen, Arthur Bennett watched his employer struggle with the maddened horse. 'Jesus Christ!' he swore. 'What have I done?'

Now that the explosions had stopped, Mark put all his remaining strength into bringing Kingston under control. The horse had almost fallen a few times already, saved only by his rider's expertise. But Mark was exhausted and knew that very soon his own aching muscles would give way. Kingston was also wearying; his sides were heaving and he was breathing raggedly through dilated nostrils. He suddenly became aware of his rider, and of the gentle voice which talked unceasingly. He spun round once more, and then stood still, legs straddled and sweat pouring from him. A gentle hand patted his soaking neck and the voice continued to soothe. But although his voice was gentle, Mark's eyes were icy as they rested on Arthur Bennett.

Alan felt Lisa's grip loosen and saw Mary Hanley wipe a tear from her cheek. From behind them came a muffled cheer.

Mark allowed the horse to catch its breath. He did not dismount, and nobody moved because nobody was quite sure what to do. And then Mark gathered up the loose reins and Alan felt a chill pass through him. The happiness he had seen in Mark's eyes was gone, replaced by a hard, unreadable expression. Kingston had no more resistance in him and walked quietly to where Arthur stood. Sally saw what Alan could not, and letting go of her husband's arm, took an involuntary step back. The rage reflected in Mark Hanley's blue eyes terrified her. Arthur stood his ground, unable to bring an apology to his lips.

What happened then was so sudden and unexpected that a spontaneous sigh echoed from those watching. Mark halted the horse in front of the man. He did not speak, but raised the hunting whip which he had somehow managed not to drop, and then brought it down across Arthur's cheek. The skin burst open and blood poured down his chin onto his clothes. Sally screamed, and Mark glanced towards her.

'Take your people home, Arthur,' he said softly. He did not regret what he had done, for Arthur had been a bloody fool. If that firework had been thrown into the bunched riders, God only knew what tragedy would have occurred. There were a lot of children here, and they could have fallen beneath plunging hooves or been bolted into oncoming traffic by terrified ponies. Considering the carnage he might have caused, Arthur had got off lightly.

Mark turned Kingston towards the people whose cause he had gone to defend. His entire body felt as though it had been beaten with sticks, and tomorrow his strained muscles would be agony. Perspiration was pouring down his face and as he impatiently wiped his hand across his eyes he saw that somebody was walking towards him.

It was Lisa. He smiled, and some colour flushed into her cheeks as their eyes met. In that fleeting moment he realised just how right his mother had been. He should never have let her go. But then he saw Alan watching them and knew it was too late. She belonged to him now.

Sally took a handkerchief out of her handbag and handed it to him to hold over the gash.

'You'll need stitches,' was all she could say.

He turned away.

'You should press charges, Arthur,' one of the men said.

'Aye,' another echoed. 'That was a brutal attack. Who the hell does he think he is? God Almighty?'

Arthur stopped at the car, one hand resting on the open door. 'Like the man said, let's go home.'

Toby Goodson pushed his chestnut gelding through the congratulating crowd. 'They're going,' he said to the weary young man. 'That was something we've all been wanting to do for a long time. I just hope there'll be no repercussions.'

'No,' Mark said. 'Not to the Hunt.'

'What about you?' Alan asked.

Marked looked at the lawyer. He was holding Gremlin's reins as though they were a length of rope.

'Nor to me either,' he tonelessly replied. 'Arthur knows he was in the wrong.'

Mary Hanley was watching Lisa, who stood at Kingston's head, her face deliberately averted. She knew that the girl was concealing not concern for her horse, but her tremulous reaction to what she had seen in Mark's eyes in that moment when his gaze, together with his smile, had fallen on her.

'I'll walk him for a while,' she said. 'He's not hurt, and he'll be fine once he's cooled off.'

'You'll miss the hunt,' Mark said.

'The least we can do is wait,' said Charles Latchcham. 'They've gone now, and Ted won't mind keeping the bar open for a bit longer.'

Toby Goodson grinned, but before he could say anything a hound yelped. 'Get those bloody horses away from my hounds!' he yelled, and turning his gelding, managed to break up the crowd.

Mark slid to the ground. His knees felt weak and he held onto the saddle for a moment. His mother placed a hand beneath his elbow. 'You're a bloody fool,' she said. 'You could have been killed.'

'You should have jumped off,' said Richard Crowder. 'Nobody would have called you faint-hearted for doing so.'

Mark looked at him. 'I wouldn't give a damn if they did. But at the time Kingston seemed the safest place to be.' He patted the horse before Lisa led him away. 'Poor boy, that wasn't very funny.'

'Come and have a tot of whisky,' said Richard Crowder. 'It'll steady you.'

George Crowder brought over the forgotten bowler. It had a large dent on one side.

'I'll buy you another,' Mark said.

Richard Crowder studied it. 'There's no need. It always looked too new anyhow. You ought to ride more often, lad.'

The blue eyes stared at him. 'Yes,' he said. 'I could do with a bit more practice.'

They caught no foxes but there were some good runs, and having recovered his second wind Kingston was able to stay out the whole day. Lisa and Mark hacked slowly home in the dark. At first they were part of a large group, but as they neared Oldenshaw only the two of them were left.

A car came round the corner behind them, its headlights illuminating the two horses and their tired riders. The driver dipped to half beam and slowed down.

'We ought to have reflectors,' Lisa said. 'I hope it isn't the police.'

'They would only lecture us,' said Mark.

He had been silent for the past half hour and now she could see why. He looked exhausted, with his shoulders hunched against the wind. She should have made him leave earlier. She had suggested it, but he had insisted on staying, for her sake, she knew.

The car drew level and someone shouted something about a good chase. Lisa could not see the driver, but his friendly greeting left a warm glow inside.

'Are you stiff?' Lisa asked.

'Stiff? I think rigor mortis has set in.'

'Then let's walk for a while. My feet are numb.'

'My dear girl, I'm numb all over.' They walked side by side on the narrow verge, the horse and pony plodding behind. 'I just trod in a puddle,' Mark said. 'Let's walk on the tarmac.'

They did not speak again for a long time, and then it was Lisa who broke the silence. 'Is Arthur Bennett frightened of you?' she asked.

'No,' he said. 'But he needs me to get where he intends going. I normally manage to keep my temper under better control, but he did a damn fool thing.'

'You don't trust him, do you?'

'I trust him to run the mill for as long as it suits him. But Arthur Bennett has dreams of greater things. He might even get where he wants through sheer, bloody-minded determination.'

'And trample you on the way up?' Lisa suggested.

'He'll try,' he said.

The girl looked at him. 'Be careful, Mark. I don't think he's a man to be lightly trifled with.'

'But my dear, I have already trifled. I have Arthur Bennett on a hook and shall play him until he begins to bore me. Then I shall throw him back into the polluted pond where he belongs.'

'Just be careful he doesn't push you in first,' she retorted. 'Even you aren't invincible.'

'I know,' he said.

They came to crossroads where they stopped. The village lay straight ahead, and to the left was the road which led to the Barlow farm. Gremlin pawed at the grass verge, and Kingston sidled across the middle of the road. They remounted.

'Shall I send Alan?' he asked.

'He's probably waiting.'

He waved, and Gremlin whinnied as Kingston trotted away. Lisa watched him go, and then she turned the pony towards home.

Chapter Seven

June was in Paris gathering information on the spring collections, leaving Lisa to cope as best she could. Theirs was a monthly magazine, and June would be back to compile the pages of fashion planned for a bumper post-collection issue, but Lisa still had to sift through the sketches and written material which were being delivered daily. So when Alan walked into her office on a particularly busy Wednesday afternoon, she was not very pleased to see him.

'You'll have to take the rest of the day off,' he said. 'We've got to see a house, and can't go after dark because the electricity is disconnected.'

'I can't leave now,' she said. 'Not with June away and this mess to sort out.'

'If June were here she'd be pushing you out of the door.'

'But she's not.'

'For heaven's sake, Lisa!' he exclaimed.

She frowned at him. 'All right, I'll come,' she said with bad grace. 'Where is it?'

'Ham,' he said. 'So Mark tells me.'

'Ham,' she repeated. 'It's obviously not the edible variety. And what has Mark got to do with it?'

'It's his wedding present, darling. If we want it, of course. He says it's a bit dilapidated, but seems pretty sure that you'll like it.'

She frowned. 'I know Mark is a bit eccentric at times, but a dilapidated house . . . are you sure?'

'I've never seen it,' he said. 'He bought it years ago, but he's never lived there, nor even bothered to rent it out. Dilapidated was his description, but I doubt if it's that bad.'

She picked up her handbag. 'Where's Ham?'

'By Richmond Park. Haven't you ever been there?'

'No.'

'Then I'll drive through it. I think you'll like it.'

She didn't like it, she loved it. Sheep and deer roamed free and she spotted two riders cantering their horses off the dirt track.

'It's beautiful,' she said. 'And so peaceful.'

'You should see it in summer,' said Alan. 'Ice-cream stands everywhere, and thousands of people.'

The property was easy to find. It was at the end of a quiet cul-de-sac, surrounded by a red brick wall with wrought-iron gates at the entrance. The house was not dilapidated, but shabby and uncared for, as was the garden.

'Why, it's beautiful!' Lisa said. He stopped the car and she leapt out, running through the calf-deep grass to an empty pond. 'Can you imagine it in summer? The trees would shade the house, and we could have tea on the lawn. Oh Alan, you wouldn't even know you were still in London.'

Alan was more practical. He stared critically at the house. It was in need of a fresh coat of paint and the guttering looked dicey. His eye followed the line of the wall, and he calculated that there must be at least three acres of ground. He knew it had cost a lot when Mark bought it, but now it must be worth a fortune.

'Let's look inside,' he called to Lisa.

'We could fill this pond with goldfish,' she said, springing to her feet.

Alan opened the door and they stepped into a spacious hall. Lisa did not stay at his side for long, she was too impatient. He could hear her moving about upstairs, and he was exploring the kitchen when she came bursting in.

'What's wrong?' he asked as she struggled to open the back door.

'There are stables! I saw them from upstairs! Why didn't you tell me?'

'Because I didn't know,' he said.

The back garden was fenced off by wooden poles, and there was a stable block with three loose boxes and a feed room. Lisa was pulling open the doors and peering in. As he watched her, he realised that it was this ability to switch from mature woman to innocent child which had attracted him to her in the first place.

'Aren't they marvellous?' she said. 'There's electricity, and everything is built in.'

'I take it that the stables are the deciding factor,' he said. 'Do you like it?'

'I love it. But even for Mark, don't you think it's a bit over generous?'

'He doesn't want it. I don't know why he kept it for so long.'

She came out of the stables, her face radiant. 'I feel as though it's asking us to come and live here. When did Mark buy it?'

'In 1955 when I first met him. I did the conveyancing, which is why I remember. He'd just offered me a job, and was rushing back to Yorkshire for his sister's wedding. Strange he never wanted to live here.'

She looked quickly away so that he could not see her face. Mark had bought this house for her, which was why he knew she would love it.

'Come on,' he said. 'Let's go back inside and decide what's going to be what.'

She shivered, and thinking she was cold, he put his arm around her shoulders.

Chapter Eight

I was in the passage when I heard her voice coming from one of the offices.

'Excuse me,' she was saying, 'but I'm lost. Can you tell me where Mr. Weston's office is?'

She was given directions and came out, turning away without seeing me standing there.

'Alan is out,' I said.

She swung round. 'Mark! What on earth are you doing here?'

'Working.'

She laughed. 'I'm sorry, but I never expected to see you skulking about the hallways. I thought you would be in a gigantic suite of offices surrounded by glamorous secretaries.'

'I don't have glamorous secretaries,' I said. 'I have Norma. She turned fifty last month, and can still run circles around every young girl employed here. Nor do I have a suite of offices, that would be far too flamboyant. What are you doing here?'

'So far I've only managed to get horribly lost. And I haven't seen even one recognisable face. Where are all your pop stars?'

'In the other building,' I said. 'This side mainly consists of offices.'

'Goodness, the place must be enormous. Did it really start with a rat-infested warehouse, or was Alan having me on?'

'It was rat heaven,' I told her. 'But they've all gone now—witness the army of cats we have to feed.'

The door behind Lisa opened, and a young girl came out. She glanced our way, and was about to say something when she suddenly recognised me. Her cheeks flushed scarlet, and she hurried away.

'I'm glad I wasn't asking the way to your office,' Lisa said. 'They would have dropped dead from the shock.'

'You would have found yourself the centre of a tantalising rumour,' I told her. 'Alan certainly would not approve.'

'Is he really out?' she asked. 'I had to deliver some proofs to the printers, and as I have the company car and June is in one of her better moods, I thought I might scrounge some lunch off him.'

'I don't expect him back,' I said.

'Oh well, no Alan, no lunch. I suppose I'd better get back.'

I took hold of her arm. 'How about scrounging lunch from me instead? I'd like your advice about a couple of things.'

Her eyes widened. 'What I know about anything could probably fit onto a postage stamp. Are you trying to flatter me?'

'Of course not,' I said. 'But I really would like you to come.'

She thought for a moment. 'All right. Where are we going?'

'That depends on you. Do you want eight courses or two?'

'I was thinking more in terms of a snack,' she said dryly. 'Don't you have a canteen here, or is that beneath you?'

'I don't mind it, but the last time I walked in there you could literally have heard a pin drop. I think I managed to ruin everyone's lunch. There's a rather quaint pub we could go to, a short way down the river. You'd love the colourful clientele. But we'll have to leave now, otherwise we won't get a seat.'

'Can we use my car?' she asked. 'I'm not sure if I'm up to your limousine and chauffeur.'

'Don't be so provincial,' I said. 'We can walk along the tow-path.'

We found a small table in a corner close to the log fire.

'I've never seen quite so many weird-looking people at once,' said Lisa as I struggled back a second time, laden with platefuls of food. 'Where on earth do they all come from?'

I squeezed onto the narrow bench beside her. 'Some are local, some work for me, and that group over there come from the television studios in Shepherds Bush.'

'Alan never brings me to places like this.'

'That's because he regards them as dens of vice. Actually, the majority of these people are pretty harmless. Here, try the ham and egg pie. It's the best in London.'

We sampled everything, drank very little, and talked non-stop. And we laughed. I couldn't laugh with anybody as I could laugh with Lisa. We stayed until closing time, and then walked back along the deserted tow-path.

'What were you going to ask me?' said Lisa.

'It's about the mill,' I told her. 'I want to expand and go in for synthetics as well as the standard cloth we've always produced. I also want to put a designer in there to create our own line of fashion. I thought you could help me find the right person.'

She looked up at me, her eyes serious. 'That's a bit beyond my capabilities. But whatever you do, you're going to have problems. You'll need someone very modern, or else an old-established designer—who wouldn't be interested in that sort of thing anyway, not unless he was no good. Personally, I think your best bet would be to find a young original to work from London. You could still tie in with the mill. Do you realise how this could escalate if you get somebody good?'

'Yes,' I said. 'That's what I'm counting on. Do you know where I can find someone?'

She shook her head. 'The art schools must be overflowing with people,' she said. 'I could always ask June.'

'I can ask her myself if necessary,' I said. 'That's the other thing I wanted to talk to you about.'

'The magazine or June?' she asked, looking puzzled.

'Both.'

She stood still. 'Why?'

'Because if I'm going to expand in one field, I need to expand in others too. Your magazine was one of the first in the field, and at the time it was the best. But now there are others coming up, many of which are superior, and the company that owns it is thinking of selling it while it can still command a good price. Now, if June Halliday is part of the package, then I shall consider buying. Do you think she would stay if I took the magazine over?'

'How should I know? She's temperamental at the best of times. I think you two together would be a disaster. But what about me?' she demanded. 'I bloody well work there too. Does that mean I'm about to become your employee?'

'If and when I do buy the magazine, you'll be married to Alan,' I said gently. 'And you're planning to stop work then anyway. I'm not trying to take you over, Lisa. That's one of the reasons why I'm telling you about this now, so that later on you don't think I was going behind your back.'

'Does Alan know?'

'Of course. I asked him not to tell you yet. This is business. Personal feelings don't enter into it.'

'They never do as far as you're concerned,' she retorted. 'Why does it have to be this magazine? As you say, there are plenty of others, and money is obviously no object.'

'The others don't have June Halliday,' I said. 'She happens to be exceptional at what she does, and I want her, and the magazine she's identified with.'

'June has been good to me,' Lisa said flatly, her anger dying as quickly as it had flared. 'She gave me a job when nobody else would look at me. I don't want to see her swallowed up into your empire.'

'You should ask Alan to tell you a bit more about my empire, as you call it,' I told her. 'Strange though it may seem, I do value good people.'

'I know,' she said. 'I'm sorry I was annoyed, but it was all so sudden. You're right, of course. Sales have been falling off, and everybody on the mag is worried about the future.'

'You see,' I said, 'deep down I'm a good Samaritan!'

'Sometimes,' she said, 'just sometimes, I wish you could be wrong. You're always so damn sure of yourself.'

'I can't afford not to be,' I told her. 'One sign of weakness and the wolves would be in for the kill.'

She smiled. 'It's no good trying to make me feel sorry for you. I presume I am not to mention this conversation to anyone?'

'Except for Alan,' I said.

I took her arm again, and we walked on in silence. We were almost at my buildings when she suddenly said, 'Martin Henderson.'

'Who is he?' I asked.

'A radical young designer who came to the office last year, soon after I started working for June. She thought his designs were awful and had me chase him away. But I liked them. They were different, Mark. I think they would need toning down, but they were certainly original.'

'I don't suppose you know how I can contact him?' I asked.

'I've got his address on the back of a sketch he gave me,' she said. 'It's stuck on the wall behind my desk. I'll let you have it when I get back.'

'You can telephone,' I said. 'We might as well go and see him now. If he's unemployed and at home, he'll be obliged to invite you in.'

'We met for all of three minutes,' she protested. 'I don't think for a moment that he'll know who I am. And June will kill me if she finds out. I've been gone for most of the day as it is.'

'I'm sure she'll forgive you,' I soothed. 'I'll ask Tim to run back the car, and we'll take a taxi.' She glared at me with pursed lips and I laughed. 'Come on. I expect the last thing you feel like doing is going back to the office.'

'Must you always have your own way?' she asked in exasperation.

'No,' I said mildly. 'But I prefer it. Let's find a phone.'

Martin Henderson lived in a dingy neighbourhood with unkempt houses and badly swept streets.

'It's creepy here,' Lisa said. 'Don't you think you should have kept the taxi? How are we going to get back?'

I held her hand tight. 'There's always public transport. But don't worry. It may be poor here, but it's respectable; these are just cheap digs. Tim will probably cause a sensation when he turns up with the Rolls.'

'You told him to come here?' she asked.

'Of course.'

Her fingers dug into the palm of my hand, and then she silently followed me up some steps to an unlocked front door. We walked into a dark hallway which had brown walls and a floor of ripped linoleum. There was a smell of dampness and boiling cabbage, and I heard a baby wailing.

'I thought this sort of place only existed in Dickens,' Lisa whispered.

I squeezed her hand. 'There are many who live much worse,' I said. 'Perhaps it's as well I made you come.'

Martin Henderson lived on the top floor, which meant climbing eight flights of stairs. I knocked at his door, waited, and knocked again.

'I refuse to come back if he's out,' said Lisa, her breath ragged. 'He's probably working. It's months since I saw him.'

Another door suddenly swung open and a young man with spots came out. 'Martin's not in,' he said.

'Do you know when he'll be back?' I asked.

The youth shrugged. 'What do you want him for?'

'That's my business,' I said, returning his stare.

He blushed. 'He won't be long. If you're not in a hurry you'd better wait,' he said, and shut the door.

We sat down gingerly on the dirty stairs.

'He wasn't very friendly,' Lisa whispered. 'And why was he staring at you like that?'

'He probably thinks I'm competition,' I said.

'Competition for what?'

I was still holding her hand, and let it go. 'I think your Martin Henderson must be a pretty boy.'

She frowned. 'You mean he's homosexual?'

'Perhaps. I think that one was.'

She laughed. It was a happy sound which reminded me of other times we had spent together. I was not so sure whether I had been wise in bringing her here today.

'I suppose you would be a good catch,' she said.

'Happily, I prefer my girlfriends to be female. Are you cold? There's a hellish draught coming from somewhere.'

'I'm used to the northern wastes. You should be as well. I think we've become too dependent on our material comforts.' She glanced up at the filthy walls. 'Why are you sitting here, Mark? It's out of character.'

'Memories,' I said.

'Memories? In a place like this?'

I smiled into the past. 'I had been in London for a year before Mark Anthony came into being. I arrived with two pounds, seven and sixpence, and after spending my first night in a remarkably crummy hotel, rented a room in a house which looked very like this one.'

'I never realised,' she murmured.

'Nor did anyone. I know you disapprove of my wealth, but brief though the experience was, I've also seen the other side of the coin. There's nothing romantic about being poor and wondering where your next meal is coming from.'

'I don't disapprove,' she said, the gaiety gone from her voice. 'I'm wise enough to know my limitations. You're right, it is cold here. Can I snuggle up against you?'

She laid her head on my shoulder and I held her close. Tim came, but Lisa preferred the stairs to waiting in the car. An hour dragged past.

She sat up suddenly. 'Somebody's coming. Let's hope it's him.'

It was. He wore an ankle-length coat of indeterminate age and ancestry, which made him look very frail. He had sandy hair which flopped across his forehead, and an intelligent face with high cheekbones and a prettiness which was almost feminine. His grey eyes lit up when he saw Lisa.

'The lady who disapproves of dirty old men staring at her legs,' he said.

'I didn't think you'd remember me.'

'How could I forget? You're the only person who has ever given me constructive criticism. Everybody else just throws me out.'

His eyes rested on me.

'This is Mark Hanley,' said Lisa. 'I'm sure you've heard of him. He wants to see some of your designs.'

I held out my hand. His was cool and soft and feminine. Everything about him was feminine, even his voice, which was half a pitch higher than it should have been.

'Come in,' he said. 'You'll have to excuse the mess, I wasn't expecting visitors.'

The room was small and impeccably tidy, and the walls were literally papered with his designs.

'I have lots more in portfolios,' said Martin Henderson. 'Would you like some tea?'

'Yes please,' Lisa said. 'That hall is like an ice-box. I've never seen so many sketches. Where on earth do you get the ideas?'

'They sort of come,' he admitted.

I moved closer and studied the nearest wall. The sketches were of leggy, shapeless females in flowing poses. In fact, everything flowed, the long limbs, the long hair, and the extremely short skirts. Lisa was right about him being an original. If I decided to take this young man on, I would be labelled as either foolish or far-sighted. I preferred to think of myself in the latter category.

'Are you *the* Mark Hanley?' he asked, his voice expressionless.

I turned round. I saw he had been knocked down too many times for his hopes to build up again now.

'You make me sound like an ancient relic which has been dug up, scrubbed and then put on display. Yes, I suppose I am.'

Lisa sat on the bed; there was only one chair, and that looked neither safe nor comfortable. Martin Henderson flushed.

'I'm sorry,' he said. 'I remember your records. And the Hanley name has a good reputation. When I tried out a couple of my designs, I used one of your heavy wool weaves. You must know it. A rich autumn brown which hangs to perfection.'

'Another fan,' said Lisa flippantly.

'Another fan,' I agreed. 'But not a very intelligent one if he has been investing in that particular weave. It only gets distributed to a handful of shops, Harrods being one of them. At the price per yard, it should fall well.' I turned back to the wall, pointing at an outfit which had caught my eye. 'This would suit you,' I said to Lisa. 'Would you wear it?'

A lazy smile curled her lips. 'When I'm married to Alan I shall have to play the correct records, choose the correct materials, and wear the correct clothes. Alan would have sense enough to put up with it, but Daddy would have a seizure if I went home looking like that.' She turned to Martin Henderson. 'I think you ought to brace yourself. He likes them.'

The young man was speechless.

'Ignore her,' I said. 'Come and sit down. Lisa will make the tea.'

Chapter Nine

Mark Hanley had visions of a fashion house which would rival the best of the Paris couturiers, whereas all Martin wanted was the opportunity to open his own boutique. He knew his designs were good, but hadn't the confidence to try and enter the big league.

It didn't take Mark long to see how intimidated the boy was. Instead of giving him the razzmatazz of a big launch, he decided first to send him north to become acquainted with the mill and the initial stages of the textile industry. Martin had covered fabric design at college, and the idea of experimenting with cloth appealed to him.

He shared a railway compartment with two other people, one an elderly businessman who was reading financial magazines, the other a woman who knitted throughout the journey. Martin sat beside the window, his threadbare coat folded over his knees. In his breast pocket was an envelope which Alan Weston had handed him at the station. It contained more money than he could possibly use, and he was terrified of losing it. He was an honest person, and had already decided to list his expenses, so that he could hand back whatever he didn't need.

The train arrived at Manchester, and Martin reached for his battered suitcase, then flung the coat over his shoulders, ignoring the frowning businessman.

'Take a taxi to Steelton,' Alan Weston had said. 'There are no trains and heaven only knows what the bus service is like.'

The man and woman were waiting for him to open the door. He did so, nervousness making him clumsy. As it slammed back he leapt onto the platform. He saw a line of taxis beyond the ticket barrier and hurried in case they were all taken by the time he got there. He was handing in his ticket when the chauffeur stepped forward and grasped his suitcase.

'Mr. Hanley asked me to meet you,' said Tim Denholm. 'You're to stay with him at the main house. I've already cancelled your room at the inn. The car's over here.'

Martin had already seen it, parked in front of the taxi rank. He followed Tim, feeling shabby in his old coat and scuffed shoes.

'Can I sit with you in front?' he asked.

Tim smiled. 'I'll be glad of the company. It's a longish drive.'

Martin saw that the elderly businessman had missed the last taxi and was impatiently waiting for another to come in. As Tim put the suitcase in the boot he stared open-mouthed at the scruffy youngster who obviously had friends, influence or money.

'I didn't know Mr. Hanley was here,' Martin said a short while later. 'I don't think anybody knew where he was.'

'There's nothing odd about that,' Tim told him. 'There are times when Mr. Hanley prefers to keep his whereabouts secret. It's the only opportunity he gets for a bit of peace and quiet.'

He communicated no more than that and Martin, not wanting to pry, lapsed into silence. It was not long before he became bored with green fields and grazing cattle.

'Doesn't Lisa Crowder also come from round here?' he asked.

'Her father farms outside Oldenshaw,' Tim said abruptly. 'Have you any idea what Mr. Hanley will have you doing at the mill?'

Mary Hanley found her son in the orchard arguing with Albert, who still treated him as a small boy and had no compunction about yelling back. Albert was purple with fury, and Mark looked very much as though he were trying not to laugh. He smiled when he saw her.

'Hello, Mother,' he said. 'You've come at just the right moment.'

She turned to the old man. 'Good morning, Albert,' she said. 'The gardens are looking marvellous for so early in the year.'

'You should tell him that,' Albert said with ill humour. 'He's got the brazen cheek to say I've no right to be pruning these trees. I was pruning them before he was born and there's never been a year when we haven't had a good crop of apples.'

Mark's lips twitched. 'I never said anything of the sort. I told you to let the younger men prune the taller trees.'

'I've been climbing trees all my life,' he said indignantly.

'For heaven's sake, Mother, say something.'

'What?' she asked.

'For a start, tell him what will happen if he slips. He was swinging about in the old oak like a monkey the other day. Maude almost had a heart attack when she saw him.'

Mary Hanley looked at the gardener. She could understand his frustration; nobody liked to be told they were getting old. 'He's right,

Albert,' she said. 'Would it be fair on Maude if you ended up in hospital?'

If Albert had been expecting an ally he showed no visible disappointment. 'They don't do them proper,' he said.

'They would if you told them what to do,' said Mark.

Albert was beaten. He glared at them both in turn, muttered something beneath his breath, and then stalked away.

'Thank you,' said Mark. 'To Albert I shall always be the young master. Maude asked me to have a word with him because she's worried sick. Are you coming in?'

'Let's walk,' she said. 'I want to talk to you about Oldenshaw, and it's too beautiful a day to be indoors. Where's Mr. Henderson?'

'Cutting out patterns in the summer room.'

'He's a nice boy,' she said. 'I do hope you don't ruin him.'

He took her arm, and they strolled beneath a grove of trees which led to the western side of the property.

'What about Oldenshaw?' he asked.

'Did you know that Jean Brewton of Ivy Cottage is dying? Dr. Ferris says she only has a day or two left. She's ninety-four and has been bedridden for the past two years. When she's gone the cottage will come back to you. What are you going to do with it?'

'I don't know. Why?'

'Somebody has been making enquiries about it through an estate agent. The villagers are worried that town planners will try and move in. I suppose you realise that Oldenshaw must be one of the few unspoilt villages left in the county.'

'Only because us Hanleys have never bothered to do anything with it,' he said. 'Who was making the enquiries?'

'I only know the name of the agent.'

As they came out of the trees she saw that he had a thoughtful, faraway look, which quickly vanished when he became aware of her stare.

'Miles Wender is the official bailiff, although I don't think he does anything more than draw a pittance of a salary. I'll see him about reletting it to some rustic who wants to keep chickens in the bathroom and goats in the kitchen. I don't think I'd like to see development round here either.'

'Thank you, Mark,' she said.

He was smiling when he stopped and pointed across some nearby fields. 'I'm going to build an airstrip over there,' he said. 'If I fence it off, Richard can still graze his cattle here. I went to see him about it this morning.'

'You have a licence?' she asked.

'Why do you think I've stayed here for so long? It certainly wasn't to coddle Martin.'

'You must have found it easy,' she said.

'It was a matter of clocking up a few flying hours,' he said. 'I bought a plane yesterday. Would you like a spin in it?'

'No thank you,' she said with a shudder.

He laughed, and then took her back to the house.

Chapter Ten

It was a year since Paul Hanley had died. During those twelve months a Russian had circled the earth in a spacecraft, and now another Russian, a ballet dancer this time, was stealing the headlines. Today, the social columns were so preoccupied with the doings of Rudolf Nureyev, who had so recently and spectacularly defected at Le Bourget airport, that they quite failed to report that Mark Hanley, Britain's most eligible bachelor, was to be best man at his lawyer's wedding.

A wedding day should be something never to be forgotten, Lisa thought. There was a gentle knock at the door, and Richard Crowder came in, bringing her a cup of tea. He was wearing his second-best suit, and looked ill at ease away from the familiarity of the farm.

'Morning, love,' he said. 'I thought you'd like this. I couldn't sleep, and nobody's about yet.'

She had moved out of the mews flat yesterday. All her belongings were at the house in Ham, and her last night had been spent at the Stewarts'. It had seemed the most suitable place, especially as Fran had offered to care for Marian during the two weeks Lisa and Alan would be away. Mary Hanley was staying with her son in his Belgravia home, and Richard had been squeezed into a small bedroom at the top of the Stewart house.

'Thank you, Daddy,' she said, watching him draw back the curtains. 'It's not a very nice day, is it?'

He stared from the window. 'The clouds are high, so I doubt if it'll rain.'

'Come and sit down,' she said. 'You look as though the end of the world is upon us. I know this isn't quite what you had planned, but I think a big wedding would be rather ridiculous. Anyway, it's better than being stuck with a grouchy old spinster.'

'Nay lass,' he said, sitting beside her, 'you'd never be a grouchy old spinster. You've not got it in you.' He looked down at his hands, which were yearning to be doing something useful. 'Could I ask you a question?'

'Of course. What is it?'

'I know Alan's a good man who'll do well by you and your Marian, but do you really love him? After all, he's a good fifteen years older than you, and he's never been married. You'll find him set in his ways and not easy to change. Have you any doubts, lass? It's not too late, even now.'

She took hold of his hands. 'He'll make me a good husband, Daddy, and Marian a good father. Do I have a right to ask for more?'

'What about love?' he asked. 'I never wanted to remarry after your mother died. She was something special and I knew nobody could ever take her place. Do you feel like that about Alan?'

Her eyes were no longer on his, but staring at the wall behind him. 'I am fond of him,' she said, her voice trembling a little. 'I think, given time, I shall learn to love him as much as he loves me.'

Richard Crowder lifted her chin, forcing her to look at him. 'You never did get him out of your system, did you? And I don't suppose you ever will now. A part of you will always belong to him.'

'Oh Daddy,' she gasped.

And he held her tight, like he always did when she was frightened.

Nobody who attended the brief ceremony at Caxton Hall five hours later would have guessed at the tears earlier that morning. Lisa was relieved to reach the hotel where the reception was being held, for then she was able to calm her nerves with a few too many glasses of champagne.

It was a small reception, attended only by immediate family and close friends, but even so, she was surprised by the number of people she and Alan knew between them. Mary Hanley had shed a tear or two, and her father looked suitably austere in his best suit, which was outdated beside the well cut, expensive clothes of the younger men. Marian was playing with Kevin and Kim, watched over by the Stewart nanny, and Mark was at his bubbling best, infecting the proceedings with a touch of gaiety. But it was not until she and Alan were about to leave that Lisa found him suddenly at her side.

'Lisa, my dear,' he said. 'I'm afraid that you're a little tipsy.'

'And you never get drunk at weddings,' she said.

'No. That came up a long, long time ago.'

She remembered that cold day when they had made love for the last time; and she remembered her father's words this morning. But she dismissed the unsettling thoughts from her mind, and said instead, 'You bought the house for me, didn't you?' He had not expected that, and she saw the surprise in his eyes. She thought for a moment that he would not answer, but he did.

'Yes,' he said. 'That's why I'm glad you have decided to live there now. I could never imagine anyone but you in it. Never let Alan know, Lisa. It would only hurt him.'

'It's our secret,' she promised. 'Aren't you going to kiss the bride, Mark? Everyone else has.'

He kissed her cheek, and then turned abruptly away. She stared after him, not noticing Alan until he grasped her cold hand.

'We must go, darling,' he said.

She didn't see Mark leave, but she instinctively knew that he had gone. She threw her bouquet and Mary Hanley, who was laughing with Martin Henderson, caught the flowers as they bounced off her shoulder.

'Good gracious!' she exclaimed. 'What a terrible aim!'

But she kept them until they died a fortnight later in her cottage at Oldenshaw.

'I bought you a wedding present,' Alan said when they reached the newly painted house.

'Oh Alan, you shouldn't have. What is it?'

'Go and look in the kitchen.'

She stared at him with raised brows. 'You've got me pots and pans,' she said. 'I may not be the world's best cook, but I do know how.'

He laughed. 'Go and see for yourself.'

In the kitchen she only found Clara Gibson, a pleasant woman in her late forties, recently widowed, who she had employed as housekeeper.

She ran out, colliding with Alan in the hall. He caught her by the shoulders, steadying her.

'Really, Lisa,' he said. 'You're worse than Marian. Try looking out at the back.'

'Out at the back?' she said.

'At the stables.'

She was gone, slamming through the kitchen and into the garden, scratching her new shoes, and tearing her stockings on an untrimmed rose bush. Alan followed slowly. This was her moment and he did not want to intrude upon it.

The horse was nervous, and thrust its head over the half door and whinnied. 'Oh my God, you're lovely,' Lisa murmured.

She held out a hand and the horse nuzzled her palm, then ran its nose along her jacket, leaving dirty streaks. She opened the door and slipped inside.

. . . *Do you still ask for a pitch black Arab stallion which runs fast as the wind . . .*

This was not a stallion, but a mare. A beautiful Arab mare.

'Do you like her?' Alan asked. 'Her name is Chanson de Nuit. I'm afraid it's a bit of a mouthful, but you can always change it. She was imported from France and has a pedigree longer than your arm. I asked Mark to choose her because I don't know a damn thing about horses.'

'She's beautiful,' she said. And because he expected it, she came out of the stable and hugged him. He kissed her on the lips.

'Come and get changed,' he said. 'We don't want to miss the plane. Mark says he'll exercise her while we're away.'

'You've thought of everything,' she said. 'Thank you, Alan. I really don't know what to say.'

He kissed her again. 'I want you to be happy, darling. I want you to have everything you want.'

She laughed. 'I can see you're going to spoil me rotten,' she said, and went with him back to the house.

Chapter Eleven

When June Halliday received an invitation to join Mark Hanley for lunch at the Savoy Grill she was curious enough to accept. The man was fast becoming a legend, and by all accounts he was barely into his thirties. It was at Lisa's wedding that she had seen him close at hand for the first time, although they had exchanged no more than a couple of words.

She arrived on time, to find he was already waiting.

'I'm glad you could make it,' he said. 'I thought we might have a drink first.'

He was treating her as an equal, and she immediately knew that he wanted something. She ordered brandy and water. 'Why are you going to so much trouble?' she asked. 'I'm sure you didn't invite me here for conversation.'

'You don't believe in beating around the bush, do you?'

'No,' she said bluntly. 'I can only think that this has something to do with the magazine. But whatever it is, I should prefer to know before we have lunch.'

'So that you can decide whether to be moderate or excessive?' Mark asked.

'Or if I should walk out beforehand. I expect that would be a new experience for you.' She raised her glass. 'Cheers.'

He smiled as he sipped his whisky. 'I think we shall understand each other very well, June. May I call you June?' She nodded her assent. 'I want to buy the magazine, and I'd like a guarantee that you will come with it.'

'I never realised you were in the market,' June said. 'But tell me, what do you have to offer that I can't get anywhere else?'

'A free hand,' he said evenly. 'And co-editorship.'

'It sounds interesting. But I specialise in fashion, not the raucous young people you promote. I presume you would wish to aim the magazine at them? Change its format completely?'

'I would overhaul it, of course. You need to get rid of your competition, and you won't do that by sticking to an outdated formula.'

'Brave words from someone who knows nothing about the business,' she said.

'I know what your readers want and can deliver it,' he told her.

'No doubt to the detriment of the fashion pages,' June said sarcastically.

'Not at all. You must know that I am also involved in the textile industry.'

'That may have some bearing on the fashion business, but it's certainly not something which will attract readership.'

He put down his glass. 'I am presently trying to remedy that situation. By the time I've finished, even you will be interested.'

She believed him. He was too shrewd to lie, and too good a businessman not to know what he was doing.

'You said co-editorship. Who would I be expected to work with?'

'Eric Stewart. He's been with me for long enough to know the music business inside out. You'd have total control over fashion and beauty, he would deal with the features.'

'The man's a creep,' she said. 'I've met him. He also has the morals of a tomcat.'

'Granted. But he is clever. Do you find it too much of a challenge?'

Her eyes narrowed. 'I find nothing too much of a challenge, especially your careful manoeuvring. Why haven't you tried to bribe me? Money is usually considered to be the best incentive.'

He laughed. 'Not to a person with principles.'

She had underestimated him. He was cleverer than she had thought.

'That being the case, you may as well tell me more about these plans of yours,' she said.

'Which is why I invited you here in the first place. Can I get you another drink, or shall we go in for lunch?' He smiled. There would still be a good deal more hard bargaining to do, but the bait had been taken, and it was really only a matter of reeling in the line.

Mark had Martin dress Patsy Hart for an interview she was having on a television chat show. The girl was horrified by the outfit he produced, and if Mark Hanley had not been involved, she would have refused to wear it. But she was more terrified of him than of the critics, and so she gave in. The next day the press crucified her, and in a flood of tears she declared that she had never been so humiliated in her life.

Martin was certain he was finished before he had even managed to get started. 'She looked absolutely lovely,' was all he could think to say.

'Good God, Martin, if I had given up as easily as you have just done, none of this would exist today,' said Mark. 'We took them by surprise, and they weren't ready for it, that's all. You'll reach them eventually. I think now's the time you should open up the boutique you always wanted. Knightsbridge is the best place, as the women who shop there will buy your creations just because they're different. We'll have to build you up gradually, buy space in the top fashion magazines. It's like promoting a new pop star. Publicity is your best weapon.'

'You're giving me another chance?' Martin asked, not quite believing what he had heard.

'I never intended to give you only one chance,' Mark said. 'Now, one word of warning, Martin. Use only the best fabrics, don't attempt to mass-produce, and keep your prices high. The women you need to attract aren't looking for basement bargains, they want quality and originality. If there's anything special you need which the mill can handle, come to me, not Arthur Bennett. He's still recovering from the shock of that pink and purple tweed you designed.'

Martin smiled. 'And what about the fabrics you can't supply? I shall need a large range in small quantities, which will work out astronomically expensive.'

'I can arrange for you to have unlimited credit. But for God's sake keep a tally of all you spend, and if there are any problems tell me, or Alan if I'm away.'

Martin nodded, and said hesitantly, 'I'd still like to dress the average girl in the street.'

Mark's eyes rested on him. 'And so you will. But not yet. Corner your market first. Where do you think that average girl gets her ideas from? She probably follows fashion more closely than the wealthy, whose prime objective is usually to get noticed. Once your name is known, and there's enough demand, you can start thinking of a ready-to-wear collection.'

'What if I foul up and don't make it?' Martin asked.

Mark smiled. 'You'll make it. You wouldn't be here otherwise.'

A couple of months later, Martin opened his boutique in Beauchamp Place, and in September Lisa paid him a visit there.

Lisa was happy. When the honeymoon was over, she and Alan, and Marian, had settled into the new house together more easily than she had dared to hope, and life had soon fallen into a relaxed, familiar pattern. Lisa found Chanson a delight to ride, and while she was away, Mark had somehow managed to get Marian interested in riding too, so that now she often accompanied her mother on Tom Thumb, a Welsh pony hired from a nearby riding school. Then there were the dogs. Alan arrived home one evening to find that his wife had acquired not one but three dogs from the Battersea Dogs Home—a Pekinese called Madame Ping, a floppy creature of uncertain breeding which she named Tipsy, and Samson, a half-bred Alsatian of about six months old, who made an immediate love pact with Marian and followed her everywhere. Two days later a kitten had mysteriously appeared. Alan, far from being angry, was delighted; he loved what was happening, for the house was now a home.

'Hello Martin, it's me,' Lisa called now, stepping over the boutique's elegant threshold. There was no one in sight, and she found him sitting cross-legged on the floor in the cramped room at the back of the shop, his nimble fingers racing along a hem.

'You look like an old fashioned cobbler,' she said. 'How are you?'

'Well,' he answered. 'And you look like the cat which got the cream. Married life is obviously suiting you.'

'Alan spoils me silly,' she said. 'And it's marvellous not to work, I can spend all day doing the things I enjoy most.'

He laughed. He liked Lisa, and was pleased that she had bothered to visit him. She looked round the room, and seeing a length of scarlet material, held it beneath her chin.

'This is a bit daring,' she said. 'Are you selling much?'

'Roughly a dress a day. Sometimes not even that. Cherry red would suit you. You have the colouring for it. Or that russet brown over there.'

She followed the direction of his arm. 'That's nice. Why don't you get an assistant to help out front?'

He threw aside the dress, and rose stiffly to his feet. 'I can't afford it, and the shop isn't busy so I can manage by myself. Would you like some coffee?'

'I'd love it,' she said. 'But you should consider getting a girl. Business might pick up a bit then. After all, it's a bit odd being fitted by a man.'

'The best designers are usually men,' he said as he plugged in the kettle.

'I know, but they stick to their designing. Do you mind if I look through your racks?'

'Go ahead,' he said. 'But you won't find much on them, they're only there for display. I prefer to make for the individual customer.'

She was standing in the doorway, and although she was dressed in jeans and a grubby jumper, he could still feel that elusive quality which had struck him the first time they met.

'Do you think there's anything which would fit me?' she asked. 'Our social life is beginning to run away with us, and I must have been through my entire wardrobe at least a dozen times. I talked it over with Alan last night, and he's happy to finance a new one . . . he's such a dear, he'd finance anything if I asked him nicely. So I decided to come here.'

'I haven't got anything on the racks that will suit you. What are you after?'

Her fingers flicked over the scarlet material. 'I wouldn't be seen dead in this colour. Otherwise you can have a free hand and let your imagination run riot . . . Well, perhaps not too much riot. But I need some daytime clothes, and a lot of evening wear. Could you cope with all that?'

'Yes,' he said. 'But are you sure?'

'Of course,' she said. 'I shall be the envy of all my friends when I glide in wearing my original Martin Henderson. I can be a genuine pioneer.'

'You'll have to fitted by a man,' he told her. 'Will you object?'

She laughed. 'As a respectable married woman I'm sure I'll survive the experience.'

'Then leave those racks alone and make the coffee. I have some designs which I'd like to show you first. And would you take some advice about your hair and make-up.'

'Do I really look that bad?' she asked, not the least insulted.

'You are perfection itself,' he purred. 'But you don't match my clothes.'

'I shall adore being your guinea pig, Martin. Sugar?'

'Yes please. One spoon.'

He was going to use some old sketches, but suddenly decided against it. He picked up his pad and very soon his hand was flying through sheet after sheet. She brought over the coffee in cracked mugs.

'Surely Mark can do better than these?' she asked.

'I dropped them,' he said. 'Now sit down and shut up.'

She sat beside him, watching in fascination.

'You shall have to be a bit more conservative than that,' she said after a while. 'Alan will have a seizure.'

'They have to be short or they won't work,' he said. 'But just for you, I'll only go an inch or so above the knee.'

'Mid-knee?' she suggested.

'No.'

'Then you'd better be there to support my naked knee caps. We're having a housewarming party in three weeks' time, and it will be as good a time as any for the new me to emerge.'

The bell over the shop door tinkled, and Martin stood up. 'Don't go,' he said. 'Stay and make some more coffee.'

She pulled a face. 'I'm not expected to work this hard at home.'

Mark could not come to the party. 'He got a telephone call, and then rushed off to the aerodrome,' Alan told Lisa. She was in the stables, fussing over the horse. 'He asked me to apologise.'

'I hope there's nothing wrong at home,' she said. 'Maybe I should ring Daddy and find out.'

'If it were anything bad he would have told me,' said Alan. 'And don't you think you should start getting ready?' She glanced at her watch, and coming out of the stable, walked with him along the path. 'I've got something else to tell you,' he said. 'I have to go to the States on Monday, and you're coming with me. We'll only be gone for a few days, so Clara can look after Marian. Mark has arranged for us to fly over in the new jet, and stay in the house at the coast.'

She kissed his cheek in delight. 'Mark certainly knows how to spend his money,' she said.

Martin arrived a short while later, and to Lisa's dismay she discovered that he was unimaginably fussy about his creations.

'Perfect,' he said at last, after she had turned this way and that, and tried a mountain of accessories.

Lisa looked at herself in the full-length mirror. She was different, but nicely different—except for the hemline. Martin had been sneaky about that.

'I could do with Mark for support,' she said. 'He wouldn't dare disapprove.'

'Don't be such a prude,' Martin said. 'There's the doorbell. It's now or never.'

Alan cornered her later on. 'Every woman in the room is talking about you!' he said.

'And women are such bitches!' said Lisa, her eyes sparkling. 'I thought you'd hate it.'

'It was a shock at first, but it grows on you.'

'It's my sexy knee caps,' she said. 'Have you seen Martin anywhere? June would like to meet him. After all the fuss she made last year, she now thinks that he is revolutionary.'

'That's probably because she'll be working for Mark once the sale of the magazine is finalised.'

'I very much doubt if that would influence her. June has always swung from one extreme to the other,' said Lisa. 'Where is Martin? Have you seen him?'

'He was talking with Len Parker a short while ago . . . Is something wrong?'

Lisa swore beneath her breath. 'Was there anybody else with them?'

'No. Why?'

She gazed around the crowded room. 'Where are they? Who was the idiot who introduced them in the first place?'

'I suppose I was. Lisa, what on earth's the matter? What's wrong with Len Parker? He's just a perfectly harmless, rather entertaining radio personality, isn't he?'

'Don't you know his reputation?' said Lisa. 'He's as queer as they come, and Martin is just the sort of promising young newcomer to interest him.'

'Oh,' said Alan. Then, 'Well, if that's what Martin decides he wants, I don't see how you can stop him.'

'I shouldn't think Martin has any idea of what he wants,' she retorted. 'And Len will only use him, and discard him like a broken doll.'

Five minutes later they had established that Len Parker and Martin had left the party together.

'Oh why isn't Mark here to deal with this?' groaned Lisa.

Alan took hold of her arm. 'Look, you cannot control Martin's private life. Nor can Mark.'

'But Len Parker? Why did I have to invite him?'

'Because I know him professionally, and you often meet him out riding.'

'Poor Martin,' she said. 'I hope he can cope.'

Dawn was creeping over Richmond Park when the telephone rang. Alan groaned and pulled the blankets over his ears, but Lisa reached for the receiver.

'We've only just got to bed,' Alan said. 'Leave it.'

She ignored him. 'Hello . . . Daddy . . . Yes. Don't worry, I'm not asleep . . .'

Bloody liar, he thought. Nobody but a maniac or a Crowder would dream of telephoning at this time on a Sunday morning. He was half asleep and determined to stay that way, but as he listened to Lisa's questioning voice it was obvious something was wrong. As she put down the receiver he sat up.

'What is it?' he asked.

'Albert. Albert Warburton. He's dead.' She wasn't crying, but shivering violently, and he held her tight.

'The Hanley gardener?' he asked.

'He was more than a gardener, he was part of the family. Daddy says he was lopping one of those tall pines along the driveway, and fell. He died this morning in hospital. I'll have to go there, Alan.'

'Of course. What about Fran?'

'Mark had her flown up last night. I know they left early, so he must have contacted her at home. Are you coming?'

He shook his head. 'Mark expects me to be in America, and it isn't something which can be put off. What about Marian?'

'I think it would be better if she stayed with Clara. Daddy says there's a train getting into Manchester at one and he'll be there to meet me.'

It was marvellous to be home, even for such a sad occasion. Later in the afternoon she telephoned Alan, and then drove into Oldenshaw to visit Mary Hanley. Maude had moved from the Manor into the largest of the cottage's two spare bedrooms; Fran, Eric and the three children had to make do with the other, smaller room. Both Mary and Eric were fractious, and it was little wonder, Lisa thought, as she tried to prevent Kim from leaving sticky fingermarks on her clean trousers.

'I thought you'd be staying at the Manor,' she said to Fran, resisting an urge to slap the persistent child. Marian would never be allowed to behave like this.

'The Manor, like everything else around here, belongs to Mark,' Fran snapped. 'He and Daddy may never have seen eye to eye, but that didn't stop him from inheriting the whole damn lot.'

'He received no money,' said her mother sharply.

Fran laughed. 'Mine's nearly all gone. Compared with what my brother got, it was a pittance.'

'Shut up, Fran,' Eric said.

'Why should I? It's always Mark this and Mark that. He only has to snap his fingers and you're grovelling.'

'That's quite enough,' Mary said angrily. 'This is my house, and while you are in it you will keep a civil tongue and refrain from behaving like a fishwife.'

Fran stood up. 'You always did put him first,' she shouted. 'If I get on your nerves so much, I'll go upstairs.'

She picked up the baby, which immediately began to scream, and then slammed out of the room. Kim started to cry.

'I'm sorry,' Eric apologised as he tried to comfort the child.

'Don't worry about it,' Lisa said. 'I expect she's under a lot of strain at the moment.'

She left soon after that, and as she drove past Olden Manor, was in two minds about going in to see how Mark was. But it was getting late, and she knew her father was waiting. And so she did not see him until the funeral on Tuesday morning.

Doesn't he ever get tired like the rest of us, she thought. He had not only made all the arrangements here, but she knew he was in constant touch with Hanley Recordings in London and Alan in America. Yet, to look at him, one would think he had nothing more important on his mind than comforting a grief-stricken old woman.

He must have been aware of her stare for he glanced up at her, his eyes smiling.

When the funeral was over, she stayed behind. 'I'll walk back,' she said to her father.

He watched Mark Hanley herd his family into waiting cars. 'Or get him to bring you?' he asked.

'It'll be all right, Daddy,' she said. 'Don't worry so much,'

Mark was not long. 'Thank you for coming,' he said. 'Maude is in a bad way at the moment. I don't think she's up to talking, but I know she's grateful.'

'What will she do now?'

'Stay at the cottage with Mother, which means I inherit Elly and all her troubles. She's split up with her boyfriend, and wants to work for me in London.' He glanced round and saw that everyone else had gone. 'Do you want a lift to the farm?'

'I was hoping you'd ask.' He took her arm and they left the graveyard.

'I'm afraid all I can offer is Tim and the Rolls.'

'I'm growing used to it,' she said. 'Did poor Tim have to drive all the way from London?'

'Poor Tim slept. We flew. I keep another car here now.'

The chauffeur greeted her, and then they were inside the car with only five miles between them and the farm. Mark did not attempt to talk and she noticed how his eyes strayed towards the windows. She wondered if he resented her breaking into his privacy without invitation.

'Will you be staying for long?' she asked.

He turned suddenly, as though she had startled him.

'I'm sorry, Lisa,' he said. 'I can't leave until I find someone to look after the Manor.'

'Can't Elly take it on? She's perfectly capable.'

'No. She wants to get away from here, and doesn't want to live in an empty house. It's a miracle she remains in service at all.'

'What about Fran?'

'Ah yes, Fran.' He closed his eyes for a moment. 'I hear you were at the cottage on Sunday?'

'Yes.'

'Then you probably want to know why she insists on staying with Mother when the Manor is empty?'

There was a touch of the old humour in his eyes, and she smiled at him. 'I didn't get the impression that you were her favourite brother,' she said.

'I'm not. I told her that only she and Eric were to come to the funeral, and she refused to come without the whole ghastly brood. I was *not* pleased, and nor was Mother.'

'It wouldn't matter so much,' said Lisa, 'if she coped better. As it is, the children run rings round her.'

'Poor Fran,' Mark said. 'I'm afraid there's not much holding that marriage together. She just has more babies and hopes everything will come right.'

'She resents you inheriting all the property.'

'She resents the world in general. But Father did leave her a substantial amount of money. The mill did very well during his last few years.'

And we all know why, Lisa thought, but she only said, 'Apparently it has nearly all gone.'

His eyes rested on her face. 'That's impossible. It was left in trust. She can only draw so much a year.'

Lisa shrugged. 'Perhaps she was exaggerating. I'm only repeating what she said.'

The car left the tarmac. They were on the farm road, and her time had practically run out.

'I know nothing about my sister's plans,' Mark said, 'but the jet will be waiting for you at Manchester tomorrow morning. It will take you to London first, and then America. I've already telephoned Alan, and he's expecting you.'

'Thank you,' she said wryly.

'You were going with him; I'm only trying to salvage what has been lost.'

She sighed. 'If you have time, you're welcome to take out Chanson. Marian is staying with Clara, so if you can put up with her chatter, you can take her too.'

'I haven't ridden since your honeymoon,' he said. 'And as for Marian, she wants to be a ballet dancer.'

'She what?'

'Have a talk with her when you get back. She's terrified you'll laugh.'

'At my own daughter?'

They had reached the last gate, and Tim got out to open it.

'Well we all know that you're not hung up on the finer arts!' he said. 'Unfortunately, Marian seems to think that your interests stretch no further than horses.'

Lisa bit back a cross retort, and said instead. 'Are you coming in?'

'I can't,' he said. 'I have to get back. Goodbye, Lisa.'

She almost kissed his cheek, but thought better of it. Only when he was gone did she remember Martin.

Two weeks had passed since the evening he had been introduced to Len Parker, weeks in which Martin Henderson wanted nothing more than to bask in his lover's presence. He had learnt what it was like to love and to be loved, and during those fourteen glorious days body and soul was sold to Len Parker. There was nothing he would not do for the man, however debasing, and not once had he thought of the shop, or Mark Hanley, or his ambitions.

Len Parker, confident now that the boy was under his thumb, began to take up the threads of normal daily life again. Martin resented being delegated into second place while Len arranged his work schedules, but then they would make love and everything would be all right, until the next time. Two weeks ran into three and Len accepted an invitation to go riding with Lady Dixon and her friends. Len was proud of his association with Lady Dixon. She admitted very few to her circle, and disliked Sunday riders, and anyone else who did not aspire to her outrageous lifestyle. She had once invited Lisa Weston to join her circle, but Lisa thought her an incompetent idiot and had politely declined, perhaps the only person ever to do so.

'I won't be long,' he said as he casually admired himself in a mirror. He was dressed in what Lisa would have scathingly referred to as 'full hunting kit', and even had a leather-bound crop with a silver handle. He wondered whether he should purchase spurs. Lady Dixon always wore spurs. 'How do I look?' he asked.

Martin was sitting on the bed, and his eyes lifted until they were level with the other man's chest.

'Beautiful,' he murmured.

Len was pleased. He was on the wrong side of forty, but his body was still trim; athletic, he liked to call himself. A slight chin sag had been corrected last year, and the grey which showed at his temples gave him, he felt, a distinguished air. A steady flow of fan mail came his way. Now he slapped the crop against his boot. 'Ah yes,' he said.

'The sport of kings.' He kissed the boy's cheek, surprised not to receive the normal delighted reaction. He stepped back. 'You're looking tired.'

Martin looked up at his lover and said nothing. Len frowned. 'Have a rest while I'm gone,' he said. 'We can go out this afternoon.'

Martin heard the slam of the front door, and then the roar of Len's sports car; but it was ten minutes before he moved. He walked to the window and stared at the trees which lined the road. Their brittle leaves were shedding like snow in the autumn wind, and the sky was mottled with fluffy clouds. He wanted more than this. He wanted to make it as a designer, but he also wanted Len Parker. Lisa . . . Lisa would know what he should do. He was amazed that he hadn't thought of her before.

He left the house, pausing to breathe in the cold air which filled his senses like bubbles of champagne. He felt a little breathless as he walked to the park gates, and didn't care that he might meet Len and his cronies. But Len had already left, mounted on a friskier horse than he cared for, following Lady Dixon, her niece and another couple at a brisk trot towards Wimbledon Common.

It took Martin forty minutes to reach the house. As he slipped through the gates the dogs came rushing down the drive, making enough racket to waken the dead. But it was Clara Gibson, not Lisa, who came to the door.

'I'm sorry,' the housekeeper said. 'She's not here. She and Mr. Weston are in America. Didn't you know?' He shook his head in dull comprehension. 'I don't expect them back until the beginning of next week. Mrs. Weston telephoned last night to talk with Marian, and told me business was keeping them there longer than expected.'

Martin felt suddenly depressed.

'How about a cup of tea?' Clara Gibson asked. 'It'll be no trouble, and I'd be glad of the company.'

He was tired and it could do no harm, so he went in.

Clara Gibson insisted he have lunch, and it was mid-afternoon before he left and made his way back to Len Parker's house. He had his hands thrust into his pockets, and was looking down at the pavement when he sensed someone watching him.

He looked up. The black Rolls-Royce was parked outside Len's gate, and Tim was leaning against it, enjoying a quiet smoke. He threw the cigarette into the gutter and said, 'Good afternoon, sir.'

'Is he in there?' Martin asked.

Tim Denholm saw the fear in the grey eyes and hoped that for once Mark Hanley would be kind.

'He's in there,' he confirmed. 'And a merry chase you've led him, to be sure.'

'I . . . Lisa . . . ' Martin stammered.

'If she knew, she never told him. He's had me up and down London like a bloody yoyo. You'd best go in. The longer you wait the worse it'll be.'

'Is he mad?'

'Not exactly mad,' Tim said, picturing that absorbed coldness. 'A little upset maybe. But then he's had a lot on his mind lately. If it helps, I think you're just a little fish in a big pond.'

Martin nodded, and pushed open the gate. Tim lit another cigarette.

They were waiting in the lounge. Martin stood in the hall, terrified. Len was sitting on the sofa, still dressed in his riding clothes, and Mark Hanley was staring from a window into the back garden. It was he who swung round first, his blue gaze on Martin's face. The boy flushed, and wished he were anywhere but there.

'Your paramour has arrived,' Mark said to Len. There was an unpleasant bite to his voice which made Martin shudder.

Len leapt to his feet. 'Martin . . .' he gasped. Then his voice hardened and he said, 'Where have you been? I was worried sick.'

'A bird in a gilded cage,' said Mark. 'I'm sorry that Lisa is away, but she couldn't have helped.'

Martin stared at him. 'How did you know where I was?'

'People talk,' said Mark. 'And Mr. Parker has been flaunting you around some of the better known night spots. Unfortunately, we missed one another. I came here first, but as nobody was in I went through to Ham to check on Lisa's horse. You had just left, but Tim was unable to find you, otherwise we could have talked in private.'

'This is my house,' Len Parker said in his best broadcasting voice.

'And it's very nice too,' said Mark. 'Shall I send over your belongings, Martin? I can see no point in keeping your flat on if you have no further use for it.'

Martin stared from one man to the other.

'Of course he wants them,' Len snapped. 'We'll collect whatever he needs this afternoon. I would hate to put you to any more trouble.'

'Have you lost your voice, Martin?' Mark asked. 'And have you looked at yourself in a mirror recently? You should do that every now and again, you know, it's good for the soul.'

It was at that point Len decided to take matters more firmly in hand. He walked over to Martin and put a consoling arm about his shoulders. Martin flushed. 'You may leave now, Mr. Hanley,' Len said.

'What about the shop?' Martin asked.

'Designers are two a penny,' said Mark. 'I thought you had talent and ambition, but obviously I was wrong. Perhaps I'll find somebody else to run it. I haven't decided yet.'

His words had the desired effect. Martin's face clouded as he pulled away from Len's grasp. 'Designers may be two a penny, but I'm an original,' he said angrily. 'You'll never find anybody as good as me.'

The blue eyes were still resting on his face. 'Then you must make up your own mind, Martin. Either you come back with me, or you stay with him. You can't have both.'

Martin stood between the two men, isolated by his indecision. He wanted the shop. He wanted to take a length of cloth and create a garment which was distinctively his own. And he wanted Len.

'Why not?' he asked.

Mark smiled and said gently, 'Because if you leave now, he'll not have you back.'

Martin swung round. 'Len . . . that isn't true, is it?'

Len Parker's eyes were narrow slits, and his mouth was twisted into an ugly sneer. 'He's right,' he said. 'Go with him, and you go for good.'

Martin was dumbstruck. He's bluffing, he thought. He has to be bluffing. He didn't even notice as Mark slipped past them into the hall. But Len did. 'Despicable man,' he said triumphantly. 'I couldn't keep him out . . . Why, you're trembling . . .'

Martin backed away, seeing for the first time a middle-aged man with a hint of debauchery about the eyes and full lipped mouth. 'Can you wait while I get my own clothes?' he called.

Mark was at the front door and he turned slowly. 'I'll be in the car.'

'I mean it, Martin,' Len warned. 'You'll never set foot in this house again.'

Martin winced. 'I don't want to come back,' he said. 'I hate this bloody house. And don't worry, I'll take nothing of yours.' He took off the gold watch he had been given, and laid it on the hall table. 'I came in my own suit and I'll leave in it.'

Chapter Twelve

Eric Stewart found it depressing to sort through six years of accumulated junk. In the new year he and June Halliday would be working together on the remodelled teen magazine. He was still uncertain about their proposed partnership, and resentful that Mark had not given him total control. He had certainly earned it.

Some photographs spilt from a cupboard. He picked one up. It was of Marty Pole in his earlier days, before dissipation began pulling at his features. He was beginning to slip in the charts now, and Eric knew it was only a matter of time before he went the way of so many others and became a nonentity.

The door opened, and Eric straightened up as Alan walked in. The lawyer grinned at the mess on desk and floor and said, 'I sometimes wonder where it all comes from. I thought Mark might be here.'

'Well, he's not,' said Eric irritably. 'I haven't seen him today.'

'I do wish he wouldn't disappear without a word to anybody. Even Norma doesn't know where he is.' Alan pushed aside a stack of papers, and perched on the edge of the desk. 'It's going to be strange without you here,' he said.

'I'm going to miss it,' said Eric, kicking the photos to one side. 'I know this magazine is a step up, but Mark intends to make some radical changes, and he could have bitten off more than he can chew.'

'He knows what he's doing,' Alan said confidently. 'And I wouldn't worry too much about June. Lisa says she won't give a damn about your content, just so long as her pages aren't cut down.'

'Why should I worry about June?' Eric asked brusquely. She was the last person on his mind. Angie had left last week. They hadn't really got along since her anticipated singing career fell through. She laid part of the blame on him, even though he had nothing to do with it—she didn't seem to realise that it was Mark who had pulled the strings to get her even as far as she'd managed to go.

'Why indeed?' Mark said, walking into the office. 'But you'll have to keep your wits about you. Too many late nights and June Halliday will have you twisted in knots.' Eric resented that, but Mark had already turned to Alan. 'Have you seen Henry anywhere?' he asked. 'I need to talk with him about Simon.'

'You could try the rehearsal rooms,' Alan suggested.

Henry Morton and Simon Townsend had been something of a joke at the beginning of the year. Henry was a clever young man who assisted Chris and would probably take over from him one day. He had discovered Simon Townsend, a Jamaican-born waiter, working in a coffee bar in Shepherd's Bush, and with Mark's reluctant blessing and a substantial amount of financial backing, had spent the past year moulding him into a singer of calibre; a popular entertainer who would appeal to a different audience. For Mark it was an experiment, a break away from the world of pop, and if it succeeded Simon, whom he had not even met, would receive a long-term contract. He would also pave the way for others. Now the day of reckoning was almost here, for Henry had got Simon onto the celebrated Sunday Night at the London Palladium, which was televised live throughout the country.

Mark was about to turn away when he suddenly stopped. 'I almost forgot,' he said. 'I managed to get hold of these for Marian. I thought Lisa could take her.'

Alan stared at the tickets Mark was holding out. 'What are they for?' he asked.

'Nureyev's debut next week. It should be sensational.'

'Good God, Mark, they'll be wasted on her! She is far too young to sit through an entire ballet. She'll be bored stiff within five minutes.'

Mark smiled. 'I very much doubt it,' he said. 'I think she'll be beside herself with excitement.'

Simon Townsend was ready too early. He had a small dressing room near the back of the theatre, and after suffering the ministrations of a young make-up girl, left it and headed for the stage.

This was the culmination of the months spent touring cheap music halls and crowded holiday resorts, and he had never been so frightened in his life. He glanced at his watch. There were still twelve minutes to go. Some acrobats were on stage, and scantily clad chorus girls were preparing to follow them. He stood watching.

'When they throw their props off stage you're going to find yourself standing in a shower of clubs and balls. They also happen to be jugglers.'

Simon swung round. A man was sitting on a stool amongst a stack of scenery.

'There is another stool,' the man said.

Simon had learnt that people in show business were invariably friendly, and warming to the stranger, he picked his way towards him.

'Are you waiting to go on?' he asked, sitting down.

'I'm waiting,' the man replied.

Simon saw the quality of his suit, and his professional interest in what was going on.

'I was ready too early,' he said, even though he had not been asked. He looked at the man's profile, started to ask who he was, and then changed his mind. Just because he didn't recognise him didn't mean he wasn't well known.

'There's something very soothing about tumblers,' the stranger said.

A couple of clubs and a multi-coloured beach ball came flying into the wings. A stagehand picked them up. The chorus girls were whispering as they jostled into line. Simon realised his palms were sweating and rubbed them together.

'This is my first time here,' he said.

'And you're nervous?' The man looked at him. He had blue eyes, bluer than Simon had ever seen; and there was something vaguely familiar about him. 'It's a natural reaction,' he contined in a soft voice which carried no further than the two of them. 'But once that spotlight finds me, nothing matters any more. I walk onto the stage as though I own it. I am myself, and because I make no concessions the audience usually responds. You should try it.' He stood up.

'You're going?' Simon asked.

'I have to.'

'I thought . . . I hoped you might stay a little longer.'

The man smiled. 'You must take courage from yourself, not me. If you want to be an entertainer, go out there and entertain.'

He slipped quickly away.

'Who was that?' Henry Morton asked. He was annoyed. He had been searching the theatre, only to find Simon chatting to a stagehand who'd taken off the moment he saw Henry approach.

Chapter Thirteen

I left the theatre after the first round of thunderous applause. I nodded to a couple of ushers who knew me from years ago, and then ran through the rain to the waiting car.

'Did Simon do well?' Tim asked.

'Yes,' I told him. 'He's on his way to a successful career.'

'I'm glad,' said Tim. 'He's a nice lad, and deserves as much, if not more, than the usual scruff you promote.'

I smiled as he turned into Regent Street's heavy traffic. It was times like these which made the months of preparation worthwhile. I certainly felt pleased with myself as I leant back against the seat. 'I'm taking Miss Cole to dinner,' I said. 'After you've dropped me at her flat, you can go home.'

He glanced at me through the driving mirror. 'Won't you want me to pick you up later?'

'No,' I said. Tonight, I intended to celebrate.

Chapter Thirteen

PART THREE
(1966–1969)

Chapter One

When I originally set up my studios on the west coast, I had done so because I liked the climate. New York was too large, too noisy, too hot in summer and too cold in winter—but the house I purchased on the Big Sur was a welcome retreat, especially when I was working. I certainly hadn't known when I bought it that San Francisco would become a Mecca for the young.

The pop breakthrough into America had finally come with the Beatles, and now anyone with an English accent was welcomed with open arms. But when I went over that October, it was to find communes of roving hippies who preached love and non-violence, and whose music was strongly anti-war in protest against the continuing carnage of Vietnam. I was aware of the changes in the music scene, almost from the moment I stepped off the plane—which was why I was still in the States in December, trying to capture some of the raw talent I saw all about me. It was rare for me to stay away from England for so long, but everything at home was running smoothly.

Martin had realised his dreams, for the mini-skirt now reigned supreme, with much of its popularity due to him. His first ready-to-wear collection had come out three years ago, and now he was being hailed as one of the best of Britain's young designers. With that collection had come the launch of an exclusive chain of boutiques, and enormous expansion, so that his workrooms now filled an entire building, and he had a team of designers working under him. But Martin had changed very little despite his success, and for himself, he preferred to work in the cramped room at the back of his original shop in Beauchamp Place.

The magazine had not been easy. Advertisers had been wary of the new format, but June and Eric proved an unbeatable team. They disliked each other intensely, but it was that dislike which spurred each of them on to greater achievement. Within a year sales had soared dramatically, and now it was easily holding its own as the top selling teen magazine in the country.

After two months, I was looking forward to going home and spending a quiet Christmas in Oldenshaw. But before I left San Francisco, Keith Long, who now ran our American company, insisted on holding a party in my honour. It was certainly a celebrity affair, with the doyens of Hollywood rubbing shoulders with the less flashy pop world. I was not a heavy drinker, but I lost count of the glasses of champagne I went through as Keith escorted me from group to glittering group.

Tim invariably came with me on these trips, and I had warned him that I would slip away at the earliest opportunity. The opportunity came when I found myself standing alone beside an open french window. I dumped the glass I was holding into a pot containing something which resembled a dwarf palm tree, and slipped out. It was a balmy night, with a light breeze which carried on it a faint salt tang from the sea. Many of the guests had drifted outside, and were scattered across the floodlit lawns, which I deliberately avoided as I made my way around the side of the house towards the drive. I saw Tim standing apart from the other drivers, enjoying a quiet smoke. He must have heard the ring of my shoes on an unexpected path, for he swung round and threw away the cigarette.

'You've been here barely an hour,' he said. 'Surely they'll miss you?'

'Impossible,' I answered. 'They're packed in there like sardines. Anyway, I promised you an early night.'

'That's neither here nor there,' he said. 'Mind you, I'll be glad to get home now. I'd hate to spend Christmas here. It's too hot. Plum pudding and swimming don't mix.'

I knew how he felt, for I was also looking forward to leaving. I got into the car and relaxed for the first time that day.

'I hope we don't meeting anything coming up,' I said dryly; and Tim, who habitually drove on the left-hand side of the road, swerved to the right of the drive.

I was thinking about Oldenshaw and Christmas when Tim suddenly slammed on the brakes. The car skidded to a halt, and he swore angrily before turning to me. 'I'm sorry, sir,' he said. 'But I could have killed the stupid bitch. Are you all right?'

'Yes,' I said. 'I think this car must have been modelled on a padded cell. Who are you talking about?'

'Over there,' he said, pointing. 'She was walking in the middle of the drive, and on a bend too.'

I saw her then, standing at the edge of the beams from our

headlights. She wore a low-cut, chiffon evening gown and her feet were bare. A pair of silver sandals hung from her fingers, together with a matching purse. As she stepped forward I saw a small oval face framed by shoulder-length, honey-blonde hair.

'I'll deal with this,' I said to Tim.

She stood still when I got out of the car.

'I'm sorry,' she said in a soft voice which had a Southern drawl. 'I guess I should have had more sense. Was anybody hurt?'

'Only my driver's pride,' I said, walking towards her. She had an unusual kind of beauty which was almost classical, but saved from perfection by something which could have been bitchiness in the set of her mouth. She was also vaguely familiar, although I could not recall having met her.

'Are you in the habit of taking barefoot strolls at the dead of night?' I asked.

She laughed. 'My shoes pinch. I was bored with the party. My escort didn't want to leave, and the cabs won't come out this far, so I decided to start walking. Did you find it equally dull, Mr. Hanley?'

'How do you know who I am?' I asked.

'Because I was introduced to you a short while ago. I thought you were looking through us all as if we didn't exist. I was right!'

For the life of me I could not remember her. 'I'm sorry,' I said. 'But I hate being put on display. Perhaps you will think better of me if I offer you a lift. The nearest town is ten miles away, and I don't think you'll make it like that.'

'If I didn't have a blister I'd be tempted to say no. And my name, by the way, is Caroline Delacey.'

I knew her then, for her father owned a plantation from where I purchased regular supplies of raw cotton. I had never met the daughter, but knew she was the darling of the international jet set and heiress to a fortune.

I took her arm and led her to the car. 'Can you hold these?' she asked, handing me the shoes. They were muddy, and I held them by the fine leather straps.

'The lady needs a lift home,' I said to Tim. I glanced at her. 'Where is home? This isn't your usual territory.'

'My daddy has a beach cottage not far from here,' she said. 'But I'd prefer you to drop me in town, and I'll take a cab the rest of the way. I gather the name rang a bell?'

'Quite a few, actually,' I said, and offered her the shoes.

She put them on. 'Do you have a handkerchief?' she asked as I slid in beside her.

I gave her one, and she wiped her hands clean. 'Keep it,' I said before she could hand it back.

'Did you know my parents wanted me to meet you?' she said. 'That was a couple of years ago.'

'Then why didn't we meet?'

'Because I also dislike being put on display. They had some odd notion that our money would make a great combination. They even threatened to cut off my allowance if I disobeyed them, but I got round Daddy in the end.' She paused. 'I think I should have walked. Does he always drive on the wrong side of the road?'

'Yes,' I said. And Tim, who must have been listening to every word, swerved across the main road onto which he had just turned. Way below us I could see the lights of the small coastal town. 'I wouldn't have thought that party was up your street,' I said. 'It was deadly dull.'

The light was dim and I could only just make out her features. She was smiling, and her pale hair formed a halo around her face.

'I was curious to see if you were anything like the newspapers say,' she told me. 'According to them, you're about as close to a demi-god as one can get. How come you're not married? Most men in your position would have a string of heirs by now.'

'Do you usually ask strangers such personal questions?'

'Why not? I can't believe you're embarrassed. Or are you still carrying the flame for some long lost love?' she asked mischievously.

'Men like me don't have long lost loves,' I said. 'We make conquests. Do you intend to be one of the contenders in the marriage stakes? You're going to face a lot of competition.'

She laughed. 'Your virtue is perfectly safe with me, Mr. Hanley. I always let the men do the chasing. If your driver turns right at those lights, there should be some cabs outside the hotel.'

'He can take you home,' I offered.

'I know,' she said. 'But it's best we're not seen together, and I also prefer it this way.'

Tim found the hotel. There were three cabs, their drivers clustered together, enjoying a quiet smoke. They watched as I leant across the girl and opened the door.

'Thanks for the ride,' she said. 'Goodbye.'

Tim turned round as she slammed shut the door. 'You should have seen her home,' he said. 'It's only proper.'

I laughed at his old-fashioned attitude. 'This is America, complete with its emancipated womanhood,' I told him. 'Caroline Delacey is more than capable of taking care of herself. I'm not yet so gullible as to believe that a girl like her would be hard up for a lift.'

One of the cabs pulled away. Caroline Delacey waved through the rear window.

'Then why was she walking?' Tim asked.

'I don't know. A prank, perhaps. She does have a reputation for being unconventional. I don't suppose we'll ever see her again, so I wouldn't worry about it.'

My beach house was a secretary's dream. There was a swimming pool, and servants to supply refreshments at the push of a button—but it was all wasted on Norma. She had been in the sea once and dangled her feet in the pool on a couple of occasions, but at fifty-six she wasn't going to change her ways, for me or anybody else.

She was on the verandah typing, while I lay face down in the sun, battling through pages of figures. I had just rolled into the shade of an umbrella when raised voices disturbed my concentration. 'Mr. Hanley is working,' I heard Norma say.

'He can't be that damn busy,' said Caroline Delacey. 'Not when he's sitting by the pool.'

I looked up, not really surprised to see here there. 'You may as well let her through, Norma. She's a determined young lady.'

She started down the steps. She was wearing tight jeans which clung to her hips, and an over-large shirt. Her hair was tied back from her face, and even bereft of make-up she was beautiful.

'If I'd known I had to run a gauntlet before reaching you I'd never have come,' she said angrily.

I stood up. 'Then why did you?'

'I wanted to return this,' she said, dropping the laundered handkerchief onto a table. 'And I also wanted to apologise for Saturday. I'd had a couple of drinks too many.'

'You did nothing which needs an apology. Your behaviour was exemplary,' I said, smiling. 'Come and sit down. Would you like a drink?'

'Thank you. I'll have a Martini.'

'At ten in the morning?' I asked, tucking the papers inside a folder.

'Well, if you'd prefer I had a lemonade,' she said scathingly.

'No, of course not,' I said. 'Hang on a minute while I give this to my secretary. How do you like it?'

'Very dry. Do you mind if I take a dip while you're gone?'

'Provided you do so fully clothed,' I said. 'Your reputation precedes you, and I will not have you shocking my staff by diving naked into the swimming pool.'

She laughed. 'You must be referring to that diplomatic party a few months ago. It was even duller than the party the other night, and I decided to liven it up. Actually, I was wearing an extremely respectable five-hundred-dollar chemise. It's not been the same since. The naked bit was the press blowing it out of proportion. They weren't even there at the time and heard it second- or third-hand. Everything I do is always reported ten times larger than life.' She started to unbutton her shirt. 'I presume you have no objection to this?'

She was wearing a yellow bikini top which set off her tan to perfection.

'No,' I said, surprised to find that I was beginning to like the girl.

As we talked, it soon became apparent that Caroline was not the irresponsible tearaway one read about. She was a little wild, yes; but she bubbled with energy, and not once did she flaunt her sex at me.

I took her to dinner that night, and on Friday I did not fly home with Tim and Norma.

'When will you be back?' Norma asked, her tone disapproving.

'Before Christmas.'

Caroline moved in on Christmas Eve.

'Plum pudding and swimming don't mix,' I said after dinner.

'What?'

'I'm sorry. I was thinking aloud. Would you remind me to book a call to England later on? Since my father died I usually try and see my mother over Christmas. What about your parents?'

'I sometimes make Thanksgiving, but they're not worried if I don't,' she said. 'You're a strange person, Mark. I thought I was getting to know you, and then something else crops up and I realise I know nothing about you at all.'

'Why? Because I'm fond of my mother?'

She did not laugh, and her eyes, when they looked into mine, were serious. 'No,' she said. 'But because I think that beneath a thick veneer of something quite hard, you really care.'

Christmas and New Year came and went. January was halfway through, and still I put off leaving. I had made no contact with anyone in England, except for the brief conversation with Mother on Christmas morning. I knew Alan could cope, although it was unfair to leave him with the responsibility for so long. But I would have to go soon. There were too many things demanding my attention.

I had taken Caroline out to dinner, and afterwards she had hauled me to a disco, where we had stayed until the early hours. Now I could not sleep, and lay awake listening to the surf crashing against the cliffs. I was dying for a cigarette, but Caroline was asleep and I didn't want to disturb her. Maybe I moved unintentionally, or perhaps she sensed my restlessness, for she suddenly said, 'I can't sleep either.'

I sat up, switched on the lamp, and reached for my cigarettes. She was lying on her side, propped up on an elbow, and her eyes were red as though she had been crying.

'You're leaving soon, aren't you?' she asked.

'I have to,' I said. 'I've already been out of touch for too long.'

'When are you going?'

'Next week,' I said. 'I'm sorry. I wanted to tell you sooner, but the time never seemed right.'

'Why be sorry?' she asked. 'I knew you couldn't stay here forever.'

'We've had a month that's worth remembering. What will you do now?'

'I don't know. Stop going on about it. Just leave. I hate long goodbyes.'

She turned away, but not before I saw tears in her eyes. I stubbed out my cigarette and switched off the lamp. I had been alone for far too long, and knew I was going to miss her.

'Caro?'

Silence.

'What?' she mumbled.

I reached out and took her in my arms, kissing her gently before wiping away her tears with the edge of the sheet.

'Caroline,' I said. 'Will you marry me?'

'I'm not in the mood for bad jokes,' she said frostily.

'Damn it, Caroline, I'm not joking.'

'You really mean it?' she asked.

'Yes,' I said. 'Yes I do.'

Chapter Two

It as one of those freezing mornings with frost stiffening the grass and a strong wind rattling the windows. As Alan Weston ate his breakfast, he wondered when they would see the sun again, for this weather meant another weekend shut in the house. Not that it matters, he thought. He had work to do, work which he was never able to finish at the office and had to bring home.

'Can I leave the table?' Marian asked.

He looked at her. She was a pretty child, but small for her age, which was just as well, considering that her life revolved around ballet.

'Yes,' he said. 'Are you going to ride Tumbleweed now?'

'I wasn't going to ride him today,' said Marian, standing up.

Alan frowned. 'I'll not have that pony shut in the stable all day. He gets little enough exercise as it is. What about your friends?'

Although she was looking at him through her mother's eyes, there was something about her gaze which was not her mother at all.

'Sandra and Donald have the flu and can't come out,' she said. 'Lesley is away for the weekend, Carol's pony has a swollen leg, and the others are at boarding school. There's nobody for me to go with, so I've decided to stay in.'

'Then think again, young lady. Aunt Judith is coming over, and if you don't go out with her, I'll sell the pony.'

Tears came to Marian's eyes. 'You can't do that,' she said. 'You can't sell Tumbleweed.'

'I can and I will,' said her father. The child ran from the room, slamming the door behind her. 'Marian!' he yelled, but she did not come back. He sighed, poured another cup of tea, and went into the study.

Lisa came in to him a few minutes later with Tipsy and Madame Ping behind her. She looked pale and drawn.

'Shouldn't you be in bed?' he asked, springing to his feet. 'Did you take your pills?'

'I'm becoming a hypochrondriac,' she moaned. 'I've never taken so many pills in my entire life. I never went through this with Marian.' She paused. 'What did you say to her? She's crying her eyes out.'

'I told her that if she doesn't start riding Tumbleweed more regularly I'm going to sell him.'

'You can't do that,' she said, echoing Marian. 'He's part of the family. And you know I won't let her go to the park on her own. She's too young.'

'What about Judith?' he asked.

'She shouts a lot, and you know how sensitive Marian is. I wish Mark were here. She'd go with him like a shot.'

'Damn it!' he swore. 'Does Mark's name have to come into every conversation we have? I bloody well wish he were here too. And if Marian doesn't ride the pony, it goes. That's final.'

Tipsy, unnoticed, crept forward, sniffed Alan's cup and then tried to lap the tea left in the bottom. The cup went flying onto the floor, and swinging round, Alan hit the dog across the side of the head. It yelped, and ran to Lisa's side.

'And keep those bloody animals out of here!' he yelled.

'We'll all stay out of your blasted way!' she shouted back, and walked out.

Soon after ten Judith Smitton arrived on the ugly bay horse which she kept at the nearby stables. She did not stay long. Alan watched through the window as she left with the frisky Arab mare on a leading rein. Lisa walked alongside, and Marian followed behind, her hat pulled over her eyes, and a look of determination on her face. He knew then that his threat had been an idle one, he could never sell Tumbleweed.

The telegram arrived much later. They had finished tea and Marian was visiting a friend. Lisa was reading a book, and Alan wondering how to apologise for this morning, when the doorbell rang. Clara went to the door and returned with the telegram.

'It's from Mark,' Alan said, tearing open the envelope. 'He must be coming home at last.'

'He probably wants you out there,' she said. 'He'd never send a telegram just to say he's on his way back. He never has before.'

Alan read it quickly, frowned, and read it again.

'What's wrong?' Lisa asked.

He smiled, and handed it to her, 'Read it,' he said.

I was married this morning. See you in three weeks time ...

Mark married? Lisa's breath caught in her throat. It was inevitable that this should happen, yet she was unprepared for it. Her father had been right, for she had never really got over him. Suddenly aware of Alan's gaze, she looked up. 'She must be very special,' she said.

She saw just how special Caroline Delacey was next morning, when the front page of every London newspaper carried a photograph of Mark Hanley and his radiant bride.

'Look at Uncle Mark and his new wife!' Marian said, bursting into her parents' room at seven, early even for her, and flinging some papers onto the bed. 'She's like a fairy-tale princess. Don't you think so, Mummy?'

'And he's Prince Charming,' Lisa agreed. 'Climb in the middle, love, otherwise you'll catch a chill.'

Alan sat up. 'Let's hope they live happily ever after,' he said.

'Of course they will,' said Marian. 'Uncle Mark is the nicest man in the world ... after you, of course.' She turned to her mother. 'Haven't you got your morning sickness today?'

'No,' Lisa said, and picked up one of the newspapers.

At least I didn't cry, she thought.

Arthur Bennett did not see a newspaper that morning. While waiting for the kettle to boil he looked through the frosted windows and wondered whether the Hunt would meet in this weather. He was certainly not looking forward to going out in it, but as president of the Society he had no choice.

As it turned out, a lot of people came, despite the cold, which was gratifying.

'I don't reckon those youngsters will be up to much good,' Leslie Moul said. 'You should send them home, or else put them in the company of a responsible adult.'

Arthur looked up. They were a gang of six youths and two girls who were obviously looking for something to tide them over the boredom of winter in a small industrial town.

'They'll be all right,' he said. 'But I'll tell them about shutting gates and so on. We don't want any angry farmers after us.'

The youths looked sulky when he spoke to them, and the girls giggled.

'All right, mister,' said one of the boys. 'We get the picture. We try and get the dogs away from the fox, and then muck up the riders without hurting anyone. We can do that can't we, lads?' The girls giggled even more stupidly.

'Just don't cause any trouble,' Arthur warned as he walked away. Their laughter followed him, and he wondered whether Leslie was right about sending them home. And then he got caught up in more important matters and forgot about them.

The hunters, on the other hand, were short of temper as they found themselves waylaid by group after group of shouting people who successfully prevented them from getting off to an early start. After a number of false starts, one of the hounds picked up a scent.

Charles Latchcham, who was hunting today, turned to the riders clustered behind him. 'At bloody last!' he exclaimed, before draining the little which remained of his flask of brandy. He was frozen to the marrow and thoroughly fed up with the young horse he was riding, which was over-excited and refused to stand still.

'They've got a fox!' Harriet White shouted angrily.

Arthur peered through his binoculars. This was what he enjoyed best. The horsemen hunted the fox, and he hunted the horsemen.

'If they keep running in that direction, we can head them off in the lane that runs through Sempton's lower meadows,' he said.

'Good,' said Harriet. She was middle-aged, dumpy and unattractive, and a devoted Society member.

'I wonder where those bloody kids are,' Leslie said.

'They've probably gone home,' said Arthur. A lot of people had gone home. It was too damn cold for enjoyment.

The youths and the two girls soon tired of following the horses and branched off on their own.

'I don't like it here,' said one of the girls after a while. 'It's bloody freezing, and its boring. Can't we go home?'

'Yeah,' the other one agreed.

All of them were fed up, and it wasn't long before they realised that they were also lost.

'Shit!' said a thin boy called Alf. 'It all looks the same.'

'Couldn't we follow the hedges?' another boy suggested. 'They'll have to take us somewhere.'

They had been walking for twenty minutes when they heard the baying of hounds.

'C'mon,' Alf shouted, breaking into a run, 'let's head them off! We might as well have some fun.'

'Maybe someone will tell us how to get home,' said a girl.

A young fox streaked past them. It had scrambled through a high hedge which was threaded with solid rails and had a ditch running beneath. The hounds were close behind, running silent now as they bore down on their prey.

'There's no gate,' one of the girls said. 'How do the horses get through?'

'They jump,' said her friend.

And to prove it, a large brown horse soared over the hedge, landing close to them. It galloped on, but others followed, some alarmingly close, their hooves throwing up clumps of mud. A man wearing a red jacket swore at them, but they couldn't hear what he said above the din. The two girls were frightened and started to run back, keeping close to the shelter of the hedge.

A bay horse took off without any help from its rider. It was barely two feet from the ground, with the considerable force of its hind legs behind it, when it saw the two people cowering beneath the hedge. One of them looked up and screamed. It seemed impossible to avoid her, but the horse twisted in mid-air, and as its chest crashed into the highest rail, it somersaulted into the ditch.

Lord Charles Latchcham, who was only three paces behind, saw what happened and pulled up his own horse. By bawling loudly and waving his arms, he managed to head off those riders who were still coming on from the far side of the hedge—those who had not already seen the horse go down.

'Christ!' Charles Latchcham swore as he leapt to the ground. The fallen animal lay on top of its rider, who was partly submerged in a stream of water.

The screaming girl was hysterical, and the other unable to move. The boys stood in a silent huddle, their earlier cockiness gone.

Don Farrow, who had now taken over his father's small farm, was the next person there, quickly followed by his wife Nancy.

'Will somebody shut that bloody girl up,' Charles Latchcham said, before taking hold of the reins and trying to calm the terrified horse. 'Don, we'll need some men to move him,' he said. 'That hind leg is broken and we're not going to be able to get him out of the ditch.'

Some riders were catching up the loose horses, and wide-eyed children, many with tears running down their cheeks, were offering to hold others as men and women leapt to the ground. Nancy, who had started up a local branch of the Pony Club and was used to dealing with petulent children, slapped the screaming girl on both cheeks, then called the frightened youths over to look after her.

Charles Latchcham, wading ankle deep in the muddy water, lifted the fallen rider's head. He was unconscious, and the only way they could pull him free was by lifting the horse off him.

From the next field came the mournful sound of the horn. Had it run a little further, the fox would have been saved, for abandoning their cars in the lane, the members of the Anti-Blood Sports Society were streaming through a five-bar gate. Arthur Bennett led them, with Harriet and Leslie at his heels. They were carrying the foul-smelling scents which they planned to lay.

'My God, we're too late!' Harriet exclaimed.

But Arthur's eyes were not on the snarling hounds. He was trying to make out what was happening in another field, where most of the riders had gathered by the hedge.

'I think there's been an accident,' he said.

Leslie screwed up his eyes, and when a horse swung round he saw the cause of the trouble.

'It's those bloody kids,' he said.

Even as he spoke, a horseman broke away from the crowd and pushed his animal into a gallop. For the first time in his life he was pleased to see the despised Society. Arthur stopped, with the others grouped about him, and as the horse came to a skidding halt he felt an awful senation which took him back to another day, another brown horse... But the young man on this animal's back bore no resemblance to Mark Hanley.

'There's been an accident,' Don Farrow gasped. 'It's pretty bad ... we need an ambulance and a gun. Bill Sempton's place is only two miles down the road, but a car would get there a damn sight quicker than I could.'

Arthur turned back to the lane, dropping his bag of scent in the grass.

'Wouldn't it be quicker if we took the rider to hospital ourselves?' somebody asked.

'We've already had to move him more than we should. Tell them he's unconscious and probably has internal injuries,' he shouted after Arthur. 'The horse fell on him.'

Arthur waved as he ran to his car. Harriet looked at the young man.

'What about the horse?' she asked. Animals meant a lot more than people to Harriet, and she could not bear the thought of any creature suffering.

'That's why we need the gun,' said Don harshly.

'I have a rug in the back of my car,' Harriet said. 'It would help keep the injured man warm.'

'Thank you,' said Don. 'We put some jackets over him, but I don't think they're much help.'

Harriet went back to the lane, followed by others who remembered having blankets and flasks in their vehicles. Don swung off his horse when it became apparent that those left were going to walk back with him, and under Leslie's scrutiny he told them what had happened.

With the unconscious man as comfortable as they could make him, Charles Latchcham turned his attention to the staring crowd. He ordered them away in a carrying voice, and in silence they drifted to the lane, hunters and antagonists united in this moment of tragedy.

Charles Latchcham had slashed the girth with a knife and pulled the saddle from the horse's back. He now sat with his feet in the water, and slipping the bridle from its head, talked gently to the shivering animal. It groaned a little, but no longer screamed as it had done when they lifted it. Harriet laid a blanket over the animal's back before she left, and Charles Latchcham thanked her.

'I didn't mean it ... honestly I didn't,' the girl whimpered as she was led away.

Nancy and another young woman stayed beside the fallen rider, while Charles Latchcham and Don Farrow sat with the horse.

When Bill Sempton arrived, Charles Latchcham took the gun and, gritting his teeth, pulled the trigger.

Mary Hanley guessed something was wrong as soon as she opened the door. Charles Latchcham stood there in filthy riding clothes, and with him was the man she recognised as manager of her son's mill.

'Come in,' she said. She knew there was a Meet today; what on earth had brought Charles here now? And what was the other man's name? Brown? Binnington? Bennett!

She led them into the drawing room where damp logs were hissing in the fireplace.

'I think you ought to sit down,' Charles said. 'I'm sorry to burden you with this, Mary, but you know the girl well, and I think it would be best for you to break the news.'

The girl! Mary shivered and sat down. Arthur Bennett sat on another chair, and Charles leant against the mantlepiece, his eyes deliberately avoiding hers.

'Can I get you a drink?' Mary asked. 'Or some coffee?'

'You'd better hear what Lord Latchcham has to say first,' said Arthur Bennett.

She looked at him. He did not turn away, but neither did he return her stare; and the scar, the ugly scar inflicted by her son, looked livid against his pale skin.

'There's been an accident,' Charles Latchcham said. 'Richard Crowder is badly injured. They've taken him to Manchester because they don't think the new hospital in Steelton can cope. It's bad, Mary, really bad.'

Alan had to hire a plane to take him and Lisa to Manchester. He wished now that he'd listened to Mark and learnt to fly.

There was nothing they could do when they got there, but wait. Lisa was allowed to see him, but Richard Crowder did not seem to know she was there. For a week he hovered between life and death; and, impassive throughout the horrendous nightmare, Lisa ran the farm and exerted herself unmercifully as she raced between there and the hospital. Alan rallied to her side as best he could, but this was her world and he was a stranger in it.

During that week he saw a change in his wife which he found distressing. She was suddenly quieter, and would often disappear for hours on end—to where or what, he didn't know. But she always came back pale and frozen and more withdrawn than before.

After six days the doctor told them Richard Crowder would live, but would never walk again.

'Will you tell him or shall I?' Lisa asked, her chin quivering.

'I think he might take it better from the medical profession,' the doctor said.

Mary Hanley had been with Alan and Lisa, and came back with them to the farm, but not until later did she realise that Lisa had disappeared.

'Where is she?' she asked.

'I don't know,' said Alan. 'I've no idea where she goes. I followed her once, and she turned round and came back home. If I ask her, she either changes the subject or ignores me. I don't know what to do, Mary. I can't get through to her any more.'

Orchid Livingstone looked up. 'She has a secret place,' she said. 'Always did have as a little 'un. They used to go there together and neither of them would tell.'

'Them?' Alan asked.

'Mark and Lisa,' said Mary. 'Mark would know where she goes and what she does. I know it's your problem, Alan, but I have a feeling that in this only Mark can help. I think you must get him back.'

Alan stared from the window. 'I don't know where he is,' he said dully. 'And how do you know he'll come? He has his own wife now.'

'Seven days is ample time for a honeymoon,' Mary said, her voice equally flat. 'He'll come if you ask.'

'How do I find him?'

'Somebody must know where he is,' she said. 'Mark isn't a person who can disappear into thin air. He's far too well known.'

Alan wondered if Eric Stewart could help, Eric might perhaps be able to alert the journalistic fraternity; but he came up with a much simpler idea. 'He has the jet,' he said. 'All flight paths have to be recorded, so you only need to find the plane and you've found Mark. Shall I do it for you? I'll probably get things moving much quicker from down here.'

Yes,' said Alan. 'Thank you.'

Chapter Three

Each time I saw Steelton I was alarmed by how much it had grown, and today was no exception. I swung the plane west, towards home, flying below the clouds, and lower than was officially acceptable. On this side of the town urban development halted abruptly, and nostalgically I circled Oldenshaw and Charles Latchcham's ill-managed estates. By the time I landed, Mother was waiting.

'I thought you were going over the end,' she shouted as I leapt to the ground. 'Why didn't you stop sooner?'

'Too slippery,' I said. 'How did you know it was me?'

'Because nobody else would skim over the tree-tops like that. I do wish you wouldn't take such risks, dear.'

I walked over and kissed her cheek. 'It's been a long time.'

'Too long,' she said, 'But where is Caroline? I was looking forward to meeting her.'

'This didn't seem the appropriate time for a family reunion,' I said, leading her to the car. I had been too long in warmer climates, and the wind was cutting through me. 'I left her in London.'

'She couldn't have been pleased,' Mother said. 'If your father had deserted me like that I would probably have run home to Mother.'

I laughed. 'Caroline is thoroughly independent and perfectly able to take care of herself. And she has to do some shopping. Here, let me drive.'

'I'm sorry about this,' Mother said. 'We didn't give you much of a honeymoon, did we? She looks very beautiful from the pictures I've seen.'

'She is,' I said. 'And in case you're wondering, she's not pregnant.'

'The thought never crossed my mind.'

'It crossed Tim's,' I said. 'I could see it in his face when he met us at the airport. One would think I had done something out of the ordinary.'

'You have,' said Mother dryly. 'I'm glad you've finally settled down, but Maude disapproves. She thinks you should have found yourself a nice English girl.'

'With rosy cheeks, a father who hunts with only the best packs and ... I'm sorry, that wasn't very subtle. How is Richard?'

'He will live. How much do you know?'

'Only that he was hurt out hunting and that I was to come immediately. I'm here, but I don't know what I'm expected to do.'

I sensed her hesitation. 'You weren't called back because of Richard,' she said slowly, 'but because of Lisa. She's changed in a way I don't know how to explain. Richard is barely alive, and they had to shoot the horse in the field where it fell, but Alan says that she hasn't shed one tear. She's always been emotional, and if she bottles everything up like this she's going to make herself ill. She also disappears for long periods of time. Orchid says you and she had secret places you went to as children. She thinks Lisa goes to one of them now.'

I knew where she went, where she would always go.

'What about Alan?' I asked.

'He's hurt that she won't talk to him, of course, but he's thinking chiefly of her,' she said. 'He knows there are bonds between you and Lisa which can never be broken, however hard you try.'

'I don't suppose anybody has bothered to ask Lisa how she feels about what you're doing,' I said. 'Our lives touch, Mother, but that's all. Do you think it fair to thrust me upon her without warning?'

'I was wondering whether the shoe mightn't be on the other foot,' Mother said, looking at me. 'I get the impression that it is you, not she, who may buckle beneath the strain.'

Olden Manor came into view. There was a Jaguar parked in the drive.

'Charles saw what happened and so I asked him to come,' Mother said.

I had hoped to find Lisa at the farmhouse, but Alan told me she had been gone for over an hour. They had come back from the hospital, and she had disappeared.

She was at the pond. I stopped at the gate, surprised to see not a tomboy but a smart young woman in tailored slacks and a contrasting jacket. Her hair was held back by a bright scarf, the loose ends fluttering in the wind. Martin's influence, perhaps. But it wasn't the clothes I was seeing, it was the girl, the girl I had loved ... still loved. Why else would I have flown back from halfway across the world without a second thought? I pulled myself together, remembering

Caroline alone in London.

She didn't see me coming because her back was to me, and my steps were muffled by the wet ground. Nor did I call out until I was practically able to touch her.

I thought she hadn't heard, and was about to call again when she turned. She did not need to speak, her eyes said everything. I held out my hand and she took it. I put an arm around her shoulders, and held her close. She shuddered once, and then the tears came.

We stayed like that for a long time, until the sobs lessened. Then I handed her a handkerchief. 'I don't suppose you have one?' I asked.

'No,' she said. 'What are you doing here, Mark? You should be on your honeymoon?'

I smiled. 'The honeymoon is over, and I have business at the mill.'

'No you don't,' she said. 'You came because of me. Is that fair on your wife?'

'Are you being fair on Alan, or yourself? I came because I care. Despite all the years, I still care.'

She brushed her fingertips across my cheek. 'Why tell me now, when it's too late?'

I caught her hand and held it against my lips. '*Because* it is too late,' I said. 'But I don't want to discuss us. We have to talk about Richard. But you're shivering, Lisa. Martin's creations may be fine for the city, but they're not much use out here.'

'I don't want to go back,' she said. 'Not yet.'

'Then let's sit under the willow,' I said, dropping my overcoat over her shoulders.

'You'll freeze.'

'I'll be all right,' I said.

We sat on the edge of the coat in the place where we had sat countless times before; as children, before Fran's wedding, before the rot set in. We huddled close for warmth.

'You know that his back was broken, and he'll never be able to walk again?'

'It could be worse,' I said, taking hold of her hand. 'He could have been killed.'

'I think it would have been better if he had,' she said. 'He's a farmer, Mark. That's his life. What life is he going to have in a wheelchair.'

'He's handicapped,' I told her. 'He will never be able to plough a field or ride a horse again, but with the help of ramps he can learn to get about the farmyard. It's less than he had before, but it's something.'

'But not enough,' she said. 'Not for Daddy. You of all people should know that.'

'It's going to be hard on him,' I said. 'And he's going to need you more than ever before. You have the strength, Lisa. Use it. I shall help all I can, and Alan would hand you his heart on a plate if you asked him.'

'I know,' she said, more tears coming to her eyes. 'But I'm frightened.'

I kissed her on the lips. 'You can do it,' I said. 'You can do anything you want.'

She smiled. 'You're the one person I can always trust. I think I'm ready to go back now.'

'No more running away?' I asked.

'No more running away,' she promised.

I stayed at the farm for lunch, and when I returned to the Manor Mother was still there.

'Was it that bad?' she asked. 'You're looking tense.'

'Reaction to all the travelling, I think. And I still have to get back to London.'

'How about a brandy?' she asked, and poured us both one. 'You spoke to Lisa?'

'Yes,' I said. 'She'll be all right now. I offered to see Richard if it would help, but she thought he might find that a bit patronising.'

'She's right,' she said, and then added, 'You should have married Lisa.'

'We have different partners now, Mother. Please don't open old wounds.'

'They're already open if your expression is anything to go by,' she said. 'I'm sorry. I really am. And won't say anything more about it.' She sipped her drink. 'I waited because I wanted to tell you that Charles has asked me to marry him. I know his reputation leaves a lot to be desired, but four years of persistent courtship shows something of the man's character.'

'And so you're going to become the fourth Lady Latchcham!' I said, smiling.

'Yes,' she said. 'I hope you don't mind.'

I laughed. 'Why should I mind? Congratulations, Mother. I hope you'll be very happy.'

'Thank you, Mark. Now, before you leave, I want to hear all about your Caroline.'

Chapter Four

The Richard Crowder who was discharged from hospital was a very different man from the one everyone remembered. Lisa had hoped that being back at the farm would give him the boost he needed, but after a week he still refused to go outside. He spent most of the time in his new bedroom at the back of the house, only enduring being wheeled into the kitchen for meals, which he picked at without interest. He never spoke except when words were unavoidable, and he showed not the slightest interest in the farm. Everything was left to Lisa, and now that she was almost five months pregnant, the strain was beginning to tell.

'You'll have to go home,' she said to Alan on the morning he found her collecting eggs. 'It's unfair on Marian for us both to stay here for so long, and you're constantly on the telephone to Mark. I know he's too polite to say anything, but he needs you, doesn't he?'

'There are one or two problems,' he admitted. 'But at least I've put the time here to good use and learnt to fly.' He took the basket from her. 'You shouldn't be working so hard. Surely somebody else can do this?'

'I don't mind. Orchid is too busy, and it's not a man's job.' She pushed a hen off its nest. 'Oh Alan, what are we going to do? We can't go on like this for much longer.'

'If he refuses to run the farm, we'll have to hire a manager and bring him down to London.'

'He'd never agree to that,' she said.

'Perhaps not, but the threat of it might jolt him out of his lethargy. He's a cripple, Lisa, and will never be anything else. He has to accept it.'

'Give me a little longer with him,' she said. 'When will you go back?'

'I think the day after tomorrow, if that's all right by you.'

'Of course,' she said. 'Be careful of that speckled hen. She bites.'

'Isn't Mummy ever going to come home?' Marian asked.

'Soon,' Alan said, watching her mount the pony.

'Why can't I go and see Grandad?'

'Yes, why can't she?' another voice said.

Alan swung round and Tumbleweed sidestepped as the child unintentionally jabbed his mouth. Mark looked fit and healthy, and happier than Alan could remember in a long time.

'Uncle Mark!' Marian yelped. She leapt off the pony, scrambled through the fence and ran to him. He swung her into the air like he always did.

'You're getting far too big,' he said. 'And look at poor Tumbleweed. If he steps on that trailing rein he's going to break it.'

She laughed, and went back to the pony. 'Will you watch me?' she asked.

'Of course,' he said, and then turned to Alan. 'I hope you don't mind me coming round, but I wanted to see you away from the office.'

'How did you know I was back?'

Mark smiled. 'A spy in the camp. Mother telephoned this morning and told me you'd left.'

Marian had gathered the reins and was pushing the pony into a reluctant trot round the stable yard. 'Daddy ...! Uncle Mark ...!' she shouted. 'Are you watching?'

'Yes, darling,' said Alan.

'Why don't you take her to the farm next weekend?'

'Lisa doesn't want her there. I'm not sure if I do either.'

'She has to find out about Richard some time,' Mark said. 'And maybe her being there will help.' He looked up as Chanson kicked the stable door. 'That horse needs exercise.'

'If you can find the time, you're welcome to take her out. I wish you would.' Alan stamped his cold feet. 'I'm sorry to keep you out here, but Marian will be disappointed if we desert her so soon. What did you want to see me about?'

Mark leant against the fence. 'Toes up and in,' he shouted to Marian. They went up, but not in. 'There's trouble brewing, and I'm going to need some help. It's Chris. Did you know that he and Henry have been fighting?'

'Yes,' said Alan. 'But their rows seemed to blow over with no harm done. Henry is an ambitious young man and it's inevitable that he and Chris should clash sometimes.'

Mark sighed. 'This time it's more than a difference of opinion.

Norma tells me they had an enormous set-to a month ago. Now the rest of the staff are taking sides. To put it in a nutshell, Chris has accused Henry of trying to push him out so he can take his place, and Henry says Chris is a doddering old fool who is letting good talent slip through our fingers because he's prejudiced towards the new groups which are coming up.'

'Shit!' Alan swore.

'Henry is right,' Mark said. 'I'm afraid that Chris is getting too old. Because of him, two groups and four soloists have been rejected by us, and then gone on to better things with other companies. Have you seen the charts recently?'

Alan shook his head. That side of the business invariably passed over him.

'There's a group called Memorial who've held the number one slot for the past fortnight. We have a test recording of them singing the same song ... And that's just one example. If it goes on like this, I'll lose Henry. I know he's had other offers. As a temporary measure I've promised him that I'll personally vet every test we make from now on. It's an extra burden for me to carry, but if I only vet the ones which Chris throws out, he's going to know what's happening; this way, he'll just think I'm a bloody nuisance with nothing better to do.'

'You'll never cope,' said Alan. 'Not on top of everything else.'

'I shall have to. I can't very well throw Chris out on his arse. I owe him too much. But I'd like you to keep an eye on them both and smooth down any ruffled feathers when necessary.'

'Can't you do something else with him?' Alan asked.

Mark shook his head. 'He's an excellent manager. Perhaps if I could find someone worthwhile ...' His voice trailed off.

'Which is easier said than done,' said Alan. 'How's your wife going to feel about you taking on extra commitments?'

The blue gaze turned to him. 'Caroline knew what she was letting herself in for. By the way, she expects you for dinner tonight. I hope you don't mind the short notice?'

'Of course not,' Alan said. 'I would come with no notice whatsoever. I'm dying to meet the lady. I think we've shown enough interest in Marian. How about coming indoors?'

'Give her a few more minutes,' said Mark. 'She's enjoying showing off. By the way, did you know that Eric has been indulging in some pretty heavy gambling?'

'I guessed he was living beyond his means.' Eric and Fran now owned a large house in Surrey, with the children attending expensive private schools. There was also Eric's succession of mistresses, and the gambling clubs he was known to frequent. 'Is he dipping into

Fran's trust again?'

Mark shook his head. 'She was foolish enough to give him the money before, but she used the rest for collateral against that white elephant of a house they've bought. I know Eric's private life is none of my business, but keep an eye on him, Alan. Something's wrong. I don't believe he can be winning all that consistently, not when he's betting four and five figure amounts. That adds up to an awful lot of money.'

'Are you sure you've got it right?' Alan asked, frowning. 'Where would Eric get that sort of money?'

'That's what's worrying me, especially as the information came from a reliable source.' He rubbed his chilled hands together. 'I think I'm ready for that drink now.'

Marian ran, crying, to her mother.

'You had no right to bring her here!' yelled Richard Crowder. 'Keep her away. I don't want to see her!'

Lisa glared at him before taking the child out of the room. 'Come along, darling,' she said. 'Don't cry. Let's see if Orchid can find something nice for you.'

Orchid had heard the shouting, and when Lisa brought Marian into the kitchen she was looking through some tins for the child's favourite currant biscuits. Alan put down his newspaper.

'I think we must have finished them,' Orchid said. 'But Harold might have some left. Let's go and see.'

The moment she and Marian had gone Lisa turned on her husband.

'For God's sake, Alan, why the hell did you bring her here? She's the last person he wants to see, and the way he yelled at her was terrible.'

'I thought it might help,' he said.

'Well, it hasn't. And what a bloody awful weekend we're going to have.'

She sat down, and reaching across the table, he took hold of her hands. They were cold, and she was looking ill. It wasn't just Marian. She was trying too hard, and working impossible hours when she should be resting.

'I'll keep an eye on Marian,' he promised.

'We all will,' she said. She was so tired that she didn't even have the energy to argue with him.

In the afternoon they visited Mary Hanley. It got Marian out of the house for a while, and gave Alan the opportunity to tell Mary about her son's wife.

'Don't expect an accurate description,' said Lisa. 'From what I've gathered, she's only missing a halo and gossamer wings!'

Lisa was outside with Marian when Mary said to Alan, 'Was it you who decided to bring Marian for the weekend, or are you covering up for someone? Mark, for instance?'

'Why do you ask?'

'Because I know you better than you seem to think, and I certainly know Mark better than he likes to think. He's not always right, you know.'

'I didn't have to take his advice,' Alan said.

'I know. But you invariably do.' She paused. 'I think you should take Lisa away from here. She's looking ill.'

'How can I?' he asked. 'She'll never leave while Richard's like this.'

'Then start showing a little more dominance. Perhaps if she isn't here, Richard will be forced to take an interest.'

Alan could not bear to be alone with Richard Crowder, and while Sunday lunch was being prepared he sat in the kitchen.

'Why can't you keep Marian company?' Lisa asked after tripping over his legs for the third time. 'Where is she anyway?'

'In her room, reading,' he said.

She glanced towards the ceiling. 'Well, if you must stay you can help me draw up a feeding chart for the calves.'

They had nearly finished when Harold came into the kitchen. He was grinning broadly.

Lisa glanced up. 'Come and tell me what you think,' she said.

Orchid slammed a pot onto the stove. 'I'll not have you trotting those muddy boots over my clean floor,' she said to Harold.

'Well, I'm not taking them off,' said the old man. 'And I never came for them charts, Miss Lisa. I wanted to congratulate you. It's grand to see him out again, even if I did get bawled at for having the bullocks in the wrong field.'

'Congratulate me for what?' Lisa asked. Her eyes widened. 'It's grand to see who out again, Harold?'

'Don't you know?' he asked. 'Young Marian has been pushing him about the yard for the past half hour. A right proper little nurse she is, too.'

'Daddy?' Lisa gasped, leaping to her feet.

'Aye. You can probably see them from here. They were with the horses just now.'

Lisa rushed to the window. The four Clydesdales were standing at the gate, Snowy with them. Marian was feeding the pony, while

Richard Crowder leant forward in his wheelchair, fondling the proud heads of his beauties.

'He's going to be all right,' she said. 'Alan, he's really going to be all right!'

'What are you going to do with them now, Grandad?' Marian asked.

Richard Crowder smiled at his grand-daughter. She was growing up, and the baby fat was disappearing. She reminded him of Lisa at that age, and there was something too, he thought, of her father in her.

'I'll harness them to the hay wagon,' he said. 'Then they can take me anywhere.'

Marian screwed up her small face and laughed. 'The hay wagon is far too big,' she said. 'It would be like driving a bus.'

She was right. He would need something smaller, like a dray. He reached up, and Jinny dropped her nose into his hands.

'Aye, my beauties,' he said. 'There'll be no more champion rosettes, but I'm not beaten yet. We'll show them all what we're made of. That we will.'

Chapter Five

It was April when Lisa went home, and by then she was so exhausted that all she wanted to do was rest. She rarely left the house at Ham, but her friends were in and out so much that she was never alone, and Mark came as often as he could to exercise Chanson. Caroline sometimes came with him, chatting with Lisa while he was out.

Mary Hanley and Lord Charles Latchcham were married in May. Lisa insisted on going to the wedding, and Mark brought his bride to Oldenshaw for the first time. The past few months had been hard on them both, and they had rowed constantly over his work. He had wasted valuable time listening to the test tapes which flowed in daily, and invariably arrived home late with a blistering headache and frayed temper. Caroline did not have the temperament for sitting at home and waiting for her errant husband. They had been inundated with invitations, but more and more often she found herself attending the parties and functions unescorted, in the company of friends. She had laughed about it at first, then grown resentful and finally angry. That was when the rows began. In the beginning he had been contrite. He would let her rant for a while, before he soothed away the anger by making love to her. But he too became more irritable as the long hours spent at work began to take their toll. The rows worsened, and their bed became part of the battle ground, with their short marriage running headlong towards disaster.

But in Oldenshaw Caroline saw an opportunity to get back a little of the happiness they seemed to have lost.

'Let's stay for a few more days,' she said on the morning Alan took Lisa back to London.

It was chilly but sunny, and they were sitting in the garden. Mark was looking more relaxed than she had seen him for a long time.

'You'd be bored silly in two days,' he said.

'No I wouldn't,' she said, kneeling beside him. 'Please, Mark. For a few days let's be only you and me. Forget about the bloody business for a while. Alan is there, and it's not going to run away.'

He laughed. 'No theatres or restaurants?' he asked. 'Nor those feather-brained friends of yours whose one purpose in life is to have a good time?'

'I don't need them, not when I've got you,' she said. 'I've never really had you, not since we set foot in this bloody country.'

He kissed her forehead. 'All right,' he agreed. 'But if you're thinking of rearranging the house, please don't fill it with modern junk.'

'You mean it? We can really stay?'

'If you want to,' he said. 'I know I haven't been easy to live with these past few months.'

'Thank you, Mark,' she said, laying her head on his knees. 'And I won't change a thing in the house, except ...'

'Except what?'

She looked at him. 'Except that we should install a pool. A great house like this should have a swimming pool.'

'We're in England, not California!' he said.

'I know. But a heated pool would be nice in summer. I should like to come here for a short while every summer. We'll both come. You're so different now that you're away from London.'

'All right, Caro,' he said. 'You shall have your swimming pool. Everyone will think we're stark raving mad. Where d'you want it?'

'Over there. At the side of the house.'

'It would be better a little further to the left,' he said, screwing his eyes into the sunshine. 'We could have the patio leading from the summer room built out onto it. And if we're to have contractors and builders in, I may as well act the country squire and have the cottages done up.'

'The village?' she asked. If Mark were to get involved with the village, their stay could last all summer. It would mean missing some of the more important social events of the season; she particularly wanted to go to Ascot next month and had already bought a new outfit. But it was worth missing everything if she could keep him out of that damn office for a while.

'Some of them are starting to look shabby,' he said. 'We'll go on an inspection tour tomorrow.'

When the new Lady Latchcham returned from her honeymoon she was surprised to find Mark and Caroline still at the Manor, and the entire village undergoing renovations. It appeared nothing had been left undone, and even the church was getting a new roof.

Mark knew Caroline was deliberately trying to keep him here, but Alan was managing without him, and truth be told, he was happy. Because she was making such an effort, he too tried to be less inflexible. They avoided London, but he took her to Ascot because he knew she wanted to go; and there were a couple of garden parties and a charity banquet. But apart from these occasions, they remained locked away from the world at Olden Manor. Charles Latchcham had offered Mark a young horse which was in training for next season's hunting, and he took it out every morning. It was on one of these rides that he met Richard Crowder in Oldenshaw. The farmer's lifeless legs were propped on the platform of a cart which was drawn by Jinny and Drummer.

'Is that Charles' new hunter?' Richard asked. 'I heard he was training one. Looks like he'll do well. Back's a mite long, but the bone is good. Are you going in or coming out?'

'Going in,' Mark said. 'But I'll ride along with you if you want.'

'Aye. I need to speak with you. Will he walk?'

'He'll walk,' Mark confirmed as he turned the horse in the same direction as the cart. 'I don't know why, but whenever someone has an under-exercised or unschooled horse, I'm offered it.'

He realised, too late, the carelessness of his words.

'Don't worry about me, lad,' said Richard Crowder. 'I've grown used to having no legs. I only regret what happened to the horse. Kingston was a good animal who'd go until he dropped. But you know that. It was a brutal end.'

And you feel you're to blame for it, Mark thought shrewdly. 'He died humanely,' he said gently.

'Aye. But he were Lisa's horse. Perhaps if it had been one of these two beauties, I wouldn't feel so guilty.'

'Rubbish,' Mark snapped with a hint of impatience. 'Would you have felt guilty about the horse if Lisa had been riding him that day? If she, not you, had broken her back? Kingston would still be dead. If Trojan here decided to bolt into a lorry I'm damn sure I wouldn't live my life feeling guilty because my stepfather's horse got killed.' He stopped abruptly and smiled. 'At my age it seems strange to refer to Charles Latchcham as my stepfather. But I suppose he is, God help him. Lisa doesn't blame you for Kingston. She never did.'

Richard Crowder was staring at the swaying backs of his horses. They had passed the last cottage, and the deserted road echoed the twelve shod hooves. Mark still handled a horse well, and Richard Crowder shuddered as he remembered the time that fool man had thrown a firework at Kingston. It was a time which belonged to another life, another world.

'You must be spending a fortune on the village,' he said, wishing he could forget the memories which haunted him more and more these days.

'I never realised how run down the cottages were until I walked round and saw for myself,' Mark said. 'As landlord I'm responsible for their upkeep. But nobody ever thinks to let me know unless a roof collapses, like it did at Nutcracker Cottage a couple of years ago. If I had any sense I'd sell the lot. If it weren't for Mother, I would. She thinks property dealers will move in and turn the place into a suburb of Steelton.'

Richard Crowder gazed at him. 'You don't think that possible?' he asked.

The young horse shied at a cigarette packet and Mark was kept busy for a few minutes, trying to bring him under control. He came back to a walk, his eyes bulging as he searched for more terrifying objects.

'Mother's not a fool, or an alarmist,' Mark said. 'Which is why I don't sell. Steelton has been able to expand in every direction except this one. We must be a constant source of irritation, because unless the developers can break through the cordon which consists of you, Charles and me, they'll get nowhere. What I can't understand is why so many farmers on the other side gave way. They sold out field by field. Perhaps they made a quick profit at the time, but once the foundations of the new buildings have been dug, nothing can bring back the land. You're a farmer, do you know why they sold?'

Richard Crowder continued to stare straight ahead. 'Take Ned Crawford,' he said. 'He sold everything last year. They were closing in all round him and there was nowt worth salvaging, and no capital to do it with anyhow. Now he's in a council house, working as a watchman, while his two eldest boys have gone into a factory. The small farmer can't stand up against an onslaught.'

The hunter was bored and kept tossing its head. Mark held him at a sidling walk. 'Why did Crawford sell out?' he asked. 'His family had been there for five generations. It would have taken more than a few houses to scare him away.'

'He sold his first field about six years ago,' Richard told him. 'After his barn burnt down, destroying the store of winter hay and killing some cows. He never did recover from the loss. After that, the fields began disappearing one after the other.'

'How did the barn catch fire?' said Mark sharply.

Richard looked at him. 'Nobody knows,' he said. 'The police say it was an accident, but there's many would agree with me that there've been too many accidents over the years. And each time something happens, *he's* there, like a bloody vulture.'

'Arthur Bennett,' said Mark.

'You knew?' Richard asked.

'Not that. Only how he's buying everything he can lay his hands on.'

'He's after my farm,' Richard said. 'He knows he'll not budge you, and that Latchcham Hall is here to stay. But he thinks I might give up. He came over last month and made me an offer. I told him that if he came again I'd get out my shotgun. I may have lost the use of my legs, but while there's breath in my body, I'll not have my land go to anyone of his sort. And that, lad, is what I wanted to see you about.'

'Do you want me to speak ...?'

'Nay,' Richard cut in. 'I'll fight my own battles. I always have. It would take more than a burnt down barn to budge me. But it's not now I'm worried about. It's later. When I'm gone. Everything will go to Lisa, and however hard she tries, I don't think she'll be able to cope.'

'That's a long way off,' Mark said.

'Perhaps. Perhaps not.'

A car passed them and the hunter broke into a plunging canter. It gave Mark the opportunity to disguise his shock, for he saw now that Richard Crowder had changed more than anyone had realised. He had accepted his fate, but there was something else, something dark and ultimate which would decide his future.

'What do you want me to do?' he asked, hoping Richard would not notice the sudden hoarseness in his voice.

'Something I have no right to ask you,' said the farmer. 'But I know you'll not let me down. I want your promise that you'll never see any harm come to the farm. I'd never rest in peace knowing that houses and factories had been built in my meadows.'

Mark had recovered, and his sombre eyes rested on Richard's face. 'Arthur Bennett will never lay a hand on a single tree. I promise.'

'And the others?' said Richard. 'Arthur Bennett's not the only one.'

'Nobody will ever build here,' Mark said.

Richard Crowder smiled in relief.

Chapter Six

Lisa had a son. He was called David, and when his parents brought him to Oldenshaw for his christening, they asked me to be his godfather. Caroline and I returned to London soon afterwards.

It was inevitable that we should slide back into our old routine. I tried to be more considerate, and Caroline did not nag as much, and somehow we managed to get through what was left of summer.

It was in September, just after Alan had come back from America, that Caroline said, 'You need a holiday. You work far too hard. What good is all your money if you never get any pleasure from it? The mill runs without you, and so does the magazine; even Martin can survive, so why can't the damn recording company?'

'All right,' I said. 'Where do you want to go?'

She stared at me for a moment, and then, with a squeal of delight, threw her arms around my neck. 'You mean it?' she said. 'You really mean it?'

'Yes,' I answered. 'I give you a rotten time, Caro. We can leave at the end of October and get back for Christmas.'

It was mid-October when Marian came to my office. I had told Norma that I did not want to be disturbed, and when the child peered round the door I could see the consternation on her face.

'Can I come in, Uncle Mark?' Marian asked.

'Of course,' I said. 'What are you doing here?'

'I have something to ask you. Mummy told me not to, but I slipped away when she wasn't looking.'

'Do you want something to drink?'

'Do you have fizzy lemonade?'

'Yes. In that cupboard. And ice if you want it.'

'*And ice*!' she said, her eyes wide with delight. 'Daddy doesn't have ice in his office. He doesn't even have lemonade.'

'What do you want to see me about?' I asked when she was sipping the drink.

'I'd like you and Aunt Caroline to come to the concert next Friday.'

'What concert?'

'The one her school is giving,' said Lisa from the doorway. 'Marian, I told you not to worry Uncle Mark.'

'He doesn't mind,' the child said. 'Look, he gave me a drink.'

I turned round, staring at her like a simpleton. 'Where is your hair?' I asked when I was able to find my voice.

'Stuffing cushions for all I know,' she said 'You sound just like Alan. And I don't care if neither of you like it because I do, and so does Martin. It matches his new look.'

Damn Martin, I thought.

'I like it short too,' said Marian.

Lisa smiled at her. 'You still have to learn that men would have us in crinolines if they had their way. Now hurry up with that drink. Daddy's waiting to take us home.'

'What about this concert?' I asked.

'You'd be bored stiff,' said Lisa. 'It's a school concert, and as doting parents we have to go. But she had no right to blackmail you into coming as well.'

Marian finished her lemonade and put the glass on a table. 'I'm dancing a solo,' she said. 'I'm the only one who is, and Madame says I'm the best in the class. Anyway, it's not only our school. It's lots and lots of schools in a proper theatre.' She looked at me with eyes which were pure Lisa. 'Please come, Uncle Mark.'

'I'll try,' I said.

'You promise? Cross your heart and hope to die?'

'Marian!'

'Cross my heart and hope to die,' I agreed.

'I knew you would,' she said. 'Come along, Mummy.'

'You run ahead,' said Lisa. 'I'll be with you in a minute.' She waited until Marian had gone, and then turned to me. 'I'm sorry, Mark. If you really want to come, you and Caroline can eat with us afterwards. But if you're wise, you'll come down with some convenient complaint. It's sure to be terrible.'

Perhaps Martin was right about the hairstyle. Now that the initial shock had worn off I quite liked it.

'I'd better go,' she was saying. 'Goodbye, Mark ... no, please don't bother to see me out.'

'I'm not coming to some bloody kid's concert!' Caroline screamed. 'You've let me down time after time, and now you expect me to sit through a couple of hours of screeching children. Well, I damn well won't.'

'As the entire neighbourhood probably knows,' I said.

She stood in front of me, her eyes furious. 'Stanley Walpole has been pestering me to go out with him for months. At least I know that he'll take me somewhere decent.'

I sighed. 'Do what you want, Caroline.'

'You bloody bastard,' she said, and slammed from the room.

I lit another cigarette, drank a couple of whiskies, and settled down with a novel.

It must have been very late when she crept downstairs. Roberts had said goodnight a long time ago, and in over an hour there had been no sound from the street. I had almost finished the book, but had no idea what it was about.

The door opened.

'Aren't you coming to bed, Mark?' Caroline plaintively asked. 'It's gone two, and I'm lonely without you.'

I put down the book. 'It won't work,' I said. 'You're wasting your time.'

She looked startled. 'What won't work?'

'Your sex, darling. Tonight I can be neither tempted nor wooed.'

'You're drunk,' she said.

'Only mildly. Go back to bed.'

She stood in a flimsy nightgown, watching me.

'Will you come up?'

'No,' I said. 'You'd only regret it. And tomorrow morning I'd regret it even more.'

'Shit,' she muttered. 'If it's that damn important then I'll come to the bloody concert.'

And she slammed the door so hard that it must have reverberated through the entire house.

When I went upstairs a short while later she was either asleep or else pretending to be. I couldn't be bothered to find out which.

The concert was terrible. Marian came on just after the interval and was very good for her age. That was the best that could be said for anyone there. I closed my eyes and was half asleep when I heard the beautifully pitched voice rendering an evergreen song from my schooldays. I opened my eyes and saw an unattractive girl of about sixteen, who stood awkwardly with her hands clasped over her stomach.

'It's nearly finished,' Caroline whispered. 'And as you insisted on coming, it's your own fault if you're bored.'

The song ended, and the girl fled from the stage.

'Caro,' I said, raising my voice above the half-hearted applause. 'Please ask Alan to come outside with me.'

She raised her eyebrows. 'Why?' she asked. And then she glanced towards the stage. 'Not *her*?'

The next act, a recital, was filing onstage. 'I think she might have something,' I said. 'I'm not sure.'

I had forgotten to lower my voice and the woman behind me tutted angrily.

'You're mad,' Caroline hissed. But she conveyed the message. Lisa looked startled, and Alan shattered.

'You can't leave now,' Lisa whispered. 'We're in the middle of a row. Can't it wait until the end?'

'No,' I said, and stood up. 'She might be gone by then.'

The woman tutted again, and then, with Alan behind me, I hurried out of the auditorium into the foyer.

'You're crazy,' he said as I led him backstage.

'In legal matters I would put my life in your hands,' I told him. 'In the music field you ought to trust me.'

Backstage in any theatre is chaos, but here it was a thousand times worse. I was wondering how we would find the girl when Marian spotted us.

'Daddy ... Daddy ... did you like it?' she shouted. 'I tried my hardest.'

'You were beautiful, darling,' he said as she ran up to us.

She turned to me. 'You were better than the lot of them put together,' I told her.

'Do you really think so?' she asked. 'What are you doing here? You're going to get into awful trouble if you're seen.'

Alan took hold of her hand. 'Uncle Mark is looking for the girl who was singing just now. Do you know where she is?'

'The fat one?' she said. 'What do you want to see her for? She wasn't very good. Everyone laughed at her.'

'Marian, you might be laughed at one day,' said Alan. 'Do you know where she is?'

'She belongs to Eastcote Secondary School. But they're awfully rough and common. I'm sure Uncle Mark won't like them one bit.'

'Uncle Mark can judge for himself,' Alan said. 'And since when did you start calling people common?'

'Well, they are.'

'Do you know where she is, Marian?' I asked. 'I really would like to speak to her before she leaves.'

'Well ... ' she answered with irritating slowness. 'Their dressing

room is along that passage, but she never went there.'
'Where did she go?' I asked gently.
She smiled. 'I'll show you,' she said. She led us further back, away from the immediate bustle. 'She went in there,' she said, pointing towards a room which looked as though it contained props. 'But she might have gone by now.'
She had not gone. She was sitting on an old trunk. Marian left reluctantly, for she was obviously dying to know what business I had with a common fat girl.
'Be careful you don't send her into hysterics,' Alan cautioned as I was about to step into the room. 'If she yells rape we're going to find ourselves in an embarrassing situation.' We should have kept Marian for a little longer, but it was too late now.
'You sang very well,' I said from the doorway.
She didn't cry rape, but she leapt off the trunk as though a bomb had exploded beneath her, and when she swung round she looked hostile rather than afraid.
'Who are you?' she asked with a broad cockney twang.
And God, she was unattractive. Beneath the make-up her skin was thick with spots, and she looked much fatter than she had on stage. 'I'd like to talk to you,' I said. 'This is Alan Weston. What is your name and how old are you?'
She took a backward step. 'Catherine Bridges,' she said. 'I'll be seventeen next month. What of it?'
I turned to Alan. 'We wouldn't have trouble with her age, then,' I said.
The girl sank back onto the trunk. 'Who the hell are you?' she asked.
'My name is Mark Hanley.'
She closed her eyes and gulped loud enough for us both to hear.
'Come off it,' she stammered. 'You're having me on. The likes of him would never come here ... not to see me.'
'Strange though it seems, he has,' I said.

Because he knew her I sent Alan to fetch Catherine Bridges. I was hoping she possessed the potential I had glimpsed at the concert; then I could hand her to Chris, and Henry could take over the recording side of the business while I got on with salvaging what tattered remains were left of my marriage.
Alan was late back. Catherine looked frightened and awed as her eyes flew around my office. She was different from the last time I had seen her, and it took me a moment to realise that the change was due to the thick black lines around her eyes, and a dress which was far too

tight and emphasised every bulge of her overweight body. I looked at her, and wondered whether I had bitten off more than I could chew.

'Hello, Catherine,' I said. 'Are you nervous?'

'I'm bloody terrified,' she replied, smiling. It was a charming smile which transformed her and gave me a ray of hope. 'Cor, this ain't half some set-up. Is it all yours?'

'Yes.' I said. 'Would you like to see round it?'

'Could I?' she asked. 'Even me mum and dad didn't believe me when I said I was coming here. What do you want me to sing? Mr. Weston didn't seem to know.'

'Sit down, Catherine,' I said, holding a chair for her. 'Alan deals with the legal side of the business. I chose this song for you. It's one of Marty Pole's old numbers. Go through the words, and then we'll try a couple of practice runs. I'm not after perfection, only an idea of your range.'

She took the score from me. 'I know this,' she said. 'I got all his records. He was the greatest, was Marty Pole. But I never hear of him any more.'

'He's gone,' Alan said sharply. 'Can I have a word with you, Mark?'

'Later,' I replied.

'Don't mind me,' said the girl. 'I think I've forgotten some of the words.'

We went into Norma's office. 'What's wrong now?' I asked.

'She's a nice kid,' he said. 'I admit she's a bit rough around the edges, but I like her, and don't want to see her tread the same path as the others.'

'Marty Pole, for instance? He never had any real talent, just a sexy way of swinging his hips. The same can be said for most of them.'

'And you want her to become another puppet?' he asked. 'I suppose once she's outlived her usefulness she'll be thrown out like a piece of junk. What kind of future is that?'

I did not reply immediately. In all the years we had been together Alan had never questioned a decision I'd made. 'She has a choice,' I said slowly. 'I cannot force her into anything.'

'What choice? She's from a poor family, and she'd be lucky to find a job at all when she leaves school. To her this is a dream come true.'

'Then doesn't she deserve the chance?' I asked. 'Not everyone goes off the rails. Look at Simon Townsend. He improves year by year, he's already rated as one of the country's top male singers. He came from a family of six immigrants who lived in two rooms. Why shouldn't Catherine Bridges get the same chance? If you're worried about her future, arrange to look after her finances. You seem to have given Simon plenty of advice and Martin, I know, leaves everything to you.'

He smiled. 'Martin needs looking after. He's hopeless with money and always will be. You won't give her any false hopes?'

'No,' I assured him.

She very nearly blew it. She looked atrociously fat and insignificant as she stood in the recording room, headphones clamped over her ears and the sheet of music trembling in her hands. Alan, Chris and I were in the control room with Tony Crane and his assistant.

'Tony will run through the music as many times as you want to hear it,' I told her. 'Listen carefully. Hum it if that helps, and when you feel ready, let us know. Do you understand?'

She nodded, then listened to it once, and in a small voice said that she was ready. Tony re-wound the tape and cued her in. She uttered a high pitched squeal which bore no resemblance to any note that I had ever heard, and dried up, staring at us with frightened eyes.

Chris swore beneath his breath. 'What the hell did you see in her?' he asked.

I ignored him. 'Try it again, Catherine,' I said. 'Take a deep breath and concentrate on the music. Don't worry about us.'

'All right,' she whispered.

But her second attempt was no better than the first, nor was the third, fourth or fifth. I could see she was reaching the end of her tether. I was about to start her off again when the door behind us opened.

'Get out, whoever you are!' I shouted.

'Sod you, too,' said June. 'I thought marriage would mellow you, but I was obviously wrong. You asked me to come, so here I damn well am. Norma sent me down. She said you were trying out a new girl.'

'I'm sorry,' I said, swinging round. 'I hoped this would be finished by now. Sit down and watch. She's the reason I asked you here.'

June walked forward, and screwing up her eyes, peered through the glass which separated us from Catherine. 'Well, she wouldn't win any beauty contest,' she said sarcastically.

'We're well aware of that,' I said, 'which is why she's going to need all the help she can get, including everything the magazine has to offer.'

'Then you want Eric, not me,' she said dryly.

'This is an exception,' I told her. 'What I intend to do falls into your department.'

I turned back to Catherine. 'Let's try it one more time.' She murmured her agreement and quickly wiped away a tear.

'She's had enough,' Alan said. 'She can't do it. Stop forcing her, Mark.'

'Stay out of this,' I warned him. 'I am more than aware of her limitations. Catherine ...'

'I can't!' she cried out. 'I'm sorry, but I can't ...'

Alan stood up. 'That's enough!' he said angrily. 'The poor kid is scared to death.'

'And any moron could see why,' said June, who'd taken a chair against the far wall. 'Only a bunch of unfeeling men would dream of putting a child like that in a room that resembles a goldfish bowl and expect her to perform like a bloody professional.'

'Why don't you go in there and hold her hand?' I snapped.

'Why don't you?' she fired back. 'Good God, you of all people should know what it's like. Take those bloody things off her ears. Sit in there with her and talk her through it. You'll be surprised at the difference it makes.'

I looked at the girl. Her face was colourless and she was trying to hold back a flood of tears.

'Pipe the music through the main speakers,' I told Tony. 'And have you got a Coke or something in here?'

He took a can from the cupboard behind him and handed it to me. 'Maybe you should forget it for today,' he suggested. 'She's pretty strung out.'

'If she doesn't calm down, I will,' I said.

I went into the recording room, and gave her the Coke. 'Peace offering,' I said. 'Let's sit down and talk this over. And if you really don't want to try it again, you needn't.'

She smiled that enchanting smile. 'I'll try,' she said. 'If you stay in here with me.'

And this time she didn't let me down. She missed the cue and came in late, but once she had caught up she sang like a nightingale.

'How's that?' she asked when it was finished.

'Good,' I said. 'Better than Marty ever did it.'

She blushed. 'You're having me on. Do I have to do it again?'

'No, Catherine,' I said. 'I'd like to listen to the tape now. Do you want to stay, or would you rather go to the canteen?'

'You got a canteen too?'

I nodded. If the tape had captured what I had heard, it was going to be a long, long time before she was let loose in a canteen again. I sent her away with Alan, and June decided she might as well join them, as the cramped control room was giving her claustrophobia.

'Her voice is good,' Chris said when they had gone. 'But what about the rest of her?'

'It can be improved on,' I said. 'But I need someone to take charge of her.'

He was silent for a moment. 'That's why I'm here, isn't it? You want me to do it?'

'Yes,' I said. 'I think she could be great, Chris. Look what you did with me. You can do even more with her.'

I hadn't expected it to be easy, but I think Chris knew what was going on behind his back, for he did not argue.

'Would I have absolute control of her?' he asked.

'Yes. You would only be answerable to me.'

He looked down at his pudgy hands and sighed. 'I'd like to have another Mark Anthony. Do you really think she'll be of that calibre?'

I squeezed his shoulder affectionately. 'She can be even greater,' I said. 'After all, she has our mistakes to learn from.'

Later in the afternoon we gathered in my office. Catherine sat opposite me, with Chris to her left, a curious look of achievement in his eyes. Alan stood beside the window, and June had made herself comfortable on the sofa.

I looked at Catherine. 'Before we go any further I want you to understand what will be happening,' I said. 'The next few months are going to be hell and by the time they're over you're going to hate the mention of my name.'

She smiled, and a blush spread upwards from her neck. 'I'd never hate you, Mr. Hanley. I know I'll have to diet, and I don't suppose the spots help much neither.'

'They don't help at all,' I said. 'But I'm afraid you need a good deal more than a diet. I want Chris to take charge of you. He knows what he's doing, and you'll be in good hands.'

'What about you?' she asked.

I saw Alan's delighted smile before he turned away. 'I won't be here,' I said. 'But you'll be kept busy, and you'll meet all sorts of interesting people. Have you heard of Martin Henderson?'

She looked blank for a moment. 'Ain't he a famous designer who makes clothes for the big nobs?'

'He's going to make you a new wardrobe,' I said.

'You'll have to thin her down before she meets him,' said June.

'I know. That's why I didn't ask him to join us.'

'You must know him awfully well,' the girl said.

'His business is a subsidiary of this,' Alan told her.

'Could you stand by that table for a moment,' I said to Catherine.

She stared at me. 'Why?'

'Because I asked you to. And because if we're to get anywhere, you have to learn to obey orders whether you like them or not.'

She pulled a face. 'I feel like something at a cattle auction,' she complained.

'Then obviously you've never been to one,' I said. 'Somebody usually chases them round a ring with a big stick. Now turn round. Right round ... slowly.'

'I feel silly,' she said as we viewed some of her worst points.

I glanced at Chris. 'She'll have to go to a health farm,' he said. 'Even then, I'm not really sure.'

But her arms were not too fat, nor were her legs, what I could see of them.

'Pull up your skirt,' I said.

She raised the hem a half inch above her knees.

'Is this really necessary?' Alan asked.

I glared at him. 'Lisa's hemlines are verging on indecency. If Martin has a hang-up on legs, I need to know what we have to offer him.'

'Martin never puts more than a quarter-inch hem on anything he makes for Lisa,' he said gloomily. 'She wouldn't be able to take them down if she wanted to.'

I smiled, and turned back to the girl. 'Stop dithering, Catherine.'

She pulled up the skirt. Her legs were long and straight, but chubby round the thighs. That would probably disappear with the other superfluous fat.

'Well?' said Chris.

'I think we could do it,' I said.

'Can I put me skirt down?' the girl whined.

'You can sit down,' I said. 'This is where you come in, June. I want you to run a series of articles showing her transformation. It would help to make her better known, and will probably give some encouragement to other teenagers in the same predicament.'

'It's already been done. Countless times,' said June. 'It would be a different matter if she were already well known.'

'I don't want to go in no magazine,' said Catherine. 'And I'm not a block of wood, you know. I do have ears.'

Alan was smiling. Even in June's eyes there was a glimmer of amusement.

'We'll discuss this later,' I told her. 'I'm sorry, Catherine. But if you want to carry on in this business, we have to create an image. Can you look at Alan for a moment? I want to see your profile.'

'Her nose is terrible,' Chris said, when he'd had a good look.

'I know. It's going to ruin the rest of her later on. Would you be frightened of plastic surgery, Catherine? You could have a brand new, beautiful nose.'

Alan frowned; and the girl looked horrified. I had forgotten that she was only sixteen, and about to be thrust into a world she'd never known existed outside the pages of a novel.

'The operation won't hurt,' I assured her. 'But we can't force it on you.'

She ran a finger along the bridge of her nose. 'It ain't very pretty is it? I dunno. It must hurt a little bit.'

'Well, perhaps a little. In another couple of years you'll be grateful for having it done.'

'All right then,' she said. 'But only 'cos you want it.'

Alan was smiling again. 'Good,' I said. 'Next, your hair. It will have to come off.'

'Not me hair!' she wailed. 'Anything but that. It took years to grow this long!'

'I'm sorry, but it really will have to go.' I turned to Chris. 'I think you should leave the hair for Martin to organise.'

'Voice?' Chris asked.

'No,' I said. 'Round off some of the rougher edges, but leave the rest intact. And concentrate on the smile. Her name will also have to be changed.'

'What's wrong with me name?'

'Too long,' said Alan. 'You could shorten it. To Cathy, perhaps.'

'Kathy with a K,' I said. 'Kathy Karn. It suits her.'

'It's horrible. Why can't I stay Cathy Bridges?'

'Because there is no romance in Cathy Bridges,' I said. 'Marty Pole's real name was Albert Jenkins. How far do you think he'd have got on that?'

'How long do I have to do all this?' Chris asked.

'As long as you want.'

'She'll need a good song.'

'I know. I want Larry Sparks to do it.'

'Would he?' Chris asked.

'Yes,' I said. 'If we can find him. The last I heard he was living in Spain.'

The girl was starting to fidget. I stood up. 'I'm sorry, Catherine, you must be exhausted. Chris can take you home, which will give you an opportunity to get acquainted. I want you to think carefully about all of this. Chris will bring you back on Wednesday, and if you want to sign a contract, the papers will be ready. You can bring your parents, and they're welcome to bring a lawyer.'

'I don't think they'll be that interested,' she said. 'All they'll want to know is if I'll be ... well ...'

'If you sign the contract you will receive an allowance until you start earning your own money,' I said.

She flushed. 'It's only that me mum will expect me to bring something in,' she said. 'Will I see you on Wednesday?'

'Yes.'

As Alan said when she was gone, it was pure puppy love.

I handed June her usual brandy and water. 'Why won't you do the article?' I asked, sitting down opposite her.

'I never said I wouldn't do it. But your timing is wrong.'

'And if I insist you do run it?' I asked.

She put down her glass. 'Don't lord it over me, Mark. I know what I'm doing. Get the girl started. I'll compile the article all right, but I won't use it until I am sure the time is right.'

'I could override you,' I said. 'I've never interfered before, but this is important.'

'Important enough for you to make a fool of yourself? The girl is immature. What if she can't take the pressure? If she cracks up altogether?'

'She won't,' I said. 'Not with the money I shall be investing in her.'

June laughed. 'That's absolute rot, and you know it. The few thousand you'll be spending on her is a mere drop in the ocean. It won't even leave a dent in your pocket.'

'You're a hard woman,' I said. 'It's little wonder you've never married.'

'I never wanted to,' she said. 'I love my work, and I know I'm good at it, so why should I get myself tied down? And why the hell are you changing the subject? You'll not get round me that way.'

'I don't intend to. I shall accede to your better judgement this time, but the moment the girl is ready, I want the article printed.'

She picked up her glass, slowly revolving it between the palms of her hands. 'Agreed,' she said. 'If that's all you wanted, then I had better get back.'

'What's the hurry?' I asked. 'Eric is there. How are you and he getting along these days?'

'Another change of strategy?' she asked. 'You know perfectly well how we get along. Cat and dog all the way. But the man knows his business inside out, I'll grant him that.'

'I hear he's been doing some pretty heavy gambling,' I said.

'Eric suffers from an inferiority complex. He craves your power, although for the life of me I can't understand why. Did you put him on the magazine to keep him off your back? There must be a lot of people in an organisation of this size who would gladly push you out if they had the opportunity.'

'There probably are,' I agreed. 'But they can't. My father practically ruined himself by selling off too many shares outside the family. It taught me a lesson. I've kept total control of all my companies, except for a negligible shareholding in the recording company. What else can you tell me about Eric?'

She sipped her brandy. 'He's running a new Jaguar. But I know nothing about his personal life, and have no intention of spying on him.'

I laughed. 'I'd never dream of asking you to do that. If I need information, there are more subtle ways of obtaining it. I was reading your sales figures the other day. You've soared ahead of your nearest competitors.'

'We've been in the lead for the past year.' She eyed me suspiciously. 'What are you getting at?'

'Nothing in particular. I've been considering expanding Hanley Publications. Do you think we could handle another magazine?'

'God forbid! Surely you own enough already. Why the hell do you want more?'

'Megalomania?' I suggested. 'I like to see things done well, June. And I enjoy the challenge of making things work that way. Catherine Bridges is a minor sort of challenge. It's what keeps me going.'

'You have to stop somewhere,' she said. 'You can't own everything.'

'I know,' I said. 'But another publication wouldn't hurt. If you're against a second magazine, what about a newspaper?'

She emptied her glass and held it towards me. 'You can get me another drink, and then amuse me with some more of your ramblings.'

Chapter Seven

It was only one week from Christmas when Lisa walked into the Knightsbridge boutique. The two salesgirls smiled at her. 'He's in the back,' said the prettiest one.

'Hello, Martin,' Lisa said. 'I don't know why Mark bought that new building. You never seem to be in it. Is the kettle hot?'

He was sitting in his usual cross-legged position on the floor. 'It was boiled not two minutes ago,' he said, grinning at her. 'Help yourself. I'm practically finished. I think this will be the last fitting.'

Lisa plugged in the kettle and ladled instant coffee into a mug. She was certain Martin must drop his mugs deliberately, for they were always cracked. She sat beside him. 'I hope the weather stays like this, otherwise Alan will have to fly into Manchester when he goes up there to fetch Daddy. Mark could land on the private runway if it did ice over, but Alan would probably go skidding off the end.'

Martin put down the dress he was working on. 'I hear he won't be back until after New Year.'

'Yes,' she said. 'Alan received a letter and piles of instructions on Tuesday. Mark added a postscript: they hired a yacht and sailed round the Caribbean for a month. Now they're in Switzerland, and they're going to America to spend Christmas with Caroline's family. Can you imagine what all that must be costing?'

'Millions,' said Martin. 'More than you or I shall see in a lifetime. Look, I've got another appointment in half an hour and I want you to come with me, Lisa. I have to look over some new premises. The reason I never use the offices I've got is that they're overcrowded – there are five designers working for me, and a clothing factory underneath them. We really have to expand, you see; I've received orders from God knows how many chain stores, and I've got all the shops to outfit.' He stood up, and walking to a rack, removed a half-finished dress. 'But for you, sweetheart, my services will always be exclusive. Here, try this on.'

She took the dress from him. 'At this rate you'll be catching up with Mark and his millions,' she said. 'Will we be long? I have to collect Marian from ballet at five-thirty.'

'We should be back before that. Be careful, it's held together with pins.'

She went into one of the changing rooms. Not that it mattered – if she walked out in front of Martin stark naked, he wouldn't turn a hair.

'It's awfully tight,' she said.

He passed a critical eye over her, and then picked up a tape measure. 'Really, Lisa, you've put on almost an inch in a fortnight. What are you living on? A diet of Yorkshire pudding?'

'I can't have!' she said.

'My tape measure doesn't lie. Neither does my dress. You'll have to lose it, otherwise you're going to look like a sack of potatoes.'

'You could let out the seams a bit,' she suggested.

'If I do that you'll just get fatter and fatter!'

'But you're the one who told me I was too thin,' she complained.

'That was months ago, after the baby. I never expected you to take my advice quite so much to heart. Turn round. I'll take the pins out half an inch.'

'I bet you don't talk to your other customers like this,' she said.

'My other customers don't get this sort of personal attention!'

'Why do you want me to come with you?' she asked. 'I wouldn't know whether the place is any good or not.'

'I don't need your opinion about the premises,' he said. 'Alan will be there for that. I want to talk with you privately.' He peered round the side of the changing room at the salesgirls. 'I don't trust them. I think they listen at the door.'

'You could have mentioned that before. Ouch! You pricked me!'

'Then for God's sake, stand still!'

'I need your help,' Martin said. 'I think I'm in love.'

He was a terrible driver, and she had been anxiously watching the road. Her eyes now flew to his face, for despite their close friendship, she never pried into his private life.

'Who's the lucky man?' she asked.

'It's a woman,' he said.

'What?' she said. 'I'm sorry Martin, I didn't mean to be rude. Are you sure?'

He blushed. 'Of course I'm sure. I even sent Philip away. I'm alone at the flat now. Do you think I'm stupid?'

'No,' she said, 'of course not. Oh Martin, please watch the road! Who is she?' She squeezed his arm. 'I promise not to laugh.'

'Kathy Karn.'

She stared at him. She could imagine nobody falling in love with Kathy Karn, or Bridges, or whatever her name was. Certainly not Martin.

'Chris brings her in for fittings,' he said. 'I don't think she knows about me. Do you think he's told her?'

'But she's only sixteen!'

'Seventeen,' he said. 'You don't approve?'

She smiled. 'Don't be silly. But what on earth have they done to her?'

'Done to her? What do you mean? Her nose has been reshaped, and I had Alexander cut her hair. It's a bit like yours, but shorter. What else is there?'

'She was fat,' said Lisa.

'She's thinner than you, and she has marvellous legs which go on forever.'

'I'm sorry, Martin,' she said. 'I don't mean to sound unenthusiastic. But I haven't set eyes on the girl since the evening Mark saw her at Marian's school concert. We all thought he was mad at the time.' How old was Martin now? Twenty-five? She remembered Mark when he was not very much older. 'I suppose Chris is keeping an eye on her?' she said.

'Yes. But it's not Chris that I'm worried about.'

'I know, it's Mark. Does she like you?'

'I don't know,' he said. 'We talk a lot, and we get on, if that's what you mean.'

She suddenly felt old and matronly. 'Have you asked her out?'

'No. Chris would probably stop her from coming, and when Mark gets back ...' His voice tailed off, and about to reassure him, Lisa stopped herself. After all, Martin was entirely responsible for his own homosexual reputation, and one couldn't blame Mark for wanting to keep Kathy Karn away from him. Anyway, after he'd dated her a couple of times, Martin was sure to lose interest.

'I have an idea,' she said. 'But I'll have to talk it over with Alan.'

He stared at her in disbelief.

'Martin ... the road! For heaven's sake! I've no intention of telling him everything, of course. Trust me, will you? It'll have to be done carefully because Alan, God bless him, might be gullible, but

Mark certainly isn't.'

He had relaxed by the time they reached the building, and if Alan suspected there might have been some plotting going on, he was too preoccupied to ask.

Chapter Eight

Our marriage had been closer to the rocks than either of us would admit, but now that Henry had taken over from Chris, I was able to devote more time to Caroline. Those weeks in Oldenshaw had helped heal some of the scars, and the time we spent together from November to January almost succeeded in bringing back the earlier magic. In a moment of madness I had promised Caroline a chalet in Switzerland and a villa in the South of France if she considered them necessary. She did, and within a week of our return to London she left for Europe, taking Elly with her. I felt sorry for Elly. Caroline had long ago promoted her to personal maid, but this was her first trip out of the country and she was obviously terrified at the prospect.

'She needs bringing out of herself,' said Caroline gaily. 'She might even meet a nice Frenchman. An illicit affair would do wonders for her!'

We laughed, but I knew Elly wasn't the kind of girl to have any sort of affair, illicit or otherwise.

'Remember you promised to come out when I find something,' Caroline said before she left.

'I'll try,' I said.

But when she was gone there were so many things to be done. Kathy was practically ready, and I had decided that a newspaper would not be such a bad purchase. Alan disapproved, but Alan always disapproved when I wanted to launch into something new.

It did not take Caroline long to find a chalet in Gstaad. She wanted me to join her for an elaborate housewarming party, but I refused, and we had a row over the telephone which resulted in her furiously slamming down the receiver. We hadn't taken long to get back to stalemate.

Kathy completed her first recording, and I knew something was wrong when Chris asked me to listen to the tape. I took Alan along.

'We've been doing this for a week now,' said Tony Crane. 'And we're all sick and tired of it. I could mix something from the material we have, but you said you didn't want that.'

'Don't you think she's any good?' I asked.

'She's good, but for some reason or another she can't do it. I have her original test recording here. I'd like you to compare the two.'

Kathy and Chris came in halfway through the first tape, the coaxed recording of Marty Pole's old number.

'Hello, Kathy,' I said. 'We're trying to find out where you went wrong.'

She grimaced, and leant against the control desk. She looked very young and vulnerable with the boyish haircut and pale eyeshadow.

The first tape finished. 'Ready?' Tony asked, watching me.

He was right. She had ruined an excellent song. Marty Pole could have done better. Tony switched off the tape.

'Do you want to hear it again?' he asked.

'No.' I looked at Kathy. There were tears in her eyes. 'What happened?' I asked.

'I just can't do it,' she said. 'I tried real hard. But it wouldn't come right, and I don't really understand what you want.'

'What do you mean?'

A tear ran down her cheek. 'I don't understand how it goes,' she said. 'I never heard it before. I never heard nobody else sing it. That other song I knew already.'

I understood now. She mimicked.

'A new song needs a new interpretation,' I explained.

'I know. But I still can't do it. Can't somebody show me how? Just this once?'

It had been done, with groups which had raw talent and no musical background, but if Kathy were going to copy, she needed to copy somebody who knew what they were doing. I turned to Chris. 'Where is Simon Townsend?'

'I don't know,' he said. 'Do you think he'd do it for us?'

'Yes.'

'He's not been in today,' said Tony. 'I think he's got a few days off. He's been working pretty hard.'

'I'll get Norma to find him,' I said. 'And in the meantime we can go through this tape piece by piece.'

Simon did not appear for another three hours, by which time we were all exhausted. But Kathy was beginning to understand, and when I explained what was needed, Simon was willing to help. He listened to the music, humming as he studied the words.

'It's catchy,' he said. 'She has a good chance of getting into the Hit

Parade if she gets it right. Can I use it on my next album?'

I couldn't very well refuse him, not when he was doing me a favour on this scale. 'Yes,' I said. 'But until Kathy's version is released I want it to go no further than this building.'

'Fair enough,' he agreed. 'I'll try a couple of test runs now.'

Simon had leart his trade the hard way, and he got it right the first time. As I listened to him, I almost regretted the song was going to Kathy. It seemed impossible that she could better him, but on her first attempt she was easily as good. I sent her home then, having decided that we would record it in the morning when she was fresh.

'Thank you, Simon,' I said. 'I don't think she could have done it without your help.'

'My pleasure, Mr. Hanley. You did as much for me. If you can get her over those nerves she's going to be good.'

Yes she was. I only hoped she'd pick up some of his resilience, for she was going to need it in this cut-throat business.

Tony and Chris were resigned to being there for the entire day, but Kathy was chirpy from the outset.

'Do you want a couple of test runs?' I asked.

'No,' she said. 'I think I got it now. Let's get it over with.'

Her confidence paid off, and after the first take I knew she would never get it any better.

'Can I have that flat now?' she said to Chris.

'What flat?' I asked.

'The one Chris promised I could have when I started earning me own money. I dunno, but it ain't the same at home no more. I feel sort of wrong there.'

I looked at Chris. 'I think it would be best,' he said. 'Especially now. She's going to be thrust into the public eye, and quite honestly, her home isn't quite what we had in mind.'

A grand-scale publicity campaign was ready to be launched, and June had promised to run her series of articles immediately the disc was released. I certainly didn't want any foul ups at this stage. 'All right,' I agreed. 'But you'll have to employ a housekeeper who can sleep in and keep an eye on her.'

'I don't need a nursemaid,' Kathy squeaked.

I frowned at her. 'You're only seventeen. When you reach eighteen you can do what you want, but until then you will do as I say.'

Chris found her a flat in Mayfair, and shortly after she had moved in Alan came up with an excellent publicity stunt. 'Have her escorted about town by a well known personality,' he said.

'Who?' I asked. 'I can't think of anyone I could trust not to have her in bed after the first date.'

'What about Martin? She seems to like him.'

'He'd never agree. Anyway, he's queer as a coot, he wouldn't know what to do with a proper girlfriend.'

'I thought that was the idea,' said Alan. 'It wouldn't harm his reputation to be seen with Kathy, and there's the added advantage that she already knows him. Just think, Mark, she'd hang on to her virginity, and there would be no awkward attachments.'

It was worth a try. I knew the press would love it.

'I'll talk it over with Martin,' I said. 'Did you know that we've got Kathy onto John Sullivan's show next Saturday? I plan to release the record the following Monday. I think it will pay dividends.'

'Does Kathy know?'

'Yes. But in case she panics, I said nothing about her having to perform live. She knows the song well enough, and Chris is rehearsing her until every movement becomes second nature.'

'John Sullivan must have taken some wangling,' said Alan. Sullivan was compère to one of the most successful pop shows ever presented on the small screen. Only the best ever got onto it, and he rarely accepted newcomers unless they were exceptionally talented.

'He owed me a favour from a long way back.' I told him. 'I was at the height of my own singing career, and forced the issue which led to him being given a small part on a television special I was recording. He's come a long way since then.'

Chris told Kathy about the show being live on Saturday morning. Because Caroline was still away I was at the office, and Norma, in her dogmatic fashion, had insisted on coming in too. Kathy dashed in just before midday.

'I can't do it!' she cried. 'I just can't do it!'

'Of course you can,' I said. 'All you do is stand on stage and sing. You'll have most of the afternoon to rehearse, and it really is no different to being in the booth with all the technicians watching you.'

'But the whole bloody country will be watching me!' she wailed. 'Thousands and thousands of them. I can't do it. Not by meself I can't.'

I liked Kathy. She was an uncomplicated child who viewed this new world with wonderment. 'Would it help if I came?' I asked.

'Would you?' she said, her eyes lighting up. 'Maybe it wouldn't be so bad then.'

'All right,' I agreed. 'I'll be there. Now run along, and make sure you eat something before you go. You'll regret it if you don't.'

Kathy had not been gone long when Norma popped her head round the door.

'June Halliday has just been on the telephone,' she said. 'She's been looking all over for you. She's coming here now and asked if you could wait.' She peered at me over the rims of her spectacles. 'She sounds agitated.'

I couldn't think why, unless something had gone very wrong with the magazine. Eric was in Holland, preparing a feature on one of my newest groups, Mantis, who were on tour there.

June looked flustered when she arrived, which was unlike her.

'You can give me a straight brandy,' she said. 'I need it. I think you will too.'

'What's happened?' I asked.

'I've just received this from a friend in Paris. The press over there are revelling in it, and the story's going to break here tomorrow. I thought you should be warned.'

She held out a large manilla envelope. I stared at it. 'What's in there?'

'A slightly blurred cutting from one of the leading newspapers. There's a photograph as well.'

I took it from her. 'Caroline?'

'Yes. Do you have a cigarette? I left mine in the car.'

I handed her one, and lit another for myself. She had put the envelope on the low table which separated us. I was reluctant to pick it up, knowing that whatever it contained could only be bad news.

'Another man?' I asked.

'You could say that. You can't avoid it, Mark. The entire country will know by this time tomorrow. I've never envied you your position, you're the butt of every columnist and news-hungry reporter. It can't be easy for her either.'

'Caroline thrives on publicity,' I said. 'Who's the man?'

She did not reply. She picked up her brandy and sipped it slowly. 'Look for yourself,' she said after a moment. 'Can you read French?'

'Well enough to get the gist of it.'

I opened the flap and pulled out the single sheet of paper. Caroline looked both vivacious and breathtakingly beautiful. She and Eric were pressed together on a crowded dance floor, and they were kissing. I glanced at the caption beneath. The nightclub was in Paris. Caroline was meant to be in Nice, and Eric in Amsterdam. I felt a chill pass through me. Why him? Of all the people she could choose, why did it have to be Eric Stewart?

I hadn't even been aware that June had moved, not until she pressed a cold glass into my hand.

'Drink that,' she said. 'They have no proof that anything happened. It's gutter press at its worst.'

Gutter press or not, the facts were there. They had come to the nightclub together. They had left together. And according to this reporter, Eric had taken Caroline back to her hotel, not reappearing until the next morning.

Tomorrow, our lives would be an open book. It would be known that Caroline and I had been apart for practically two months, and the gossip columnists would he predicting that our marriage was finished. I wondered if they would be so very far from wrong.

I took a sip of the whisky June had given me, but it left a sour taste.

'Get out there today and sort out the whole damn mess,' she said.

'I can't,' I said flatly. 'I have to be at the television studios this afternoon. I promised Kathy.'

'Christ! Is that chit of a girl more important than your wife?'

'Yes,' I said. 'At the moment she is. When is Eric due back?'

'Next Wednesday. Why? Are you going to instigate a witch hunt? Don't be a fool, Mark.'

I walked over to the window. The sky was grey and the Thames murky, which all seemed to fit in with my mood. 'I can't afford a scandal, not when nearly everything I'm involved with is aimed at the teenage market. Thank you for taking the trouble to tell me.'

There was a rustle as she stood up.

'Sort it out, Mark, before it's too late,' she said.

When she had gone I held my lighter to the sheet of paper. As the flame flared upwards, I dropped it into an ashtray, watching as the two dancers gyrated obscenely before they dissolved into dust.

The last thing I wanted was the clamour of a live show. But I went because I had promised, and I didn't want Kathy to break down at this crucial stage in her career.

'I told you to take the afternoon off,' I said to Tim as he battled through the traffic. The Hammersmith shops were open all day on Saturday, and one would think half of London was there.

'You did,' he said. 'But I thought you might need me.'

Tim and Norma were constantly thrown together during my trips abroad, and had developed a close friendship. Norma must have asked him to come in after June had left.

Once we were clear of the heavy traffic Tim put his foot down.

'I never realised the speed limit had been raised,' I said as he went through the third set of orange lights which turned red when we were less than a quarter way across the intersections.

'Show must have started ten minutes ago,' he said. 'I hear Miss

Karn is one of the first on.'

I glanced at my watch and cursed. I should have left earlier.

'And if the police stop us?' I asked.

'You'll think of something.'

'One of these days you really will end up in jail, and I won't do a damn thing to help you.'

'Nobody else would fret over you like I do,' he said, smiling.

I began to feel better. Caroline would never have an affair with Eric. She didn't even like him.

'If you're sure the car won't be towed away in our absence, you can come and watch,' I said when we reached the studios.

'I'll park her down there,' said Tim, pointing towards an alley full of No Parking signs. I thought it best not to say anything.

I was hardly inside the door when Chris pounced on me.

'Damn it, Mark,' he said, 'I thought you weren't coming. She did fine during rehearsals, but now her nerves have got the better of her, and she's hysterical. If we can't get her out in time, they're going to cut the number. And to make matters worse Martin is fighting about her dress. They say it's too short and refuse to photograph her below the waist unless he puts on a false hem.'

We reached the crowded studio which was hot and noisy. Sullivan always had a live audience, and some couples were dancing while a group on stage belted out tuneless music. Chris led me through to the back, where we bumped into Sullivan himself.

'Thank God you came,' he said. 'Look, I've managed to swop round one of the groups, which gives you another ten minutes to get her out here. I'm sorry, Mark, but I can't play for more time than that.'

'Thank you,' I said. 'Have you seen her?'

'Yes,' he answered. 'And even you might not be able to get her out in time. I've got to go. Good luck.'

I was already in half a mind to call this off and release her record in the normal way. I would make the final decision when I had seen her. Chris opened the dressing room door, and what first struck me was the silence. After the babble outside it was unbelievably quiet. Kathy was sitting on a chair, a handkerchief in her hands. Martin hovered over her, dressed in a suit which looked as though it had been designed by himself for himself. A young make-up girl was leaning against the dressing table. Martin glanced up when we came in, and gave me a relieved smile. Kathy's back was to the door, and she hadn't heard us. I wondered whether the hysteria had passed into something more easily controllable.

'Kathy?'

There was a pause before her head shot up. She swung round. Her eye make-up had made filthy circles around her swollen eyes, and the face powder was blotched. To clean up that mess would take more than ten minutes ... by now there could only be eight left.

'You look terrible,' I said.

Whether those were the wrong words, or whether she was on the verge of breaking anyway, I don't know; but as she looked at me her face puckered, and then she began to cry.

'I can't do it!' she wailed. 'Nothing can make me go out there, nothing!' She finished on a piercing scream.

Martin had already started forward, but I moved quicker still, and did the only sensible thing. As I slapped her hard on both cheeks Martin looked at me in horror. Even the make-up girl recoiled.

'Mark!' Chris exclaimed.

But Kathy ... Kathy stopped crying. Her mouth fell open and she ran her hand over the livid marks left by my fingers.

'You have five minutes to get cleaned up and out there,' I said. 'If you don't go, I shall wash my hands of you. Do you understand?' Her lips formed a silent yes, and I looked at the make-up girl. 'Can you do it?'

'If she doesn't cry any more,' she said.

'Chris will stay with you,' I told Kathy.

It was then that a look of defiance came into her eyes. 'I want Martin to stay,' she said, her voice trembling.

'I'll see that she comes,' he promised. 'And in the meantime, perhaps you could use your influence and get them to back down over the dress. She's standing all the time, so there's no question of indecency.'

I nodded as I walked to the door.

'Car's fine. I parked it in a director's bay,' Tim said when I reached the studio. 'He won't be in this evening.'

'And if he is, he'll be yelling bloody murder. Have you seen John Sullivan anywhere?'

'Aye,' said Tim. 'He's talking to that mob with the long hair.'

I saw him. 'Tim, tell Chris where I am and have him bring Kathy to me when she's ready. He's up that passage, waiting outside her dressing room.'

'Trouble?' he asked.

'When isn't there?'

Because they had no argument, I got my way over Kathy's hemline, and by the time Chris and Martin brought her to me, the cameramen had been instructed. The make-up girl had done a good job and although Kathy's eyes were still swollen, I didn't think they would show up under the subdued lighting. Sullivan was sitting on a stool, stalling for time, his eyes flitting from the camera to us. The stage manager pointed at his watch, muttering beneath his breath as he tried to pull Kathy away before I could speak to her.

'I'm frightened,' she said, refusing to move.

'I'll stay here,' I promised. 'Watch me and pretend you're in the recording booth. You can do it, Kathy.'

She smiled nervously as the stage manager led her away. I glanced towards Sullivan, and heard the relief in his voice when he announced her name.

'There was no need for you to hit her so hard,' Martin said. The continuity man glared at him. 'There was no need ... ' he began again in a whisper.

'I'm not deaf,' I hissed back. 'And I didn't notice any of you bubbling over with ideas. I got her out here, despite my brutality.'

The backing group struck the first chord, and Kathy's eyes were suddenly on mine. She was very pale, despite the heavy make-up, and her forced smile did little to hide the fright. I forgot Martin. I forgot everyone. I concentrated on Kathy, bringing her in at the right moment.

'She's good,' Chris said from behind me. She could manage alone now, but she was still watching me, and so I silently helped her.

Then it was finished, and Kathy Karn was on her way.

Chapter Nine

Caroline was only in Paris because she had joined some friends for a shopping spree. They had flown over in a private plane, and rather than return the same day, decided to stay overnight. The party was being given by a friend of a friend, and it was quite by chance that they went to it. As was usual these days, LSD was being passed freely about, and although Caroline had never been into hard drugs, she wasn't averse to smoking a reefer or two. She'd smoked three when she ran into Eric Stewart. She was surprised to see him there, this wasn't the sort of company he'd normally mix in, but he told her he had come with one of Mark's groups, who might even play later if they could be rounded up. Caroline lit her fourth cigarette, discarded a glass of champagne, and accepted an invitation to dance. She couldn't remember when they had left and begun a tour of the nightclubs, only that the tour was prematurely cut short when the effects of too much champagne and marijuana began to take their toll.

Eric took her back to the hotel, where she discovered another reefer at the bottom of her handbag. They shared it, he taking no more than one drag to her three. By now she was so spaced out that she was putty in his hands. A gentleman would have left, but Eric was no gentleman, and Caroline was not his usual conquest but Mark Hanley's wife, and by that virtue alone, tantalizingly, overwhelmingly, desirable. She had put on the radio and was swaying rather unsteadily to the music. He was in two minds about staying, but when she beckoned him to join her, he went. He was playing with fire and knew it; but what the hell, this would probably never happen again. He put his arms around her, kissing her on the neck and then the mouth. She responded to his embrace, and he ran his hand up the inside of her thigh. There was no protest, no slap in the face. It's his own damn fault, Eric thought, for neglecting her like this.

She woke the next morning with a foul-tasting mouth and a brutal headache. She sat up, aware of somebody lying beside her. 'Mark?' she murmured. And then she saw who it was, and gagged.

He opened his eyes on her revulsion, and felt last night's triumph slip away.

'Oh Christ!' she said, her face ashen. 'What the hell have we done?' She reached for a discarded robe and wrapped it tightly around her nakedness.

He sat up and swung his legs over the bed. 'I didn't force you, Caroline,' he said quietly, his back to her. 'You wanted it.'

She closed her eyes. 'I'm not blaming you, Eric. Does anyone know you're here?'

'No,' he said.

She breathed a sigh of relief. 'Then don't tell anyone. Please.'

He remained silent for a moment. If this got out, it wouldn't do him much good either. 'I wonder if Mark realises how lucky he is,' he said. 'I won't say a word.'

'Thank you.' The room was beginning to spin around her. 'Would you mind leaving now?' she asked, and ran to the bathroom to be violently sick. She came out half an hour later to find him gone.

She did not bother with her friends, but took the next flight back to Nice. She felt awful, and went straight to bed, where she stayed until Elly woke her the next morning. The maid had not been with her in Paris, and her face was stricken as she held forward some of the air mail editions of the English Sunday newspapers.

Caroline did not have to see them to know what had happened. You bastard, Eric, she thought. 'Start packing,' she said. 'We're going home.'

Roberts had left the Sunday newspapers folded on the breakfast table, but Mark ignored them. He poured himself strong black coffee, and declining any food, shut himself in the study.

But when the barrage did come, it was from the least expected quarter. Roberts interrupted him shortly after eleven to say that his sister was in the drawing room.

'What do you want, Fran?' he asked, standing with his back to the door.

'To see how you like playing the cuckold. Your wife and my husband. It's not only disgusting, it's practically incest.'

'Do you always have to dramatise?' he said. 'What do you really want?'

'To know what you intend doing. This scandal affects us all, especially my children. *Your* nephews and nieces,' she emphasised.

'It's too late,' he said. 'Whether or not it's true, the harm has already been done. The best we can do is bluff it out.'

'And Eric? Are you going to take your revenge on him?'

His eyes focused for the first time on the brooch Fran wore. He had given Caroline enough jewellery to know good quality diamonds and sapphires when he saw them. He walked across the room and lifted the lapel of her jacket.

'Where does he get the money?' he asked. 'This is no child's bauble, nor is your house, or that damn car he drives. And what was he doing in Paris?'

'Presumably the same as your slut of a wife,' she said maliciously. 'You don't know how long it's been going on, either. Eric is always sliding off somewhere, but what about Caroline? Did you really think she was as pure as the driven snow? I wonder how many men she's had behind your back.'

He stiffened. 'Get out,' he said coldly. 'You're not welcome here. You know I can't do a bloody thing without making matters worse. But if Eric puts so much as one foot out of line, then I swear I shall break him.'

'And make yourself the laughing stock of the entire business world?' she mocked. 'I know you better than that, Mark. You value your reputation too much.'

He reached forward and rang a bell. 'Goodbye, Fran,' he said in a hard voice. 'Roberts will see you out.'

Caroline did not bother with the Hanley jet because she thought it would take too long to come out to her from England. In the end, she wished she'd waited: there were no direct flights to London until later that evening, and when she and Elly reached Orly there was a two-hour delay before they could get a connection. By this time Heathrow was fogbound, and after wasting an hour circling London, their plane was redirected to Gatwick. From there they took a train to Victoria, and finally a taxi the rest of the way. It was after nine when they reached home, and shivering with cold, Caroline cursed as she waited for Roberts to open the door.

'Welcome home, madam,' he said, unflustered by her unexpected appearance. 'Mr. Hanley never told me you were due back.'

'He isn't expecting me,' she said. 'Is he home?'

'Yes, madam. In the drawing room. Would you like anything sent in?'

He took her coat, and she flung her hat and gloves onto a table. 'Coffee', she said. 'And crumpets. Do we have any?'

'Of course, madam.'

She turned to Elly. 'Go and get something to eat,' she said. 'Anne can unpack my cases.'

'She'd never do them proper,' Elly said, relieved to be back in familiar surroundings with people who spoke English. 'I'll do it.'

Caroline nodded absently as she paused for a moment outside the door. And then, taking a deep breath, she turned the handle and walked in.

The radio was playing softly, and Mark was sitting on the sofa reading a book. She paused, wondering where he found the time and energy to do all he did; and then she closed the door hard enough for him to hear. He did not look up, and halfway across the room she stopped, staring helplessly at him.

He had, of course, heard her arrive, and putting down the book, had lit a cigarette while she was talking with Roberts and Elly. And although she did not realise it, he had been watching her from the moment she came into the room.

'Why did you come back?' he asked suddenly.

She shuddered and went over to the fire, stretching her cold hands towards it. He always insisted they have coal fires, despite the adequate central heating.

'Caroline?'

She turned to him. 'I saw some newspapers,' she said.

'And decided to make matters worse by running home.' The sudden ferocity of his voice frightened her into taking a backward step. 'Why couldn't you bloody well stay where you were? Christ, how the press are going to love this.' His furious eyes rested on her shocked face. 'How did you get here? Everywhere is fogged in.'

'I took a commercial flight which landed at Gatwick, and I came because …'

'I don't give a damn why you came,' he cut in furiously. He stood up. 'Is it true, Caroline?'

'For God's sake, you don't think I meant it to happen, do you?'

'Then it is true?'

She flung herself forward, catching hold of his arm. 'Yes,' she said. 'But it's not like you think. I swear it.'

'He shook her off, and like two strangers they stood staring at each other. Had Caroline not been so preoccupied she would have noticed how colourless his face had suddenly become, and how heavily he was breathing, as if after some fierce physical exertion.

For a moment Mark wasn't sure what was happening to him, but within seconds the odd sensation began to pass. He found his voice again. 'I don't want to discuss this any further, not tonight,' he said. 'I shall have Roberts move my things into one of the other rooms for the time being.' With an effort which she missed, he walked to the door.

'Jesus!' she swore. 'I deserve a chance to explain!'

'Why?' He turned a little, so that she could see the mockery in his face. 'It's a little late for feeling guilty, Caroline. You're the one who committed adultery, not me.'

'You bastard!' Tears welled up in her eyes, and without thinking, she reached for the nearest object she could find. She flung the heavy glass ornament at him. It missed, shattering as it slammed into the wall.

'My God, Caroline,' he said, 'why are you acting like a ravished virgin?'

'Leave me alone!' she screamed. 'Just go away and leave me alone!'

She closed her eyes tight, and when she opened them again he was gone. The glass dog had been worth nothing but memories; he had bought it for her in Windsor shortly after their marriage. She dropped to her knees, gathering up the shreds of glass, not realising that she had cut her finger until she saw the drops of blood on the carpet.

Alan had never seen Mark quite like this in all the years he had known him. The accountants had already been through the magazine's books once, and with single-minded determination, Mark was insisting they go through them again. Even Alan could not dissuade him.

'You're making a fool of yourself,' he said.

'The man has to be getting his money from somewhere. Even you can see that the sales are up, while the profits have increased only marginally. Eric owes a substantial amount of money to various gambling clubs, and very soon they're going to start calling in their markers. The magazine is the only source he can tap. Fran's money has gone, and they're both living way beyond their means.'

'That does not mean he's embezzling magazine funds,' Alan said. 'I can understand how you feel Mark, but what you're doing is an utter waste of time. If you want to sack him, then sack him outright. Don't go through this ridiculous farce.'

'If you don't like it, then don't get involved,' said Mark. 'Actually, I'd like you to go over to the States for a while.'

'I'm not in the habit of running away from trouble,' said Alan.

'I'm not asking you to run away,' Mark said irritably. 'I'm sending Simon on tour, and although Keith is arranging everything at that end, there are some legalities which I'd prefer you to deal with.'

'Simon never told me,' Alan said.

Mark stubbed out his cigarette and reached for another. 'He doesn't know yet. Will you go?'

Alan sighed. 'When?'
'Next month. The tour is in April. Take Lisa with you and make it a working holiday.'
'She'll want to stay here. David is teething, and Marian will be auditioning for that new ballet school. She'll need Lisa to get her through it.' He took a deep breath. 'How is Caroline?' It was two weeks since her dramatic return from Nice.
Mark had been pacing the floor. He paused. 'Why do you want to know?'
'Because we've been friends long enough for you to be able to trust me,' said Alan. 'It was only a damn photograph and a lot of speculation. Surely Caroline told you what actually happened?'
'Of course she did,' Mark snapped; and he began pacing again, getting on Alan's nerves.
'Would you like to talk about it?' he asked.
'No, thank you. This is something that Caroline and I must work out between us. Anyway, she's going to Oldenshaw for a few days. And talking of relationships, I'm not sure whether it's such a good idea for Kathy to be seeing so much of Martin. He's a bad influence. Before we know what's happening she'll be acquainted with every queer in London.'
Alan realised too late that Mark was deliberately steering the conversation away from the turmoil of his personal life. 'She's much more confident,' he said. 'She likes Martin, but in a brotherly sort of way, I think. And let's face it, nothing could possibly develop between them.'
'I hope you're right,' said Mark.

Mary and Charles Latchcham had left for Liverpool that very morning, which meant Caroline had to spend a miserable three days waiting for them to come back. Mary learnt from Hugh Latchcham, her husband's son, that her daughter-in-law was at Olden Manor, and drove immediately to her old home. She found Caroline in the conservatory at the back of the house.
'Caroline!' Mary called from the doorway.
She swung round. Mary knew Caroline as a young woman bubbling with vitality; now she could not fail to be moved by the dramatic change in her, and when Caroline ran into her arms, her heart went out to her.
'Let's go into the drawing room,' she said.
They sat in front of a log fire, and Mary asked for tea to be brought in.
'He's been hard on you, hasn't he?' she asked.

Tears sprang to Caroline's eyes. 'He won't forgive me, Mary. I don't think he ever will.' She stammered to a halt as tears began to pour down her cheeks.

Mary took her hand and squeezed it. 'If it had been anyone other than Eric,' she said. 'Give him more time. Once he's thought it over, he'll realise that what the newspapers insinuated was pure rubbish.'

'That's the trouble,' said Caroline. 'It wasn't.'

Mary was shocked. 'You mean it's true?' she asked. 'But in heaven's name, why? I know you and Mark have had your fair share of troubles, but Eric of all people ... There must have been countless other men to choose from.'

'It happened,' said Caroline. 'He was there, and Mark so rarely is.'

Mary looked into Caroline's grief-stricken face. 'You love Mark very much, don't you?'

Caroline met her gaze. 'I always thought love at first sight was the sort of thing that only happens in cheap novels,' she said after a moment. 'I know it sounds ridiculous, but that's what it was like with me. I'd never chased a man in my life until I met him. I think I shall always be a fool where Mark is concerned, and I'm never going to stop loving him, whatever happens.' She wiped the tears from her cheeks. 'I wish you would tell me about him. Help me to understand him a little better.'

How could anybody unravel the knotted skeins? Mary thought. 'I can't,' she said. 'He's built a wall round himself which I thought you would be able to break down. At times I think you did – but you only had to turn your back for him to start desperately building it up again. If it helps, I think he loves you more than he realises. If he didn't, he would never have reacted in the way that he has. What about Fran? I haven't heard a word from her.'

'The other servants told Elly that she came to the house that Sunday morning and there was a row. Apparently she didn't stay long.' She stared into the fire. 'I don't know what to do any more,' she said.

Mary took hold of the girl's hands. 'Then you must leave him. You can't go on like this, my dear. You are starting to look ill.'

'I can't leave,' said Caroline. 'Not now. I'm pregnant. I don't want my baby born without its father.'

'How long have you known?' Mary asked.

'I saw the doctor last week.' She looked up, suddenly horrified. 'Good God, surely you don't think Eric had anything to do with it? I'm three months. Even Mark can't twist that round; he and I were together the entire time.'

'And you haven't told him yet?'

'No.'

'You must,' Mary said.

Caroline's eyes were pleading. 'I'm frightened that he won't believe it's his. That's why I came to you. He's going to notice soon. Would you tell him?'

'I can't, Caroline,' said Mary. 'Not that. Do you want him to believe what he is already thinking? I'm afraid, my dear, that this is something you must do yourself. But if it will make you feel better I shall have a chat with him when he comes up.'

'He's not coming!' said Caroline, crying again.

'Everything will turn out all right,' Mary said. 'Just you wait and see. Go back to London, Caroline. It's not a good idea for you to stay alone in this enormous house. I shall be coming down myself in a few days' time to stay with Hugh and Sarah. We can talk again then, and I'll somehow contrive to have a chat with Mark.'

Caroline leant forward and kissed Mary's cheek. 'Thank you,' she said. 'I feel much better now that you know.'

Caroline returned to London, but Mark was colder than before; day followed day, and still she was unable to summon the courage to tell him about the baby. There was nobody else to whom she cared to turn, and as her friends did not know she was back, nobody tried to get in touch with her. She waited for Mary to come, moping miserably about the house during the day, and going to bed at an hour when the old Caroline Hanley had always been on her way out. If Mark noticed the change in his wife, he ignored it.

She rarely slept well, but because of the baby she didn't want to take pills. Tonight, for some reason, sleep had come easily, and she did not hear the slam of the front door, nor the hurried tread on the carpeted stairs; nor did she hear her bedroom door open. But she sprang up when the door thudded shut and the overhead light came on. It took her a few moments to gather her wits and adjust her blinking eyes to the glare.

Mark stood at the foot of the bed, his face pale and his eyes furious. She stared at him, the sheet clutched beneath her chin.

'Why didn't you tell me you were pregnant?' he demanded.

She shivered. 'I was frightened,' she said. 'How did you find out?'

'I've just been with Mother. She thought I knew and let it slip,' he said. 'Do you know whose it is, or are you merely bluffing things out in the hope that it will resemble nobody in particular?'

He was being deliberately cruel, and she knew it. 'You bastard!' she hissed. 'If Mary told you I was having a baby, then she'll also have told you when it was conceived.'

'How do I know what other men you've had?' he asked. 'You're always running hither and thither. God only knows where you are half the time.'

She could feel hysteria building up inside her. She couldn't break down. Not in front of him. 'Get out of here!' she screamed.

He turned away. As he shut the door, a tear rolled down her cheek. She brushed it away with her hand.

She was tired and upset, pushed beyond the level that her taut nerves could endure. There was only one way to escape this mess, and she would take it. She padded barefoot to the bathroom where she found a full bottle of the pills her doctor had prescribed when she was having trouble sleeping before she and Mark went on holiday. She filled a glass with water, and then spilt the pills onto the top of a cabinet where they rolled and spun, a few of them dropping to the floor. There were an awful lot, but methodically she began cramming them into her mouth. She gulped them down with the help of the water.

I shall be able to sleep now, she thought. I shall sleep and sleep, and he will never be able to hurt me or his child again. She returned to the bedroom, and feeling strangely at peace with herself, switched off the bright lights and got into bed.

The small bedside lamp was still on, but she couldn't be bothered to turn it off. She closed her eyes and waited for the nothingness which was to come.

Chapter Ten

It was past three when Mark went up to his own room. As he passed Caroline's door he saw that a light was still on. He loosened his tie, walked on, and then hesitated. She had probably cried herself to sleep—except that Caroline had a phobia about lights in the bedroom and could never sleep unless it was pitch black. Or maybe she was still awake; in which case, perhaps he would go in. He had not meant to hurt her—or at least, not quite so much.

She was asleep. There was a smile on her lips, and her breathing was slow and regular. He was about to switch off the lamp when some inner sense told him that something was wrong. She was sleeping too soundly. He shook her, gently at first, then violently, but her eyelids did not even flicker.

'Oh Christ!' he muttered.

He hurried to the bathroom and saw the empty bottle lying on its side, and a glass standing beside the washbasin. Something crunched beneath his foot, and when he stepped back he saw a pill. He searched round, found others, and put them in his pocket, together with the bottle. He remembered that she sometimes used to take sleeping pills.

He went back to the bedroom, aware that had it not been for the lamp she would have been found dead in the morning. He telephoned for an ambulance, then hesitated, not wanting the servants roused and chattering. There was a telephone extension to Elly's room, and he asked her to come down; she was the one person he could trust.

She was half asleep when she crept into the room wearing an ankle-length dressing-gown and slippers with bobbing pompoms. She looked at her mistress, and then at Mark Hanley who was sitting on the bed. She was unable to tell what he was thinking, she could only see he had received a severe shock.

'Will she be all right?' she asked.

He looked at her, his eyes a little unfocused.

'I hope so, Elly,' he said. 'Could you wait downstairs for the ambulance, and show the men up when they come? I'd better stay with her.'

She nodded.

'Elly,' he said suddenly, 'do you know the name of her doctor? Maybe I should let him know.'

'Barlow,' she said, 'Dr. Terence Barlow. His surgery's near Sloane Square, but I don't know where he lives.'

'I'll find out from enquiries,' he said.

The operator connected him to the Barlow number, and briefly Mark explained what had happened. The doctor said he would meet them at the hospital. Mark put down the receiver and glanced towards the window. Where was that damn ambulance?

He picked up the telephone again, and ignoring the angry voice that eventually answered, asked for his mother.

'Caroline has taken an overdose of sleeping pills,' he said. 'I've just found her.'

There was a pause. At last he could hear the sirens, still a long way off but coming closer.

'I have to go,' he said. 'Shall I send Tim for you?'

'I'll get a taxi,' Mary Latchcham answered. 'Where are they taking her?'

By the time he rang off the ambulance had arrived and he could hear Elly's voice on the stairs. He leant across the bed and flicked a strand of hair from his wife's face.

'Caro,' he said. 'Surely there was a better way than this?'

Lisa Weston had been out to dinner with friends, and did not get home until late. She felt as though she had only just closed her eyes when the telephone started to ring. It's sure to be the wrong number, she thought. She sat up and fumbled in the dark for the receiver, found it, but, not gripping the thing properly, managed to knock the telephone to the floor. With a curse she switched on the lamp, and blinded by its glare, groped around the floor until she found the telephone. She was surprised that the call had not been cut off.

'Hello,' she said irritably.

'Lisa ... are you all right?'

She was suddenly wide awake. 'I dropped the telephone. Is something wrong?'

'I'm sorry for waking you, but I need a favour.'

'Of course,' she said. 'What's happened, Mark?' He sounded overwrought, and barely in control of himself.

'I can't very well tell you everything over the phone, but Caroline has tried to commit suicide. She'll be all right, but I have to stay at the hospital with her, and wondered whether you could come over and collect Mother. She's staying with Hugh Latchcham and his wife, but she doesn't know them all that well, and I'd rather she was with you—just at the moment. She looks exhausted, and she's refusing to leave. I know she'll listen to you.'

Caroline ... suicide ...

'Of course,' said Lisa. 'But Caroline? I don't understand. She's not the sort of person to do something like that.'

'Well, she did,' Mark said. 'Look, Tim is already on his way—it's pouring with rain, and far too late for you to be driving alone. I'll explain the rest when you get here. And Lisa, thank you.'

Only Mark and his mother were in the waiting room. Mary Latchcham sat in a corner beside a window, looking small and hunched, and showing every one of her sixty-three years.

'Thank you for coming,' Mark murmured as Lisa walked in. And she, who knew him so well, saw just how badly shaken he was.

'How is Caroline?' she asked.

'Still unconscious.'

Mary Latchcham stirred, saw who her son was talking to, and straightened up. 'Lisa, my dear, you shouldn't have come out at this time of night. There's nothing we can do but wait.'

Lisa kissed her cheek. 'There's nothing we can do here,' she said. 'I thought you'd like to come home with me.'

'Thank you, dear. But I ought to stay.'

'Go with her, Mother,' Mark said. 'I promise to telephone immediately there's any change.'

Mary gazed at her son. 'I suppose you're right. But I can go back to Hugh's.'

'What?' asked Lisa. 'With my family wide awake and dying of curiosity? When I left the dogs were barking, David was screaming, and Marian was yelling out of a window wanting to know where I was going. You may as well come back because I can promise you that nobody will be getting any more sleep tonight!'

The old woman took hold of Lisa's outstretched hand. 'All right, dear,' she said. 'Thank you. But I'll have to telephone Hugh and let him know what is happening.'

While Mary put on her coat, Lisa turned to Mark. In the harsh light she could see the sleepless rings about his eyes, and the beginning of the blonde, barely noticeable stubble.

'What happened?' she asked.

'She took pills.'

Lisa frowned. 'I don't suppose it would be any good my asking why?'

His expression hardened. He was in no mood to counter Lisa's head-on attack. 'No,' he said sharply. 'I don't suppose it would. That is a question best left for Caroline to answer.'

'And naturally you had nothing to do with it,' she bit.

He didn't answer, but his eyes were furious as they rested on her face. She did not flinch, but held his stare until she turned away to take Mary's arm.

Caroline did not have to open her eyes to know she was alive and in a strange room. She could not immediately remember what had happened, but then it came back in a rush, and she was grateful. She wanted to live, she wanted her baby; and however cruel he was, she still wanted her husband. She opened her eyes and stared at the ceiling, then moved her head slowly until she saw him standing in front of the window, watching her.

'How did I get here?' she asked, the words coming out in a hoarse whisper.

'I brought you,' he said gently. 'How do you feel?'

'Terrible,' she croaked.

He smiled. 'They had to pump out your stomach. But the baby's all right. Why did you do it, Caroline?'

She closed her eyes. 'It seemed the easiest way at the time. I suppose it was you who found me?'

'Yes. You know, I would have given you a divorce if you had asked for it.'

She felt too tired to cry. 'I don't want a divorce,' she said. 'I don't want my baby born without its father.'

He moved a little, as though he were shifting his weight from one leg to the other. 'What can we do, Caro? Even without this, I don't think anything can ever be the same between us. I should never have married you, and I think you would be wise to leave me now before I ruin your life altogether.'

She was very tired, but determined to see this through. He had called her Caro, an endearment he had not used for longer than she cared to remember.

'We could try,' she said.

He moved so suddenly that she jumped. 'It wouldn't work. There would always be that shadow hanging over us.'

'It was one misbegotten night, Mark. Don't you think I've paid a hundred times over for what I did? I don't want to go back to the beginning, I know we can't do that. But surely we can compromise, try and make something more than a mockery out of our marriage?'

'If that's what you want, I'll try,' he said. 'But I am what I am, Caro; I can't change overnight.'

'I don't know if you can change at all,' she said. 'But we must both do our best, and perhaps we can find some middle course.'

'Don't be too generous, Caroline,' he said softly. 'Now, before you fall asleep I want you to listen. As Alan isn't here to advise me, I'm not sure whether this incident will be reported to the police or not. If it is, I shall try and keep them away from you. But you must tell everyone, including your doctor, that this was an accident. Say you were tired and sleeping badly, that the baby was kicking, anything that sounds plausible—but not that you deliberately swallowed a bottle of pills.'

She wanted to laugh, but her throat hurt too much. 'Babies don't kick at three months,' she said. 'What about the press? Do they know yet?'

'No. The staff here are discreet, and if the worst should happen I will arrange for a suitable release saying that you're pregnant and in for a routine check-up.'

'What about Eric?' she asked.

His eyes hardened. 'What happens to Eric is none of your concern. Do you understand that?'

'Yes,' she murmured.

He reached forward and ran his fingers along her cheek. 'Try and get some sleep,' he said.

Eric Stewart had been scared witless when he'd seen the newspapers after his night with Caroline. He had gone home to Fran, who refused to speak to him, and every day he went to work, dreading the moment when he would receive a summons from Mark. He heard that Caroline was in hospital, but was unable to discover why. He could only surmise that some massive bribes had been paid in order to ensure such a high degree of secrecy. And then Norma telephoned him, asking if he could come to his brother-in-law's office that afternoon.

Mark was sitting behind his desk, studying a document, and writing notes in the margin. He glanced up. His eyes were dangerously bright, and his expression steely. Eric shifted uneasily, not daring to speak.

'I'd like you to take a look at the papers inside that file,' Mark said, pointing towards the coffee table.

Eric opened his mouth and then clamped it shut. Mark wasn't

even looking at him, he was concentrating on the document again. Eric sat down and stared at the unmarked buff folder. It wasn't very thick. 'What's in here?' he asked.

Mark ignored him. Eric's hand trembled as he reached forward. The folder contained photostat pages whose contents made his blood run cold. As soon as he saw them, he knew everything would be there, but he flicked through them all the same, to be sure. When he had finished he closed the folder and stood up.

'What are you going to do?' he said.

'How much of that money are you able to pay back?'

'None of it. You know that.'

'I am amazed you managed to get away with it for so long. You could go to jail if I decide to press charges.'

What little colour was left in Eric's face drained away, leaving him white as a sheet.

'However,' said Mark, 'there has been enough scandal already. I am not placing my business, or my private life, in further jeopardy because of your idiocy. I don't suppose you would like this made public either. If you clear your desk at the magazine and get out today, I won't take it any further.'

'What about the money?' Eric asked.

'I shall see to it.' Mark gazed at him with cold eyes. 'That file will also be destroyed, together with the original documents.'

'You seem to have planned everything,' Eric said bitterly.

Mark frowned. 'Don't push your luck, Eric. If it weren't for the fact that you're married to my sister, I'd have no compunction about throwing you to the wolves.'

Eric stood there for a moment longer. All those years of work. All that striving. Now he had lost everything, and for what? He turned away, defeated, with an uncertain future and a dubious past.

Mark was about to leave when June Halliday stormed into his office, slamming the door in Norma's indignant face. 'I quit!' she said, throwing an envelope onto his desk. 'You've bloody well done nothing for almost a month, and then you pounce on him like a damn cat on a mouse! Well, if you're going to let personal feelings influence you, I'm out too. You can run your own magazine.'

Mark had a pounding headache, but glaring into that calm, composed face, June would never have known it.

'I didn't realise you thought so highly of Eric,' he said quietly. 'You've certainly been pulling the wool over my eyes all these years.'

'That has nothing whatsoever to do with it!' she said angrily. 'He was excellent at what he did, and I disapprove of the way you have thrown him out.'

'What did he tell you?'

'Nothing. There was no need. I have eyes in my head. I had a great deal of respect for you, but not any more.'

'Sit down, June,' he said, and pressed an intercom button. 'Norma, do you still have that file I told you to shred?'

'Yes. It's in the safe. I was going to do it after you'd gone,' came back the efficient reply.

'Good. Please bring it in here.'

June was watching him suspiciously. 'What the hell are you up to now?' she asked.

'Nothing,' he said. 'I know you won't babble this around.' Norma brought in the file. 'Give it to Miss Halliday,' he said.

June gazed at the folder. 'What's in here?' she asked.

'Proof that Eric has been fiddling the magazine's books. He was very clever. It took two firms of accountants to run the discrepancies to earth, and a hell of a lot of money to pay them off. Add to that Eric's twenty thousand pounds in gambling debts, and another forty thousand he skimmed from the magazine, and you have a rather substantial amount, all of which has been settled from my own pocket. I think I have treated Eric very well in the circumstances. Everything is there. Read it.'

June's eyes narrowed, and with a look of distaste, she dropped the folder onto his desk. 'I believe you,' she said. 'What about the editorship of the magazine?'

'It's all yours, of course.' He picked up her resignation and handed it back. She tore it in half.

'And what if I don't come up to your exacting standards?' she asked.

'You will,' he said confidently. 'You'll also be interested to learn that I have more or less completed the negotiations to buy the *Threepenny Post.* I'm just waiting for Alan to come back from America so that we can finalise the purchase.'

She had known the paper was in financial difficulties, but not that Mark was interested in it. The *Threepenny Post* was a small but prestigious newspaper which had been owned by the same family for the better part of half a century.

'Don't you ever reach a point where you feel you own enough?' she asked.

'No,' he replied. He glanced at his watch. 'I really do have to go. Caroline is expecting me. Is there anything else you want?'

'Only to say that you're a bastard, and a damn cool one at that.'

Chapter Eleven

Lisa visited Caroline in the mornings when there was less likelihood of meeting Mark. It was after her final visit—for Caroline was to be discharged the next day—that Lisa arrived home to find a red sports car parked in the drive. She left her station wagon in front of the garage and went to look at the car, which was obviously brand new and very expensive. Her first thought was that it belonged to Mark, but he rarely moved without Tim these days, and since his own accident, had hated sports cars.

Well, she thought, there's only one way to find out. She was in the hall unbuttoning her coat when someone stepped from the shadows and slid the garment from her shoulders.

'You really should pay more attention to accessories,' Martin said. 'A long scarf would have set this off to perfection.'

She spun round as the coat came away in his hands.

'Martin!' she said. 'What a horrible fright you gave me!'

He kissed her cheek. 'I'm sorry,' he said. 'Will you forgive me for not having seen you in such a long time?'

'There's nothing to forgive,' she said, taking the coat from him and shoving it into a cupboard. 'Is that your car outside?'

'Yes. What do you think of it? I only bought it last week.'

'I think you're a bloody fool,' she said. 'You're a terrible driver at the best of times, and those things are lethal.'

'Oh Lisa,' he said, his smile fading. 'Are you against me as well?'

'Against you?' she asked. 'What do you mean?'

He turned his head away. 'I should never have come here . . involved you in this ...'

'In what?' she asked sharply. 'What on earth is going on?'

'You're the only person I can really trust,' he said, his eyes troubled. 'But it was silly of me to come.'

'Let's sit down and you can tell me about it. Have you quarrelled with Mark? That's easy enough to do these days.'

His eyes darted towards the drawing room. 'Could we talk somewhere else? Kathy is in there.'

Lisa was aware that she must be staring at him open-mouthed. It took an effort to pull herself together. 'The dining room should be nice and warm,' she said.

It was at that moment the telephone rang. At once Martin went pale, and she could hear the sound of his uneven breathing. She wondered what Kathy must be thinking.

'Shall I get it?' Clara asked, popping her head out of the kitchen.

'Yes please,' said Lisa, watching Martin's terrified face. 'Whoever it is, tell them I'm not back yet.'

She gripped Martin's arm, feeling the tension surging through him; they both stood waiting while Clara made a few routine responses, then put the 'phone down.

'It was Mrs. Smitton,' said Clara. 'She'll be taking out her horse at two and will wait at the Ham Gate for five minutes. If you don't come, she'll carry on.'

Martin sagged like a deflated balloon.

'Thank you, Clara,' Lisa said. 'Please could you bring us some coffee in the dining room? And you'd better ask Miss Karn if she wants anything.'

Clara nodded as she walked away.

'Nothing can be that bad,' Lisa said to Martin.

When they reached the dining room he did not sit down but stood beside the window, watching the horse and pony pull hay from their nets. Lisa knew better than to hurry him, and sat on a chair at the opposite end of the room, her elbows resting on the table.

'Mark has forbidden Kathy and me to see each other except when it's unavoidable, and then only with Chris present,' Martin said. 'He had us both in separately this morning. He told Kathy that she's still a child with a career to think of. I suppose you know she's reached Number One in the charts? As for me, I was told that if I tried to see her on her own he would tell her about ... about ...'

'Your boyfriends,' she said flatly. 'So you genuinely love her, Martin?'

He swung round, and the expression on his face was something she had been unprepared for.

'I do,' he said.

'Does Mark know that?'

He sat down. 'He suspects enough to try and part us. He's determined to make a success of her, and he won't let anything stand in his way.'

'But he can't stop you seeing each other,' Lisa said. 'I know Kathy is young, but she's not an infant. What about her parents? Can't they help?'

'They signed legal documents placing her under Mark's guardianship,' he replied. 'Need I say more than that Alan drew them up?'

She sighed and wished Alan were here now. 'What are you planning to do?'

'Marry. He can't touch us then.' Everything suddenly tumbled out in a breathless gush. 'We knew immediately what we had to do. Kathy pleaded a headache and had Chris take her home. As she was upset, he cancelled her appointments. She told the housekeeper she didn't want to be disturbed, locked the bedroom door, and then climbed out of the bathroom window and down the fire escape. I was waiting and we went to the Town Hall, but you have to have a licence, and there are God only knows how many forms to be filled in. We forged a letter of consent from her father, and managed to find a sympathetic old dear who didn't ask too many questions once she realised who we were. She's rushing everything through. If we go back at two-thirty we can be married.'

'And so you came here to kill the time,' Lisa said.

'There was nowhere else to go. I'm always moving from place to place anyway, so it's difficult to keep track of me, but once it's discovered that Kathy has gone, all hell is going to break loose. Will you help us, Lisa?'

'Of course,' she said, smiling. 'What are you going to do after the ceremony?'

'We were thinking of going to Cornwall for a few days. By the time we get back Mark should have cooled down. He's sure to come here, though, and I don't think he'll be very pleasant.'

She laughed. 'I've known him too long to be frightened by him. Don't worry about me.'

'Lisa, sweetheart, nobody could ask for a better friend than you.' He pulled her up, and hugged her. 'You haven't met Kathy, have you?'

'No,' she said. 'And the poor girl must be terrified. You shall both stay for lunch and we'll have a celebration.'

'What if Mark 'phones?' he asked, frowning. 'Perhaps it would be better if we left now.'

'Don't be ridiculous. Where on earth would you go?' She kissed his cheek. 'I think I can hear Clara coming. Let's have coffee in the drawing room with Kathy.'

Kathy was sitting on the sofa, staring into the fire, her face creased with worry. Lisa would not have recognised the girl who had sung at the school concert. And she's so young, Lisa thought, watching her run into Martin's arms. They're both so young ... so happy ... so much in love.

'It's all right,' Martin whispered to Kathy, and in them both Lisa saw the heedless passion of youth. It was strange to think that she, too, had felt that once—and much more besides.

Kathy Karn smiled nervously. 'Thank you, Mrs. Weston. Thank you for everything you're doing for us.'

'Call me Lisa,' she said. 'I only wish I could do more. Come and sit down.'

Lisa liked Kathy. She was natural and unpretentious, and talked in muted tones about Mark and all he had done for her. None of them could do justice to the meal which Clara prepared, or the bottle of champagne which Lisa insisted on opening. At fifteen minutes to two, they started to stir.

'Who's going to witness it?' Lisa asked.

Martin stared at her. 'I don't know. I expect we'll find somebody.'

'I'll do it. Look, I'll follow you in my own car. Then you'll have at least one friendly face there.'

'Lisa ... there's no need,' Martin began.

'I insist,' she said. 'Just give me a couple of minutes to change into something more respectable.'

She left them in the drawing room and dashed into the hall, shouting to Clara that she was going out for a while. She could hear David crying and suddenly remembered she had not seen him since early that morning. But there was no time now, and Pat was there. She would make it up to him this evening.

She changed into a plain dress, brushed her hair and hurriedly put on some lipstick. She was at the door when the jewellery box on the dressing-table caught her eye. Lisa had never much cared for jewellery, but Alan had given her some pretty pieces during their married life, several of them quite valuable. Surely there was something here she could give to the bride? She opened the overflowing box, emptied its contents on the bed and started rummaging through the gold and silver and sparkling stones. She was trying to choose between two brooches when she saw the case jammed at the bottom of the box. With trembling fingers she pulled it out. The case was scratched and discoloured in places, but when she opened it the bracelet looked as wonderful as it had when he first gave it to her.

... '*It sparkles nearly as bright as your eyes*,' he had said.

She snapped the case shut, pushed the rest of the stuff back into the box, and then ran downstairs.

'Scarf!' she shouted to Martin, holding it up. 'Be a dear and get my coat, will you?' She walked over to Kathy and held out the case. 'This is not new, I'm afraid, but I want you to have it. And I hope, my dear, it brings you as much happiness as it did me.'

Kathy's eyes widened when she saw what lay inside. 'It's beautiful!' she gasped. 'But I can't take this. Honest I can't.'

'Of course you can,' Lisa said, throwing the scarf around her neck.

Martin came up from behind, his hands smoothing the scarf into place. 'It's far too valuable,' he whispered.

'Perhaps it was valuable to me once,' said Lisa, 'but not any more.' She was silent for a moment. 'I haven't worn it in years.'

He gripped her shoulder, almost as though he understood.

'I'll never part with it,' Kathy said. 'It's the most beautiful thing anyone has ever given me.'

'And it's only the beginning,' said Lisa.

She did cry later, as she followed the sports car down the drive. But with a toss of her head she gulped back the tears. After all, the past was the past and she was better off rid of its memories.

She was kissing Marian goodnight when she heard the car. So soon, she calmly thought. She had expected all hell to break loose tomorrow, but not as early as tonight.

'Who's that?' Marian asked.

'Nobody important, darling. Go to sleep now.'

Doors slammed and the bell rang. Somewhere on the stairs Madame Ping started to yap, and Samson pricked his ears and growled deep in his throat. She heard Clara in the hall, shouting for the Peke to be quiet.

'Goodnight, love,' she said.

'Goodnight, Mummy.'

She went to the top of the stairs and looked down at the housekeeper. 'Tell him to help himself to a drink,' she said. 'I'll be there in a few minutes.'

I don't even feel nervous, Lisa thought. She looked into the nursery. David was asleep, and so she went to her own bedroom. She had no inclination to hurry, and looked at herself slowly in the full-length mirror. Her weight was back to what it had originally been, and she still looked much younger than she was. Her jeans were filthy, but it was impossible to work with horses and stay clean. Had Alan been home she would have changed for dinner, and wondered whether she should do so now, but decided against it. Her only concession was to run a comb through her hair.

She had run out of delaying tactics. Feeling confident and self-assured, she started down the stairs.

'Hello, Mark,' she said.

He was pacing the room, but stopped when she came in. His eyes were furious, as they had been the last time she had seen him in the hospital. But tonight he was sharper altogether, like a finely honed blade. She knew he would forgive her anything, except for this. She had deliberately meddled in his business empire, and was about to face the consequences.

'Good evening,' he said coldly.

She clenched her fists. This was going to be more difficult than she had thought.

'Would you like a drink?' she asked, aware that her own voice had hardened.

'No thank you.'

'Then I'm sure you won't mind if I do,' she said. 'Sit down, Mark.'

He did not sit, but stood beside the fireplace. Her hands trembled as she poured herself a generous gin laced with a few drops of tonic. She sat on the sofa, glad when Madame Ping jumped on her lap, staring at Mark with popping eyes.

'Where is Martin?' he asked, so suddenly that she practically choked on a mouthful of her drink.

'Try checking under the beds,' she retorted. 'How the hell should I know where Martin is?'

He had his back to the fire, and the lamp threw strange, almost frightening shadows across his face.

'For God's sake, Lisa, stop playing games with me. Where is he? He hasn't visited any of his usual haunts today, and his car has been gone since early this morning. The one consistent thing about Martin is that he's loyal to his friends, and if he was in trouble I think he'd turn to you. So where is he?'

'Is he in trouble?' she said innocently, and when he did not reply, 'Please note that I am also loyal to my friends. I don't know where he is.'

'And even if you did, you wouldn't tell me?'

'I don't, so the question doesn't arise.'

As she watched him, she wondered where the laughter had gone, that irrepressible humour they had once shared.

'Then let me put it this way,' he said. 'Have you seen him today?'

'Why?' she asked.

She saw the glint in his eyes and the way his lips pursed, and took another sip of gin. She knew he could not harm Martin and Kathy now, but she was determined not to give in to him too easily. Let him fight every inch of the way, she thought. He always gets what he wants just because everyone is frightened of him. It never occurred to her that his questions were not so very unreasonable.

He seemed to take a long time before answering.

'I have just come from Kathy's flat,' he said. 'A locksmith had to break into her room after the housekeeper went into hysterics thinking she'd killed herself. But instead of a corpse we found no Kathy at all. A suitcase and some clothes have also gone. I have every reason to believe she is with Martin. Is she?'

'What?' she asked. 'A dirty weekend?'

She felt then the anger which he was fighting to hold down.

'Perhaps you could enlighten me,' he said. 'The girl happens to be only seventeen.'

'And what would you do if she had gone with him?' Lisa asked.

A look of exasperation passed through his eyes, and she knew that anybody but her would long ago have been subjected to a verbal lashing. She thought it prudent to accept defeat now, before he lost control of his temper.

'You are too late,' she said, gazing into his eyes. 'It's ridiculous. At seventeen she can't vote, or control her own life, but she is no longer considered a child. They were married this afternoon. And I wasn't lying, I don't know where Martin is. I don't know where either of them is, but they'll be back in a few days.'

He had been expecting anything but this, and she saw a wave of shock pass over him.

'Would you like that drink now?' she asked.

'No thank you,' came the curt reply. 'Did you help them?'

'I was there,' she said. 'It didn't seem right that they should have to sneak away without a friendly face in sight. They came here because there was nowhere else to go, and I helped them because I felt sorry for them. I know what it's like to feel the world is against you. I only did what I thought was best.'

'Lisa ... Lisa ... If wishes were horses ... Do you really understand what you have done with your misguided goodwill?'

Her brow creased, but her voice remained steady. 'They are young and very much in love. Why couldn't you let them be?'

He sighed. 'Because Kathy is a child. In an incredibly short time she's seen and done things which have been beyond her wildest dreams. Doors of experience have opened which she never even knew existed. Surely you can imagine the effect of all that on an immature girl from a background as deprived as Kathy's? Like it or not, Lisa, you just can't treat Kathy like any ordinary young girl—she's hardly living in the real world at all. She had an adolescent crush on me for a while, but when she met Martin the puppy love transferred to him, and he became her white knight in shining armour. But Martin is fundamentally homosexual. How long do you think it's going to take before he strays back to his pretty young men?'

She stared past him into the fire. 'If you hadn't forbidden them to see each other, this might never have happened,' she said. 'Why did you have to play God? Why couldn't you leave them alone?'

'Because they are not ordinary people,' he snapped. 'And I'll be surprised if that marriage lasts for three months.'

Her eyes found and held his. 'I suggest, Mark, that you set your own house in order before meddling in their affairs. I think there's a lot more to Caroline taking those pills than either of you will admit. And what you did to Eric is nothing to be proud of. The jilted lover taking his revenge—isn't that rather adolescent?'

The coldness of his eyes sent chills down her back, and the silence seemed to hang between them for ever.

'I have learnt all I need to know,' he eventually said, 'and shall waste no more of your time.' He walked past her and had the door open before he swung round. 'I expect you'll be pleased to hear that Alan is coming home tomorrow. He's probably trying to get through to you now with the news.'

'You bring back my lord and master to keep me under control?' she asked.

His frown deepened. 'Don't flatter yourself, my dear. I'm bringing him back to look after the business. If you hear from your lovebirds you can tell them it's safe to return. I shall be putting my house in order, as you put it. Caroline and I are going away.'

He closed the door without even saying goodbye. She heard him call Tim, who must have been in the kitchen gossiping with Clara. Her hands gripped the Pekinese as she listened to them leave.

She was crying.

'Damn you, Mark!' she shouted to the empty room.

Chapter Twelve

By the time Mark and Caroline returned to London, spring was in the air. Kathy was back at work and Martin was preparing his spring collection. Mark certainly saw an improvement in the girl, and Martin's designs were amongst the best he had ever produced; yet there was still a niggling doubt at the back of his mind. They were happy, they were in love, but it was altogether too perfect to last.

They had wasted no time in settling into an enormous four-storeyed house in Kensington, with more servants than they could possibly need, three of the latest in the Rolls Royce range, and the Aston Martin. Nothing was spared, and they lived in a luxury which was the delight of the press, but which Mark could all too easily see crashing down about their ears. Kathy, oddly enough, derived her greatest pleasure from a Dalmatian puppy that Martin gave her. She took it everywhere, and more than once Mark wondered which was more important to her, Martin or Sofie.

Mark deliberately stayed away from Lisa, and she did not go near Hanley Recordings. Nor did Mark attempt to make any contact with his sister. He learnt that the Stewart house was up for sale, and that Eric was doing some freelance journalism, and earning enough to keep the family solvent; but they were out of his life now, and he no longer felt obliged to keep an eye on them.

And Caroline. A change had come over Caroline. Perhaps it was impending motherhood, or maybe it was guilt for what she had done. She became strangely domesticated, and although her swollen stomach neither bothered nor embarrassed her, she preferred to remain at home. Even when Mark was at work she invited her friends over rather than visit them. He found her extraordinarily subdued—something she had never been—and he made a genuine effort not to neglect her quite as much as he had done in the past. But he did not share her bed, using her pregnancy as an excuse; although she said nothing, Caroline knew that this situation was permanent, and that their relationship was altered for ever.

In mid May she left London for Oldenshaw, where she idled away her days, watching her stomach expand to enormous proportions. She did not expect Mark to follow her, but he did come during the first week of June and, even more unexpected, he stayed. She was delighted that he should want to be with her.

Many others were equally delighted, though for different reasons. Simon Townsend was exhausted after an intensive American tour which had been followed by long recording sessions, and he was now able to escape with his family to Sardinia. Martin and Kathy, the pressure temporarily lifted, disappeared to an unknown destination in Spain. At the recording company the wheels of business barely turned, and almost ground to a halt when Alan Weston departed for Greece with his wife and daughter, leaving David and his nanny at the farm with Richard Crowder.

For Caroline it was a time which she would not easily forget. Oldenshaw always cast a strange spell on her husband, although she was not sure whether he realised it. Only here was he really happy and at ease. This time, too, the place worked its magic—Mark did nothing unless she were with him, and in everything he was sympathetic to her and mindful of her needs. When Charles Latchcham brought his hunters up from grass during July she almost had an argument with him over his refusal to ride. And so he went daily to Latchcham Hall, with Caroline usually accompanying him. Looking back later, it was on these days she liked to remember him best, astride one of the tall hunters, his eyes happy and his windswept hair like a gleaming crown. In the afternoons he would take her to faraway villages with quaint pubs, or they would walk together over the summer meadows.

She could have stayed there forever, but in the end it was because of her that they left. They had finished dinner one evening and since it was still light outside, they decided to go for a walk. They were in the orchard when she felt the strange sensations. The baby was not kicking as it usually did, but actually moving inside her.

'Perfectly normal,' the elderly doctor said half an hour later. 'Turned over, that's all. It'll be a few days yet before it comes.'

But when he had gone Mark told her they would be returning to London in the morning.

That night she cried into her pillow. It was over.

The child was born a little before dawn.

Mark was alone in the waiting room, staying because it was his duty. Any emotion he felt was not for the child, but for Caroline—and even for her, his feelings were not strong. Nothing remained of their marriage, as far as he was concerned, and he had only helped her through these past months to make them more bearable for her. It had cost him nothing, and had given her the strength to carry on.

He was looking through the window when the doctor came in. 'Is it over?' he asked without turning round.

Dr. Terence Barlow disregarded the strange question. 'You have a son,' he said.

'And my wife?'

Terence Barlow was beginning to feel uncomfortable, as though he had committed a crime by bringing an innocent child into the world.

'She is tired, but well,' he said. 'You can see her now, but only for a few minutes.'

She was waiting for him. But when he kissed her she felt no warmth in the touch of his lips, and his eyes, when she searched them, were guarded. He was performing the duty expected of him; nothing more. She had hoped the baby might bring them together. 'He is your son,' she said awkwardly. 'He already has your eyes. But you don't care, do you, Mark?'

'I care, Caro,' he said gently.

Her eyes widened with accusation. 'You don't want him! You've never wanted him. I'm sorry for keeping you here when you must have better things to do. If you go home now you can still get a couple of hours sleep and be at work on time.'

'Caroline ... '

'No!' she said, hysteria edging her voice.

The door opened.

'Doctor thought you might like to see him together,' said the nurse. She was holding a small bundle in her arms.

Caroline screamed, and kept on screaming until they tranquillised her. Her husband stayed and watched, and when she was quietly sleeping he left. He made no attempt to see the child.

The servants were eager to hear the news, and after telling them, Mark asked Elly to come into the study. She was aware of Roberts' eyes on her back, and of the others glancing at each other. Mr. Mark did not look as a new father should. There was no pleasure in his face, and his voice had been expressionless.

'Close the door, Elly,' he said. 'Would you like a drink?'

'Why, Mr. Mark,' she gasped, 'it's barely breakfast time!'

He smiled. 'Then you must excuse me if I do. Please sit down. I won't keep you long.'

She sat on a hard chair by the door, and watched as he poured himself a large whisky. It was obvious that something was very wrong. He leant against the desk.

'Is Mrs. Hanley all right?' she anxiously asked.

'Yes,' he said. 'She'll be home in a few days. Meanwhile, I should like to know whether she's done anything about finding a nanny for the baby.'

Elly sighed with relief. 'She thought she would wait for a while,' she said. 'She wanted to look after him herself at first, with me helping. I'm to move into the room next to the nursery. Why do you ask?'

He took a cigarette from an antique box which Caroline had bought at Sotheby's.

'Because I didn't know. But I doubt Caroline will want to nurse him now.'

'Is something wrong with the baby?'

He shook his head. 'No. As all of you must be aware, it is our marriage which is at fault. I was thoughtless enough to upset her when I went to see her today, and when the child was brought into the room she became hysterical.'

Elly smiled. 'She's had a trying time, Mr. Mark. She'll come round. Just see if she doesn't.'

'No, Elly,' he said. 'I don't think she will. You should have married, you know, not stagnated in service; if this were you instead of Caroline, I know you'd have taken that child to your heart, no matter what.'

She flushed with embarrassment, and looked down at the floor. When she looked up again he was sipping the whisky. He was the most dynamic man she would probably ever know, and despite his reputation as a hard businessman, he had always been kind to her. She wondered whether the child was like him.

'I'd like to take care of him,' she said.

He put down the glass. 'That is an enormous undertaking, Elly. I didn't bring you in here for that. I'm sure I can find a suitable person before Caroline comes home.'

'I want to care for him,' she insisted.

'Won't my wife mind losing her personal maid?'

'Anne could manage if I showed her, and we can easily get another parlour maid in her place.'

'I think you ought to ask Caroline first,' he said. 'You can come with me when I visit her this evening.'

'Thank you, Mr. Mark,' she said. 'I'd like that.' She stood up. 'What are you going to name him?'

He looked at her in surprise. 'I don't know. What was Caroline's preference?'

'Kathleen. She wanted a girl. Kathleen Tina Mary. Tina after her mother, and Mary after yours.' She hesitated, wondering if she were being presumptuous. 'You should name him after your father, Mr. Mark. After all, he is a Hanley.'

'Paul? My mother would approve of that. Thank you, Elly. I'll talk it over with Caroline.'

As she was about to open the door she paused and turned back to him.

'Don't you think you should eat something, Mr. Mark?'

'What? Oh yes, I suppose so,' he said. 'Ask Roberts to arrange for something light.'

She bobbed her head and slipped out of the room. Mark finished the whisky, and then turned to the telephone. Mary Latchcham would want to know about her grandson.

Chapter Thirteen

It was a strange year; a year of student protest and riot, and for Mark Hanley, a year of mingled success and failure. By the end of it, the *Threepenny Post* was back on its feet, and June Halliday had a good grip on the magazine, changing the format just enough to boost the sales figures even further. Everything Mark Hanley touched turned to gold, except for his marriage; that rapidly deteriorated after the birth of his son. Young Paul Hanley spent his first birthday with Elly, neglected by his father, who was too busy working, and by his mother, who flitted gaily around the world with her friends and an occasional, discreet lover.

Lisa had seen neither of them in months. But she had other things on her mind now. At Easter she went to the farm, and returned home depressed and worried. It was not the pains in her father's back which upset her, but something else which she could not quite put her finger on. The Westons did not holiday abroad that year but went to the farm, taking their horses in a recently acquired double box pulled by Lisa's station wagon. Lisa drove up with Marian and the dogs, and Alan flew in at the weekend with David and Pat. He could not promise them the entire summer, but he would be there during August.

And so, for a while, Richard Crowder's flagging spirits received the boost they needed. David had got past the walking stage and required constant supervision, and Marian started to ride every day—something she rarely did at home any more, because ballet was taking up so much of her time.

The day before Alan was due to join them for the summer, Lisa came in from an early morning gallop and found her father alone in the kitchen. Marian was putting Chanson and Tumbleweed into a field with the Clydesdales. There were only three Crowder horses now, for Ben had died the previous autumn, and Snowy had succumbed when winter began to set in.

'We had a lovely ride,' she said, throwing her arms around his neck. 'I never realise how much I miss this place until I come back.'

He abruptly manoeuvred the chair sideways, then forwards, so that her arms fell flatly to her sides. She stared at the back of his neck, not even sure whether he had heard what she said.

'Is something wrong?' she asked.

He turned, his expressionless eyes meeting her anxious ones. 'I've just heard it's spread to Wilkinson's farm. His entire herd have to be destroyed.'

She thought for a moment. 'But Daddy, that's a good thirty miles from here. And you know the foot-and-mouth's been concentrated in that area all along. The chances of spreading this far are very slim. The Wilkinsons were bound to be hit. They were isolated in the middle of it.'

'It'll spread like wildfire now,' he gloomily declared. 'Harold swore that he'd seen a badger the other day. God only knows where it walked from. Then there's that bloody fox which took three of my chickens last month.'

'We could bring the cattle further in if you're worried,' she said. 'But it'll mean giving them extra feed. Really, Daddy, I think you're over reacting. We've seen it come much closer than this. Do you remember the year you sent me to stay with the Hanleys, and then barricaded yourself in? It never hit us then.'

'Aye,' he said, watching Marian through the open window. 'But this time will be different. I can feel it in my bones. I'd like to go into the village,' he said. 'Could you harness the team for me?'

'I can take you in the car if you like.'

'No,' he said, 'I'd prefer the team. I don't rightly know how long I'll be.'

Marian heard the tail end of the conversation as she came flying into the kitchen.

'Can I come with you?' she asked, flinging the bridles into an untidy heap on the kitchen table.

Richard Crowder eyed his granddaughter, then thrust the chair forward. 'No,' he said, propelling himself into the passage. He slammed the door behind him.

A comical frown creased the child's brow. 'What did I say?' she asked.

'Nothing,' said Lisa. 'He's got something on his mind, that's all. Do you want to help me harness the horses?'

'Drummer is filthy. He's been rolling in the mud by the trough.'

Lisa grimaced. Cleaning Chanson was bad enough, but brushing down a filthy grey Clydesdale was like tackling a double-decker bus.

'I'll take a look,' she said. 'If he's too bad we'll have to turn the hose on him.' Marian was about to follow her when Lisa pointed to the tangle of leather. 'First things first, young lady. Wash the bits, and then hang those bridles up properly.'

It spread like the plague. By the end of August it had reached the far side of Steelton and the cattle were brought into the immediate fields around the house. Lisa and Marian met up with Charles Latchcham during the last week of their stay. He was riding an elderly hunter, and a groom was following behind on a younger animal which was difficult to control.

'It's going to crucify the hunting season,' he said, with the same air of despondency which had spread throughout the farming community. 'If it reaches Steelton's southern boundaries I'm going to close off the estates altogether. I'd advise your father to do the same.'

'We've already brought up the cattle,' Lisa told him. 'We've also posted No Trespass signs all over the place. Only our own people are allowed in at the moment, and I think Daddy's on the verge of stopping them too, just in case.'

'Wisest move,' Charles Latchcham agreed. 'I'm breeding some bloody good stock from that young bull I bought off your father a couple of years ago, and I've no intention of losing them all now. Whatever the younger men say about artificial insemination, I still don't think you can do much better than one of your line of bulls.'

Lisa smiled. 'They come from generations of selective breeding. Daddy has papers which trace some of the stock as far back as a hundred years. That's an awful long time.'

'Too long to lose now. We won't be able to take out these buggers for much longer either. Will you be staying on to help?'

'I don't know,' said Lisa. 'I hadn't actually thought about it.'

They parted company, and Marian thumped the pony up beside her mother's horse.

'Why did you say you don't know?' she asked. 'We've got to go home next Tuesday. I go back to school the following week.'

'Let's trot,' Lisa suggested.

Their hoofbeats were dulled by the mossy path. 'Would you mind very much if I weren't there?' Lisa asked. 'I know it's wrong, and that I should take you to school at the beginning of the new term, but you will have Clara and Daddy. Your grandfather has nobody, and if this spreads much further, which I think it will, he's going to need all the help he can get.'

Tumbleweed broke into a jarring canter. The child pulled him back.

'Who'll drive the horses and dogs home?' she asked, her voice trembling.

'You can all go back with Daddy in the plane,' Lisa said. 'But you'll have to keep the dogs off him, otherwise he'll go mad. Perhaps you could tie them to something near the back.'

'Their leads could go round the seats,' said Marian. 'But we can't take the horses in the plane, and if they stay here ...'

Lisa looked at her daughter, who was far more upset than she would admit.

'Horses don't get it,' she said.

'Are you sure?'

'I'm positive. Nor do dogs and cats. They are only carriers. Thank you for taking it so nicely, Marian.'

'Let's gallop,' Marian said, pushing the pony forward.

Chanson snorted and tossed her head. But Lisa held her in for a few seconds, watching the retreating back of the small girl, her plaits flying out from beneath her riding cap. Then, with a sigh, she let the horse go.

It was a warm September afternoon, and Martin Henderson, who had been watching for Mark's car from a first-storey window, rushed cheerfully down the stairs. As he came out Tim gave him a warning nod, and pulling his hands from his pockets, Martin stepped forward with an exaggerated air of authority. Mark looked at him, but there was no reciprocating smile, or any of the usual pleasantries.

'I hope you haven't called me out on a fool's errand,' he said sharply. 'What are you doing here, anyway? I thought you never came near the place.'

'I don't very often,' said the designer. 'I prefer to work from the shop. It's more peaceful. This would normally be dealt with through official channels, and I wouldn't know a thing about it. But I was expecting a delivery of wool weave from the mill, and was here when the whole damn lot arrived.'

Mark asked no questions as he followed Martin through the bustling workrooms to the storeroom where the rolls of fabric were kept.

'All this,' Martin said, stopping beside some rolls which had been kept apart from the others. 'It's all the same.' With a yank he overturned a roll of his favourite brown wool weave and pulled out about four yards, which he then dropped to the well-swept floor. 'Perhaps you can throw some light on it. For a start, I think the orders got muddled up. I never ordered this one, the grey.' He yanked at another roll. 'It's a colour I never use. So if I'm not meant to get it, I wonder who is.'

Mark picked up the material, seeing the flaw immediately. It stretched along the grain of the cloth in a faint, irregular line, like a catch which kept repeating itself. The inexperienced eye might not notice it at first, but this was reject stuff, and following his father's standards, Mark never let such material leave the mill.

'It's begun, Martin,' he said, not even sounding angry. 'I didn't expect him to be quite so brazen. If it weren't for this, I wouldn't have found out until I began losing my buyers. You were quite right in asking me to come.'

'What's begun?' Martin asked.

The material slithered through Mark's loose fingers to the floor. 'This is inexcusable. If much of it has already been circulated, my reputation for good quality could go down the drain.'

Martin frowned, and pushed back some hair which had fallen into his eyes. 'Arthur Bennett?' he asked.

'Arthur Bennett,' Mark confirmed. He remembered something Lisa had said a long time ago. Arthur was now on Steelton's Town Council and there was a rumour that he could be the next Labour Party candidate. He was well established in the community, and was making a fair amount of money from his real estate business. The mill was no longer essential and if he were planning to leave soon, this was retribution for what had happened at that Boxing Day Meet.

'Would you mind going to Oldenshaw for a few days?' he asked. 'The main production might have to be moved to the RIEL mill at Talon-Under-Water, and I'd like you there to check the quality.'

'RIEL? But I thought ...'

'It's still a secret,' Mark said. 'I'm buying it from them. The deal is meant to be finalised in January, but as the papers have been signed there should be no trouble if I jump ahead a few months. It hasn't been doing well and I offered them a good price. I'll have Alan sort out any legal difficulties, but I'd like you to fly there tomorrow. And your stay must remain secret, at least until I can come up in a few days' time. Arthur doesn't know what happens in Talon, so unless you advertise your presence he's unlikely to find out.'

Martin hesitated, the unspoken question clearly reflected in his eyes.

'I'm sorry,' Mark said. 'Kathy has to fulfil her television contract. You'll be back in a week, so she won't even have time to miss you.'

Martin smiled. 'At least I'll have Lisa for company.'

Mark was rolling out another bale of cloth. 'See this?' he said. 'Different machines, yet a similar pattern. By the way, Martin, I doubt you'll see Lisa. They have foot-and-mouth up there at the moment, and you'll find that every farmer who hasn't already been scourged will be barricaded in. Alan wanted to go up last weekend, but Lisa told him he wouldn't be allowed on the farm.'

'What's foot-and-mouth?' Martin asked.

'A contagious disease which can only be caught by cloven-hoofed animals. They can inoculate, and even cure some cases, but it's never a hundred per cent certain. There's only one sure way to stamp it out, and that's to destroy the infected animals. One case of foot-and-mouth on your farm, and the Ministry of Agriculture will slaughter every beast, whether it's diseased or not. That's the reason for the fortifications. People can't catch it, but they can spread it by walking from an infected field to a clean pasture, as can any animal which moves around freely. It's a nasty business, and you'd better not wander through any fields or you're liable to find yourself riddled with buckshot.'

'Can I telephone her?' Martin gloomily asked.

'You can telephone the whole damn world if you want,' Mark told him.

Every day, twice a day, every cow, bull and pig was inspected for the first tell-tale sign of blisters on the tongue or between the feet. Lisa watched her father's deterioration with growing anxiety. She knew his quickfire temper was caused through lack of sleep, and the pains which were now with him day and night—but he refused to leave the farm or let the doctor in. So she did the best she could over the telephone, and arranged for a prescription to be left outside the padlocked main gate with their provisions.

This self-imposed isolation had been fun at first, but in a short while the strain began to tell. The only time Lisa was able to get away by herself was when she rode Chanson through the grazing herds of dairy cattle. Her father depressed her, Orchid seemed to grow more crotchety with the passing years, and Harold told and retold the same stories she had heard since childhood. Bill Simpson and Ned Dooley, both single men, had volunteered to stay on the farm and help out. They shared a room in Harold's small cottage, and although their combined brawn and willingness was appreciated, Lisa found them as dull and uncommunicative as two clods of earth. After three weeks she felt ready to be condemned to an institution.

Every day she prayed that the disease would leave the area. But it did not. One by one the farms to the north and east of Steelton fell prey; then slowly but surely it began to slink southwards, eating its way west towards them. It has to miss us, she thought. It always has before, and it will again.

It was a Wednesday morning when Harold sought her out.

'Christabel's down,' he said. 'Do you want to see her, or should we call the vet first?'

The nightmare of waiting was over. Lisa felt tears in her eyes as she looked at the old man.

'Are you sure?' she asked.

'Aye, pretty well. All I need is official confirmation, and you know as much as that young upstart who's taken over from Mackingsaw.'

Jim Croxley was a first rate vet whom Lisa remembered from university. He had been a year ahead of her, and was a quiet, dedicated man who had always been top of his class.

'Where is she?' she asked, unable to look at him. Harold had aged visibly this past month. The cattle were his life. How would he survive without them? How would any of them survive?

'I'll show you,' he said.

They took the Land-Rover, having to pass through herds of healthy animals whose eyes followed the vehicle. The heifer was lying where Harold had left her. Lisa stroked the animal's damp neck, and as Harold prised its mouth open she tried to recall her old text books. But there was no need for text books. There was no doubt whatsoever. She walked to the Land-Rover, and reached with shaking hands for her father's revolver.

'Will you do it, Harold?' she asked, holding the weapon towards him.

'The Ministry people will want to see for themselves.'

'To hell with the Ministry people,' she said. 'They can see as much from a dead cow as a live one.' Her voice was trembling. 'If you won't do it, I'll have to.'

He took the revolver from her. 'Fine vet you'd have made,' he said gruffly.

She stayed beside the Land-Rover, tears streaming down her cheeks.

Her eyes were still swollen from crying when she faced Orchid. 'Where's Daddy?' she asked.

The housekeeper put down the plate she was drying. 'It's happened?'

'Yes, it's happened,' Lisa replied. 'I have to tell him. Where is he?'

'You're a brave young lass,' Orchid said, hugging her. 'He's been practising with the shotgun behind the barns. I'm surprised you never heard the racket he's been making. But he's been quiet for some time now, so I expect he's cleaning it. Richard knows better than to muck up my kitchen with oil and rags after all these years. Where's Harold?

I thought I saw him come back with you.'

'He's taken Bill and Ned to round them up.' She gulped back a fresh onslaught of tears. 'He's quite right, you know, I'd have made a rotten vet. I'm far too sentimental. Could you 'phone Jim Croxley and tell him what's happened? He'll contact the authorities.' She turned towards the door. 'The sooner this is over, the better.'

'Daddy?'

She saw his chair at the back of the barn. His back was to her, and he did not seem to have heard her call. She walked towards him, wishing she could soften the blow. But there was no way to tell a man who had already lost a large part of his life that the rest was about to be snatched from him. There would be nothing left but the dogs and cats, the horses and poultry.

'Daddy?' she called again, her voice echoing in the rafters.

The shotgun was lying beside the chair, a thin shaft of sunlight glinting on its barrel. He was sitting very still, with his head strangely slumped.

'Daddy?'

She stopped, her mouth falling open in a soundless scream. Where his face had once been was a nightmare of blood and flesh and bone. She stared in horror, hypnotised by the dreadful thing which had been her father.

Then, as the bile rose in her throat, she turned away, and falling to her knees, gagged uncontrollably in the blood-spattered straw. It was only when her stomach was empty and her throat raw that she screamed; the screams reverberating round and round the farmyard.

Chapter Fourteen

I was just getting into the car when Norma ran into the yard.

'Thank goodness!' she gasped. 'I hoped to catch you before you left. Martin's on the telephone. He wanted Alan urgently, but when I said he'd left for Paris an hour ago he asked for you instead. He sounds upset about something.' Tim already had the door open. 'The switchboard is holding the call,' Norma was saying. 'It would be quicker to take it on the caretaker's extension.'

I nodded. What the hell could have happened in the short time Martin had been up there? I turned to Tim. 'Are we late?' This was an important meeting which I did not want to miss.

'Will be now,' he said, glancing at his watch. 'Can't be helped.'

I smiled, and then followed Norma into the small back room. 'Don't go,' I said to her. 'I might need you ... Martin?'

I heard a sigh. 'Thank God you're still there. Can you get Alan back?'

He should be over the Channel by now. 'If I have to,' I said, before remembering that Lisa was also up there. 'What's happened?'

There was a pause, and from somewhere behind Martin I could hear the hum of voices and a dog barking.

'I'm at the farm,' he said. 'I can't go into much detail, there are too many people in and out, but Richard Crowder blew his head off with a shotgun, and Lisa found him not half an hour ago. The doctor is here now. He's sedated her.'

The colour must have drained from my face, for Norma stepped forward before checking her impulsive movement.

'That's not all,' Martin continued. 'Lisa was about to tell him that she'd just discovered their first case of foot-and-mouth. The housekeeper tells me he couldn't have known. In fact, she's adamant that he was in fine fettle all morning.'

'He knew,' I said. 'You don't farm all your life and not sense what's going on around you. I'll have the jet radioed to return immediately. If I leave now I can collect Alan in Manchester, and we should be at the airstrip at about eleven. Can you be there with a car?'

'Yes,' he said. 'And Mark, I'm sorry.'

I put down the receiver. I could not believe what I had heard. Not Richard Crowder. Not Lisa's dependable father. But I think I'd had a feeling that this might happen ever since that morning when he asked me to watch over his farm; for the day on which Richard broke his back was the day on which he died. His body had merely waited a little longer until the right excuse had presented itself.

'Mr. Hanley?'

I had forgotten Norma. 'Lisa Weston's father is dead,' I said. 'I shall have to go up there immediately. Can you get through to Air Traffic Control and ask them to turn back the jet? Tell Peter he's to fly direct to Manchester. I'll meet them there. And make sure Alan knows Lisa is all right, otherwise he'll be a nervous wreck by the time he arrives.'

'I'm sorry,' she said. 'Shall I cancel your appointments for the next few days?'

'Yes. And telephone Toddington. Tell them to have my plane fuelled and ready for take-off.' I paused. Clothes? I always kept an adequate supply at the Manor. Caroline? 'And try to locate my wife. You should be able to contact me at either the farm or the Manor.'

She nodded, and as I walked outside, the sun did not seem as bright as it had before.

The jet must have gone further than I thought, for I reached Manchester a good twenty minutes before it. I paced up and down as I waited. So much time was being wasted when I could be doing more important things. I knew I would have to take charge at the farm, make sure that what had to be done was done properly.

It arrived at long last, and as he rushed towards me Alan looked pale and shaken. In less than half an hour we were over the airstrip. I could see Martin waiting, smoking with jerky movements as though he despised every puff. He probably did, for I had never seen Martin smoke before. As soon as I pulled up Alan sprang out.

'How's Lisa?' he shouted.

'Heavily tranquillised. I told her you were coming.'

I missed the rest because I wanted to turn the plane before shutting off the engines. They were still talking when I joined them.

'I'll drive,' I said.

I questioned Martin closely, and learnt enough to give me a rough picture of the situation.

'The vet is there and some other men,' he replied to my probing. 'From what I can see everything is in turmoil. Surely they can't kill them all? An inoculation?'

'Nothing can help,' I said more harshly than I meant. 'Alan, I want Lisa taken away from the farm before the slaughter begins. Go to the Manor, and you as well, Martin.'

'I could help at the farm,' he suggested.

I glanced at him through the rearview mirror. I could see he was repulsed by the whole situation, yet he was still eager to assist. Martin had a lot more backbone than met the eye.

'No,' I said. 'It's not going to be a pretty sight, and I don't think you could stomach it.'

'What about you?' Alan asked.

'I have no choice,' I said. We were nearly there. 'I expect everything is in hand, but remember not to leave until you have been thoroughly disinfected, otherwise you're going to spread the disease even further. Alan, please make sure that Lisa changes her clothes before she goes, even if you have to strip her yourself. And none of you are to go out of the grounds. There are a few smallholdings around the village, and many of the villagers own a milk cow or a few pigs. The Latchcham Estates are also to be avoided.'

'Talking of Latchcham Estates, Mary came immediately she heard,' Martin said. 'She's with Lisa now.'

'But I thought she couldn't ...' Alan began.

'She can come out,' I said. 'But if Charles has any sense, he won't let her back in.'

We travelled the rest of the way in silence, waved past a hastily erected barricade by a young policeman who recognised Martin and the car. As we drove into the farmyard I saw a uniformed constable standing in front of the largest barn, talking with a stocky young man who Martin told me was Jim Croxley. Behind them was the blood-stained wheelchair. Two labourers stood nearby, and I saw Harold leaning against a gate. Nobody knew more about the Crowder cattle than Harold. They were his life. I looked away, parking the car just beyond the main barn.

Alan was staring at the house.

'You'd better go in,' I said.

He needed no further bidding. Martin stayed with me for a moment longer. 'This is such a bloody waste,' he spat, before following Alan to the house.

The cattle were spread through two large fields in the lee of a low range of hills. Later on, they would be herded into one smaller meadow, but for the moment they had been left here, where they could not be seen or heard from the house. Before the farmhands began their thankless task of driving the creatures to their deaths, I wandered amongst them, away from the bustle of the yard, and away from Lisa whom I had not seen and whom, at the moment, I could not bear to face.

When I went back Jim Croxley was waiting for me.

'Everyone has gone except for the housekeeper,' he said. 'She refuses to leave. She's making the men a spot of tea, and then we'll have to begin. I think we ought to put the horses in the stables.'

I went with him. Harold was still leaning against the gate.

'Perhaps we should ask him to help,' the vet said. 'Better than standing there brooding.'

'Harold is a cattle man,' I told him.

The old man turned as we approached, unashamed tears running down his cheeks.

'It's time then?' he asked, directing the question to me.

'Yes. We're going to put the horses inside.'

He straightened up. 'Then I'd best get down there. They know and trust me. I'd not like them to go feeling alone and frightened.'

He walked past us, an old, old man.

'This is the part of my profession I hate,' Jim Croxley said. 'All those healthy animals, and there's not a damn thing I can do to help them.'

I called the horses. They came, nervous at the unusual activity and wanting reassurance. Afterwards, we coaxed the dogs into the kitchen. I watched the men walk towards the fields. They liked this job no more than the rest of us. But it had to be done.

'Thank you for coming, Mark,' said Orchid. 'This is a black day to be sure. Can I get you something to eat or drink?'

'No thank you. I think I'll walk round the yard.'

She nodded, and I left quickly, knowing she wanted to cry.

The pigs would be done last, together with the two bulls, sterling animals which were worth a fortune. Piglets were squealing in ignorant bliss, and a tabby cat sat washing itself at the feet of Crowder's Tempest, a beautiful animal which had won a string of champion rosettes at local shows.

I don't know why, but I was drawn to the barn where some forgotten chickens scratched, and a cockerel strutted ridiculously in front of them. Blood still stained the straw, and as I stared at it I seemed to hear Richard's voice coming from nowhere.

'I promise nothing shall ever happen to your farm,' I said aloud.

* * *

The black, foul-smelling smoke was rising beyond the hills and drifting sluggishly towards Oldenshaw when Martin returned. He was carrying fresh clothes for me, neatly folded over a hanger and covered with polythene.

I was mixing horse feed when he arrived, and Bill Simpson was helping. The horses were nervous and kept kicking their doors, wanting to be outside, not shut in, where they were engulfed by the nauseating smell of burning flesh every time the wind changed.

'What's that?' Martin asked.

I straightened up, rubbing damp bran from my hands.

'A funeral pyre,' I said, watching the smoke whirl in the upper currents of air. 'It's a lifetime of hard work and devotion literally gone up in flames.'

Behind him were the deep marks made when the tractor had dragged away the dead bulls. I turned to Bill. 'Could you hand out the feed? It's already mixed.'

'Aye, sir,' he said. 'I'll do that.'

I did not want to go back to the farmhouse. I knew the Ministry men were in the kitchen, talking in subdued tones, while Orchid kept herself busy feeding them. They were dog-tired, and still had the barns and other buildings to disinfect. Jim Croxley had left when the slaughter was finished. Ned Dooley was somewhere round the back, trying to gather up straying poultry, and Harold had gone alone to his cottage, neither asking for, nor wanting sympathy.

I leant against a gate and offered Martin a cigarette.

'I thought you didn't smoke,' I said, 'but you've never stopped today.'

'I don't usually. But sometimes it helps.'

'You may as well put that down,' I said, referring to the clothing. 'Did you make sure the rest was burnt when you got to the Manor?'

'Yes,' he said. 'These are the oldest Mary could find.'

We did not speak for a few minutes, both of us lost in our own thoughts. I heard a chorus of whinnies. Bill must be handing out the feed.

'Your mother noticed,' Martin suddenly said.

'Noticed what?'

'How you deliberately avoided the house after you arrived. Lisa has also been asking after you. She's still in a daze, but she wants you to go through her father's papers. Mary will telephone the relatives if you can find me their numbers.'

'I'll do it,' I said. I heard a hum of voices from the direction of the farmhouse. They were coming out to finish the job. 'Did Norma or Caroline telephone?' I asked.

'Shit, I forgot. Norma 'phoned and said she hadn't been able to find Caroline, but had left messages for her.'

Where the hell was she? Since Paul's birth we had gone our separate ways, and didn't even attempt to try any more. I straightened up. 'You'd better get back.'

'Is there anything I can do to help?' he asked with genuine concern. 'You look done in.'

'Thank you, Martin, but it's finished now, bar the cleaning up. Do you know where they took Richard's body?'

'To the mortuary in Steelton. Alan will make the necessary arrangements tomorrow.'

'Good,' I said. I dropped my half-smoked cigarette, grinding it beneath my heel. 'I'm sorry to get you involved in this.'

An unexpected smile lit up his face. 'What are friends for? Lisa has done as much for me. In fact, both of you have done more for me than any other person alive. I only wish …' He paused.

'What do you wish?'

He turned to watch the men sorting through their equipment.

'I only wish you would allow yourself to become a little more human a little more often.'

So saying, he walked away, hopping impatiently from foot to foot as both he and the car were once more disinfected.

'I must smell like a bloody dry-cleaning factory,' I heard him complain.

Later, when I walked over to the house, he was gone.

I don't know what time the Ministry men left, but they came to tell me they had finished for the time being, and would be back in the morning for a final check. I know it was dark, and the farmyard eerily silent. Orchid was still bustling about the house, but the two farmhands had gone to Harold's cottage, dead on their feet.

The three dogs were in Richard's office, watching me anxiously in case I too should leave. Every so often one of them would whine softly, walk to the door, then back to me, placing a paw or chin on my knees as their eyes pleaded to understand. Three of the cats had also sneaked in, and sat watching me with unblinking eyes.

Richard Crowder had worked hard on his books over the last few months, probably harder than he had worked on them in the rest of his life put together. He had known what he was going to do, and had meticulously prepared for the day when he would take his own life. If it had not been for this outbreak of foot-and-mouth Lisa would have inherited a prosperous farm. But now she would only have the land, for to bring the farm back to the state which had reigned here this morning would mean years of work. Richard had been no fool when he extracted that promise from me.

The sudden ring of the telephone made me jump. The dogs sprang to their feet, eager and excited, only to sink back to the floor when I picked up the receiver. It was Caroline, and she sounded drunk.

'I'm sorry,' she apologised with maudlin grace. 'I've just been speaking with Mary. She told me what happened. I tried to get through earlier, but the connections are bloody awful, and telephoning Oldenshaw is like trying to speak to the other side of the world.'

'Where the hell are you?' I asked angrily.

'Mark, darling, is that any way to greet me? Where am I? Let me think ... Christ, I don't know. I'll find out if you're that interested.'

'Forget it,' I said. 'If you can sober yourself up I want you here tomorrow morning. Mother can't cope alone, and if only for appearance sake, you should be here.'

She hiccuped loudly, and giggled. 'Who could resist such a charming offer? And seeing it's so long since you wanted me at your side, I suppose I should feel damn well flattered.'

A cat stood up, stretched, and brushed, purring, against my arm.

'Then I suggest you telephone Norma in the morning and she can arrange for Peter to fly you up.'

She laughed. 'Don't bother, darling. I'll have Ferdy fly me. He's got a cute little plane, and has been itching to take me for a spin.' She paused. 'I'll let you know what time I'll be arriving so that you can send a car.'

'There's nobody here to spare. You'll have to find a bloody taxi.'

I slammed down the receiver. My hand was shaking. 'Oh God!' I exclaimed.

Orchid came in a short while later. 'I've brought you some hot tea,' she said. 'Leave that for now, it's late and you've been on the go all day. I'm off to bed. Would you shut the dogs and cats in the kitchen when you leave? There are car keys on the hall table. Take any vehicle you want.'

I stood up and took the mug from her.

'Thank you,' I said. 'I've nearly finished. If you don't want to be alone, I can stay tonight.'

A thin hand clutched my arm. 'Nay lad, don't fret over me. I'm fine, and there are plenty of menfolk in the cottage should I want them. I'll have to get used to being without him now, at least until Lisa decides what she wants to do with this place.'

'Nothing will happen to the farm,' I assured her. I kissed her cheek. 'Goodnight, Orchid.'

'You're a good lad when you've a mind to be,' she said.

'Goodnight.'

As I sipped the tea my eyes strayed to a shelf full of books and files. There was an overflowing box file which I lifted down. I wished I had let it be, for as I sat reading until the early hours, I learnt the history, past and present, of that smouldering mass beyond the hill.

God! What a bloody waste.

Arthur Bennett had never moved into my father's office. It remained a hallowed place which was only used when I was at the mill. I didn't go near it today, but walked unannounced into Arthur's office. He did not look surprised, but I sensed an uneasiness in his manner.

'I heard what happened at the Crowder farm,' he said. 'I'm sorry.'

'Are you, Arthur?' I asked. 'I should have thought you'd be rejoicing. After all, if the farm is sold you stand a good chance of getting a foot in the door, so to speak. But I haven't come here to trade pleasantries. To be blunt, I want your resignation today. If I don't receive it, I shall have no option but to give you notice.' He stared at me. I could see the bitter hatred, not only for the scar I'd inflicted so long ago, but because I was everything he wanted to be and never would be. I didn't give him an opportunity to speak. 'I wouldn't argue if I were you,' I said. 'I've let Martin Henderson loose downstairs. He's checking the quality of the cloth, and expects to find the same defects which were in the last batch you forwarded to him. I also want to take charge of the books.'

'You'll find nowt amiss with the books,' he said.

'Not the account books, the order books. It seems strange that RIEL have recently received orders from some of our oldest customers. Stranger still that I knew of no problems here.'

His eyes glinted evilly. 'Get rid of me and you'll have nobody who can run mill. You'll be back where you were when I took over after your father died.'

'I came to you, Arthur, because at the time we could help each other. We can't any more. I also want Tucker to go.'

He smiled at that. 'Sack him and you'll have a walk out.'

'If he doesn't leave I'm going to shut the mill down for renovations and the installation of improved safety precautions. As sole owner I have every right.'

He was nervous now. 'You'd not get away with it,' he said. 'The unions would never let you. And you'd lose your customers. Every one of them.'

'I omitted the best part,' I told him. 'I'm buying the RIEL mill. I planned to expand production, but it can always take over on a temporary basis. I shall, of course, arrange to transfer the majority of my people there. Sam Tucker and anyone else in your pocket will not be included amongst them. So you see, Arthur, whatever happens I can't lose.' I walked to the door. 'Martin will be here for the rest of the day. If you hand your resignation to him, he will give you a cheque covering three months salary and whatever refunds you are due.'

That was the worst insult. Not me, nor Alan, but Martin.

He was shaking with rage and humiliation. 'The day will come, Mark Hanley, when you'll live to regret what you've done.'

I surveyed him coldly. 'On the contrary, Arthur, he who plays with fire gets burnt. Badly burnt if he persists in dabbling.'

I closed the door behind me, and went in search of Martin.

Arthur Bennett left, taking Sam Tucker with him. I knew there would be problems at the mills, but for the moment the energetic young man from Talon-Under-Water seemed able to cope with them both, and they would get by until I was able to come back and tend personally to their reorganisation.

I was surprised by the number of people who came to the funeral. Even with foot-and-mouth on their doorsteps the majority of farmers who knew Richard came, and also Charles Latchcham. When it was over they quickly dispersed, and Lisa, even in her grief, tried to show her gratitude for a foolhardiness which was unexpected.

A few hours after the funeral the will was read. The farm went to Lisa, with generous allowances being made to Orchid and Harold. But the surprise came at the very end when we thought it was finished. All eyes turned curiously as I learnt that I was now owner of Jinny and Drummer. By bequeathing me his two horses, Richard Crowder was stressing an obligation which, if the time ever came, I would be obliged to fulfil.

The next day Caroline and Martin returned to London, while I stayed a little longer to help out at the farm. I thought Mother was moving back to Latchcham Hall, but when I came home she was waiting for me.

'Fran is here,' she said.

I stared at her. 'What the hell does she want?' I was not in the mood for a confrontation.

'To talk to you,' Mother said.

'I have no desire to see her, let alone talk to her,' I said. 'If you brought her here, then I suggest you take her away again. I'm going to have a bath and then an early night. I ate at the farm.'

'Mark,' she said, taking hold of my arm. 'She is your sister. Don't turn your back on her.'

'It would be a total waste of time.'

'Please, Mark. For my sake.'

She too had been under a lot of strain this past week, and it was beginning to show in her face.

'Why does she want to see me?' I asked.

'That's not for me to say. Just talk to her.'

I glanced towards the drawing room. 'Is she in there?'

'Yes.'

'All right. I will do it for you, but for no other reason.'

'Thank you,' she said, and releasing my arm, she stepped back.

I hesitated outside the door and then pushed it open and walked in. 'Well, Fran?' I asked.

She was drinking tea and leapt to her feet when I spoke. She had lost some weight and her face was haggard.

'Thank you for seeing me,' she said. 'I wasn't sure if you would.'

'Thank Mother, not me,' I told her. 'Why are you here?'

'Because we're broke,' she said.

'What has that got to do with me?' I asked coldly. 'You and Eric should learn to handle your finances better.'

Tears sprang to her eyes. 'Damn it, Mark, he can't get a job. He's done a little freelancing, but not enough for us to live on. Since you threw him out nobody will touch him.'

'That's not my fault,' I said. 'Nobody knows exactly what happened. Surely you don't think I would release that sort of information?'

'No,' she said, the tears starting to spill down her cheeks. 'It might harm your bloody business. But when you paid off his gambling debts, people began wondering what else you were trying to hide. I was always jealous of you because I thought you had everything. I'm not any more. You might be successful, but you've become hard and unfeeling, and of us all you are the one who should be pitied. I'm sorry to have troubled you. I don't know how we'll do it, but we'll manage somehow. I don't ever want anything from you.'

She would have swept past me, except that I was blocking the doorway.

'How bad is it?' I asked.

'What do you care?'

I took a firm grip of her shoulders. 'Stop being so self-righteous and tell me the truth. Are things really that bad, or are you exaggerating?'

'Would I be here if they weren't?' she asked. 'Without Mummy the children wouldn't even have decent shoes on their feet.'

She broke down then, her shoulders heaving as she sobbed uncontrollably. What could I do? She was still my plain little sister.

Nothing could ever change that. I put my arms around her and held her tight. 'Don't cry, Fran,' I said. 'Everything will be all right. I'll arrange a position for Eric on the *Threepenny Post.* I own it now.'

'Oh Mark,' she murmured, crying even harder. It was a few minutes before she got control of herself. She pulled away from me and dabbed her eyes with a tissue. 'He won't let you down this time. I swear it.'

'I know he won't,' I said. 'You do realise that he will only be a reporter, not editor, nor even assistant editor?'

'Yes,' she said. 'And it's enough. At least he won't be able to have his women. I know you always thought I should leave him, but I'm not like you, and Eric is all I have—him and the children.'

'Where are you living now?' I asked.

'In Holland Park. We found a cheap basement flat. It's worse for the children than us. They can't understand why everything had to go so suddenly.'

'I'm sorry,' I said. 'I honestly never knew.'

'You weren't meant to,' she said. 'Is Mummy still out there?'

'I expect she's got her ear to the door. I'll call her in.' As I turned away something else struck me. 'How much money do you need? To keep your heads above water for the time being?'

She coloured. 'We can manage a bit longer.'

'I'll write out a cheque anyway,' I said. 'And I don't expect you to pay it back.'

Her smile was unexpected. 'I wish we could have got along better, Mark.'

'It's not too late,' I said.

'You're being kind. You know we shall never see eye to eye.'

'Then perhaps we can both try and be more tolerant,' I said, and kissed her on the cheek.

Chapter Fifteen

Martin had lost his way a half dozen times already, and then would have walked past the studio had it not been for her voice. She was pre-recording a lavish spectacular which was scheduled to be shown on Christmas Eve. It was practically finished now, this being the final number, in which she had to sing and dance with the chorus cavorting energetically about her. She saw him immediately and grinned. Chris turned round to see what had attracted her attention, and beckoned him forward.

'Cut!' the director yelled. 'Kathy, you're meant to be on this camera.'

'Oh, to hell with it!' she said. 'I'll do it proper for you later.' She ran out of the bright lights, dodging past the cameras and into Martin's arms. 'Cor, I missed you,' she whispered. 'It's been forever and forever.'

'Only a fortnight,' he said, and tilting her head, kissed her on the lips.

'Everyone is staring at us,' she hissed.

'Let them,' he answered, kissing her again.

There was a yap, and the young Dalmatian escaped from Chris and leapt between them, not knowing where to lavish her love first.

'Oh Sofie!' Kathy exclaimed, laughing as she tried to push the dog away.

'Kathy,' the director called across the floor. 'I think you'd better take a fifteen minute break. And please take the hound with you ... Chorus please ...'

Kathy caught the dog's trailing leash, and then swung her husband round in the direction from which he had come.

'C'mon, the canteen's down here,' she said. 'Let's have a cuppa, and you can tell me everything that's been happening. How's Lisa? Chris should have let me come. If it weren't for Mr. Hanley being there I think I'd have defied him and come anyway. But he frightens me sometimes. Don't he ever frighten you?'

'Not any more,' he said. He would never forget the anguish in Mark's eyes on that warm evening when, side by side, they had watched the clouds of black smoke rising from the Crowder farm.

In the canteen they drank tea and, ravenous, he ate a couple of ham rolls. She listened while he told her what had been happening, and it was half an hour later when Chris came looking for them.

'They want you to finish the number,' he said to Kathy. 'After that you can wind up for today.'

She smiled at him. 'I'll just be a couple more minutes,' she said. 'Can you take Sofie for me?'

He took the leash and coaxed the reluctant dog from beneath the table.

'Make sure she comes, won't you, Martin?'

He nodded. 'We'll be right behind you,' he said. He watched Chris drag the dog from the canteen, then turned back to his wife. She was looking at him with sparkling eyes.

'I got something special to tell you,' she said. 'I'm pregnant. The doctor told me last week.' Her eyes searched his face. 'Well, ain't you going to jump in the air, or yell, or sweep me off me feet?'

He was still staring at her in disbelief.

'Are you sure?' he asked.

' 'Course I'm sure. I missed me period, and was worried 'cos you know how regular I always am. So he did all the proper tests and it's confirmed.' Her face fell. 'You're not angry, are you?'

He took her hands in his, and then leant across the table, kissing her open lips.

'Do I look angry?' he laughed. 'When is it due?'

She laughed with him for a moment, then sprang to her feet. 'Christ! They'll be yelling bloody murder. C'mon. About the middle of May. I've been told to eat proper, but if I put on too much weight me doctor will give me a diet which won't harm the baby. He's going to be real angry now, ain't he?'

'Who?' Martin asked.

'Mr. Hanley, of course.'

'He'll probably tell us that we should have consulted him first . . . and I'll have to design you some clothes. I can start on that tomorrow. In fact, it might be an idea to do an entire range. I've never thought about pregnant women before, but the market must be pretty considerable.'

'C'mon,' she said, breaking into a trot. 'I've not put on an inch yet, so I don't know why you're talking about draping me in horrible maternity clothes.'

It only really struck him that he was to become a father when he was sitting at the side of the set, holding Sofie's leash. As he watched Kathy skip through the dance steps she had been taught, he hoped they would have a daughter. He would like a girl to pamper and spoil.

He was glad this show was almost completed. It was strenuous, even for Kathy, and the following day she was to start recording the new album Mark wanted to release before Christmas. There were also a few personal appearances to be made, but nothing demanding. If she wanted to keep working in the new year he would have to talk with Chris and Mark, ensure they kept her on a light schedule.

Halfway through the toe tapping number the chorus filed on stage, boys from the right, girls from the left. As they came face to face the couples linked arms. Martin Henderson's mind was suddenly empty of all thought as he gazed not at his wife, but at the leading pair of dancers. Not the girl, but the boy. He was tall and thin with jet black hair and dark eyes. He was beautiful.

Mark was not angry when they told him Kathy was pregnant. He called them a couple of fools and then dismissed the subject as being relatively unimportant. Kathy plunged into her recording sessions, being of the opinion that the sooner she was finished, the sooner she could spend time at home planning for her future family. She slaved long hours, often staying at the studios until midnight or later, so that the recordings were being taped in double the usual time. She was determined to have her own way, and neither Martin nor Chris were able to persuade her otherwise. Only Mark had the authority to take matters in hand, which he did on occasion.

It was on such an evening that he walked into the studio where she was working. It was almost ten, and he was going home himself. He took one glance at Kathy's earnest, but pale face, and called a halt to the session. Enough was enough.

She flung off the headphones and came storming into the control room. 'It was going so well, too!' she shouted angrily.

'Not everyone possesses your remarkable stamina,' he answered with rare and excellent humour, considering how trying his own day had been. 'And Kathy, I do wish you would keep that dog outside. Every time she scratches the tapes pick up a most peculiar range of noises.'

'She likes to be with me,' the girl said defiantly. 'I ain't leaving her at home, and Tony don't like her in here. He's got a cat which sleeps on that shelf and Sofie keeps worrying it.'

Mark glanced at Tony Crane. He shrugged. 'It's your cat,' he said.

'At least it's one of the many which has access to the building. It keeps me company when I work late at night.'

Mark smiled, then turned back to Kathy. 'Would you like a lift home?' he asked.

She shook her head. 'No, thank you. The car's been waiting for me. I told him to be here by six just in case I wanted to leave early, but then Martin rang to say he'd be working late, so I changed me mind.'

As she bent down to clip a leash onto the dog's collar she missed the frown which swept away his smile.

'Kathy, has nobody ever told you that employees are people with feelings, not scraps of dirt to be ground beneath your feet? I take it you have simply left your chauffeur sitting in the car for close on four hours without any indication of when you would be ready to leave?'

She glanced up at him. 'Why not?' she asked. 'He gets well paid, and that's what I got him for, ain't it?'

His eyes narrowed dangerously, but then, changing his mind, he walked out.

'Goodnight, Kathy,' he said.

She stared after him, unable to understand his curt rebuffal. What the hell had she done wrong now?

Kathy felt very tired by the time she got home. The house was in darkness except for one dim hall light, and the servants had obviously been dismissed for the night. Martin must have come home earlier than expected, and gone to bed.

She did not go upstairs immediately, but threw her coat over the bannister, then took Sofie into the kitchen for a bowl of milk and some biscuits. She watched for a moment as the animal ate, and then left her to follow later.

As she walked wearily up the stairs she could hear the sounds of laughter, and whispered voices. She smiled. He'd probably fallen asleep with the television set on. She wondered whether she could be bothered with a bath. The hot water would be relaxing. She paused outside the bedroom door, and then opened it. A hand flew to her mouth, and her eyes widened in horror.

Martin was naked; leaning over a woman who was dressed in one of Kathy's nightgowns. But when Martin turned his head she saw that the woman was a man. She uttered a low, animal moan, then backed from the room. Tears scalded her eyes as she ran down the stairs. She heard Martin call her back, but visualising those two male bodies being so vilely intimate, she kept on running. She slammed out of the house, leaving the dog whining frantically in the hall.

She ran until her legs were trembling and unable to move any more. She was crying hysterically, not caring about the few people on the streets who paused to stare. She stopped, her back against the cold glass of a shop window. Where to go? What to do? She had no money with her; not even her coat. She started to walk; on and on into the early hours of the morning, and all the time she wished she were dead.

Chapter Sixteen

Lisa came out of the room looking much paler than she had when she went in a half hour before. There was a set expression on her face, and a look in her eyes which told me that her own cure had begun. She was ready to face life again, to stare it defiantly in the face, and not run back into her silent world of mourning.

It was the first time we had been alone together since that evening in her house when she told me Martin and Kathy were married. Now she came straight to me, and I held her tight.

'He'll be all right,' she said softly. She moved from my arms, and sat on a velvet chair beside the empty fireplace. 'You were right, Mark. I didn't want to believe you because I thought you were being spiteful, but you weren't.'

I stayed where I was, watching her.

'Another man?' I asked.

She nodded. 'Upstairs in their bedroom. He swears he had never brought his lover here before, but he forgot something and dropped by the house to pick it up. One thing led to another, and I don't think he expected Kathy to come home so early. Apparently, she never gets back before midnight when she's working. Anyway, she found them together and although he tried to stop her, she ran out of the house and he has no idea where she could have gone. Do you know the worst of it? Deep down, he still loves her. He doesn't know why he did it. God, I wish I had listened to you in the first place.'

I took her hands in mind.

'None of us are really to blame,' I said. 'If I hadn't sent her home early she might never have known. Equally, if you had refused to help them, they would have found some other way.'

'What are you going to do now?'

'Try and find her. A girl like that can't just vanish into thin air. She's too well known. I only hope the press don't find out, otherwise they'll go to town.'

She smiled. 'This has been one hell of a year, hasn't it?'

Kathy had disappeared from the face of the earth. Even the detective agency I hired was unable to find her. After a fortnight I knew I would have to inform the police. I got no further than thinking about it, for at ten o'clock on a Monday morning she walked into my office, drawn but calm.

'Will you get Sofie for me?' she asked.

I looked at her. She was different. The innocent girlishness had gone.

'Where have you been?'

'Bobby put me up. I knew I could trust him not to tell nobody.'

Bobby Milton was lead singer to Mantis, who were now on their way to becoming one of the top groups in the country. He and the rest of the group were also into drugs, and none of them were desirable companions for an impressionable young girl. But was Martin much better?

'Will you get her for me?' she asked.

'Yes,' I said. 'Is she all you want?'

'No. I want a divorce too, but I'll have to get a lawyer for that.'

'And the baby?'

She shrugged. 'I got rid of it.'

I stood up and walked to the window. Autumn leaves were falling into the sluggish water of the Thames. Seasons come and seasons go, and Lisa was right. This had been one hell of a year.

PART FOUR
(1972–1974)

Chapter One

'Can't you think of anything but work? Caroline asked as she walked into the room. 'Making a fortune may make you feel wonderful, but at this rate, you'll be heading nowhere except to an early grave. Why don't you get some enjoyment out of life for a change?'

I put down the papers I had been studying, and looked up at her. 'I take it we are in for a pleasant evening of husband-baiting? Don't tell me you've nothing better to do.'

'I thought we could have dinner and talk,' she said. 'God only knows how long it is since we managed to do such a simple thing together. And I don't want to quarrel. Not this evening.'

'What do you want to talk about?' I asked.

'Us.' Her steady gaze held mine. 'But after dinner. I meant what I said about your getting some pleasure out of life, Mark. You've built your kingdom, so why not let somebody else sweat over it for a change? The day is going to come when you look back and regret having thrown away so much of your life.'

I sighed. 'What would you have me do? You know your lifestyle doesn't interest me.'

'Well, you're ridiculous to be a slave to work,' she snapped. 'Carry on like this and you'll be dead before you reach fifty.'

I closed my eyes. 'Caroline, I've had a hellish day. Are you going to give me a hellish night as well?'

'No,' she said. 'I'm sorry. I suppose what it boils down to is that we don't seem to be able to communicate any more. Let's have a drink.'

We clung to useless, neutral subjects after that, and not until dinner was finished did Caroline broach what was on her mind. I felt her eyes on my face and glanced up, a smile coming to my lips. Caroline at thirty-three was still breathtakingly beautiful, but very different from the girl I had married six years ago. She had matured, and her figure had smoothed into a maternal roundness which suited her.

'I think we've had a pretty long run,' she said suddenly, her fingers toying with a glass. 'We've certainly lasted longer than most of my friends. But we're not working out are we, Mark? I thought Paul might help, but he didn't. We go our separate ways, and when we're together ... well, that speaks for itself. I'd rather get out now than wait until the marriage grinds to a bitter end filled with hate.'

I had been wondering when this would come up. Caroline was right; ours was no longer a marriage, we were just two people who on occasions shared the same house.

'You want a divorce?' I asked.

'Yes.'

'When?'

'I can see no point in prolonging it.'

'What would you want?'

She looked tranquilly into my eyes 'Whatever you think fair. I don't want a long drawn out fight any more than you do. I'll be happy to settle for a little property and a respectable alimony. I shall take Paul, of course. You'd have to provide for him as well.'

'You can arrange the monetary details with Alan,' I said. 'And you can have anything you want, except Olden Manor.'

She laughed. 'I don't want that, nor this place either. I'm going back to America. I've seen enough of your bloody awful climate to last me a lifetime. But I'd like the houses in France and Switzerland. You rarely visited them, so they hold no memories.'

'What about the beach house at Big Sur?' I asked. 'It's no longer in the company name.'

Her face shadowed, and she looked as though she were going to cry.

'No,' she said after a moment. 'I know this sounds corny, but I loved you in that house, and I like to think you loved me too. I don't want to take on its ghosts ... Shit, now I'm saying all the things I was determined not to. Can I have a cigarette?'

I gave her one, and also poured her a strong drink. When I sat down again she was composed.

'The divorce laws are so damn complicated in this country,' she said 'I've been told the easiest way is if you commit adultery and then you don't oppose when I file for a divorce.'

'Good God, Caroline, I could have caught you out a half dozen times this year alone.'

Her face flushed, not with embarrassment but anger.

'And what about those cute model girls your precious Martin Henderson keeps in supply? From what I can see they have the morals of tomcats.'

I looked at her. 'I never realised you knew.'

Her anger was gone as quickly as it had flared. 'You weren't devious enough, Mark,' she said. 'You were seen.'

'Over-confidence,' I said, and then as her lips pursed, I wished I could retract those thoughtless words. 'All right, Caroline,' I agreed. 'We'll do it your way. I'll tell you where and when, and you can arrange for a detective to watch from outside. There are to be no photographers, no cheap sensationalism.'

'I said I wanted this to be quick and painless,' she said. 'And there'll be no smut, Mark. I promise. I'm going to bed now. Goodnight.'

As she leant forward to kiss my cheek, I took hold of her hand and squeezed it. 'Goodnight,' I said, feeling closer to her than I had in a very long time.

When she had gone I poured myself a drink and took it into the study. I'd got into the habit of working late at night, when the servants had been dismissed and I was left in peace. Despite the general air of gloom in the business world, nothing I owned was suffering. There was always a demand for music, although the gaiety and optimism which had characterised the early and mid Sixties had faded away. So too had that vast supply of originality, and I often felt now that we were merely plodding forwards while waiting for something new to inspire us.

This was certainly not a good time to be thinking of expansion, but I hadn't got where I was by treading a safe path. I had gambled before and was prepared to do so again. The high quality women's fashion magazine I had been offered at a bargain price by the bankrupt publishers struck me as a particularly good investment, but only if I could persuade June Halliday to take over as editor.

I was also contemplating making Eric Stewart assistant editor, as he and June together were an unbeatable combination. He had spent the past three years as a desk man on the *Threepenny Post*, where his talents were largely wasted. He was in his mid-forties now, and had finally come to terms with what he was. He still had the occasional affair, but they were only mild flings which came to nothing. He and Fran had moved back into Surrey, but to a far less flamboyant house, and although their marriage wasn't perfect, they had managed to find a level of content.

It was past one o'clock when the telephone rang, the shrill bell ear-splitting in the silence. I quickly picked up the receiver, hoping Caroline hadn't been woken. I expected it to be a wrong number, but it was William Denning, Martin's lover for the past two years. He was a likeable, inoffensive young man who had been a reasonably successful model until he gave up his career to move in with Martin. After Kathy left him, Martin had been unable to settle into any satisfactory relationships, with either men or women. But William was different. He kept discreetly in the background, and was an anchor to which Martin could cling when the professional pressures became too great.

'What's wrong?' I asked, knowing he would never phone at this hour, not unless it was important.

'Practically the entire summer collection has been stolen,' he said. 'We're at the workrooms now. Can you come over?'

'Christ!' I swore. 'I specifically told him not to keep them there.'

'I know,' said William passively. 'But he hates secrecy, and he refused to believe that anyone would attempt to steal them. The thieves circumvented the alarm system and got in through a skylight. They hit the security guard over the head and he'll need a couple of stitches, but otherwise he's okay.'

'I'll be right over,' I said. 'What about the police?'

'They're swarming all over the place looking for fingerprints and clues. They called us out. I personally don't think there's much chance of them getting much of it back.'

And even if they did it would already be too late. Patterns were probably being cut at this very minute. Those clothes were more than special, for they formed an exclusive collection which Martin was preparing for a charity fashion show. The tickets had been sold out months ago, and it had been confirmed that royalty would be present. This was going to be the fashion event of the year, and it was scheduled to take place in three weeks time.

I didn't wake Tim, but ordered a taxi. I was in the hall when Caroline came down the stairs.

'Where are you going?' she asked.

'Martin's collection has been stolen,' I said. 'Go back to bed. There's nothing you can do.'

She stood on the bottom step, looking at me. 'What about the show?' she asked.

'I don't know,' I said. 'I'm going there now to see what can be salvaged.'

'Try not to stay out all night. I know you don't believe me, but you're working far too hard. These long hours are unnatural.' She turned away. 'Perhaps our marriage would have been more successful if you'd cared as much about us as you do about everything else.'

I watched as she walked slowly up the stairs. Wherever it was that we had gone wrong, it was too late now for recriminations. At least there was no bitterness between us, nor the unsavoury prospect of prolonged court battles.

The thieves had been no ordinary burglars. They had known what they wanted and only the partially completed collection models had been taken. Nothing else was touched. Martin was sipping tea and looking totally shattered. I took him and William into one of the small side offices, where he slumped into a chair with William standing beside him, one hand resting on his shoulder.

'How many do you have left?' I asked.

'Six ... seven ... out of forty. The original drawings are still in the safe, but I won't be able to use them now. The show will have to be cancelled. We can't possibly meet the deadline.'

'Why not?' I asked. 'Ten years ago you were able to roll off umpteen designs without a second thought.'

His head shot up. 'I still can!' he said angrily. 'But even working flat out, we could never get them made up in time. New fabrics and accessories would have to be chosen, patterns cut, and every outfit has to be made up in cotton first, to see if it's going to work. We took three months to get where we are now, so how the hell do you expect us to do it again in just under three weeks?'

'By keeping your head, working flat out, and cutting corners. You'll have to use the same accessories and colour schemes as before, and whatever fabrics you have available, supplementing them as best you can with what's easily obtainable. Make them straight up, and pin the damn things onto the models if they don't fit.'

'Cut straight into brocades and velvets?' he asked in horror. 'Each gown costs thousands. One slip of the scissors would be catastrophic.'

'Not nearly as catastrophic as cancelling the show altogether.' I said. 'Do you have any better suggestions? After all, it's your own bloody fault that this happened. You're no longer running a couple of trendy boutiques. This is big business, and it's not only money that's involved; now your reputation is at stake.'

William shifted his feet. 'Where is he going to work?' he asked. 'The security here is obviously dicey. If they got in once, they could easily do so again.'

'He's right,' said Martin. 'This building is far too public, and there's nowhere else large enough.'

I could probably make room for them at the studios, but there was another alternative. A better one.

'Go to Olden Manor,' I said. 'You won't be disturbed there, and we can take the extra precaution of hiring a security firm to patrol the grounds.'

Martin grimaced. 'You make it sound like a bloody concentration camp.'

'It's the only chance you have,' said William.

'What about the people who have families? They might refuse to come.'

'Ask them,' I said. 'I think you'll find that in a crisis everyone will rally round and do all they can. And sitting on your backside moaning is certainly not going to get that collection re-done.'

'You're asking a lot, Mark,' he said, standing up. 'Too much. I'll do my best, but I think it's going to take a miracle to bring this off.'

'You won't know until you've tried,' I told him.

I think Martin learnt a valuable lesson during those three crucial weeks, about himself and the people who worked so devotedly with him.

The fashion show was a success in more ways than one. For Martin it was not only a personal achievement, but with it he came of age, veering away from his beloved mini-skirts and producing a collection of sophisticated garments which rivalled those of the top Paris fashion houses.

It was also the last time Caroline and I appeared together in public. We may have seemed happy enough to the gossip columnists, but two days later she and Paul and Elly moved into a rented flat, where they stayed until custody had been settled, and Caroline was able to leave the country.

Chapter Two

Later that year Charles Latchcham's son was forced to give up his parliamentary seat because of heavy business commitments. A by-election was held and Arthur Bennett became the first Labour candidate ever to win the district, the bulk of his votes coming from Steelton, which was now a good-sized industrial town. The result was greeted with less enthusiasm in the rural areas, but as the summer days swept past, so too did indignation. At the Crowder farm, cattle once more grazed in the fields and pigs squealed in the styes. But the dairy herd was not a quarter the size of the one Richard Crowder had not lived to see destroyed.

Alan Weston gave his wife a free hand with the farm, but Lisa had lost heart. She was unable to leave it rotting, and had employed Edward Wainwright, a young man from the Cotswolds, as manager. He was trying to save enough money to purchase a small farm back home, and for him this job was a temporary arrangement, which suited Lisa well. Wainwright was a good farmer, but preferred to use the land for crops, and more and more of it was coming under the plough.

There were other changes as well—changes which kept Lisa away. Harold was gone. Within two months of the destruction of his beloved cattle he was found dead in the cottage where Edward now lived. Nobody had been quite sure how old he was, but most people said he must be well into his eighties. The official cause of death was given as pneumonia, but in and around the village it was rumoured that a broken heart had finished him off. Orchid left after Harold's death, moving to Cambridge to live with her widowed sister. She did not want to live alone in the empty house, and Lisa no longer needed her support and guidance.

Betsy, the oldest of the Clydesdales, had been destroyed the previous year. Her teeth were loose, and she had reached a stage where she could eat nothing with ease except for mushy foods. Mark had been there on one of his regular visits to the mills, and made the decision on Lisa's behalf. Jinny and Drummer stayed on at the farm with Bill Simpson employed to care for them.

In August, Alan had to go to Steelton on business and since it was going to take anything between a week and a month, and there was still a fortnight before school started, Lisa decided to go with him. Chanson and Tumbleweed were loaded into the horsebox, and the dogs into the station-wagon. Madame Ping had also died the previous year and had been replaced by another Pekinese called Wang.

Lisa had given Edward Wainwright complete control at the farm, with freedom to draw whatever money he required. She was therefore surprised when he came to her a few days after their arrival, a dog-eared catalogue in his hand. Marian was indoors working at her ballet exercises, and David's nanny had taken him to the village, wooing him with the promise of ice cream. Lisa was reading on the lawn.

'Excuse me, Mrs. Weston,' Edward Wainwright said. 'There's a stock sale on t'other side of Steelton tomorrow. There's some good beasts being put up, and I might be able to pick up one or two at a fair price. Here.' He thrust the catalogue at her. 'I've already marked the possibles.'

'You don't have to consult me, Ed,' she said. 'I've told you that before.'

'Aye,' he replied, reddening a little. 'But it's your money, and as you're here I thought you should see for yourself.'

He walked away, and she started to leaf through the catalogue pausing at his markings. There were not many, but as he said, they were good stock. She flicked through to the bulls. The farm still needed a bull. Ed was all for artificial insemination, but like her father, Lisa preferred the old methods.

'What's that?' Marian asked.

She half turned. The girl was still dressed in a leotard, her long hair tied back back from her face.

'A catalogue. There's a cattle sale tomorrow, and Ed wants to buy some more cows.'

'Oh, let me see!' she shrieked, running forward. 'Can we go too? I've never seen a proper sale. It must be lots of fun.'

'They're filthy dirty and stink of cattle,' Lisa said. 'The place will be milling with farmers, the real rustic types, and the majority of them will be roaring drunk before we get halfway through the afternoon. You would hate it.'

Marian flung herself onto the grass and started turning the pages. 'I won't. I promise,' she said. 'Look, there are horses as well. Please Mummy?'

Lisa smiled at her. It was rare for Marian to get enthusiastic about anything other than her ballet.

'All right,' she said. 'Just remember, I don't want one word of complaint from you.'

'Not a murmur,' Marian promised.

It had been hot and dusty, and the noise intolerable. David loved it and Marian was fascinated. They purchased four heifers but no bull. The prices were high, and although Lisa was willing to bid, Ed convinced her she would only be throwing away good money. They left at three-thirty, and arrived home an hour later. David was asleep on the back seat, and Marian chatted excitedly to her mother, who felt less enthusiastic as she wondered what Alan would say.

'Don't worry,' said Marian at her adult best. 'Daddy can't possibly beat the two of us. And we did do the right thing, didn't we?'

'Of course we did,' she said. 'He's not back yet, so we can break the news to him this evening. I wonder where the dogs are?'

'Dora is probably feeding them.' Marian turned round, looking for the hired lorry. 'How can they possibly be so slow?'

'You can't expect them to go as fast as us,' she said. 'We should have time for tea.'

Marian shook David. He woke abruptly, crying out before he realised where he was.

'Are they come?' he asked, sitting up and rubbing his eyes.

'Have they come,' Marian corrected. 'No. Not yet.'

'Take him in, darling,' said Lisa. 'Ask Dora to make tea. I'd better warn Bill.'

She couldn't find him, and on the way back to the house paused by the gate to watch the grazing horses.

'What are you up to?'

She swung round to find Mark standing not two feet behind her. He was smiling, and the sun on his hair was like gold on spun gold.

'Mark!' she exclaimed with delight, and throwing her arms about his neck, kissed him upon the cheek. 'I never heard a car come in.' She stood back, studying him. Even here he exuded power, and for a man in his forties was still lean and irresistibly good looking. Lisa found so-called 'laughter lines' depressing, but they suited Mark, adding to his character.

'I was here all the time.' he told her. 'But I parked round the side of the barn in the shade.'

She squeezed his hand. 'It's good to see you again. You shouldn't shut yourself off from your friends. Even Mary hasn't seen you since the divorce.'

'It's not been deliberate,' he said. 'I've been busy, that's all.'

He rested a foot on the lower bar of the gate. He works too hard, Lisa thought, and the strain is beginning to show in his face. She asked, 'Have you heard from Caroline?'

'No,' he said, his eyes on the horses. 'She was in Spain a couple of months ago, but God only knows where she is now. The decree nisi came through last month.'

'Do you miss her?'

He turned his head a little.

'It's too late, Lisa,' he said.

'And Paul?' she persisted.

'I doubt she's trailing him across Europe,' he stiffly replied. 'As I'm sure you are aware, Elly went with her.'

'Yes, I know,' said Lisa flatly. He had closed up and she knew she would get nothing further from him.

Chanson came up to them.

'She has white whiskers,' Mark said, surprised.

'She's sixteen,' said Lisa. 'I ought to think of retiring her soon.'

'You should put her to foal.'

'I suppose so.' She fidgeted with her scarf. 'I don't know what Alan's going to say. He's so tolerant, but—'

He was staring at her again. 'I knew you'd been plotting something. What is it?'

'We've just bought some horses at an auction.'

'How many?'

'Only two, but one is in foal. It was a case of the knackers or me.'

He smiled. 'What did you buy? The two most knock-kneed, sway-backed hacks you could find?'

'Of course not! One of them is a Clydesdale mare. She's the pregnant one. And the other Marian begged me to buy. I think they're coming now, so you can see for yourself.' She watched the truck bounce along the rutted lane. 'I'd better call Marian and David.'

'Too late,' he said. Marian was already running across the lawn, her eyes on the tall man who stood beside her mother. Samson loped alongside her, and a few feet behind Wang bounced and scrambled. She dashed straight into Mark's arms, as she always did, and he swung her in a half-circle before putting her back on the ground.

'You're just in time to see our horses,' she said.

She took hold of his hand and would have pulled him after her at a trot, except that her mother told her to run back and call David, and then ask Dora where Bill was.

'It doesn't seem very long since she was David's age,' Mark said, watching her.

Lisa linked an arm through his. 'It seems only yesterday since you and I ran down this very same path, sharing every bit of her enthusiasm. I sometimes wonder where all the years went.'

David appeared at a run, with Pat trailing behind; Dora came, still clutching a dishcloth, and Bill strode out from behind the barns. He and Edward went into the truck, while Lisa instructed the children to stand back. A brownish-beige colt was first out. The animal wasn't as tall as either man, but scared out of its wits and obviously unused to being handled. It came down the ramp in a rush, dragging both men behind it.

'Isn't he beautiful?' said Marian.

Mark half turned. His eyes found Lisa's, and for a moment unreleased laughter hovered between them. The colt was ugly, with impossibly long legs, skinny body, and a large head with eyes which showed white at the corners. Ed and Bill were both strong men but could hardly hold it.

'Knackers?' Mark asked.

'Yes,' said Lisa. 'Who else would want him? He's only a baby and still has his milk teeth. I don't think he can be more than a year old.'

Mark looked at the plunging animal. 'If you got anywhere near his teeth I can only commend your bravery, if not your common sense. I hate to think what his parentage is.'

'He's beautiful,' said Marian. 'Can I name him, Mummy? Can I?'

'I suppose so. But try and choose something sensible.'

'Bucephalus,' the girl said.

'I'll get the other one,' said Mark, and Lisa could tell by his voice that he was trying not to laugh.

'You'd better put him in the empty paddock next to the other horses,' she told the two men.

Mark, composed again, appeared at the top of the ramp, a placid black mare at his shoulder.

'Richard would have approved of her,' he said.

'I know,' said Lisa. 'Her name is Metcalfe's Beauty. We've even got papers. I think it's such a shame that nobody wants the big horses any more.'

'Where shall I put her?' he asked.

'I think one of the stables would be best.'

She went with him. The mare settled immediately, more interested in the hay-net than in exploring her new quarters.

'You'll stay for dinner, won't you, Mark?' Lisa asked. 'I know you want to discuss business with Alan, but you can do that tomorrow. Tonight we're going to enjoy ourselves.'

He turned to her, and in his smile was something which struck her as being almost unbearably sad.

Chapter Three

For Simon Townsend to show any temperament was exceedingly rare. His popularity extended not only to the public but also to those who worked with him, for he was a remarkably undemanding person who was always ready to accept advice. But he was now pacing Alan's office, pounding his palms against each other.

'He won't even see me!' he said angrily. 'I've been trying for two days, and I can't get past that bloody secretary. I know he's there.'

'He's busy,' Alan said. 'And half the time even I get shown the door. But one song, Simon? There must be a hundred and one others from which you can choose.'

Simon paused in mid-stride. 'I don't want a hundred other songs. I want that one. He said I could have it, and while I was away he gave it to his high-and-mighty Kathy Karn.' He spun round and dropped into a chair. 'Have you heard what she's done? Murdered it!'

Alan shook his head in sympathy. He had heard the song, of course, but it had made no clear impression on him. He heard so many, and they all sounded the same.

'It's nothing personal, Simon,' he said quietly. 'Kathy always makes the top three. The kids like her, and it's the kids who buy most of the records.'

Simon pouted. 'If she could make it, so could I,' he said. 'It's been released for a fortnight now and it's still no more than halfway up the charts. I don't think she'll get into the top five this time, despite all the publicity she's been given. I could have, I know I could.'

'Then why don't you?' said a pleasant voice from the doorway. 'I quite agree with you, Simon. Kathy has ruined it, and if you push her off the Hit Parade, it'll give her a rather nasty fright.'

Alan was used to Mark's sudden appearances and gave no more than a tight-lipped nod, but Simon was genuinely startled. Mark walked across the office, dropping a wad of papers in front of the lawyer.

'I made notes in the margins,' he said. 'Well, Simon, cat got your tongue? If you want it, I suggest you record tomorrow morning, and by pulling a few strings we should have it in the shops by Monday. Kathy will have less than three weeks up on you, and if you're as good as you think you are, it'll be interesting to see who comes off best.'

'Mark!' Alan spluttered. 'You can't possibly run two of your own people against each other, certainly not with the same song. It's unethical!'

'You should know by now that ethics don't count in this business,' said Mark. He turned back to Simon. 'I hope you realise that she'll never forgive you if you succeed? Well?'

'I still think I could do it a hell of a lot better than her,' Simon said, a timid smile coming to his lips.

Mark was at the door. 'I'll make sure Henry knows. And Simon, if you make a belly-flop, don't come crying to me. Or Alan either, even if he is a good listener.'

'Did that really happen or am I dreaming?' Simon asked when he was gone.

'No, you're not dreaming,' said Alan. This was a small matter, but he had seen Mark make the same snap decision where millions were involved.

'I don't believe I respect any person more than Mr. Hanley,' Simon was saying. 'But there are times when he gives me the shivers.'

Like a bloody iceberg, Alan thought. Yet there had been nothing cold or hostile about him during that evening at the farm, when Lisa had insisted he stay for dinner.

Chris was fed up with being turned away by Norma, and so he left early and drove to the house in Belgravia, prepared to wait all night if necessary. Mark might avoid him at the office, but was unlikely to order him out of his house.

He accepted tea from Roberts, and was pouring his third cup when he heard the front door open and voices in the hall. He couldn't make out what was being said, but Mark's voice was raised in anger, and Tim was shouting back, equally angry. Then there was a moment of silence before the front door slammed. Chris walked to the window of and saw the chauffeur running down the steps. He pulled open the car door, glanced back, and then got in.

More voices sounded in the hall before the drawing room door opened and Mark walked in. Chris was momentarily taken aback, and it showed in his face. Mark's eyes flashed dangerously.

'Not you too?' he snapped. 'What the hell is wrong with everyone today? One would think my face had turned green.'

His face wasn't green but grey, an unhealthy, colourless pallor. Chris stared at him, not realising that behind his employer's anger was a desperate need to sit down before he fell. These attacks came to Mark at odd intervals, not regularly, but each one a little worse than the last; and they passed so quickly that it hardly seemed worth the effort of consulting a doctor. It was unfortunate that this one had come when he was walking out of the building with Tim's sharp eyes on him. The chauffeur had known immediately that something was wrong, and had refused to take him to his meeting, bringing him home instead. He would have been more insistent—rest, a doctor—but with his breathing returning to normal, Mark had cuttingly dismissed him. That was what Chris had heard in the hall.

'Now I know why you've been avoiding me,' said Chris. 'You look bloody awful.'

'I'm tired,' Mark said, seizing the opportunity to sit down. 'I'm not growing any younger, and I work a good deal harder than I ever did before.'

'Then why are you buying another magazine?' Chris asked. 'And you're only forty-four. That's not old. I'm fifty-eight, and I know I get a bit puffed now and then, but there's still plenty of fight left in me. You should have a check-up.'

The cold eyes turned to him. 'There is nothing wrong which a good night's sleep wouldn't cure,' he said. 'First of all Tim has tantrums because I trip down some steps, and now you start because I look tired. I assume you've come to enquire about more than my health?'

Chris glanced towards the window. The Rolls Royce was gone, together with its irate driver. 'You should be grateful for Tim,' he said. 'Loyalty is not something to be treated lightly.'

'Loyalty can go a little too far at times,' came the acid reply. 'Tim would never survive with anybody else.' A smile came to his lips, and for a moment the sallowness seemed to fade. 'Roberts was disgusted. On more than one occasion he has subtly suggested that Tim be reprimanded; I thought he'd burst a blood vessel this time. I've asked him to bring coffee. If you want something stronger, ring the bell. He refuses to admit it, but he misses Caroline like mad. While she was here the house was a challenge to him, with a constant flow of people in and out.'

'But he stays,' Chris said.

Mark felt a little better. He would have preferred Chris not to be here, but knew that as long as he remained seated and kept his wits about him, Chris would forget this incident. He had always found it ridiculously easy to fool Chris in anything.

'Why did you come?' he asked.

Chris pursed his lips. He wasn't entirely convinced that Mark was suffering from nothing more than a combination of sleeplessness and overwork. But he knew when to keep his peace.

'Kathy is none too pleased about Simon Townsend. She thinks you deliberately had him record that song, then pushed through enough publicity to send her version crashing.'

'Simon wanted the song. All I did was let him have it. Can I help it if he shot up to Number One?'

'And is still there three weeks later?' Chris asked. 'You know, Mark, I think I'm getting too old for this business. She was such a lively young kid when she started out. Look at her now. Heavens knows, I've tried to set her straight often enough. But she won't listen to me any more. She won't listen to anyone but you.'

Mark sighed. 'I can no longer devote my entire life to Kathy Karn. I've had her in four private clinics during the past two years. She comes out, and in a few weeks she's back on those bloody drugs. It's Bobby Milton who started her on them, and I wouldn't be surprised if he's the one who keeps her supplied.'

'Then why not kill two birds with one stone and let him go?' Chris asked. 'I hear you've refused to let him out of his contract.'

Mark shifted a little, his eyes resting on Chris's face. 'Mantis is presently riding on the crest of a wave. It's taken years to get them there, and I've no intention of letting them go just because Bobby takes it into his head he wants to leave. Their contract has another eight months to run. I don't give a damn what they do after that, but until then they stay together.'

'There was a time,' Chris said, 'when a certain Mark Anthony wanted out of his contract. Health clause or not, if I'd put my foot down you wouldn't have had a hope. But I let you go.'

Mark didn't say anything for a few minutes, but when he did, his voice was cold.

'Bobby is an addict who's susceptible to every passing whim. And despite what you're thinking, I'm not a fool. I've sounded out the rest of the group, and none of them want to leave. If they did, I'd let them go. Therefore Bobby remains, whether he likes it or not. You never had anything to do with them before, so why this sudden interest?'

'Because he is desperate and came to me,' Chris said. 'You should let him go. You'll still have a group, and Pete does most of the song-writing anyway.'

'No!' Mark snapped, and as with the subject of his health Chris knew he would get nothing further from him.

He was grateful Roberts chose that moment to come in with the coffee. He also brought sandwiches and a cake. Mark took his coffee black and refused any food. Chris could have sworn those capable hands were shaking. But he said nothing.

Chapter Four

During the next two weeks Chris and Tim watched my every move, and even Alan shot me the odd quizzical look. But as I had known they would, the breathlessness and dizziness left me, and months could pass before they would bother me again—if they did at all.

It was Simon's success which took Chris off my back, for it brought Kathy's testy temperament well to the fore, and with November and the crowded Christmas schedules upon us, he had his hands full. I suspected Kathy was becoming a strain on him, but did not interfere.

Bobby Milton was also making trouble. Mantis were presently on tour in Scotland, and reports kept trickling back that although he never actually refused to perform, he was being as disruptive as possible. He was upsetting not only the rest of the group, but everybody even vaguely connected with them. If things got much worse I would have to go up there and sort him out myself.

Then there was Martin, who was no longer content to have a monopoly on the clothing market. He had become involved with cosmetics the previous year, and now he was into health foods. With his name cropping up on more labels that I cared to count, he was becoming an enormous headache to Alan and the rapidly expanding legal department. He was another one with whom I would need a few words. A few words, a bit more organisation, and a lot of wasted time and frayed tempers could be avoided.

And June was being temperamental over the new magazine. She wanted to keep hold of her present position on the teen magazine and become co-editor with Eric on the new one.

'You'll never cope with the two of them,' I had said. 'And why this sudden desire to have Eric up-graded?'

'I'll manage,' she had said confidently. 'The one practically runs itself, and as for the other, if you want to do follow-ups of the major news items then you'll need Eric's skills and not mine. And it's an insult to the man's intelligence to offer him an assistant editor position.'

'If anything goes wrong, it's your head which will roll,' I told her.

'Even a fool doesn't make the same mistakes twice,' she had said. 'Eric might be many things, but he's not that much of a fool.'

I hoped she was right, for after a lot of consideration, I'd decided to accede to her wishes.

It was only the amalgamated mills which were giving me no worries. They were running smoothly, with production up threefold. I was going through the combined figures when Norma came through on the intercom.

'There's a young lady out here who wishes to see you,' she said.

'Who?' I asked.

'Me,' a voice squeaked in the doorway. 'I thought I'd give you a surprise. But you don't look very pleased.'

Marian was now seventeen and had grown into a stunning young woman, although she seemed unaware of the fact. She was wearing a short dress which could only have been designed by Martin, and knee-length boots. A coat was flung over her arm, and her hair hung in wet strands down her back.

'Marian,' I said, standing up. 'What on earth are you doing here?'

'Taking advantage of both Mummy and Daddy going up north for the day. I wanted to see you.'

'Shouldn't you be in school?'

She turned up her nose in an unbecoming manner. 'Mummy let me stay off because I complained I was getting the flu, but I told Clara I felt fine and wanted to go to ballet this afternoon. Unfortunately, I forgot to bring an umbrella, and it's pouring with rain.'

'Give me your coat,' I said. 'I expect Norma can do something with it, and even find a dryer for your hair. Go and sit beside the radiator. Do you want something hot to drink?'

'Coffee please,' she said. 'But not too strong.' She dropped cross-legged to the floor, arranging her skirt to its best advantage. Marian had a refreshing naivety, due partly to Lisa's upbringing and partly to the fact that she had no time for boyfriends or adolescent hang-ups. She was determined to become a ballerina, and nothing was allowed to get in the way of her chosen profession.

Norma took the coat, and said she would have a hairdryer sent up. I leant against my desk. 'Why did you want to see me?' I asked.

'I need your help,' she said. 'I've saved up ten pounds and I want to buy Daddy something special for Christmas. You always wear such nice things that I thought you could help. Maybe I could get him some pretty cuff links or a tiepin. I rather like the one you're wearing now.'

That particular tiepin had been a present from Caroline, and had cost a good deal more than ten pounds—she never dreamt of doing anything by halves.

'What about your mother?' I asked.

'She's easy. I can always buy her a china horse or some perfume. But I never know what to get Daddy. He must get awfully tired of ties, handkerchiefs and socks.'

'Have you brought your money?'

'Of course.'

'Then I know just the place. You'll love their selection of tiepins and cuff links.'

Her eyes lit up. 'Can we go in the Rolls Royce with Tim driving?'

I laughed. 'Well, I have no intention of traipsing about the muddy streets in the rain. But you'll have to make yourself a bit more presentable. I refuse to have you dragging on my arm like some poor relative.'

'Uncle Mark, you're marvellous! I knew I could rely on you.'

I glanced at my watch. 'I suppose you expect lunch first?'

'I was hoping you would suggest it,' she said. 'I'm famished. Will you take me somewhere expensive and exotic which is full of famous people?'

I practically choked. 'I most certainly will not,' I said. 'I have no intention of having all the gossip columnists accuse me of cradle-snatching in tomorrow's papers. A hamburger from the canteen would be much more suitable.'

'Oh well, it was worth a try,' she said. 'To tell the truth, I never thought you would agree. But don't tell Mummy and Daddy, will you, or they'll be furious with me for daring to impose on you.'

'I won't,' I promised.

Norma came in carrying a tray with coffee, and a small hand-dryer. Marian leapt to her feet.

'Would you like something to eat?' Norma asked.

'Yes please,' Marian said. 'I'm starving!'

'No,' I told her. 'I'm not treating you to lunch just so that you can leave half of it on your plate. You can use the plug behind my desk.'

Norma peered at me over the rims of her glasses. 'Is there anything else?' she said.

'Ask Tim to have the car at the front entrance in about an hour.' I glanced at Marian. 'And telephone Caldwells. Tell them to have an assortment of cuff links and tiepins for me to see, and say that the young lady only has ten pounds. Anything above that is to be charged to my account.'

Norma looked from me to Marian, and back to me again. 'That

child has you wound round her little finger,' she said. 'I wish I knew her secret.'

I smiled as she left the room.

'Uncle Mark?' The dryer had stopped.

'Yes.'

'You shouldn't smoke so much. Cigarettes are bad for you. They'll ruin your wind.'

'Then my wind must have gone years ago,' I told her.

The rain had thinned into a drizzle when I dropped Marian at her ballet school.

'Thank you for a marvellous time,' she said. She kissed my cheek, and then leapt out of the car, waving before she disappeared into the building.

Tim was about to pull away when the telephone rang. He picked it up, and then turned to me. 'Norma,' he said. I picked up my extension and listened to Norma's expressionless voice.

'No,' I said. 'I don't want to speak to him. Give him something to calm his nerves, and tell him to wait in my office. I'll be there in about twenty minutes.'

'Trouble?' Tim asked.

'Isn't it always? Something to do with Mantis.'

Chris was sipping whisky, which was a bad sign. He bounced to his feet when I walked in.

'What have they done now?' I asked.

'They've done nothing,' he said harshly. 'It was on the one o'clock news. How come you never heard anything?'

'Because I don't spend my life with one ear to the radio,' I retorted. 'I'm not in the mood for games, Chris. What's happened?'

He sank back into the chair. 'Bobby killed himself.'

I stared at him in stunned silence.

'How?'

'Slit his wrists and bled to death in the bedroom. They found him this morning. The police think he was high at the time, his luggage was full of dope. And the others have been arrested for possession. This is going to cause one hell of a scandal.'

I was already thinking ahead. I knew adverse publicity could be twisted in our favour, but first the remainder of the group had to be released from jail and put into seclusion. Thank goodness Alan was in Oldenshaw with his own plane. He could fly to Edinburgh this afternoon and have them free and on their way home by this evening.

'Where's Kathy?' I asked.

'I let her go home. She was fond of Bobby and badly shaken when she heard the news. The show is shaping up nicely and they're going to rehearse some of the other acts in her absence.'

I flipped on the intercom. 'Norma, get Alan on the telephone, and I'd better talk to Mantis's agent as well.'

Chris was eyeing me with disapproval. 'You don't give a damn, do you? I warned you he was being pushed too far, but you wouldn't let him go. I don't think you care that the boy is lying on a slab in a mortuary.'

I stiffened. 'Bobby Milton was one of life's many failures who managed to hit the jackpot for a while. His popularity wasn't due to his rather limited talent, but to the power and money I poured into him and his second-rate group. Better people than he was die every day. If he wanted out, he should have fought me. I might have respected him then.'

Chris stood up. 'You make me feel sick,' he said angrily. 'Sick and ashamed of what I've become.'

He slammed out of the office. Marian and her carefree world could not have been further away than at that moment.

The remaining members of Mantis returned to their London homes that night, with strict instructions not to talk to the press. Alan had decided to stay in Oldenshaw for the night, and return to London the following morning to salvage what he could from the mess. When I telephoned Chris later in the evening, he refused to speak to me.

The next day Alan and I made the best we could of a bad situation. But by lunchtime he was looking jaded and I sent him home. He touched my shoulder as he left.

'Don't worry, Mark, he'll come round. Chris may be old and stubborn, but he loves you like one of the family.'

Two days later I heard that Kathy Karn had not turned up for rehearsals of her TV show, and unless she had a good excuse, she was to be replaced. It was the day Bobby Milton's body was to be flown to London for burial, and biting back an impulse to investigate the matter, I waited. That afternoon Chris came to my office. He was cool and formal, but he came.

'I can't get anywhere near her,' he said, his eyes studying the painting behind me. 'She's locked herself in her house, and no amount of shouting or cajoling will get her to open the bloody door. I suppose you know that if she doesn't show up tomorrow they're going to throw her off the set? They're fed up with her temperament.'

'Did you tell her that?' I asked.

'I shouted through the letterbox, if you can call that telling her.'

I frowned. It was a large house, too large for a single person. In fact it was the one which Martin had purchased after their ill-fated marriage, and it took an army of servants to run efficiently.

'What about the housekeeper? The servants?' I asked, trying without success to catch his averted eyes.

He looked at me then, briefly. 'What servants? You're out of touch, Mark. Kathy can't keep servants. They never stay longer than a few days. There's nobody there at the moment except for her and the dog. Hell, I'm not even sure whether she has the dog any more. She never takes it anywhere. She said something about it being pregnant, but that was months ago. There's a chauffeur who lives in a small flat above the garage, but he can't get into the main house either.'

'What do you want me to do?' I asked, already knowing the answer.

He was gazing at his hands. 'I think she might listen to you. You seem to be the only one she still respects.'

I should have felt sorry for Kathy, but could find no pity in me. She could have had everything. Nobody had driven her into this corner, only herself.

'I'll try,' I said.

'Thank you. And while I'm here, there's one other thing,' he said 'That son of mine has got himself engaged to an Israeli girl. They want to marry in January. Deborah thinks Israel might be a nice place to retire to.'

I looked into his eyes, which no longer tried to avoid mine.

'You want to leave?' I asked.

'Yes. Kathy doesn't need me any more. And I'm growing too old for all this. I can't understand the young people of today. This terrible urge they have to destroy themselves. Bobby was twenty-eight. At twenty-eight you were well on your way to becoming a millionaire. And Kathy's twenty-two. She's done everything and seen everything, she's virtually no place left to go but down. Are we the ones who ruined her, Mark?'

'I am perhaps,' I replied.

'No,' he said. 'It's not you. It's this monster you've created. It swallows people whole, then spits them out chopped into a thousand tiny pieces.'

'Not all of them,' I said. 'The tough ones survive. And nobody is forced. Whatever they do, they do of their own free will.'

'Everybody wants to be another Mark Anthony,' he said sadly. 'But he was one of a kind. I'll stay until Christmas, and then I never want to set eyes on this place again.'

* * *

Tim's biggest weakness was that he loved scandal, and he had an uncanny knack of gathering an unbelievable amount of gossip. I turned to him now because I was out of touch with Kathy and did not want to blunder back into her life unprepared.

'Doesn't it seem odd to you that only the chauffeur stays?' I asked. The obvious should have been staring me in the face, but somehow I still thought of Kathy as an unsophisticated young girl, not the scheming, drug-addicted bitch Tim described.

'Miss Karn prefers to keep a young man about the place,' he bluntly replied. 'I understand she pays generous stud fees.'

I wondered whether Martin knew. He still cared for her despite what had happened, and only because of his persistence had she been hospitalised so regularly.

'I'd advise you to be careful, sir,' he warned as he pulled up in front of the house.

The house was different from the way I remembered it. It was shabby and tatty, with an air of dereliction.

'I'll think I'll be able to hang on to my virtue,' I said, smiling.

A flush spread up his neck. 'I mean't, she can get irrational,' he said.

'Then if I yell for help you can come and rescue me.'

He did not smile, but looked remarkably grim as he opened the door. I clasped his shoulder. 'Don't worry, Tim. If I'm not capable of looking after myself at my age, I never shall be.' I looked up at the house, its windows caked in grime, and most of the curtains drawn. 'Anyway, she probably won't let me in.'

I think he would have been relieved if she had left me standing on the doorstep. I rang the bell three times, and then shouted through the letterbox. I wondered about Sofie, for she didn't seem to be there. I was also wondering how long Tim could restrain himself when, without warning, the door swung open.

'Come in,' she said.

Even before I stepped into the dark hall I could smell the sickly-sweet odour of incense. And there was something else as well which, after a moment, I recognised as decay. When she slammed the door my senses swam, and I thought I was going to throw up, but the feeling quickly passed. I turned to her, my eyes still adjusting to the semi-darkness. She was wearing a long, shift-type dress and I could see she wore nothing beneath the flimsy material. I was unable to see her face clearly, but she was smiling.

'What a privilege! The high and mighty Mr. Hanley coming here!' she said in a dry voice which was barely recognisable. She waved a hand in the general direction of the drawing room. 'Come in, Mr.

Hanley. You'll have to excuse the mess, but hired help is getting impossible these days. They just don't want to work no more.'

I followed her to a filthy room with scented candles burning in the fireplace. The radiators must have been on full blast because it was like a Turkish bath, and with the closed curtains I felt as though I were entering a tomb.

'Sit down,' she said. 'Oh ... do they bother you? I'll put them out if you want.'

'There's no need,' I said, and walking to the windows, pulled back the curtains and thrust them open.

'It's about time we had a heart to heart talk,' I said, turning to face her. 'Kathy ...'

A hand was across her eyes, and she was backing away from the light as though it caused her physical pain.

'I don't want it,' she groaned. 'Close them again ... please.'

I didn't close the curtains, but went over to her and roughly pulled down her hand. She struggled and tried to spin away, but I was too strong. I gripped her arm tightly, and tilted her chin towards the daylight. Her eyes were large and unnaturally dark.

'What are you on?' I demanded.

'That's none of your bloody business!' she spat, and pulled away. As her arm twisted she stopped, glaring defiantly at me. 'You're not me bloody keeper!' she yelled.

'No,' I said, letting her go. 'But you certainly need one. It's no wonder you can't keep any servants. Nobody decent would want to stay in this.'

Her eyes flamed with something of her old self, but it died away almost immediately, to be lost in a sea of nothingness. She walked to the door and pulled it open.

'I don't want you here no more,' she said. 'You can go now. You know the way out.'

'And if I refuse?'

'I'll call the police.'

'And have yourself thrown into jail for possession of drugs? I don't suppose they'd be hard to find, either.'

She shuddered, and sat on a chair. 'What to you want?' she asked. 'With all your airs and graces you ain't no better than the rest of them. You killed Bob. You wouldn't listen to him. You wouldn't listen to no one.'

'He killed himself,' I said, 'Just as you are killing yourself. Neither of you has a backbone.'

'When I first met you, I thought you was the most wonderful person in the whole world,' she said. 'I'd have done anything for you in those days. But it was all fake. You use us. You're not interested in talent. All you want is the money. You and the others like you.'

'And where would you be without me?' I asked.

'I dunno,' she answered, rising to her feet. Her movements were erratic, like those of a sleepwalker. She went to the fireplace, where she snuffed out the incense candles, and then sank to the floor as though the effort had exhausted her. She looked at me over her updrawn knees. Perhaps it would have helped if I had shown a little compassion, but I was incapable of it. She was shuffling amongst the litter in which she sat, and suddenly found something which she held up. It glittered obscenely in that filthy room.

'I loved him too,' she said, rubbing the thing against her sleeve. 'I loved him, and look what he done. You knew, didn't you? You knew all along.'

I frowned at her senseless meanderings. 'Knew what?' I asked with a great deal more patience than I felt.

'What he was. That's why you never wanted us to marry.'

She flung the bracelet across the room with a suddenness which startled me. It struck the wall to my left, then bounced back and landed at my feet. I picked it up. The catch was broken, but the stones were still bright and undamaged.

'Where did you get this?' I asked.

'A present,' she said. 'A wedding present. Keep it if you want, as a gift for services rendered. For all them great and marvellous things you gone and done for me.'

Enough was enough. 'I want you back at work, Kathy,' I said.

She smiled. 'I'll go back when I'm good and ready. You wouldn't do nothing to me. I still bring in a lot of money, and I don't think you can afford to lose me yet.'

'Don't over-value yourself,' I warned. I walked to the door.

She laughed. It was a thin, nervous sound.

I'm not sure what would have happened next if it hadn't been for the dog. I had forgotten Sofie, and when I opened the door I saw her in the hall. Every rib stood out against her harsh coat, and she looked at me with pathetic eyes before turning away and loping up the stairs. I heard her whine as she scratched at a door. How long was it since Kathy had thought to feed her?

I was taking the stairs two at a time when Kathy's lifeless voice trailed after me.

'If that's Sofie, she's being punished. She went and had horrible things. Horrible mongrel puppies. But she'll know better now. So don't you go and ruin everything by petting her.'

She laughed again, and I shuddered. What had she done?

The dog cringed as I approached her. I think she expected to be beaten. I could see there had recently been puppies, despite her emaciated condition, but even if they were still alive she would never be able to feed them. I held my hand forward, but she backed away, her eyes never leaving the door. The paintwork was badly scratched, as though she had spent many hours clawing to get in. I dreaded what I might see when I opened the door. It was a bathroom, and the dog pushed past me, standing up against the side of the bath and whining as she peered in.

Nothing in this house of horrors could compare with what I saw.

There were six puppies, pure white, blind, their bloated bodies lying in the half-filled bath. My stomach heaved as I grabbed the bitch's collar and dragged her out of there. In the passage, I stood with my back to a wall, breathing deeply, while the frightened dog tried to pull away. Kathy was sitting on the stairs, staring at me with a senseless grin on her lips.

'I told you,' she said. 'All mongrels. Every single one of them. I couldn't keep them, could I?'

It took a huge effort, but I managed to hold back my anger. I swept the dog into my arms and started down the stairs, pushing past the sprawling girl. She scrambled to her feet, using the bannister for support.

'What are you doing with her?' she demanded. 'She's mine. You've no right to touch her.'

'Dalmatian puppies are born white,' I told her with barely bridled rage. 'I'm taking her away from here, and don't try to stop me.'

'You can't,' she wailed, tears of remorse in her eyes. 'Not Sofie. She's all I got left. I love her.'

At the sound of her voice the dog shrank deeper into my arms. Kathy sat down again, her eyes enormous. 'I'll be back at work tomorrow,' she whispered. 'I'll do anything, but don't take her away from me.'

'I don't give a damn what you do,' I said. 'But you'll never get within touching distance of this animal again.'

She started to cry, her sobs loud and uncontrolled. 'I never meant nothing ... I love her ... I would never hurt her ... please ... it won't happen again ... please ...'

I carried on, while behind me the sobs became hysterical. I glanced back and saw that she was stretched along the length of the stairs in an almost classical pose of grief. I could still find no pity. I was not even sure whether her grief was genuine or drug-induced.

I struggled to open the door, my nerves shattered by her piercing screams. Tim was already halfway up the steps, and I thrust the dog into his arms.

'Put her in the car,' I told him, and then reluctantly went back into the house.

But reaction had set in. If Kathy heard my voice she chose to ignore it, and when I bent forward and touched her shoulder she rolled violently away, the screams even louder.

I was holding the telephone receiver, and running down a list of names and numbers in the book beside it when Tim returned. He closed the door behind him, shutting out what little daylight had managed to filter in.

'Lady over the road is peering out of her window,' he explained. 'She's making enough din to waken the dead. Can't you stop her?'

I shook my head, found the doctor's number and dialled. The line was dead.

'I hear she's not one for paying bills,' Tim said. 'Better try from the car.'

I went with him, for there was nothing I could possibly do for Kathy, and already a headache was hitting me behind my eyes. Even outside her screams sounded impossibly loud.

'He's coming right over,' Tim said. 'He says to leave her, otherwise she'll just get worse.'

I looked at the dog which was huddled in a corner of the car.

'She used to love Sofie,' I said. 'I think she still does, in a demented sort of way.'

'What happened to the pups?' Tim asked.

'She drowned them. They're upstairs in a bath.'

He was silent for a moment. 'I thought you looked a bit peaky when you came out. I'll call the Health Department to get rid of them. Sit down, Mr. Hanley, the doctor will be a while yet.'

I sat only because the throbbing in my head was becoming unbearable.

'Why, Tim?' I asked.

He shrugged. 'Can't handle it, I suppose. Will you let her have the dog back?'

'No.'

I reached into my pocket for my cigarettes, and pulled out the bracelet instead. I must have pushed it in there when I grabbed Sofie. I rubbed my fingers over the stones. Life had been so different then. So clear-cut and uncomplicated.

'Get the catch mended, Tim, then return this to Lisa Weston. It belonged to her once. Kathy seems to have no further use for it.'

I found my cigarettes and lit one, wishing I could escape those blood curdling screams.

Kathy surprised us all by reporting for work the next morning; and even more surprising, she kept on working. I personally doubted whether she could stand the pressure for long, but if she could make it into the new year I would take stock of the situation then.

She made no comment when Chris introduced the young man who was to take over from him, and to the best of my knowledge Sofie was never mentioned. I had the dog now, and there was no way she would get near it again.

The days passed slowly, without incident. June and Eric got together to discuss the new magazine, and on the couple of occasions I joined them, they seemed to have their ideas well in hand. Christmas was finally upon us, and because it was expected, I attended the annual office party, giving a suitably short speech before slipping away with Alan.

'You're too lenient,' he said. 'In a few hours they'll all be rolling drunk.'

He had always disapproved of these parties, especially as I put no ceiling on the amount of money spent to make them a success.

'Happily drunk,' I said. 'I'm surprised Kathy never showed up.'

'I thought she was working tonight.'

'No,' I said. 'She has a live show tomorrow, but nothing else until the new year.' I glanced at him. 'I don't know why you stayed. Nothing stopped you from going to Oldenshaw this morning.'

'You have obviously never driven to Oldenshaw with Marian and David. They never stop bickering. And then there are three dogs, two horses and the cat. Clara went off yesterday, and Lisa was determined to bring the cat—she'll lose the bloody thing for sure. With that load and the luggage that accompanies them, I can assure you there's no room for me. By the time I get there, they'll be settled in. I've learnt over the years that if you want to maintain a happy marriage, you separate in times of stress. Lisa can manage very well, probably because she's so busy looking after the animals that she leaves the human element to cope for itself.'

As we stepped into the cold night I heard high-pitched squeals, and from somewhere nearby a chuckle. I had invited Alan home for dinner and he left me to fetch his car.

'Nice party?' Tim asked.

'You should have come and seen for yourself,' I said.

Alan's headlights swung round, and leaning back, I closed my eyes. This promised to be a quiet Christmas, and I was looking forward to a rest.

I think I was hoping for too much. We ate an excellent dinner, and afterwards, Alan dropped the first bombshell.

'I shall be fifty-four next March,' he said out of the blue. 'I may sound selfish, but I've been thinking a lot lately about retiring. I would like to phase myself out over two or three years. Nothing hasty, of course. I'd never do that to you. But I want to spend some time with Lisa and the children, and try to help put the farm back on its feet. Lisa loves the place, but since Richard died she's frightened of it. I had to force her to go there this Christmas.'

Christmas after Christmas returned to my memory. I reached down to fondle Sofie's ears.

'She has too many memories, Alan. She needs time to adjust.'

He stared into his brandy. 'And me?' he asked.

Less than a week ago Chris had turned his back on Hanley Recordings, and now Alan wanted to leave.

'I would never stand in your way,' I said. 'But I shall miss you. We've done a lot together.'

'*You* have done a lot,' he said. 'You've built an empire single-handed. I've never been more than one of the pillars. I would never have the guts to do all you've done. But now you have an army of sturdy young pillars to support you.'

I looked at him. Alan had aged a lot since we first met. The change was not only in his bulging waistline and receding hair, which was now more white than brown, but in his face.

'There will always be a need for you,' I said. 'And sturdy young supporters are liable to be headstrong.'

'*You* were always headstrong,' he said. 'You still are. I shouldn't be telling you this, but I've heard from a reliable source that you're to be included in next year's Honours List. A knighthood, no less.'

I grimaced. 'God only knows why.'

'For services rendered to your country. You've brought in millions.'

In the hall the telephone began to ring.

'When will you begin phasing yourself out?' I asked, not wanting to talk about myself.

'Next year. But it'll be a slow process, and I shall always be available if you need me. I'd never cut myself off completely.'

I would always need him, but did not say so. I was glad when Roberts came in. Sofie ran to him, standing on her hind legs as she pawed his immaculate suit. He would never admit it, but Roberts had a soft spot for the Dalmatian, and walked her daily.

'My apologies, sir,' he said, pushing her down. 'Mr. Henderson wants to speak to you. He says it is urgent.'

'Thank you, Roberts.'

Alan's eyes met mine, and although neither of us said anything, we knew my peaceful Christmas was about to be shattered.

'Perhaps he's fallen out with William,' he suggested.

'If that were the case, he'd be making a trunk call to Lisa,' I said.

It wasn't William. It was Kathy.

'Bad news?' Alan asked.

'Kathy has taken an overdose. Martin thinks it was heroin, but that she did it by mistake, realised what had happened, and telephoned him in panic. She'd passed out by the time he reached the house. She's in hospital now, in a coma. I promised him I would go immediately. What a bloody mess this is going to be.'

He was on his feet. 'An even bloodier mess once the drug squad have searched the house. I'd better come with you. If the press hear about it, all hell is going to break loose. She couldn't have chosen a better time to hit the headlines.' He gulped down the remainder of his brandy. 'There's no need to bring Tim out. We can use my car.'

'Too late,' I said. 'I've already asked him to bring the car round. Anyway, he'd probably sulk for a month if he was excluded from a scandal like this.'

We arrived at the hospital at midnight and found Martin pacing an empty waiting room.

'I'm sorry to call you out,' he said. 'But she's been unconscious for such a long time.'

'I thought this had only just happened,' said Alan.

Martin looked at him, his face lined with worry. 'No,' he stammered. 'She telephoned as William and I were on our way out. It must have been around seven.'

That was five hours ago. No wonder he was looking bloody awful.

'Who else knows about this?' I asked.

'Only us three, and the hospital staff. The chauffeur wasn't there, I checked. She was alone in the house, and I had to break a window to get in.' He paused. 'I called an ambulance and came here with them. That's it.'

'Perhaps I should try and find out what's happening,' Alan suggested.

I nodded. When he had gone I went and stood beside the window. Martin must have telephoned for the nearest ambulance, for this was no private clinic but an overworked public hospital.

'What will happen now?' Martin asked, his voice a whisper.

'I'm not sure,' I said. 'The police will probably be informed, and what they do will depend on whether they find any dope in the house. Are you sure it was heroin?'

'I guess so,' he said. 'I found this. What else would she use it for?' He pulled a small syringe from his pocket and held it forward on the palm of his hand. 'What shall I do with it?'

'I'll take it,' I said.

'To the police?'

'No, Martin,' I said. 'I'll throw it away. I don't want trouble any more than you do. It would be bad publicity all round. Bad for Kathy, and bad for the company.'

'She's finished, isn't she?' he asked.

'What makes you say that?'

'It's obvious. She's unreliable and a junkie. If Simon Townsend can push her out of the charts, anybody can.'

'You underrate Simon,' I said. 'He's bloody good.'

'But not a chart-buster. He never was.'

I sat down, wrapping the syringe in a handkerchief before pushing it into the pocket of my overcoat.

'What else can I do but chuck her, Martin? I can't keep carrying her. I might even be doing her a favour. If she keeps on like this she'll kill herself. Alan has invested her money well, and if she's careful she could live the rest of her life in comfort. Think about it, but not now. Somebody's coming.'

At this hour a sleepy silence enveloped the hospital, and brisk footsteps on the tiled floors echoed loudly. Martin leapt to his feet, his fists tightly clenched.

'It's probably Alan,' I said. 'Doctors don't make so much noise.'

I was wrong. It wasn't Alan but Tim, and directly behind him was my brother-in-law.

'It's bedlam down there,' said Tim. 'Nobody's being allowed beyond the main hall. They know I'm with you, so they let me bring Mr. Stewart up when I explained who he was.'

'Thank you,' Eric said more curtly than he probably meant. 'Good God, Mark, the whole of London's press knows Kathy Karn is here except for the *Threepenny Post*. We were in the middle of a Christmas party and they sent me because everyone else was too damn drunk.'

'I only heard myself less than an hour ago,' I said, surprised. 'How did it leak out?'

Tim closed the door, and leant against the wall beside it. I knew nothing short of a physical eviction would budge him now.

'Martin,' Eric said.

'I told nobody but Mark,' Martin objected.

'I'm not saying that you told anybody,' Eric said. 'But you were seen coming in with a stretcher, and a diligent wait by a news-hungry young reporter paid off when Mark and Alan arrived. Any moron would have known that something was up. As for the rest, some nurse could have been persuaded to give out Kathy's name, I don't know. But somebody might have had the decency to inform *us* earlier.'

'Do you think this was meant to be public knowledge?' I asked. 'It's something I would have preferred the press not to know.'

I looked at Martin. His head was buried in his arms. We had not been here very long yet, but for him the going was becoming decidedly rough. I wondered why William hadn't come, but then remembered that this had nothing whatever to do with him.

'You may as well sit down, Eric,' I said.' She's still unconscious, and all we can do is wait.'

Dawn was breaking when Kathy regained consciousness. She asked for Martin, and he was allowed to see her for a few minutes; after which we left. Eric said he was going back to the office, but the rest of us went home. I slept until eleven-thirty, when Roberts woke me to say Alan was here.

'I wanted to wish you a merry Christmas before I left,' he said. 'You ought to come up, Mark. It won't be much fun down here by yourself.'

I shook my head. 'I'm getting past the age where one Christmas is any different from another. But I won't be alone, Fran has asked me over for lunch—and I shall be flying up to Oldenshaw on Boxing Day.'

'Charles has offered Lisa one of his hunters for the Meet, and Marian and David want to follow on foot. Do you remember the time you rode Kingston and that bloody fool Arthur threw a firecracker? A lot of water has flowed under the bridge since then.'

I poured us each a whisky. 'At least Kathy pulled through,' I said.

He smiled. 'Even she wouldn't be spiteful enough to die at Christmas. Are you going to let Chris know?'

'No,' I said. 'Not unless he asks. He's out of this now.'

The telephone began to ring and we both listened as Roberts answered it. A moment later we were on our way back to the hospital. Kathy wanted to see me, and Alan, instead of going to the aerodrome, insisted on coming.

Martin was waiting in the hall. 'I'm sorry,' he said. 'But she wouldn't relax until she knew you were on the way.'

I had always suspected Kathy possessed the constitution of an elephant, and today was to prove me correct. Martin must have brought in some of her belongings, for she was wearing a frilly pink nightdress, and had smeared on some eyeshadow. But when she looked at me, her eyes were not quite focused.

'Thank you for coming,' she said. 'Martin told me you was here last night, so I didn't think you'd mind.' She paused, but I wasn't sure whether it was for breath or effect. 'You can sit on the chair over here. I won't keep you long. Not that they'd let me anyway. They chucked Martin out just before you come.'

I'm not sure why, but I felt uneasy, even though she appeared calm. I sat on a chair which had been placed close to the bed.

'How do you feel?' I asked.

A smile came to her colourless lips. 'Not too bad, considering. They got me doped up, but it's only temporary. They're going to take me down gradual-like. I didn't do it on purpose, you know. That's why I rung Martin. I was frightened, and I knew he'd come. You believe me, don't you?'

'Yes, Kathy,' I said. 'I believe you.'

I suddenly remembered the syringe which I had been too tired to throw away.

'Martin didn't say nothing, but the way he was talking, sort of roundabout, made me suspicious-like,' she said. 'That's why I wanted to see you. What are you going to do?'

'To do?' I repeated, although I knew what she meant.

'About me? I know you must be angry, but they still love me.' She waved an arm about the room. 'Look at all the flowers. I've never seen so many flowers. And the nurses tell me people keep ringing. Lots and lots of people who don't even know me. They care.'

'We all care,' I said gently. 'But why do you keep on doing it, Kathy? Why are you throwing your life away?'

She stared at me with frightened eyes.

'You don't understand what it's like,' she said. 'It's lonely. And I get frightened sometimes, real frightened. It weren't so bad when I had Martin ... but even Martin, look what he done to me. I didn't do it to him. I didn't do nothing to him.' She plucked a flower from a vase and smelt it. 'But *they* love me, and they're the ones who matter most. You know that, don't you?'

'I know,' I answered, wondering what she was getting at.

'And because they love me they won't mind. You know that too, don't you, Mr. Hanley?'

I knew now what she wanted to hear, but could see no point in lying.

'They send flowers because they feel sorry for you,' I said harshly. 'How long are you going to survive on sympathy? They'll send you flowers this week and spit in your face next. I'm sorry Kathy, but this has to be the end. Some other company will probably sign you up if you're determined to continue in this business, but as far as I'm concerned you're finished. Your contract will be terminated at the end of the month.'

'You can't do that!' she gasped. 'You can't do that to me!'

I looked at her. 'I can and I will. You might even thank me one day.'

A flush spread up her neck and spilt into her cheeks. Her breathing was laboured, and she leant forward, her eyes malicious.

'Bastard!' she hissed. 'Fucking bastard! You can't do that to me. Nobody can do that to me. I'll get lawyers. I'll sue you for every fucking penny you got ...'

I walked to the door. 'Do what you want, Kathy. It's over. Finished. You're a junkie and a has-been, and I'm not going to carry you any longer.'

'Bastard!' she screamed. 'Filthy, fucking bastard! I hate you ... I wish you in hell ...'

My fingers were on the door handle when I turned. I knew I could never persuade her to see reason, but decency stopped me from walking out on this bitter note.

Too late I saw the object in her hand. I tried to avoid it, but the glass vase struck the right side of my head, above my eyes. It shattered, the impact sending me reeling against the wall. Semi-conscious, half blinded by the blood which was everywhere, I tried to find the door; while behind me Kathy began to scream.

The door I could not find flew open, and people were running into the room. A steadying hand took hold of my arm.

'Christ!' Alan said.

And unable to hold on any longer, I crumpled, my feet slipping in the mess made by blood and water and trampled flowers.

I opened my eyes slowly, and saw a white-coated doctor and two nurses.

'Try not to move,' said the doctor. 'I've nearly finished. How do you feel?'

'Awful,' I said.

'You were lucky,' he told me as he worked. 'It's a deep cut, but clean, and there's no damage to the eye. I'm afraid you'll have a permanent scar, and a hellish headache for a day or two. There, I've finished. Can you sit up, Mr. Hanley?'

I managed to do so with a little assistance. I saw my jacket was lying across a nearby chair, and my shirt was patched with drying blood-stains. The younger nurse, who looked like a student, was putting dirty instruments into a kidney bowl.

'Hold still while I cover it,' said the elder one, tearing the protective paper from a pad of gauze.

The doctor was writing on a small pad. I judged him to be around my own age, kindly, with none of the briskness of younger men.

'What time is it?' I asked.

He glanced at his watch.'Two minutes to three. You've been unconscious for almost half an hour, and I think you should stay overnight for observation.'

The nurse taped the pad into place. 'Do I have to?' I asked.

'No,' he said. 'You can leave whenever you want to.'

'Then I'd rather go,' I said. The last time I had been in a hospital was after that car crash in the Fifties. Hospitals were not my favourite places.

I thought he would argue, but he only shook his head. 'Then I'll let you have some pills to help with the pain,' he said. 'And you'd better consult your own doctor within the next day or two.'

'Over Christmas?'

He smiled. 'We can't choose our working hours. But if you don't suffer dizzy spells, blackouts or violent headaches, I can see no harm in waiting until after the Christmas break.' He paused. 'You'd solve a lot problems by staying.'

'Probably,' I said. 'But I have a hard skull.'

He tore a sheet from his pad, and sent the young nurse to collect the prescription from the pharmacy.

'I've given you enough to last three days,' he said. 'Stay there until she comes back, and when you get home, go straight to bed.'

I nodded, and wished I hadn't, for the pounding in my head took on a fresh urgency.

'Does it hurt?' he asked.

'It's bearable.'

'The anaesthetic is starting to wear off.'

He picked up a syringe which looked similar to the one Martin had found in Kathy's house. 'Can you roll up your sleeve?'

I swung my legs over the side of the couch, and for one horrible moment everything spun crazily and I thought I would pass out. But when I sat still the feeling passed, and the doctor had his back to me so he didn't notice.

'This usually causes drowsiness,' he warned.

'How is Kathy Karn?' I asked as he put the needle in my arm.

'She had to be sedated. What happened in there?'

'I said something which upset her.'

'You should never have been allowed in her room without a nurse or orderly present. Her mind is unstable and she can't be held responsible for what she does.'

'Will she ever be cured?' I asked.

'If she wants to be. But if she carries on at her present rate, she is very quickly going to reach a stage where we are powerless to help her.'

I should have liked to lie back and close my eyes, but no sooner had the doctor gone than the door opened again.

'I thought you were meant to stay overnight,' Alan said abruptly. 'You look bloody awful.'

'I feel bloody awful,' I agreed. 'But I'd rather feel it at home than here. You should have left by now.'

'I don't see how,' he said. 'Kathy was in hysterics, and you literally passed out in the most dramatic circumstances. Why did you tell her? You must have known she was unhinged.'

'Unhinged, yes,' I said. 'But I never realised she had superhuman strength. All that shattered glass must have made an awful mess. Where's Martin? Or won't he speak to me for chastising Kathy?'

'He and Tim are looking for another way out,' said Alan. 'The main hall is still full of reporters, who have now been joined by some of Kathy's fans.'

'I'd scarcely expect them to be mine,' I said dryly.

He handed me his overcoat. 'You'd better wear this. What are you going to do now?'

'What d'you mean?'

'Well, you can't fly yourself to Oldenshaw on Boxing Day now. I wish Lisa were here. She never wanted to go up there in the first place. Perhaps you should come up with me.'

'No thank you,' I said. 'I'll telephone Mother tomorrow with an excuse for not coming. I'd rather she didn't see me like this.'

He was frowning. 'You shouldn't be alone.'

'With a house full of servants?' I asked. 'And Fran within shouting distance?'

'I shall also be here,' said Martin from the doorway. 'I'll probably never have the courage to say this again, but you're a bloody fool, Mark.'

I looked at him. 'You knew why she wanted to see me,' I said. 'But you still asked me to come.'

Martin closed the door and stood with his back against it. 'You should be in bed, not on your feet. But what's the use, I expect Alan has told you the same thing. Tim is taking the car round to the staff entrance. Alan will go with you while I keep the reporters occupied.'

'I have to wait for some pills,' I remembered as Alan helped me with the overcoat.

* * *

Alan came home with me. It had been a long day, and I insisted Tim drive him to the aerodrome. I even wanted to call back Peter who was staying with some friends; Alan looked too tired to fly.

'I'll use the car,' said Alan. 'But I'll not ruin Peter's Christmas.'

Tim had gone for petrol, and I went upstairs to change into clean clothes, leaving Alan drinking tea in the drawing room. I told Roberts to bring some neat whisky, and after I had drunk half a tumbler my head began to clear. I no longer felt like lying down, and decided to go with Alan to the airport. He protested a little, but only after an argument with Tim did I get my way.

At the airport, it was cold and wet, and as I stook beside the runway I could feel the rain soaking into me despite the umbrella Tim held over my head. I shivered as I watched the small aircraft position itself for take-off.

'If you must watch, you can see just as well from inside the car,' Tim said. They were the first words he had addressed to me since leaving the house.

The plane was moving, gathering speed as it raced along the runway.

'All right,' I said. 'Let's go.'

'And about time. You should be in your bed.'

I smiled. 'I know. And that's where I intend going.'

'Then why did you insist on coming?'

I shrugged. 'I'm not sure. A feeling I had. But I'm ready to leave now.'

I watched the plane climb into the dreadful night. I did not envy Alan the flight, but I envied what was waiting for him at the other end.

'You'll be running a fever,' Tim said. 'He's gone, so let's get out of here too. It'll not be easy getting back into London with the traffic and this bloody rain.'

I was about to turn away and get into the car when something, an almost imperceptible movement of Alan's wing lights, caught my attention.

'What now?' said Tim impatiently.

My eyes ached as I tried to follow the plane.

'Is something wrong?' he asked after a moment.

I couldn't be sure, not in that rain, at that distance and in the dark. Altitude could easily be misjudged. But then I saw it again before the plane veered sharply to the left. I heard the irregular whine of the over-strained engine, and even as I opened my mouth it was too late.

The plane fell, plunging nose-first to earth and exploding with the impact of a bomb. Flames soared skywards, illuminating the area like a beacon.

I stumbled back against the car, closing my eyes as I tried to fight off a wave of nausea. Sirens started to whine, and a bell clanged urgently. Although my stomach must have been empty I was sick, vomiting helplessly onto the wet grass.

'Oh my God ...' I heard Tim mumble again and again.

I was still retching when Tim took hold of my arm and forced me to sit down. I felt numb.

Vehicles were speeding along the runway. They looked far away and detached, lost in a clamour of nerve-wracking noise.

'Here, drink this,' said Tim, pushing a glass into my hands. I stared at the crystal tumbler. 'Drink it,' he repeated.

A spotlight was fixed on the burning plane. I saw the upended tail, and then it keeled over, disappearing with a roar.

'Drink it,' Tim repeated, and I gulped down the whisky. As I lowered the empty glass he bent forward to refill it.

'You have it,' I said.

'I've had some already,' he told me. I was surprised to hear his voice trembling. 'There's not much left. It'll steady you.'

He poured the rest of the whisky into the glass.

'He could never have survived that,' I said.

Tim was right. The whisky was steadying me. I became conscious of more than the burning plane. Alan was dead, and Lisa would have to be told. The police ... the press ... here was a story beside which Kathy's disaster would pale into insignificance.

The first of the engines had reached the wreckage. More lights lit up what did not need lighting up. People were running, and the sirens were less strident. I wished I had turned away, and not witnessed the cruel end of a man who had been so much more than a friend.

'Take me to the control tower,' I said.

I stood up and the whisky glass dropped to the ground. Tim bent over, searching for it.

'Leave it,' I said. 'There are more important things to do.'

He turned towards me, and I was shocked to see tears in his eyes.

'Aye,' he said harshly.

As he turned the car on the slippery grass, I saw that men were already cordoning off the area with ropes, preparing to keep away the curious and the morbid. The death-crash of an aircraft would enliven the conversation of many a family this Christmas ... I thought of Lisa waiting at the farm, and wished the doctor had never given me that injection. The nagging pain would be better than this constant battle to keep my wits about me; for during the next few hours I was going to need my wits as I had never needed them before.

Chapter Five

Eric Stewart had been too exhausted to drive home after a night without sleep. He managed a few hours on the sofa in someone's office, and then he was needed, and it was dark before he finally left for home. He cursed the heavy traffic; everyone seemed determined to get out of London tonight.

The car phone which Mark had suggested he have installed began to ring. It would be Fran, complaining because he had promised the children he would be home early.

'I'm sorry,' he said, propping the receiver between shoulder and chin as the traffic suddenly started to move. 'I'm on my way now. Are the children very upset?'

There was a pause. The traffic came to a halt, and he grasped the receiver in his right hand.

'Mr. Stewart?' a deep voice said, startling him.

'Who is that?' he asked.

'Tim Denholm, sir.'

'Tim?' He stiffened. Mark wouldn't have the chauffeur call him, not unless something were very wrong. 'What's happened?'

'Mr. Hanley wants you here immediately,' Tim said. 'There's been an accident ...'

Eric felt his pulses race as he eased the car forward. He could hear sirens at the other end of the line. 'Mark?' he asked.

'No,' said Tim. 'Mr. Hanley is all right .. more or less. It's Mr. Weston. His plane crashed and he's dead. We're at Toddington now. Can you come quickly?'

'I'm on my way,' Eric replied. 'I'll be there in about half an hour.'

'Thank you,' said Tim. 'We're at the control tower. The police have just arrived so I'll have to go, but I'll try and keep him here. Perhaps you can talk some sense into him.'

The line went dead, and Eric wondered what Tim meant by that last remark. He pushed his way into an adjoining lane, ignoring a torrent of hooting horns. He had to cross to the opposite side of London, from south to north, and mentally he planned the route which would be quickest and least clogged. As he raced through the traffic, desperately hoping that he wouldn't be stopped by the police, it suddenly struck him that perhaps he was no longer out in the cold as far as Mark was concerned. He would still have to tread carefully, but it looked as if he had finally been accepted back into the magic circle.

Mark had been right about the curious and the morbid. They came from everywhere, and when he reached the narrow access road to the airport, Eric Stewart met his first major obstruction. He could see by the lights and crowds of people that the plane had crashed on a small patch of waste land a half mile past the aerodrome.

He hooted his horn impatiently, and swore at all who could hear, but it was his press card, shown to an equally frustrated policeman on a motor-cycle, which got him through in the end. The policeman escorted him to the gates, and while he was waiting for them to open he noticed a small plane position itself at the northernmost tip of the runway. It must be a brave pilot to take off tonight, Eric thought, for the plane would have to fly over what was left of the wreck.

The gates swung open and he turned towards the control tower. He could see the Rolls Royce parked in a dull pool of light. He halted behind it, and stepped out as the plane's engines gave a final rev. Like many others that night, he watched the plane lift off, climbing higher and higher until is disappeared in the mist and rain.

'He's gone,' said Tim. The chauffeur looked haggard, his mouth set in a grim line and his eyes anxious. 'I tried to stop him, but he wouldn't listen. He's in no condition to fly such a distance, and they shouldn't have allowed it.'

'Nobody else could tell her except for him,' said Eric dully. 'I think she's the only person he's ever really cared for in his entire life.'

He turned towards the control tower, and only then did Tim remember that he knew nothing of what had happened this afternoon.

'Why did they let him go?' he asked after the chauffeur had told him everything.

'You know how persuasive Mr. Hanley can be. The people up there gave him something, some kind of pep pill, I think. He wouldn't tell me. But on top of the other medicine, and in his frame of mind, it can do him no good. That's why I was hoping you'd get here before he left. He'd have yelled bloody murder, but I think he might have listened to you.'

Eric was staring at the sky. The rain had petered out to a fine drizzle.

'Why didn't he call Peter? Or get another pilot?'

'On Christmas Eve? I asked, but there was no other pilot obtainable, and Peter's in Kent. Mr. Hanley wouldn't wait for him to get here. He said it would be too late.'

'He'll be all right,' said Eric. 'He's no fool.' A couple of policemen came out of the control tower. 'There's a lot to be done, Tim, and I shall need your help.'

'Aye,' said the chauffeur. 'You go ahead. I must telephone Oldenshaw and have them put on the landing lights. They're keeping Steelton Airport open especially for him, but he insists on landing at Oldenshaw. It's nearer, he says. I'll use the car phone, it's bedlam up there.'

Eric now understood the urgency behind Mark's hasty departure. Time was obviously the important factor, not for Lisa but for himself. He was fighting a battle against his own body; he must inevitably lose—but there were important things to be done before he finally accepted defeat.

It was a successful party, and everybody was having a good time. They had just settled down to a buffet supper when Bertha patted Lady Latchcham on the arm and said her son was on the telephone. Charles was deep in conversation with the new doctor, George Ferris, who had taken over his retiring father's practice. Mary caught his eye and, with a gracious smile which took in the rest of the company, stood up.

'You'll have to excuse me,' she said. 'It's Mark.'

She took the the call in the hallway, listening in appalled silence to the little her son had to say. She put down the receiver and called for Bertha to fetch Lord Latchcham and then bring her a coat. Charles came quickly, and she told him what had happened.

'I'd better send them home,' he said.

'No, let them enjoy themselves. This is Christmas, after all.'

'Would you like me to come with you?'

'No, Charles,' she said. 'I can always telephone if I need help. But could you ask Simpson to prepare rooms for Lisa and the children? I shall have to bring them back here. And Mark as well. He can't stay alone at the Manor.'

The maid returned with the coat. 'Drive carefully,' said Charles, and kissed her cheek.

'You're a pretty good cook when you want to be,' said Marian, taking her third mince pie. 'What would you prefer to watch?' 'A Christmas Carol' or 'The Comedy and Musical Christmas Spectacular'?'

'Neither,' her mother said. 'I'd prefer to listen to records.'

'All right. I wonder why Daddy is so late.'

Lisa smiled at her daughter, who was unable to understand that today of all days Alan thought it best to remain in London as long as he was needed, helping Mark sort out this latest crisis with Kathy Karn.

'He's not due into Steelton until about now,' she said. 'And if you carry on eating like that, you'll be at least ten pounds heavier by the time we go home.'

'It's the cold,' said Marian cheerfully. 'I'll exercise it off after the New Year. You should have gone to Aunty Mary's party. I'd have looked after David.'

'And leave you alone on Christmas Eve? I wouldn't dream of it. I think I'll make some more coffee. And someone ought to check the horses. It's beginning to ice up outside.'

Marian pulled a face. 'You check the horses and I'll make the coffee.'

Her mother pushed her out of the kitchen door, and groaning in a good-natured sort of way, Marian disappeared down the path with Samson at her heels.

There was fresh coffee, but Lisa took a jar of instant granules from the cupboard and was just ladling them into two mugs when Wang, always sharp of hearing, started to growl deep in his throat. As the growl turned into a shrill yap, Tipsy took up the tune, closely followed by the farm dogs. Lisa yelled for them to be quiet and then looked out of the window.

She saw the headlights of a car and heard Marian shout something. He was home. She checked the oven to see that the baked potatoes and cauliflower cheese were not burnt, then took the steak she had been saving from the refrigerator.

He did not come to the kitchen door, but knocked at the front instead. She wiped her hands, and leaving the steak on the table, rushed into the hall. Marian must have forgotten to tell him that the back door was unlocked. Wang followed her, but Tipsy stayed in the kitchen.

The little-used catch was stiff, and when the door swung open it was Mark who stood there, not Alan. He looked ill, his eyes dark pits. Perhaps the bandage covering his forehead made him look worse, for it was white against white.

'Mark,' she said. 'What are you doing here? Your head ... what happened?' She paused, and stared past him into the darkness. 'Is

Alan there?'

'Can I come in, Lisa?'

Her heart was thumping with the irregular beat of a steam hammer. 'Where is he?' she demanded.

Mark looked at her. How could he say that Alan would never set foot inside this house again, inside any house again? That he had burnt to a cinder in a wet and empty field?

'He is dead.'

The look in her eyes sent a cold shiver running along his spine. He trembled, partly from the cold and partly from reaction which he was finding it difficult to control.

Wang was sniffing his feet, and Lisa swept the small dog into her arms, burying her face in his hair.

'You'd better come in,' she said. She looked at a print of a hunt in full cry. The horses were stiff-legged in the way artists used to draw them; their riders leaning back and brandishing long whips.

It was impossible. She had only spoken to him this afternoon, kissed him goodbye yesterday morning. How could someone be there one moment and gone the next? Not Alan...

'*I am fond of him*,' she had said to her father on the morning of her wedding. '*I think, given time, I shall learn to love him as much as he loves me*' ...

'What happened?' she asked, still looking at the picture.

'The plane crashed.'

She closed her eyes.

Mark stood behind her, watching her even breathing. There were no hysterics or tears, just an appalling shocked space in time. He was grateful that Marian had gone to the stables on some errand, for her presence would have made this harder still.

'The kettle must be boiling,' Lisa said, her voice too controlled. 'I was about to make coffee. Do you want some?'

He did not answer, but followed her to the kitchen where the farm dogs were watching Tipsy wolf down the last of the steak. She went to the stove, picked up the kettle, and then put it back on the ring.

'It's not boiling yet,' she said. 'What happened? Were you there?'

He sat on the edge of the old wooden table. His head was throbbing with a fierce intensity, and he had left the pain killers in London. There was nothing he could do but hang on. 'Yes,' he said.

She could not turn her face to him. If she did, she would break down completely.

'You saw it?'

'Yes'

'What happened?'

'He crashed just after take-off.'

She bit deeply into her lower lip, and then turned, her eyes seeking his.

'There will be an enquiry,' he said in reply to her unspoken question. 'We shall know the reasons then.'

Still her eyes held his. 'You're a pilot, Mark, and a bloody good one so I've been told. You must have seen something.'

He took a deep breath. 'I saw the plane take off and turn. I think it turned before he had the height and speed to manoeuvre properly. The instruments should have shown him that he needed to climb higher. I could be wrong, Lisa. I was too far away, and it was too dark to see properly.'

Pilot error? 'Was it quick?' she asked.

'Yes,' Mark said. 'He would have known nothing.'

She closed her eyes. She knew he would not lie about that.

The kettle started to boil, but when she lifted it up another horror struck her.

'Did ... did ... was there any fire?'

Mark's face contorted with the bitter memory which had accompanied him during his intolerably long journey. He summoned his fast failing strength and went to her.

'Don't ask,' he said. 'Don't torture yourself any more than you have to. Come and sit down.'

She sat as he had asked. She felt no better, only dazed, as though this were happening to someone else. She looked up at him.

'I have to know, Mark. If you won't tell me, then I shall find somebody else who will.'

'Yes,' he said after a moment. 'There was fire.'

Her indrawn breath was a long hiss, and her knuckles were white as she clenched her fists.

'He ...' she began.

'... would have died on impact,' he said.

She sat very erect, not even stirring when Tipsy laid his head on her knees. Her eyes blurred as she tried to visualise what Mark had seen.

One of the dogs growled. Mark looked up and saw the headlights.

'I'm sorry,' she said in a faded voice. 'The coffee. Would you mind making it yourself? I don't think I can ... do you mind? And the steak ... can you see the steak?'

She began searching for it, but he laid a restraining hand on her shoulder.

'It doesn't matter, Lisa,' he said.

'Are you sure, Mark? Are you sure he didn't know?'

'I'm sure,' he answered, taking hold of her cold hands. 'I have never been more sure of anything in my life.'

The front door had not been properly closed, and Mary Latchcham brought Marian in that way. The girl was crying, and ran upstairs to her bedroom, leaving Mary staring helplessly after her. When she had gone Mary looked into the parlour, but it was empty. She took a deep breath and went into the kitchen.

Lisa was sitting down. She was white as a sheet, and Mark stood over her, paler still if that were possible. Of the two of them it was her son who gave her the worst shock. He sensed her presence and looked up, a warning in his eyes.

'I'm sorry for ruining your party,' he said.

'Aunt Mary,' Lisa gasped, and ran to her.

'I'll wait outside,' Mark told his mother.

She looked at him anxiously.

'I'm all right,' he said, and touched her arm in passing.

But as she held Lisa, she couldn't help worrying, for both of them.

Mark went no further than the hall, where he stood with his back against a wall and his eyes closed against the waves of pain. The pill which he persuaded the flight controller to give him had kept him awake and would probably continue to do so until tomorrow morning. Many of the charter pilots took them; they were essential to men who had long flying hours ahead and reckless night-lives behind them. But with careful calculation, he had set one drug against the other.

'Uncle Mark?'

He opened his eyes. Marian was standing at the foot of the stairs, tears streaming down her cheeks.

'You know?' he asked, straightening up.

'Yes,' she said. 'Aunty Mary told me. Why did he have to die like that?'

'I wish I could tell you, sweetheart. But I can't.'

He held out his arms and she clung to him. He led her to the stairs, where they sat. She sobbing against his chest and he gently stroking her hair. He lost track of time, and was conscious of nothing but the throb in his head.

'I want you to have something,' Marian suddenly said. She leapt to her feet and ran into the parlour. She wasn't long. She came out holding a small box which she handed to him. 'It's the tiepin,' she said.

He remembered how thrilled she had been when they chose it. 'Thank you,' he said.

'Is Father Christmas come yet?' a young voice asked from the top of the stairs.

They both looked up. David was standing on the landing in crumpled pyjamas and bare feet, smiling sleepily at them. Mark stood up, using the bannister for support.

'Father Christmas isn't coming here tonight, David,' he said. 'But he will be at your Aunt Mary's. I've come to take you there.'

'Why?' he asked, puzzled.

'Because he isn't,' Marian said. 'Because ... because Daddy is ...'

'Marian.'

She stopped, staring wide-eyed at Mark. He hunched a little as he bent down to her level.

'He's too young,' he explained. 'Even if you tell him, he won't understand. Christmas is a time for presents and fun, so try not to ruin it for him. I'd like you to go upstairs now, and pack whatever you need for tonight and tomorrow. Can you manage some things for him as well?'

'We're leaving?' she asked.

'You can't stay here.'

'What about Mummy?'

'My mother will look after her. Do you want any help?'

She shook her head. 'No. I can do it.' She looked at her brother, and after blowing her nose, smiled weakly. 'Come on, David. We're going to have an adventure.'

'Why isn't Father Christmas coming here?'

'Because he's late and ... and one of his reindeer hurt its leg. But he'll be at Aunty Mary's very soon.'

She ran up the stairs and took him by the hand. 'He should buy himself a great big lorry,' the child said. 'Why are you crying, Marian?'

'Because I'm happy,' she told him. 'Now stop asking so many silly questions, otherwise Father Christmas won't come and see you. He only visits good little boys, you know.'

Mark watched them go, thankful that Marian had the presence of mind to understand. He glanced towards the telephone and wondered whether Eric was coping, and then, exhausted beyond belief, he walked unsteadily into the parlour. There was so much to be done. Arrangements had to be made for the funeral, the disposal of the estate. Everything would go to Lisa, but there were sure to be problems.

In the little-used parlour Christmas was all around him; in the gaily lit tree, the logs crackling in the fireplace, the cards, the presents stacked under the tree, and a plate of mince pies on top of a bookcase.

He sat by the fire and closed his eyes.

'I've brought you some tea,' said his mother.

He did not turn. 'Thank you,' he said. 'But I couldn't touch it. How is Lisa?'

'Crying. But she'll be all right. She has a lot of strength. It will be hard on her for a while, but the pain will pass.' She paused. 'And you?' She came and stood over him. 'Try and drink it,' she said. 'It might help.'

'Nothing will help,' he said. 'I'm sorry , Mother, I didn't mean to alarm you.'

She frowned as she put the tea on a table beside him, and leaning forward, passed her hand over his forehead. He winced, and his eyes flew open.

'God save us from our parents,' he said, his voice blurred. 'I'm sorry to disappoint you, but I'm not burning up with fever. I have a headache, that's all. A damnable, nagging headache.'

'And the plaster?'

'A rather dramatic covering for a small cut. Kathy Karn threw a vase at me in a fit of rage.'

She was convinced that he had more than a minor cut. Alan would know; but Alan was dead.

'I've told Marian to pack some clothes for her and David, and not to tell him what's happened,' he said suddenly, his voice clear as a bell. 'I presume you're taking them back to the Hall.'

'Yes,' she said. 'Charles is arranging rooms. I'd better ask him to come over, I won't be able to fit you all in my car, and I certainly don't think you should drive again tonight. Try and drink the tea, Mark.'

He would normally have known what she was up to. But tonight he was too numb to think any further than was essential.

'I'm on my way,' Charles said when she telephoned him.

'And one more thing,' she murmured, glancing towards the half-open parlour door. 'Could you ask George Ferris to come with you? I think we need him here.'

'Lisa?' Charles asked.

'No,' she said. 'Mark. Maybe I'm being silly, but I'm frightened. He looks like death. I don't know how he got this far, or how he's managed to keep going at all.'

She put down the receiver and went back to the kitchen, leaving the door ajar so that she could hear any sound from the children or her son. And she prayed that Charles would not be too long.

Chapter Six

Clara showed June Halliday into the lounge where Lisa sat flicking through a magazine.

'Good God!' She said as the housekeeper closed the door behind her. 'You look bloody awful. Are you eating?'

Lisa stood up. 'Hello, June,' she said. 'Yes, of course I'm eating. Clara never stops trying to tempt me. And I don't look that bad.'

'You look terrible,' said June bluntly. 'And from what I hear you're deliberately keeping out of circulation.'

Lisa sank back into the chair. 'It's only a month. I need some time to myself.'

'Rubbish!' June snapped. 'That's the last thing you need.' She picked up the magazine Lisa had dropped. 'I see you've bought our first edition. What do you think?'

'It's certainly different,' said Lisa. 'But I didn't buy it. Mark left it here.'

'You and he seem very close,' June remarked.

'We go back a long way. He's the best friend Alan and I ever had. I'm sorry, would you like some coffee or something? I'm still rather disorientated.'

'I've already told Clara not to bother, for whether you like it or not, I'm taking you to lunch.'

'Not today,' said Lisa. 'I really don't feel up to it.'

'You're coming and that's that,' June stated. 'I want to talk to you, and you need to get out of this place for a while. Where are David and Marian?'

Lisa's lips twitched. 'It's easy to see you've never had children. They're both at school. Where else did you think they would be?'

'How on earth would I know? Is Marian still determined to get into ballet?'

'More than ever. What do you want to talk to me about?'

June held up the magazine. 'This,' she said. 'Mark Hanley is mad as a hatter. Nobody else would think of investing in a high quality magazine at the moment. But he just goes ahead, throws Eric and me headlong into it, and expects miracles.'

'It really is a good magazine,' Lisa said. 'And Mark told me about you and Eric. How you were the one who insisted he come in on equal terms.'

June smiled. 'I've been stagnating,' she said. 'We've already had a couple of tiffs about the cover. He's as infuriating as ever, and just as clever. I've quite enjoyed this past month.'

'And what has all that got to do with me?' Lisa asked.

'You were coming along very nicely before you left to get married, and I want you to come back as my assistant. Mark was quite right. I've bitten off much more than I can chew, and I'm swamped in work.'

'I don't need a job, June. I don't even want one.'

'I know. But you have to start thinking about what you're going to do with your life. And I think the diversion will do you good. I'm not expecting you to work full time. You can choose your own hours.'

'I don't want a job,' Lisa repeated. 'And I certainly have no intention of working for Mark.'

'I was under the impression you would be working for me,' said June. 'Mark has sense enough to keep his nose out of what doesn't concern him.'

Lisa's eyes widened. 'He owns the magazine!' she said.

'He owns two magazines, as well as a newspaper, two textile mills, a recording company and all of Martin's subsidiaries. He can't possibly run them all himself. He prefers to keep a fatherly but distant eye on us. Now run upstairs and get changed. You're coming with me for lunch, even if I have to drag you out of this house.'

Lisa stood up and walked to the door. 'I'll come to lunch, but I won't work for you,' she said. She paused, her hand on the knob. 'It's funny, but when I was younger I was always a little frightened of you. It was sheer desperation which made me speak up at that interview.'

'Most people are frightened of me,' June proudly declared. 'Mark, of course, is frightened of nobody, while Eric manages to hold his own too—although there are times when I think he'd like to crawl into some dark corner and forget I exist. You're not frightened of me now, are you?'

'Good God, no,' said Lisa. 'Beneath that brazen exterior, you're all heart. I hope we're not going anywhere fancy.'

'I'd advise you to wear a dress. I booked a table at the Savoy Grill. That's where Mark successfully wooed me to his side. And if it worked for me, it might work for you too.'

Lisa grimaced. 'I won't be long,' she said.

It was on a warm mid-June day that Mary Latchcham attended the monthly meeting of the Women's Institute in the church hall. Afterwards, she went to the grave of her first husband. She stood there for a short time, and was about to leave when a solitary figure at the other end of the cemetary caught her eye.

'Lisa?' she said, hurrying over.

The woman swung round. 'Why Mary, what on earth are you doing here?' She kissed the old woman on the cheek.

'I'd hate Paul to think I'd forgotten him,' said Mary. 'When did you arrive? Our grapevine rarely fails, but I never heard you were here.'

'We came this morning. David got mumps, and Marian caught them from him. They're both past the infectious stage but can't go back to school for another week, and as I wanted to come up, it seemed an ideal opportunity. I was on my way to see you, but decided to come here first.' She paused. 'I'm glad Mark brought him here. I'd almost forgotten how beautiful it is. Oldenshaw never changes.'

Perhaps Oldenshaw had not changed, but Lisa had. She had become pale and sad.

'You've lost weight,' Mary said.

'I know. And it's not through lack of food. I just don't seem able to put it on again. Martin used to complain every time I put on an ounce, and now he says that it's like dressing a scarecrow.' She fell silent, her gaze drawn to the grass-covered grave.

'Would you prefer me to leave?' Mary asked.

Lisa shook her head. 'No,' she said. 'Let's go and have a drink at the Jolly Farmer. We can sit outside. Or will the sight of you there scandalise the village?'

'It thrives on scandal,' said Mary.

She ordered sherry, and Lisa gin and tonic; and they sat at a table in the empty garden. This was the first time Lisa had been back since the funeral, and reaching across the table, Mary took hold of the younger woman's hand.

'Are you managing?' she asked. 'It's hard for a while. I can still remember how I felt after Paul was gone.'

'It's been hard,' Lisa admitted. 'But I'm beginning to find my feet again. They say that in times of crisis you learn who your friends are. I think I'm extremely lucky, I've had Martin and William and June all worrying themselves sick over me.'

'And Mark?'

'And Mark,' said Lisa. 'He's not a friend, Mary. He's always been much more than that. He's someone very special, and he's been my main prop through all of this. He sorted everything out for me, and he's made sure that I'll never lack for anything. It probably sounds ridiculous, but Alan always paid the bills and kept up our joint account, so money was something which never worried me. But afterwards ... when I saw how much everything cost, I thought I'd be broke in no time at all.'

'But you won't be?'

'No,' said Lisa. 'Apparently Alan has owned a small share of Hanley Recordings since its beginning. I can live in luxury on that alone. What Mark makes from it is mind-boggling.'

'And what of the future?' Mary probed.

Lisa's cheeks flushed. 'I have the children,' she said, toying with her glass. 'Marian is determined to get into the Royal Ballet Company next year. And David ... well, he's too young to know what he wants. I'd like him to follow his father's footsteps and study law, but I'll not force him if he doesn't want to. I've also been working for June on the magazine. I don't need the money, but it's helped me to get everything back into perspective, and I'm quite enjoying it. But whatever happens in the future, I'll be staying in London.' She paused. 'I've decided to sell the farm. I know it's been in the family for God knows how many generations, but I think Daddy would understand. I can't cope any more, not by myself. Do you think I'm making a mistake?'

'No,' Mary said. 'It must have been a hard decision.'

'Yes. But I really have no choice. It's never been the same since Daddy died, and Edward wants to leave anyway. He put a down-payment on some land just before Christmas, but never said anything at the time because of Alan. I've already made the arrangements, which is the reason for my coming up. I have to clear my things out of the house. It's being auctioned next week. I thought that best, private sales can drag on forever.'

Nothing stays the same, Mary thought, but for the Crowders to pack up and leave would be a heavy blow for this small community.

'Have you told Mark?' she asked.

'No. I was afraid he might try and stop me. He had to go away, and he won't be back until the end of July. It will all be done by then. And if you're worrying about a housing estate going up on your doorstep, it's impossible. Nobody could do that without government permission, it's zoned as agricultural land. I checked that out first. You might even get some competition again. Latchcham Estates seems to be thriving these days.'

'Don't you know why?' Mary asked.

'Should I?'

'Alan did,' said Mary. 'I thought you did too. Charles was in financial trouble, and just to keep the property in the family name he was thinking of handing the Hall over to the National Trust. It's costly to run, and even though we tried tourists for a couple of years, the profits were too small to be of much help. I don't know how Mark found out, but he offered Charles an interest-free loan for which he required no collateral. But Charles insisted there be a proper transaction, and now Mark has the deeds to the land. He poured in a vast amount of money, which is why it's doing so well today.'

'He did it for you, Mary,' Lisa said. 'And he can certainly afford it. He must be one of the richest men in the country.'

It wasn't easy going through the farmhouse, it was too full of memories. They were in every drawer she opened, and in every bulging cupboard. David thought it all great fun and wanted to keep a wide variety of useless objects, but Marian could feel her mother's despair and whenever Lisa faltered, the girl was there, making the heart-breaking decisions for her.

The attic was the worst. It was crammed full of dust-covered furniture and boxes, with cobwebs hanging everywhere. David loved it, and armed with a torch and a jam jar, went in search of spiders.

'Be careful that something doesn't fall on you,' Lisa said. She turned to her daughter. 'I never realised all this was up here. I don't know where to start. It'll take a week to clear it.'

'We only have a day,' Marian said. 'I think we should get some of the men to carry everything down into the yard where we can see it properly.'

'There are times when your common sense amazes me,' said Lisa.

'Be careful that you don't frighten the spiders,' David shouted from some gloomy corner. 'There must be lots and lots of them up here.'

Marian shuddered. 'He really is awful,' she said. 'I don't know where he gets it from. D'you want me to go down and get a work force organised?'

'Could you?' Lisa asked. 'I'll look around and try to get a general idea of what all this is. David, are you all right over there?'

'I think I've found a spider's nest,' he shouted back gleefully.

'I'm going,' said Marian with a shudder.

While David continued to explore the murkier corners, Lisa poked about beneath filthy sheets and in closed boxes. There were stacks of rotting farming magazines, and some old newspapers dating back to

World War Two; discarded clothes which were moth-eaten and green with mould, a couple of dolls which had been hers but never played with. She had never liked dolls. She found a stuffed elephant, also moth-eaten, and with an ear and both its eyes missing. Her father had given it to her when her mother died. That was before Orchid had come. And now she was no longer here. Lisa fought to keep back the tears. She dropped the elephant and turned quickly away, only to trip over a pile of records which scattered across the floor. As she bent down to pick them up, Mark Anthony smiled up at her. She couldn't stand it any longer. She had to get out of here.

'Bill's coming,' said Marian cheerfully. 'And he's got a couple of other men to help him. What's wrong?'

'Nothing,' said Lisa, keeping her head averted.

But Marian had always been sharp. She saw the pile of records and other discarded oddments.

'You shouldn't be doing this,' she said. 'You're getting upset all over again. Why don't you go downstairs and have a cup of tea, then we can sort through it together. It won't seem so bad in the daylight. And maybe you should take David with you.'

'I want to stay here,' her brother yelled. 'It's a treasure trove of spiders. And I just found some caterpillary things.'

Lisa could hear the men coming up the stairs. 'All right,' she said. 'But don't get in the way.'

'You're not leaving him here, are you?' Marian asked.

'Try and be a little more tolerant, darling. You were his age once, and although spiders were not quite your thing, I could relate one or two embarrasing incidents if I tried.'

'Don't bother,' said Marian. 'What are all these records?'

'Just old records,' said Lisa, walking towards the staircase.

Marian bent down and picked one up. 'Mark Anthony,' she said aloud. 'I heard him on the radio the other day, on a programme of top songs of the Fifties. They were really ... Mummy, it's Uncle Mark!'

'Yes,' said Lisa hesitantly. 'I know. He was very good in his day. If he hadn't given it up he could have become a legend.'

'He looks ever so young.'

'We were all young once.'

'You're not going to throw them away, are you?'

'We can't possibly keep everything,' Lisa said abruptly. 'Anyway, they're probably warped. They must have been up here for years.'

Marian watched as her mother stood aside to let the men into the cramped attic, and when she had gone the girl stared at the smiling young man on the cover before she started to sort through the rest of the records, putting aside all those which featured Mark Anthony.

She wasn't quite sure why, but she knew that these were probably more precious than anything else in the attic.

'Where to you want us to start, Miss Marian?' Bill Simpson asked.

'Anywhere,' she said. 'It'll all have to come out. I'm taking these downstairs, but I'll come back to help you. Oh, and David is somewhere or other.'

'I'm here,' the boy said. 'Look.'

Marian stepped back as he held up his jar, the bottom of which was covered in spiders and other things, all trying to crawl up the slippery sides.

'That's disgusting,' she said. 'What are you going to do with them?'

'Take them back to London, of course.'

'They'll be dead by then, if they don't eat each other first.'

'D'you really think so?' he asked with renewed interest.

She scowled at him, and as the men started to haul out the furniture, she hugged the records to her stomach and fled down the stairs.

Lisa and the children spent their last night at Latchcham Hall. Chanson and Tumbleweed were put in the stables under the care of the groom, Barnes, and the other horses were temporarily moved into the old stable block at Olden Manor. Lisa had intended to leave before the auction, but at the last moment changed her mind. She wanted to know who purchased the farm, for her own peace of mind, and for the sake of her father who had loved it.

She let Edward take the dogs, but kept Harvey, the last of the strain of Crowder border collies—the strain from which Mark's Whisky had come.

Charles Latchcham needed no additional stock or equipment, but went to the auction out of curiosity, while Mary accompanied him more for Lisa's sake than because of any real interest in the proceedings. David did not understand the enormity of what was happening, but Marian clung unhappily to her mother's side.

Lisa hated to see people wandering through the house and farmyard, prodding the stock and criticising everything with loud voices. When Arthur Bennett and Sam Tucker appeared, she panicked, for he wasn't interested in the livestock or the house. He wanted the land. She remembered that he was now the MP for this area, and would have the connections to press for building rights. He might not get them immediately, but given time ... Unable to watch any longer, she went and sat in the car, Marian silent at her side.

'I wish we hadn't come,' the girl said as she watched a group of cows huddle together in confusion.

'It has to be done,' Lisa said.

A car came hurtling down the lane towards them. There was no room in the yard, and many vehicles were parked alongside the lane or in an adjoining field, but the black Rover stopped alongside Lisa's own vehicle, all but blocking the only exit. It was driven by a heavy-set man with greying temples and a severe face. Lisa watched him pick up a shooting-stick and bowler, and then step from his vehicle, nodding a polite greeting to mother and daughter.

'I wouldn't mind if someone like him bought it,' Marian said. 'He looks as though he'd care for it.'

'He's probably after more livestock,' said her mother. 'He doesn't look as if he's in the market for a farm.'

'He could be expanding,' Marian suggested.

Lisa closed her eyes and prayed that her father would forgive her for what she was doing today.

Sam Tucker saw the man first, and nudged Arthur Bennett in the ribs.

'Steadman's here,' he hissed.

Arthur swung round. He recognised the tall, impeccably dressed man who was leaning against a shooting-stick. Steadman made money on commission. He travelled about the country on behalf of rich clients who did not wish to be known, buying properties, and occasionally selling them. He usually got what he was after, and Arthur wondered how high he was prepared to go today. He'd come up against Steadman twice before, losing the first time and winning the second—but at a highly inflated price after the man had suddenly lost interest. Arthur wanted this land badly, and was prepared to mortgage everything he possessed to get it. He would then be able to hit Mark Hanley where it hurt most, by having a housing estate built on his doorstep ...

Arthur wasn't the only person to notice Steadman.

'He must have a client interested in the place,' Charles Latchcham told his wife.

Mary looked round and said, 'I think I ought to take Lisa and Marian home. This is painful enough for me to watch, let alone for them.'

'Go ahead. I'd like to stay. I think things will hot up later. Bennett's already looking anxious.'

Mary wished that she had let Mark know what was happening. But it was too late now, and she could only hope that Steadman had sufficient financial resources behind him.

'Will you keep an eye on David?' she asked. 'I think he's somewhere by the pigs.'

As she walked towards the car another thought hit her. Steadman could just as easily be here on behalf of a business consortium who wanted the land for the same purposes as Arthur Bennett.

'Who the hell was he buying for?' Arthur muttered over and over again.

Sam Tucker was watching the road, for they were close to Oldenshaw and Arthur was driving far too fast.

'The village is just ahead,' he said uneasily. 'You'd best slow down.'

'Who the hell was it?' Arthur raged, ignoring him. 'I put up every penny I had, and he still outbid me. He paid almost twice what it's worth. Who the hell would have that sort of money?'

The road was winding, with high hedges on either side, and Arthur did not see the two children driving a small herd of sheep towards the village until he was almost on top of them. The animals were spread across the road with no room to pass.

Sam Tucker opened his mouth in horror and Arthur slammed on the brakes, wildly swinging the wheel to the left. The terrified sheep scattered, and the children swung round, open-mouthed, as the car bucketed over a cement culvert, crashed through a stone wall, and rolled across an empty meadow.

Arthur Bennet was bruised and barely conscious as the car came to a halt on its side. He was aware of Sam Tucker lying lifeless beneath him. He tried to move, but his legs were caught by something which held on to them with the grip of a vice. There was blood in his mouth, and he could smell something which should be familiar but wasn't. He struggled to escape, but it was useless and he lay back exhausted. Help must come soon, he thought, for his had not been the only car travelling on that road.

People were already leaving their vehicles in the road and running across the field. The first of the rescuers were almost there when the leaking petrol exploded and the car burst into flames. It drove back the men who were closest, and helplessly they watched the desperate clawing of the semi-conscious man inside.

Sam Tucker was lucky, he was already dead; but Arthur Bennett died most horribly.

Later on, the area was cordoned off, the burnt bodies removed, and the car taken away. None who passed grieved for Arthur Bennett and his henchman, not when the two of them had brought ruin to so many. It was unanimously agreed that their death was just punishment, an eye for an eye and a tooth for a tooth.

Sam Tucker's wife wept when they told her. Sally Bennett realised she was a rich widow, and turned quickly away without shedding a tear.

Mary persuaded Lisa to stay until the following day, and as they were not leaving until after lunch Lisa let Marian take out Chanson, but insisted she take David with her on Tumbleweed. She warned them to stay away from the farm, but Marian had already decided to ride over to Olden Manor and check on the other horses. David was more interested in seeing the place where the car had crashed, and sulked when his sister told him that they would be by-passing it.

They had only been gone for a short while when Steadman arrived. Charles had been supervising the laying of some new flower beds, and came around the side of the house when he heard the car.

'I understand Mrs. Weston is staying here,' Steadman said bluntly. 'I'd like to speak to her on behalf of my client.'

Charles took the man into one of the smaller reception rooms. 'If there are any problems, perhaps my wife or I could help?' he said.

'My business is with Mrs. Weston,' Steadman insisted. 'But I'm sure there would be no objection to you and Lady Latchcham being present.'

He would not be put off, and so Charles sent for his wife and Lisa.

'Good morning, Mrs. Weston,' said Steadman. 'I'm sorry for disturbing you, but I've been given instructions which are to be carried out before I leave here.'

Lisa sat on a chair and, watching her anxiously, Mary seated herself close by.

Steadman took a notepad from his pocket, opened it and cleared his throat. 'Firstly, I have been instructed to tell you that the horses are to be returned to the farm, together with ... with a Mr. Simpson, who I understand is in charge of them.'

Lisa was staring at him. 'Horses?' she asked.

Steadman felt uncomfortable. 'There are horses?' he said, feeling less certain of himself.

'Yes,' Mary Latchcham confirmed. 'But tell me, Mr. Steadman, who is your client?'

'I thought you knew,' he said.

Lisa looked even more confused, but Mary guessed immediately. He would do it like this; he knew Lisa would never have accepted it otherwise. She wondered how he had found out about the sale. 'Lisa, my dear,' she said. 'What Mr. Steadman means is that Mark has bought the farm.'

She saw momentary panic in the green eyes, and then Lisa stood up and ran from the room.

Chapter Seven

When Mark came back from Europe he neither explained how he had known about the farm, nor condemned Lisa for what she had done.

'I'm going to put a permanent manager in Harold's old cottage,' he told her. 'It will need extensive renovations, but I'll make sure it blends in with the other buildings.'

'Why not use the main house?' she asked.

'Because it belongs to you, and always will.'

She argued until she was blue in the face, but he had made up his mind and nothing would budge him. She saw less and less of him after that; her life had returned almost to normal, she was making her own decisions, working part-time on the magazine—and now that she was obviously able to stand on her own feet Mark was deliberately staying out of her life.

Autumn came. She dreaded Christmas, and as early as October arranged for June to come over, and Martin and William. She wondered about asking Mark, but thought better of it.

She went to the opening of a new play with Martin and William during the first week of November. They had dinner afterwards, and it was almost two in the morning when they dropped her at home, declining to come in for a nightcap. She was surprised to find Marian sipping cocoa in the kitchen.

'Do you want some?' the girl asked.

'No thank you,' said Lisa. 'I'll make myself a cup of tea. Couldn't you sleep?'

'I watched television until late, then thought I might as well wait up for you. Was the play any good?'

'Bloody awful,' her mother said, switching on the kettle. 'It was one of those dreadful avante-garde things. William and I got lost halfway through the first act, and spent the second half in the bar. Martin watched the whole thing, but I think he was just showing off.'

She made the tea weak, and then sat down.

'Can I ask you something?' said Marian.

'Yes. What is it?'

'When I join the ballet next year I want to move out and live in a flat. I'll be earning my own money, and I'll be old enough. Will you try and stop me?'

'*If* you get into the ballet,' Lisa corrected. 'You're going to face a lot of stiff competition.'

'I'm the best dancer in my school,' said Marian without any trace of humour, and even less of humility. 'If anything is certain, it's that I'll get in.'

'I was always taught that pride comes before a fall,' Lisa retorted. 'I suppose that's considered old-fashioned these days.'

'Just irrelevant,' said Marian, her voice equally sharp. 'Will you stop me?'

Lisa sighed. 'How can I? You'll be eighteen years old. But I hope you realise that the corps de ballet live pretty close to the breadline.'

Marian stood up. 'I'll manage,' she said.

Lisa was tired, and perhaps because of that she spoke carelessly, without thinking. 'For God's sake, Marian, you're being as pig-headed as your damn father.' She saw the girl's eyes widen. 'Go to bed,' she said dully, gazing into her half-empty cup.

Marian did not move. 'I assume you're not talking about Alan,' she said, her voice trembling a little. 'Who is my father?'

'It happened such a long time ago,' said Lisa. 'Too long ago to start discussing it at this time in the morning.'

'Why not?' asked Marian. 'I have a right to know.'

Lisa said, 'Go to bed.'

Marian was very pale, and her fists were clenched at her sides. But it had gone this far and she was not about to let go.

'You're frightened to tell me, aren't you?' she said. 'Why? Or don't you know who he is?'

This time she had gone too far. Lisa stood up, and raising her right hand hand, brought it down hard against Marian's cheek. The girl's mouth opened in shock, and then she fled from the kitchen.

The next morning she sneaked out a suitcase and left home. She did not go to school or to her ballet class, and none of her friends knew where she was. It was almost midnight when Lisa's nerve finally broke, and she telephoned Mark.

He came at once, and stood by the fireplace in her drawing room as she told him what had happened. Her voice was flat, and she paused every so often to wipe a tear from her eyes.

'I'll find her,' he said when she had finished. 'She may be defiant, but when the anger wears off I'm sure she'll come to her senses. Why don't you tell her the truth? What harm can it possibly do after all these years?' He paused. 'Have you ever told anyone?'

She looked at him and smiled.

'You're right, of course. What does it matter now? But I think nearly everyone guessed the truth a long time ago. Everyone but you. I've only ever slept with two men. One of them was Alan.' His expression did not change, except for some darting shadow which passed through his eyes. 'She is so like you, Mark, in so many ways.'

He took a step forward, then hesitated, as though he had thought better of it. As he looked at her she saw understanding, and something else she had not seen since their youth.

She was not quite sure how she got there, but she was in his arms, and his lips were brushing across the top of her head.

He knocked at the door, and was about to knock again when it opened.

'Hello, Marian,' he said, pushing past her into the room.

'What are you doing here?' she demanded, sounding frightened despite the angry bravado. 'I don't want to talk to you.'

'That's a pity,' he said calmly. 'Because I intend talking to you. But first of all I want to know if you've slept with him.'

The colour drained from her face. 'Go away,' she said. 'It's none of your business.'

He swung round. 'Well,' he persisted. 'Have you slept with him?'

'No,' she said, her voice a little too shrill and uncontrolled. 'I have not slept with him. Stephen is my friend, not my lover. But if I change my mind there's nothing you or my mother can do about it. I'm almost eighteen.'

She flinched when his eyes rested on her face.

'Almost eighteen,' he said. 'Which means you're still seventeen. Now you're to go home and give your mother no more trouble. She has suffered enough already.'

'I'm not leaving here,' said Marian, not realising how close Mark was to losing his temper. 'I don't have to listen to you.'

'And where do you intend going when Stephen throws you out tonight?' he asked. 'I spoke to him before I came here, and he's sensible enough to understand my point of view.'

'You have no right to interfere in my life!' Marian shouted.

'Haven't I?' he said. 'I have more right than anyone to interfere, except your mother, of course. I've never interfered before, and I probably never shall again—but I'm not leaving here without you.'

Marian opened her mouth, clamped it shut, and then sat down on the bed. It all fell into place now, with such remarkable clarity that it was hard to believe she had not seen it before. Her mother and him. Those records, and the tears she had tried to hide by quickly turning away. And that bracelet she never wore, and which Marian knew had never been a gift from Alan.

'Is it ... is it you?' she asked in a whisper.

'Yes,' he answered unemotionally.

Green eyes and blue met, and Marian felt the loathing rise up like bile in her throat. She couldn't speak immediately, but when she did, her voice was like ice. 'You deserted us,' she said 'You let her marry somebody else, and you didn't even care. All you ever thought of was making more money.' She stood up. 'I'll go home. But I don't ever want to see you again. My father died in an air crash, and you don't exist any more.' She turned away from him with an unexpected violence. 'I'll call a taxi. I don't want to go back with you.'

She did not see the moment of helplessness as he stared at her rigid back.

'Tim will take you home,' he said after a while. 'You can't object to him. I'm sorry if I hurt you, Marian, but when you started this you should have realised that someone had to get hurt.'

She said nothing, and so he left. He was in the passage when he heard her begin to sob, and as he paused to listen he suddenly began to feel old.

Chapter Eight

After the incident with Marian I stayed away from Lisa and her family. Gaping wounds had been opened, wounds which only time would heal.

I went to America at the end of March, and was still there in May when Martin came over on a two-week promotional tour. His final destination was San Francisco, and it was there I found him. He left William at the hotel pool and took me to his penthouse suite.

'Why didn't you reply to any of my messages?' he asked as he poured us drinks. 'I've been trying to contact you since we arrived.'

'I was busy,' I said.

We sat in comfortable chairs overlooking the bay.

'It's beautiful here,' he said. 'I can understand why you keep a house up the coast. It must make a pleasant retreat.'

'I use it more for convenience than pleasure,' I told him. 'Why did you want to see me?'

'Because I need your advice. I've had a fantastic response to my shows here, and I've been thinking of opening an exclusive chain of boutiques, much like we've done in England. I know it would cost a lot initially, but if we manufactured locally we could bring down the overheads. I think, in the long run, it would be worth the outlay.'

Martin had no business sense at all and did not realise that capital would be the least of our worries.

'Before you go any further, I think you should know why I came here this afternoon,' I said. 'I have a proposition for you.'

He looked at me blankly. 'What kind of proposition?'

'I want to set you free,' I said. 'We've been tied together for almost fifteen years, and quite honestly you no longer need me. We've had a good run, and I think you're capable of organising your own affairs.' I let the words sink in. 'There are no strings attached, Martin. It's a genuine offer.'

He walked to the window, where he stood with his back to me.

'You know I'm no businessman,' he said. 'I wouldn't know where to start.'

'There's no need to start anywhere. What the hell do you think I've been doing since Alan's death? Too much rested on him and me. If I wasn't there to make the decisions, Alan was. When he died I started thinking about the chaos there'd be if anything happened to me. Since then I've changed the organisational structure of everything, including your multiple concerns. The main decisions must still come from you or me, or whoever happens to be in charge ... the important decisions such as policy. But apart from that, every department is capable of running itself. Titular heads have become obsolete.'

He turned round. 'I always was obsolete, in that sense. I'm a designer, and if somebody asked me about a change of policy I wouldn't have the faintest idea what they meant. I still need you, Mark. I always shall. I like our arrangement, and it can go on forever as far as I'm concerned.'

'You ought to think it over more carefully,' I cautioned.

'Why? I'm not that ambitious. Unless, of course, you really want to dump me.'

I laughed. 'I thought I was doing you a long-overdue favour. I'm not always the ogre people try and make out.'

'I never thought you were,' he said, and then changed the subject. 'I saw Caroline in New York. She said she was coming to the coast for a while, so I told her you were here. I hope you don't mind?'

'No,' I said. I hadn't seen Caroline since the divorce, but I had heard of her. Everybody heard about Caroline. 'How is she?'

'Radiant. She asked after you.'

I finished the whisky. 'Are you now going to tell me every detail of your meeting?'

He sat down. 'There isn't that much to tell,' he said. 'But if you really aren't interested ...'

'There's nothing about Caroline which fails to interest me,' I told him. 'She's blossomed since the divorce. I don't think marriage suited her.'

'Oh, I wouldn't say that,' he said 'She's getting married again. Didn't you know?'

Being with Martin made me realise how long I had been away from England, and that night I told Norma to make arrangements for us to go home at the end of the week. I gave her and Tim Thursday off to drive into San Francisco for any shopping they needed, and I also arranged for them to have an early dinner, followed by a popular show which had been booked solid for months. As this happened to coincide with the housekeeper's day off, Norma was reluctant to leave me alone, but I assured her I was capable of looking after myself, and that Vicky, who came daily to clean, would be here. Shortly after nine-thirty Vicky telephoned to say that her little girl was running a fever and she couldn't get in to me. I told her to stay at home until the child was well, and then settled in the drawing room with some paperwork.

It was strange I didn't hear the car.

'I knocked, but there was no reply. The door was unbolted, so I came in.' I looked up with a start. 'I hope you don't mind.'

It was Elly. A different Elly from the one I remembered. She was plump, with a face as round as a full moon.

'Why Elly,' I said. 'Come in. It's good to see you.'

'Hello, Mr. Mark ... I'm sorry, I suppose it should be Sir Mark now.'

I smiled. 'After all these years your addressing me as sir would sound pompous. You look well.'

She glanced down at herself. She wore a sleeveless cotton frock and flat sandals.

'I'm too fat,' she said 'But you're not much different.'

'I feel a lot older,' I admitted. 'Sit down. Are you alone?'

'Yes. We live not far down the coast, but I've never been able to pluck up the courage to come here until now. Paul is in school and I don't have to fetch him until this afternoon.'

'Would you like to sit on the verandah?' I asked.

'No thank you,' she said. 'I get fed up with the sun. It never stops shining out here.'

I detected a longing in her voice. She was homesick, and trying not to let it come out in a display of nostalgia.

'I'm afraid I have no staff today,' I said. 'But can I get you something to drink?'

'Coke ... if you don't mind, that is.'

'Of course not. Nothing stronger?'

She shook her head. I found a Coke for her, and then, even though it was barely midday, poured myself a straight whisky. She bounced to her feet when I handed her the glass.

'Thank you, Mr. Mark. It's this stuff which puts on the weight. I live on it. And Paul is as bad. I'm surprised he's so skinny.' A blush spread up her neck, and she sat down abruptly. 'I'm sorry ... I didn't mean ...'

'He's my son, Elly,' I said, sitting opposite her. 'I know you must think it terrible that I don't even know him, but he has you and

Caroline. I'd only add confusion to his life. I can see you are proud of him.'

'Aye,' she answered, a fading Yorkshire brogue creeping into an adopted American accent. 'He's a fine boy. He's already like you, and he's going to be tall. But tell me, how is Mrs. Hanley? I'm sorry I keep forgetting ... Lady Latchcham. And Miss Fran ...'

I told her because she was eager to know. She soaked up every word in concentrated silence.

'It's a long way from the old days,' she said after a while. 'That night you came to the front door and gave me such a fright, who would have thought that we'd be sitting talking like this on the other side of the world?'

I picked up her empty glass. 'Another?'

'No thank you, Mr. Mark. I must be going. I have to fetch Paul, and Miss Caroline is probably wondering where I am. I learnt to drive. Can you believe it? I was terrified at first, but Miss Caroline insisted. I'm glad now that she did.'

'Didn't you tell her you were coming here?' I asked.

She shook her head.

I wondered if the air conditioning were on the blink, for the room seemed very hot. I put down the empty glass and leant against the bar.

'Why did you come, Elly?' I asked. 'It wasn't just to talk over the past. You were never much good at concealing your feelings.'

'No,' she said. 'I suppose not. Had you heard that Miss Caroline is getting married again?'

'Yes.'

'She never did want him. She took him because it was her duty, but I've been more of a mother to Paul than she has ever been. I'm frightened of what will happen once she's remarried. He's too like you for either of them to forget.'

I frowned, but before I could say anything Elly stood up, her handbag clutched against her stomach.

'I'm sorry,' she said. 'I should never have said that. I shouldn't have come here, either. It wasn't my place. I enjoyed talking with you Mr. Mark ... don't worry, I can find my way out.'

My vision suddenly seemed to blur, and the stifling heat engulfed me so that I couldn't breathe properly. I swayed, and groped blindly for the bar.

'Mr. Mark ... are you all right?' Elly sounded as though she were talking from a long way off. Then something inside me exploded and I felt myself falling. I was gasping for air, and incomprehensible pain flashed red and violent through me. I must have hit my head, somehow lost consciousness, because the blackness dropped over me with the impact of a sledge-hammer.

My mind was blank. I opened my eyes to blinding light, and quickly closed them again. But in that split second of time I was conscious of people, and of machines, and of air being pumped into my lungs. I didn't want to know what was happening, and returned to the oblivion of darkness.

The next time I came to consciousness, for a moment as fleeting as the last, I could have sworn I saw Caroline, her cheeks wet with tears. Later on, when I drifted back into semi-oblivion, her place had been taken by other shadowy figures. I was cold and did not want to think, and the blackness was much more inviting.

The fourth time I opened my eyes I was able to focus on the machines and tubes, and on Caroline. She looked tired, with tiny lines of strain beneath her eyes, but she was no longer crying.

'Mark,' she said, a hand closing over mine.

'Caro,' I murmured with an effort.

I saw tears come to her eyes, and she said in a trembling voice, 'You're a bloody bastard, Mark Hanley. Don't you ever do anything like this to me again.'

'What?' I asked, falling back into unconsciousness. But even that was not so black and hopeless as before.

Later on, I was told that had been the turning point. For forty-eight hours I had hovered between life and death, and during that time Caroline had stood vigil as near to my bed as they would allow her. When I heard that, I felt guilty for the shabby way I had treated her during our marriage.

It was another forty-eight hours before they allowed me to see her again, and for once in my life I was content to be coddled, to stare from the window at the blue sky and shifting ocean, and to study the tasteful prints which decorated the walls.

I dozed away a large part of the afternoon, waking when a shadow fell across my bed. It was Caroline. She was looking out through the open window, and the sun had formed a halo about her head. She was thirty-five now, and still a strikingly beautiful woman.

'You must have bribed the guards,' I said. 'Nobody's allowed in here, not unless they've come to poke and probe, or pass derogatory remarks.'

She spun round. 'How long have you been awake?'

'A couple of minutes. I feel like a chicken trussed for market. I'm not allowed to move from this bed.'

'I should think not,' she said. She kissed my cheek, and then sat down. 'You scared the hell out of me. I always said you'd damn well kill yourself with work.'

'Caro, sweetheart, I thought an invalid deserved kinder words than these.'

'Not this invalid,' she said.

'Thank you for bringing me here. I presume it was you?'

'Elly yelled for the nearest ambulance, and while she was waiting for it to come she telephoned me. I told them to bring you here. Do you know where you are?'

'No. But it's obviously no ordinary hospital.'

'It's called Palm's Sanatorium,' she told me. 'It's the most exclusive place on the entire west coast, and it's a haven for the film colony, because even to get in through the doors you have to be checked and double-checked. If you'd been taken to a general hospital the reporters would have settled like vultures.'

I wished I didn't feel so helpless. I had joked about getting up—because I couldn't move from the bed even if I wanted to. The stroke had left my left side semi-paralysed; although the doctors had told me I was lucky, for neither my brain nor my speech had been affected, and in the arm at least there would be total recovery.

'Who else knows about this?' I asked.

'Only me, Elly, Norma and Tim. And I guess any other servants you have at the house. Norma was about to telephone the police when I thought to let her know, and so I had to tell her the truth.'

'Did you telephone Mary?'

She didn't answer immediately.

'No. I very nearly did, but then I had second thoughts. She's an old woman, and I don't know what the shock would have done to her. Even if she came over, there's nothing she could do. And there wasn't anybody else I could think of. Alan perhaps, if he'd been alive.'

I looked into her eyes. 'Then promise me you will tell nobody. I'd prefer it that way.'

'I had a feeling you would,' she said. 'I wasn't married to you for all those years for nothing. You look tired, Mark. Would you like me to leave?'

'Not yet. I'm fed up with staring at these walls. You might as well stay until they put you out.'

'That won't be long,' she said, squeezing my hand. 'I think you've become more moderate.'

'Only because I have no way of fighting back.'

'Perhaps we're both getting more moderate as we grow older. The trouble with us was that we were always too much alike. Someone's coming.' She stood up. 'I'll come again tomorrow. Can I bring you anything?'

'A cigarette?' I suggested.

'No cigarettes,' she said, frowning. 'If you have any sense you'll give them up.'

Caroline came each day, and I found myself looking forward to her visits.

'Norma should be going on holiday to Italy the day after tomorrow,' I found myself telling her three weeks later. 'She's sure to lose her deposit, and I shudder at the names Tim's family must be calling me. Did you tell them to go back to England?'

'Yes,' she said. 'Time and time again. But they won't listen. None of them ever took much notice of me. I tried to steal Roberts after the divorce, but he wouldn't leave you. The only reason Elly stays is because of the child. She's not happy here, and never has been. Why don't you tell Tim and Norma to go yourself?'

'No,' I said, 'I don't want them seeing me like this. D'you know what excuse Norma has made about my sudden disappearance?'

I saw her hot temper flare, and then quickly subside. 'That you're taking a well earned holiday. Nobody knows what you're doing or where you are half the time, anyway. Don't start thinking about the bloody business, Mark. Please. You may feel much better, but you still have a long way to go.'

I suspected she knew more about my medical condition that I did, for everyone from doctors down to the lowliest orderlies had been irritatingly vague about the projected length of my stay here. They were even more vague about the maddening paralysis which had so far shown not the slightest improvement. I had always been an active person, and there was nothing I could do but chafe for my freedom; frighten the nurses and try, without success, to intimidate the doctors.

'How much longer will it be, Caro?' I asked.

'How much longer will what be?'

'How long am I to be confined here, helpless as a babe?'

'I'm not sure. It could be a couple of months. Maybe longer. I'm trying to persuade Dr. Robson to let you go outside. This place has the most beautiful gardens, and a little sunshine would do you good. You're looking pale.' She took told of my right hand and lifted it to her lips. 'Mark, would you do something for me? One small favour?'

'How can I refuse you, Caro?'

She ran her forefinger along my forehead and into my hair.

'You're lucky, you're turning silver, not grey,' she said. 'Let them take this scar out, Mark. It's ugly. That awful Arthur Bennett kept his scar as a reminder of what you did to him. Don't you keep this one as a reminder of Kathy Karn.'

I laughed. 'It has nothing to do with Kathy. And I've no intention of undergoing plastic surgery.'

'Not plastic surgery, just a minor skin graft,' she purred. 'Dr. Robson says you'll be strong enough in a couple of weeks. And it would give you a reason for being here if anything should leak out. I'm sacrificing everything to be with you. Dennis thinks I'm holidaying with friends. He'd die if he knew the truth. The least you can do for me is let them remove the scar. On some men it might look dashing, but not on you.'

'No, Caroline,' I said. I'd forgotten how persistent and bloody-minded she could be.

It was six weeks before some feeling started to come back to my arm, and only then was I allowed to go outside in a wheelchair. Caroline was there, of course, sitting beside me on the grass.

'They made a good job of the scar,' she said. 'Once the redness goes you won't know it was ever there.'

I had given in to her, and now it was done I didn't really mind. I looked down at her, remembering those early days we had spent at the beach house so long ago.

'What is your Dennis like?' I asked.

'Very serious. Nothing like you.'

'I'm serious,' I said.

She laughed. 'Not always. He's not good-looking either, but he is a decent man whom I respect.'

'Why are you marrying him?' I asked. 'It doesn't sound like a perfect partnership.'

'Is any marriage? Dennis adores me. He'll place me on a pedestal and worship the ground I walk upon. And for a while I shall love the adoration.'

'Only for a while?'

'Even being a goddess gets boring. I know this is going to sound corny, but I loved you, Mark ... oh, how I loved you. But I was too late. A lifetime too late. I was always nothing more than a substitute, and we both know it.' She stood up. 'It's getting chilly. Shall I wheel you in?'

'No,' I said. 'I'd prefer you to finish what you've started.'

'That's for you to do, not me. You always loved her to the exclusion of anyone else. Even on our honeymoon you went back home because of her. What more can I say? I think the nurse must have forgotten you, and you shouldn't overdo it on your first day out.'

She wheeled me back to the building. I couldn't see her face, but reaching up I touched one of her chilled hands.

'I hope he puts you on that pedestal, Caro. You deserve to be there.'

She said nothing, but I felt the chair speed up as she walked a little faster.

The leg started to improve, and after two months I was given a cane and allowed to take short walks. It wasn't easy, but I gritted my teeth and persevered.

Caroline and I had avoided mention of Dennis or Lisa since that first day in the gardens. Nor did we speak of our past life together. We deliberately kept to neutral subjects. I told her of Alan's horrendous death, of my distant promise to Richard Crowder to care for his farm, of Chris retiring to Israel to be close to his son and newly arrived grandchild, of Maude passing quietly away last year, and of Arthur Bennett's demise, undeserved even by him. I told her of Sofie and Kathy Karn, the latter still making a living on the strength of her name. And in return, she told me of her butterfly friends and the Riviera, and touched more than once on the one thing we had made together, which neither of us could escape ... our son.

I had been in the hospital for two and a half months, and Caroline and I were sitting in my room when Dr. Robson walked in. He was a thickset man, probably in his early fifties. He had a quick wit and an efficient manner, and over the weeks we had developed a healthy respect for each other.

'I've decided you can go,' he said. 'There's nothing further we can do for you here. Would tomorrow suit you?'

I nodded, speechless for once in my life.

'But before you leave I think you should know where you stand,' he continued. 'I've already talked it over with Mrs. Hanley, and she thinks you should be spared nothing.'

'I'd better go,' said Caroline.

I took told of her hand. 'I'd rather you stayed.'

The news was not good. I could tell by her expression. Dr. Robson stood at the foot of the bed, his hands clasped behind his back. I waited for the blow.

'You realise, of course, that this was no minor attack,' he said. 'You were lucky this time, but if it happens again you'll either be killed outright or permanently paralysed. I cannot believe you've had no warning that your health was not quite what it should be. It's rare for an attack of this magnitude to happen completely out of the blue.'

'I occasionally felt breathless or dizzy,' I told him.

'Then it's a pity you didn't consult a doctor earlier,' he said. 'You've had almost three months of convalescence, and now the rest is up to you. For the next nine months, preferably a year, you should do nothing whatever. You're a wealthy man who doesn't have to work, and I would strongly recommend that your retire, Sir Mark.'

'And if I don't? I asked.

'I doubt you'd survive another twelve months. Your heart could never take another attack of that intensity.'

It didn't look as if I had a very promising future. I saw that Caroline was close to tears.

'And my chances if I do as you say?' I asked.

'A normal life, if lived in moderation,' he said. 'You'll have to keep to a specified course of medication, but it'll be in the form of pills. The stresses of overwork have brought about this condition, and without them you could outlive us all. I'm afraid I can't guarantee your leg ever being normal again. In time you'll be able to dispense with the cane, but you will have a permanent limp. Exercise will help.'

'He likes to ride ... horses,' said Caroline. She was trying not to cry.

'You can still do that, but nothing strenuous like racing. Riding might even help strengthen the leg muscles. I'm sorry if all of this has come as a shock.'

'No,' I said. 'I expected it.'

He nodded and left. I looked at Caroline, and saw a tear roll down her cheek.

'It's my life,' I said.

'It was a part of mine once.'

I limped in bare feet to where she sat.

'You shouldn't be out of bed,' she whispered.

'To hell with it. They're discharging me tomorrow. Don't cry, Caro. I hate to see you cry.'

'Oh Mark,' she said, and flinging her arms around my neck, wept bitterly against my shoulder.

There was very little to put together, and I spent most of the morning saying goodbye to the staff. Maybe Caroline was right, maybe I had grown more moderate, for I dreaded leaving this place, and even worse, I dreaded what was to follow. What would I do with my life? I could see only idle days stretching into infinity.

I was resting when Caroline came.

'You've done nothing but complain about being here,' she said.

'And now you can leave, there's not so much as a smile. Do try and look more cheerful when Tim comes. The house has been decked out in flags for your homecoming. You should be flattered. I never thought Norma could work herself into such a state.' She paused. 'Let's go into the gardens. They'll call us when Tim arrives.'

I looked at her. She was fresh and lovely, smelling mildly of the same perfume she had used ever since I had known her.

'I've spent all morning on my feet,' I said.

'Then we can sit down. Don't refuse me this last request, Mark.'

We didn't walk far.

'What are you going to do now?' she asked, pulling petals from a flower which she had plucked.

'You have a destructive nature, Caro,' I said, watching her.

'I think we both have, but in different ways. You didn't answer my question.'

'I don't know yet,' I said. 'This isn't a situation I've faced before. But I shall probably stay at the beach house for a while, and then return to England. After that, I suppose it'll be a matter of doing what I feel like at the time.'

She took my hands between hers, holding them tight.

'Go back to Olden Manor, Mark. It's your home and you'll never be lost there. Up until now you've always neglected it so. I don't suppose you've done a damn thing to the cottages or the main house since I was there.'

'Essential repairs.'

'In which case the place is probably falling apart. You make a sympathetic country squire, you should practice the role more often. And you have the farm now. This is your opportunity to make good your promise to Richard Crowder.'

I looked into her eyes. 'And you, Caro?' I asked. 'What do you think of our chances if we tried again? The circumstances would be different now.'

She stood up. 'Now I really know you've been ill,' she said. 'Somehow that doesn't ring true. It wouldn't work, Mark. You know it, and so do I. You may feel you need me now, but once you get out of here and back into the world, you'll find your feet again. Do you know why I lied to Dennis and stayed here when I should have been in Philadelphia with him? Because you needed me. You never did before, and you never will again. This afternoon I'm catching a plane out of here. I'm going to get myself placed on that pedestal.' She ran her fingers lightly across my cheek. 'And if you have a grain of sense you'll go back where you belong, to the people who love you best. And one last piece of advice. Do what you should have done years ago and marry that damn woman. You'd be a fool to let her go a second time. Now I think I am going to cry. You'd better go, they're beckoning.'

I stood up. 'You're not coming with me?'

She shook her head. 'I never did believe in dragging things out,' she said. 'I've planned this farewell down to the last detail. Look after yourself, Mark. And remember that happiness is where you find it. I can reach my car if I follow the path. I'd rather do that.'

I took her in my arms, tasting the salt tears when I kissed her. It was she who broke away first.

'One final thing,' she said. 'I've left something for you at the house. I think it might help. I hope so. Goodbye, Mark.'

I watched her go. She didn't look back. She had been a crutch for a while, but I would survive without her, without anyone. I always had.

Tim fussed all the way home, and Norma was as bad once we got there. By then I was very tired; I'd been up since dawn, and I was still unused to a lot of activity.

'We thought you would prefer the verandah,' said Norma as I was about to sit on the sofa. 'Mrs. Hanley told us to make sure you had plenty of fresh air.' Tim stood behind her, clutching my suitcase in both hands.

The french windows were open, and I was about to step outside when I stopped.

'I'm glad to see you looking so well, Mr. Mark,' said Elly, rising to her feet. 'Come Paul, say hello to your father.'

My alarmed eyes left her face, to stare at the small boy who stood at her side. I felt a moment of surprise. He had grown, and in him I could see myself, and something too of Caroline.

'Good afternoon, sir,' he said politely.

I was glad of the supporting cane which was bending beneath my weight. I gulped deeply. He was seven years old and we were strangers. Caroline had no right to leave him here like this. But then, had she been so wrong? I straightened up. In this she knew me even better than I knew myself, for it was in the neglected child that my future lay.

Chapter Nine

Marian was accepted into the Royal Ballet Company and would be dancing her first season in the autumn. She had two free weeks in August, and partly because she wanted to please her, Lisa put the question of summer holidays to the family vote. She was surprised when Marian and David looked at each other and, in unison for once in their lives, said they wanted to go to the farm.

'You and David should go up for all of the summer,' Marian said. 'I can join you later.'

It would be the first time they had been at the farm since Mark had bought it, and Lisa would have to accept that she must forget the past. Then, tongue-in-cheek, David asked whether his friend Anthony, together with his pony Galahad, could go with them. Marian grimaced, but Lisa thought it a good idea, as David by himself was sure to get bored within a week. And so they set off on the familiar route ... horses, ponies, dogs and children, filling the motorised horsebox Lisa had purchased in place of the double trailer.

The new farm manager was Oliver Crawford, the youngest son of Ned Crawford, whose barn had been burnt out many years before. Lisa had no idea where Mark had found him, but he came with a wife and two young children, eager to get back to the soil he loved. He knew he could never afford to buy his own farm, and unlike Edward Wainwright had no ambitions in that direction. He was an old-fashioned farmer who loved the beasts, and was now re-establishing the Crowder bloodline with a young bull purchased from Charles Latchcham.

Lisa often wondered whether it was fate that Mark now owned most of the land west of Steelton, because as long as it was his, no land-shark such as Arthur Bennett would ever get in. It was more than a pity that he was never there long enough to appreciate what he had achieved.

Perhaps because she had not expected it, Lisa enjoyed being at the farm. She didn't see much of the boys, who usually left early in the mornings with haversack lunches, not getting home until late. On the warmer days they spent their afternoons in the swimming pool at Olden Manor, their ponies grazing in the apple orchard. It was here Lisa was with them most, for she liked to sit beside the pool, in a place which was so much a part of her life.

She had another horse now, although she still rode Chanson. Claret was a dynamic chestnut gelding who was proving a handful to control in the open countryside. David had his own pony, Truffles, and Tumbleweed had been retired to the farm at the beginning of the year. Jinny and Drummer were still there, together with Beauty and her magnificent son, Nocturne; and Bucephalus who, against all probability, had grown into an enormous well-built animal.

Marian came up in August by train. Although she spent an hour each morning exercising, she was determined to forget the stresses of ballet and enjoy herself. She was thrilled when she was Bucephalus.

'You'd never think he was that stringy colt we brought home,' she said.

'Do you realise that he's three years old?' said her mother. 'He should be trained. We ought to sell him to someone who can give him a useful life.'

'You can't!' Marian said, horrified. 'He might end up at the knackers again. Can't you train him? I can help.'

Lisa had trained Kingston, and knew that it would take a lot more time than the two weeks she had left. And even if she had the stabling to spare, which she didn't, she couldn't take Bucephalus to London, not when he was unused to heavy traffic. But to please Marian she started a daily programme of lunging and basic training. She put a bit in his mouth and a saddle on his back, and he didn't flinch a muscle. 'See, it's easy,' said Marian.

The two weeks fled by far too quickly. It was already Thursday, and they were leaving on Monday. Mary Latchcham telephoned late that evening, obviously upset about something, although she refused to say what it was. Lisa promised to call at the Hall next morning, but forgot about it until Marian asked if she could drive the car.

It was a little after nine when the maid took them into the breakfast room. Mary came forward to greet them, her eyes resting doubtfully on Marian's eager face. She was looking alarmingly frail, and with surprise Lisa realised that she must be nearly seventy.

The maid went to fetch fresh tea, and Lisa asked about Charles. He had suffered a bad fall during the last hunting season which meant that hunting, indeed any form of riding, was now forbidden him. And then, to add insult to injury, he had come down with gout, which had left him bed-bound these past few weeks. They talked about the weather and the crops, and Marian gazed through the window and wondered whether she could excuse herself without seeming rude.

The tea came, and after the maid had gone Marian waited for the conversation to pick up. But Mary still held back and Lisa thought she knew why. 'Would you prefer Marian to leave?' she asked, not daring to look at her daughter.

Marian bristled. At eighteen, almost nineteen, one did not expect to be put out of rooms like a child.

'No,' said Mary. 'Of course not.' She paused. 'I'm sorry, Lisa, but I really don't know how to begin. I've said nothing to Charles, because he already has enough on his mind. What I am about to tell you is to go no further than this room. I know I can trust you, but can you keep this to yourself, Marian? Not even David is to know.'

The girl nodded, her eyes resting on her mother's taut face. 'She won't repeat anything,' said Lisa.

Mary nodded, and said, 'Caroline telephoned me yesterday.'

'From America?' Lisa asked.

'Yes. She was at the coast. With Mark.'

Marian clenched her fists.

'He wanted nobody to know,' Mary continued, her voice monotonous in its effort to keep calm. 'He made her promise she would never tell anyone, including me. But Caroline is still fond of him, despite what happened between them, and she was worried.'

'What doesn't he want us to know?' Lisa asked sharply.

'That he almost died from a stroke, and has been hospitalised for the past three months.'

Lisa stared at her. Not Mark ... never Mark ... he was indestructible. She did not notice Marian, who was staring at her with a mixture of pain and condemnation.

'Is he ...? Will he ...?' Lisa began, her tongue tripping over the words.

'Caroline says that he has to rest for at least a year. She has given him Paul, because she thinks the boy will help.' Her voice cracked, and Lisa reached forward and took hold of her hand. 'He needs someone, Lisa. Someone who can help him through this. Caroline took the burden upon herself while she was able, but he'll be coming back soon, and she thinks it should pass to you. That's why I asked you to come here today. There was a time when I could have managed him myself, but I can't any more. He's grown too austere and withdrawn, too much a part of his own legend.'

Marian had tears in her eyes; not for a man who could be dying, but for her mother, who was once again being drawn into his wretched affairs.

'He has done so much for us all,' Mary said. 'And for you, far more than you will ever know.'

'None of us can ever hope to repay him,' said Lisa. 'But even if he comes here, will he accept our help? I haven't even seen him this year.'

Mary tried to smile. 'I'm sorry,' she said. 'I shouldn't have asked you so thoughtlessly.'

Lisa wiped a tear from her cheek, and putting her arms round Mary's shoulders, held her tight.

Marian concentrated on her driving on the way home, and didn't speak until they reached the farmyard.

'It doesn't matter what we say or think, does it?' she spat. 'You'll stay anyway, however cheap it makes you look.'

Lisa looked at the girl. 'He is your father, Marian,' she said after a moment. 'And although it may be hard for you to grasp, there was a time when I loved him very dearly. If circumstances had been different, I would have married him.'

'I hate you,' Marian said coldly. 'And if you go to him now I'll hate you forever.'

She flung herself from the car and ran to the house, not stopping until she reached her room. She sat on the bed, waiting for her mother to follow. But when she had not come after ten minutes, Marian stood up and walked to the window.

The car was empty. Her mother was in the field with the horses, a bridle slung over her shoulder. It wasn't Claret's mouth which accepted the bit, but Chanson's. Lisa led the horse from the field, vaulted onto its back and disappeared down the lane at a canter. Marian saw her wave to Oliver, who was coming in from the fields with the larger of the two tractors. He waved back and shouted something. Then her mother was out of sight, and all the unsaid words hung heavily on the air.

Marian went downstairs. Dora was cleaning the front parlour, and she purposefully avoided her. It was sunny outside, and would probably be hot later. She wandered around the yard, making for no place in particular. Oliver had driven the tractor onto the ramp, and was poking about underneath it, his arms splodged with oil and his curly hair clinging to his forehead.

'What's wrong with it?' she asked.

He gazed at her with bright eyes. 'Dunno. She's been making funny noises, and she isn't pulling proper. I thought you was out.

Your ma just left, and the boys went off early this morning.'

'I know,' she said. 'It's not your tractor, so why don't you get a mechanic up here, or simply buy another one? Mark Hanley can afford it.'

He looked at her solemnly. He was not very old, only about twenty-nine or thirty, but there was something about Oliver which made her feel that she was talking to a much older man.

'That's not the point, is it?' he asked, turning back to the tractor.

She was about to walk away when it occurred to her he might be able to help.

'Oliver?'

'What now?'

'Is a stroke a bad thing?'

He peered at her from beneath the tractor. 'Now what would you be wanting to know about strokes for?'

She shrugged. 'A character in the book I'm reading just had one. I've never known anyone who did. Are they very bad?'

'Hearts are dicey things,' said Oliver. 'A proper heart attack can kill you outright.'

'And a stroke?' she persisted.

'Will do the same, or else paralyse you. Best to be dead than an invalid. Funny things they are. Come on just like that ...' He snapped his fingers. 'Then it's over.' He pulled at something. 'Found the bloody thing. Why don't you go and see the missus? She's been baking a batch of scones, and you always enjoy her scones.'

'I'm not hungry,' Marian muttered ungraciously. 'Thanks, Oliver.'

The boy had been standing for a long time in the sun. He was watching the Clydesdales, his imagination fired by his grandfather who had told him to come here. He was certain his nose must be burning, and pulled the cap a little further forward. He squinted down the dirt road, wondering how much longer she was going to be.

'Who are you?' a voice suddenly asked from behind him.

He swung round, and pulling the cap from his sandy hair, stared down at his feet. 'Brian Bell, Mrs. Weston,' he mumbled. 'Me dad's blacksmith down at village.'

Lisa slid from Chanson's back, frowning a little as she tried to recall the family lineage. He must be Philip Bell's eldest boy, and in turn grandson to his namesake, Brian Bell, who had retired when she first moved down to London.

She smiled at him. 'Yes,' she said. 'I know your father well. What can I do for you, Brian?'

'I'd like to learn to do the horses, ma'am,' he nervously replied. 'Me grandad told me there was only you left hereabouts who knew how. I've finished with school, and have to help me dad at forge, but I'd be able to get away for a few hours every day.'

'Do the horses?' she repeated, stroking Chanson's nose. 'I'm sorry, Brian, but there's really no need for anyone else. We already have someone looking after them full-time. Have you tried one of the riding stables outside Steelton? I'm sure they would let you help.'

His skin was beetroot, and he wished he had never come. 'No, ma'am, it's not the ordinary horses I want. I want to learn how to handle the big ones.' He pointed towards the Clydesdales. 'I'd like to learn to use the plough. I'm not afraid of hard work, Mrs. Weston. I'd do anything you said.'

She slipped the bit from Chanson's mouth and swung open the gate. She could handle the plough after a fashion. Her father had shown her how—and then doubled over with laughter at the shallow, weaving furrows. It had been hard work, and needed a strong man. She felt tears, sentimental and misplaced, sting her eyes. She let the horse loose and then turned back to Brian Bell.

'I'm sorry, Brian. I'm leaving, and I don't know when or if I shall be back. And if you learnt, it would have to be with Jinny and Drummer, neither of which belong to me.'

The boy sensed something was wrong, something more than his enquiry about the horses. But he was still disappointed. 'Thank you,' he said dully, and turned to where his bicycle was propped against the stable wall. 'I'm sorry to have bothered you.'

She watched him walk away. 'Brian,' she called. 'Would you like some lunch ... or a cool drink?'

He half turned, avoiding looking directly at her.

'No thank you, ma'am. They're expecting me home.'

She watched him steer his bicycle around the potholes, and in the distance saw the two ponies walking behind their riders who were also on foot. She glanced at her watch. It was nearly lunch time, and if the boys were home they could leave for London directly after.

'Who was that?' Marian asked.

Lisa looked at her daughter, aware of unusual tension behind the girl's eyes. 'Nobody in particular,' she answered, holding the dirty bit under a tap and then hanging the bridle over an open half-door.

Marian was scuffing up dirt with the heel of her shoe. 'I'm sorry about what I said in the car. I didn't mean it.'

'Didn't you? Perhaps you're sorry now, but you certainly meant it then. As you don't seem to be doing anything, will you wait for David and Anthony? Tell them to put the ponies in the stables, then come in to pack. And you pack as well. We're leaving after lunch.'

Marian's eyes widened. 'But we're not meant to go home until Monday.'

'I have changed my mind,' Lisa said. 'I don't want to quarrel with you, Marian. As far as I'm concerned, you've won. Please bring Claret up while you're waiting. Bill went into town for feed, and I don't think he'll be back until this afternoon.'

'What about Chanson?' Marian asked, her voice starting to tremble.

'Leave her. I've decided she can stay here.'

'But you always take her everywhere,' said Marian.

'Not any more,' Lisa said, a tear rolling down her cheek. 'Those days are finished.'

She walked quickly towards the house, leaving Marian staring after her. She was still standing in mindless confusion when the two boys bounced into the yard. David gauged his sister's mood immediately.

'What's happened now?' he asked. 'Has Mum been shouting at you?'

'No,' she said, glaring at him. 'But she says we have to go home today. You're to leave the ponies in the stables.'

The boys looked at each other with dismay. 'But we can't,' her brother said. 'We planned our longest ride yet tomorrow. That's why we came home early, so they'll be well rested.' He looped the reins over a post and struggled to loosen the girth. 'It's you,' he said angrily. 'You've upset her. You always upset her. You're a perfect beast, Marian, and I wish you'd move into that flat you're always talking about and go and upset someone else. I bet she's crying. You always make her cry.'

Marian was about to lash back at him, but stopped herself. They all blamed her.

'Oh, do move out of the way,' David muttered, brushing past her with the saddle dangling untidily from his arms.

Marian felt she had to talk to someone who would understand, who would help her to understand. She went to the car, but the keys were no longer in the ignition and she didn't want to go into the house for them.

'Can I borrow Truffles, David?' she asked.

The boy stared at her. 'What for?' he asked.

'I want to go and see Aunt Mary. I daren't go into the house for the car keys, so I'll have to go on horseback.'

'Use Chanson,' he said. 'They're too tired, both of them.'

'Mother has already been out on her this morning.'

'Then you'll have to go on Tumbleweed. You're not having

Truffles, and if you dare try and take him I'll yell for Mum.'

She swept her mother's bridle from the door. 'I'll bloody well take Claret then!' she furiously retorted.

Anthony peered at her over the top of Galahad's back. Even David hesitated. 'You can't,' he said. 'You've never ridden him before, and she'll kill you when she finds out.'

'She won't know unless you tell her,' Marian answered.

'We won't tell,' Anthony said. He liked Marian. She was petite and pretty, and could be a lot of fun when she wasn't fighting with her brother. 'Will we, David?'

'She'll be hopping mad.'

Marian was walking towards the field. 'I don't think she can get much madder than she is now,' she muttered to herself.

Mary Latchcham had spent the morning pottering about the house. She was trying, without much success, to arrange some freshly cut flowers, when Bertha burst into the room.

'I'm sorry, my lady,' she gabbled, 'but you'd better come quick. It's Miss Marian.'

'What's happened?' she asked, dropping the bloom she was holding.

'She came off the horse and she's in a right state, and won't come in and leave him. She's out front now. Mr. Simpson has sent for Barnes.'

Mary remembered Mark and Lisa as children; and later on, Richard Crowder; and then Charles. She wasn't sure what to expect, but it was a shock to see Marian with her bare arms scratched and her jeans and shirt ripped. Her hair was tangled and a bruise was spreading over her left cheek. She also looked as though she was using the horse for support.

'Oh, my God,' said Mary beneath her breath. She took hold of Simpson's arm before starting down the steps.

'I'm sorry,' Marian said, tears running down her face. 'I wanted to see you, but now I've ruined him, and Mummy will never forgive me.'

'I'm sure he'll be all right,' said Mary. 'I've seen my son bring home his pony in a much worse state than that after a day in the hunting field … and your mother as well.'

She wondered whether she had said the wrong thing, for Marian looked as though she were going to cry even harder.

'Are you badly hurt, my dear?' she asked quickly.

'It's my ankle. I can't stand on it properly, and I'm too frightened to look.'

'Can you walk?'

'Sort of. We hobbled in together.'

Then it can't be broken, Mary thought with relief. Barnes was coming, hurrying around the side of the house, his lips silently moving as he studied the horse.

'Come down on top of you, did he, Miss Marian?' he asked.

Marian swung round, grimacing as her weight shifted onto the injured ankle.

'Yes,' she said. 'Something frightened him. I think it was a pheasant. He reared, and then fell over, and rolled down that gully by the aspen patch. I've lost a leather too. I looked, but I couldn't find it in the heather.'

The old man stroked Claret's damp neck, whistling soothingly to the animal between clenched teeth. Mary Latchcham took hold of Marian's arm and helped her to the steps, where she could lean against the stone balustrade. The groom ran a gentle hand down the animal's leg. When he reached the swelling Claret started back.

'Nowt here to worry yourself about,' Barnes said. 'He's more frightened than anything else. He'll be good as new in a couple of weeks. I'll get him cleaned up before your mother sees him, and do something about the leg. One of the lads can find the leather. Everything will be put right in no time at all, so don't fret your head over it.'

'Are you sure he'll be all right?' Marian asked.

'Aye. I'd not be saying so if I wasn't, would I?'

She smiled at him. 'Thank you, Mr. Barnes.'

'Now come along, dear,' Mary coaxed. 'Simpson can help you up the steps.'

They took her into a room which overlooked the rose garden. Mary sent the servants for the medical kit, and ice packs for the bruised cheek and swollen ankle. While they were gone she removed the girl's shoe, and rolled up the soiled jeans.

'Is it bad?' Marian asked. 'I'm meant to be dancing in three weeks' time. It won't be strong enough by then, will it?'

'Not for ballet,' Mary told her. 'Why did you take him, Marian?'

She was crying again, and wiped away the tears with the back of her hand. Mary gave her a handkerchief.

'Mother said we were leaving after lunch, but I wanted to talk to you first,' said Marian. 'She took Chanson out for a long ride after we left here, and when she got back she told me to start packing.'

Mary sat beside her. 'I thought that was what you wanted all along,' she said. 'I saw your face this morning. You were terrified she'd decide to stay.'

'I know, but only because I didn't want her to be hurt all over again. He deserted her once before, didn't he? Is he coming back to die, Aunt Mary?'

The old woman stiffened at the one question she had not dared ask herself. She managed a forced laugh.

'Which goes to show how little you know my son! If Mark were dying, you can be sure he'd do so in the most spectacular fashion, not hidden away in Yorkshire. You always adored him before. What happened to change all that?'

'You don't know?' Marian asked in a whisper.

'Obviously not.'

'But you must know he's my father,' she said. 'He left, Aunt Mary, and never gave a damn what happened to my mother or me. I can remember when I was very small how I would sometimes hear grandfather and Orchid talking in the kitchen. I couldn't understand it then, but now all the pieces seem to fall into place. He went to London to make his fortune, and deserted us.'

Mary Latchcham leant forward and brushed some hair from the girl's face.

'I always suspected he was your father,' she said. 'But I was never certain. And he didn't desert you, Marian. He didn't even know about you until after his father died. Your mother wanted it that way. And I know she didn't tell him then, so you and he must have learnt the truth at about the same time. I'm not defending him just because he's my son, but because, you see, I know so very much more about this than anyone else.'

Fresh tears streamed down Marian's cheeks, and Mary waited until they had subsided a little. Then, holding the girl at arm's length, she said, 'I think we must have a serious talk. Now wipe your eyes and stop all this crying. You're not a little girl any more, and it's about time you learnt something of life and the extremes that people who love each other very deeply will go to.'

Marian blew her nose. 'Are you going to tell me about my parents?' she asked.

'No, not your parents as such,' said Mary. 'You must never think of Alan as anything less than your father. It would be unfair to his memory, and to yourself as well. What I am going to tell you is everything I've pieced together over the years concerning Mark and your mother.'

'What happened?' Lisa asked when Mary met her in the hall.

'She came off the horse. I should be immune to these accidents by now.'

'She should have known better than to take Claret,' said Lisa. 'He can be a bastard at the best of times. I've been worried sick.'

Mary was surprised at how calmly Lisa had taken the news. After Richard Crowder's accident, she herself had dreaded those days when Charles hunted.

'Be gentle with her,' she warned. 'She looks a lot worse than she is. I telephoned George Ferris to come and look at her ankle. He should be here soon. He had to call at the Bradley farm first.'

Lisa might have sounded calm, but her nerves were playing havoc, and had been since she discovered both Claret and her daughter missing—with David and Anthony denying any knowledge of their whereabouts. Mary's telephone call had been such a relief that it had taken the edge off the news that there had been an accident.

Marian looked grotesque with her swollen cheek and puffed ankle.

'I'm sorry about Claret,' were the first words she said. 'I didn't mean to hurt him. But he was so strong that I couldn't hold him.'

Lisa stopped in the doorway, seeing not Marian but her father. He too had apologised for her horse, his crushed spine being of secondary importance ...

'Oh Marian,' she said, 'I can always buy another horse, but you're irreplaceable. And just look at you. What about your ballet? That ankle is going to take weeks to heal.'

The girl had been prepared for anger, not sympathy. She began to sniff. 'I'll just have to wait a bit longer for my debut,' she said.

Lisa sat beside her, gently sweeping her fingers through the red-gold hair. 'I thought you wanted us to go back to London,' she said.

'I did. But then I got confused, and you were so angry.' She looked at Mary Latchcham, who was smiling. 'Aunt Mary has been telling me all about you and Uncle ... my father. And I know it's a complete about-face, but of all the people we know, I'd rather it was him than anyone else. I kept all those records, you know. And an old scrapbook I found. They're at the back of my cupboard. Somehow it didn't seem right to throw them away.'

Lisa hugged her. 'Marian, you are an absolute twit sometimes. But I love you.'

Lisa watched anxiously as the two boys sorted through the food they had put together to sustain them on the journey. Their ponies were pulling at haynets, and the dogs sat on their haunches with drooling mouths.

'You will remember to check on them, won't you?' she asked.

Marian smiled. 'I promise,' she said. 'Although the very worst that can happen is that they'll eat themselves sick. David, how can you possibly get through all that in a little under four hours?'

'There are seven of us,' he said, pointing to the three dogs and two ponies.

'Horses don't eat sausage rolls and meat pies,' she retorted.

'But dogs do. They'll eat anything. I don't know why you want to travel in a rotten compartment when you could be having lots of fun back here.'

'And I could arrive in London with straw in my hair, and stinking of horse.'

Their mother intervened in case they bickered all morning and the train left with Marian still standing out on the platform. She didn't like the idea of them travelling back to London alone, but Marian wasn't a child, and both Clara and Judith would meet them.

A warning whistle sounded further down the platform. Doors began to slam.

'We'd better shut them in,' Marian said.

'I suppose so,' Lisa agreed, watching the stationary engine. In her childhood there had been the filth, yet special magic of steam; but now the trains were electric, the thrill of a chugging engine was gone. She turned back to her son.

'Aren't you going to kiss me goodbye, David?'

He stood up reluctantly, and coming to the door, gave her cheek an embarrassed peck. Anthony watched, and when she held out her arms, he ran forward and hugged her too.

'Thank you for the marvellous summer, Mrs. Weston,' he said.

'You'll have to come again.'

The train jerked forward a couple of inches.

'If you don't get a move on you'll have to travel with us, or else get left behind altogether,' said David to Marian, pushing an apple tart out of the reach of Harvey's inquisitive nose.

'Be careful,' Lisa cautioned, and slammed shut the door.

It was odd to see her children off like this. They quickened their steps.

'I'm sorry about the ballet,' Lisa said.

'It's only temporary.'

'You'll probably have to postpone moving into a flat with your friends.'

The girl slipped a hand through her mother's arm.

'I was thinking about that last night. If I move into a flat I won't have Clara, will I? I shall have to clean, cook, shop, and even do my own washing and ironing. I think I might stay at home after all.'

'That's mercenary!'

'But sensible,' said Marian. 'And I bet you'd prefer to keep a motherly eye on me … I'm in this carriage. When I'm a ballerina, I shall have my own flat with lots of servants.'

Her mother pulled open the heavy door and said, 'Which means I shall be supporting you for another twenty years, if not forever. Can you manage?'

'Sort of.'

She hopped awkardly up the steps, and Lisa closed the door behind her. She opened the nearest window and leant out.

'Don't worry about David,' she said. 'Clara and I will keep an eye on him. Can I ask you something?'

'Of course.'

'Would you marry Mark if he asked you?'

'Really Marian!' Lisa exclaimed. 'On Friday, the mention of his name was enough to send you into a rage. And now you're asking if I would marry the man.'

She was trembling, despite the frivolity of her words. If Mark really did need her …

'Well, you're not getting any younger,' her daughter said. 'And he's a jolly good catch. He's stinking rich, and for his age he's very good-looking. You may never get a chance like this again.'

'No,' said Lisa. 'At forty-one years old I'm verging on the borders of senility. And what do you expect me to do, walk up and propose to him? If I did that, the shock would probably bring on another heart attack, which would defeat the purpose of my remaining here in the first place.'

Mary Latchcham had said that her mother and Mark Hanley had been very much in love once. The idea of a courtship such as the old woman described seemed too distant for Marian to grasp, but she could understand that they still cared deeply for one another.

The train jerked forward. Marian glanced towards the lights and saw them change from red to green.

'You never answered my question,' she said quickly. 'Would you marry him?'

Lisa's face was pale as she walked alongside the barely moving carriage. Could she go back? Or would it be going forward?

'Yes,' she said. 'Yes I would. But only if you and David didn't object.'

Tears sprang to Marian's eyes, and she suddenly realised that the train was picking up speed. 'Mummy!' she cried.

'What is it?'

'Only that I love you!'

They somehow managed to embrace, the one straining upwards, the other leaning dangerously forward over the partition. Then the train was moving quickly away, and waving frantically, Lisa shouted goodbye.

'I mean it!' were the last words she heard from Marian.

She stayed on the platform until the train had disappeared. She felt strangely alone as she turned towards where she had left the Latchcham Land-Rover and horsebox. Only after she had handed in her platform ticket did she realise that for the first time since Marian's birth she was free. She hurried across to the horsebox, which was parked on a thick yellow line but had been ignored by a patrolling policeman because of the prominent Latchcham coat-of-arms stamped on its side.

There was so much she wanted to do. She revved the engine and switched on the radio. She would start schooling Bucephalus in earnest, and that boy ... What was his name? ... Bell, Brian Bell. She would find him right now, for if he meant what he said about the horses, there was a lot of work ahead. The harness had been stored away for years, the plough was rusty, and Jinny and Drummer fat and lazy.

She pushed her way into a heavy stream of traffic. A familiar voice came over the radio, announcing Simon Townsend's new song. She realised with a shock that it was Len Parker. She and Alan hadn't long been married, and David not even born, when Len Parker seduced Martin. It was ironic that he was now praising Simon, someone who, like Martin, owed his career to Mark. And then Simon's voice surged round her. It was a pleasant song, and she began to hum along with him. She was out of town, speeding along deserted country roads, when she realised that the song was 'Sad Man', the last song ever recorded by Mark Anthony.

Chapter Ten

I had walked further than I intended, and found it necessary to stop and rest awhile. I leant against a rotting stile and lit a cigarette as I watched Sofie explore the tangled hedgerows. Perhaps because I had been away for so long, or perhaps because I had tasted death, I thought the countryside had never looked lovelier than it did this morning. Although it was nearly October, the sunshine was warm, and late flowers grew in a profusion of colour along the lanes. Cattle were grazing in the fields—my cattle and my land, stretching as far as the eye could see.

Two crows began quarrelling in a nearby tree, their cries raucous as they echoed across the countryside. I was amused by their antics, and watched them chatter and scold, hopping from branch to branch and sending dead leaves and twigs swirling to the ground. I was so absorbed that only when Sofie growled a warning did I hear the sound of hooves. As I turned the horse shied towards the hedge, neck arched, eyes boggling at both me and the dog. I put a restraining hand on Sofie's collar, and she sat down. Bucephalus decided I was not going to attack him, and stood suddenly still, watching me with pricked ears.

'Hello, Mark,' Lisa said.

I looked at her. The sun was a glaring ball above her head, and I saw again a young red-headed girl.

'Hello,' I answered, focusing on the woman. She was older and wiser, but not much changed from that earlier image.

'When did you get back?' she asked. 'I hadn't heard.'

I released the dog's collar. 'Last night. We came into Steelton quite late and went directly to the Manor. I've not even contacted Mother yet.'

'We?' she asked. And I thought I heard a tremor in her voice.

I smiled. 'I've decided to stay here for a while, and my staff have been uncommonly faithful. Roberts has come to take inventory, and will be returning temporarily to London tomorrow. Elly is here too, with Paul. He was exhausted by all the travelling, and he was still sleeping when I came out. It's such a beautiful morning that I couldn't resist going for a walk.' She slid from the horse, and stood facing me. 'Why are you here?' I asked.

There was a long pause. Bucephalus sidestepped and impatiently shook his head.

'Because Marian thought he should be trained,' she answered after a while.

'Are she and David with you?'

'No. David is back at school, and judging by my telephone conversation with him yesterday he's not missing me at all. And Marian is growing up and away from me. She's sorry for all that bitterness, Mark. She and Mary had a long talk, and she understands better now.'

The crows had fled, leaving their tree for a more distant perch. I reached for my cane, left lying beside the stile; and as I swung round, saw the horror in Lisa's eyes. I also saw that she knew what had happened.

'My leg aches when I walk long distances,' I said. 'And these lanes are in terrible condition. Who told you?'

'Caroline,' she replied. 'She was worried and rang Mary, who confided in Marian and me. Nobody else knows, not even Charles.' She stopped. She was twisting the reins round her fingers. 'Oh Mark, I've been so very frightened. I've lost so much. I couldn't bear to lose you as well.'

She left the horse, and came into my arms. She was shaking as she buried her face in the roughness of my jacket. I closed my eyes as I held her, and the walls that I had erected over the years started to crumble.

'Lisa ...'

'No,' she said. 'Don't say anything.'

I raised her chin until her eyes were level with mine. And then I kissed her, tenderly upon the lips, with understanding and love.

'Will you walk a short way with me?' I asked.

The look she gave me was answer enough. She broke away from my grasp and caught up the loose reins of the grazing horse.

We fell into step, Bucephalus breathing down the back of my neck, while Sofie ran ahead, chasing a thrush which broke suddenly from a ragged section of the hedge. The crows were yelling again, their squabbling filling the air. And beside me ... Our fingers touched and entwined.

Our lives had turned full circle. I had come home.